Chloë Mayer is a journalist whose work has been shortlisted for several awards, including newcomer of the year and reporter of the year. She has lived and worked in Tokyo and Los Angeles, and now lives in east London, not far from where she grew up. *The Boy Made of Snow* is her first novel.

The Boy made of Snow

CHLOË MAYER

WEIDENFELD & NICOLSON

First published in Great Britain in 2017
by Weidenfeld & Nicolson
an imprint of the Orion Publishing Group Ltd
Carmelite House, 50 Victoria Embankment
London EC4Y 0DZ

An Hachette UK Company

1 3 5 7 9 10 8 6 4 2

A CIP catalogue record for this book is
available from the British Library.

ISBN (Hardback) 978 1 4746 0479 6
ISBN (Export Trade Paperback) 978 1 4746 0480 2
ISBN (eBook) 978 1 4746 0482 6

Typeset at The Spartan Press Ltd,
Lymington, Hants

Printed and bound in Great Britain by Clays Ltd,
St Ives plc

MIX
Paper from
responsible sources
FSC
www.fsc.org FSC® C104740

www.orionbooks.co.uk

For my parents

*O*nce upon a time there was a troll, the most evil troll of them all; he was called the Devil.

One day he was particularly pleased with himself, for he had invented a mirror which had the strange power of being able to make anything good or beautiful that it reflected appear horrid; and all that was evil and worthless seem attractive and worthwhile . . .

'It is a very amusing mirror,' said the Devil . . .

It was so entertaining that the Devil himself laughed out loud. All the little trolls who went to troll school, where the Devil was headmaster, said that a miracle had taken place . . .

At last they decided to fly up to Heaven to poke fun of the angels and God Himself.

The nearer they came to Heaven, the harder the mirror laughed, so that the trolls could hardly hold onto it; still, they flew higher and higher: upward toward God and the angels, then the mirror shook so violently from laughter that they lost their grasp; it fell and broke into hundreds of millions of billions and some odd pieces. It was then that it really caused trouble, much more than it ever had before.

Some of the splinters were as tiny as grains of sand and just as light, so that they were spread by the winds all over the world. When a sliver like that entered someone's eye it stayed there; and the person, forever after, would see the world distorted, and only be able to see the faults, and not the virtues, of everyone around him, since even the tiniest fragment contained all the evil qualities of the whole mirror.

If a splinter should enter someone's heart — oh, that was the most terrible of all! — that heart would turn to ice.

From *The Snow Queen*, by Hans Christian Andersen

Kent, 1944

I

———∞∞∞———

All right, we will start the story; when we come to the end we
shall know more than we do now . . . There once lived a
poor little girl and a poor little boy . . .
From *The Snow Queen*

When she was twelve years old, the enchantress shut her into
a tower, which lay in a forest and had no stairs or door.
There was only a little window, right at the top . . .
From *Rapunzel*

Annabel was gathering magnolia petals from the front lawn when she first saw the strange procession making its way down the lane.

She couldn't abide the sight of the stray blossoms; they were beached on the grass in the watery spring sunshine like a school of dead white fish. So she had come outside as usual – as she did every day of the tree's brief season – to tidy away the fallen flowers.

And it was then, while she was clutching fistfuls of the tough fabric-like petals outside her cottage, that she glanced up to see the gang of men heading down the street towards her.

She stared for a moment or two but quickly regained her composure and hurried towards the house so she could watch properly – unobserved – through the bay window.

As she crossed the lawn, she kept her gaze fixed on the approaching men. There were seven of them and they were still in their uniforms. Nazi soldiers, just walking down the lane.

They were being escorted by two British officers, so she assured herself this wasn't an invasion. She knew from the wireless that most towns had a Prisoner of War camp on their outskirts now, and she'd heard that the village, or rather old Mr Dawson's farm, had been selected as such a site. But Annabel wondered why this first batch of Germans was arriving on foot.

She rushed through the open front door and into the sitting room where she positioned her body flat against the wall by the window. Then she leaned over, partly hidden by the wall and partly obscured by her net curtains, to peek out into the lane.

The soldiers were still a little too far away for her to scan their faces, but she squinted against the sunshine to make them out. An intoxicating mix of fear and excitement made her heart thump painfully in her chest. She felt furtive, as though she were doing something wrong, but she was desperate to catch a glimpse of the captured prisoners as they passed by.

The war seemed to have made government officials suddenly aware of the existence of the village. First a steady stream of evacuated children were sent to Bambury and now Jerries were being transported here. Should she be afraid of them? With Reggie away fighting, she was alone in the house with their nine-year-old son. And Dawson's farm wasn't far from her cottage. She wondered if the old man was worried about having a load of Krauts just a short distance from his farmhouse, where he too lived alone since his wife had died of the cancer.

There were some rumblings in the village, of course. Fears of Germans escaping, biding their time until they were free to slit dozens of throats in the dead of night as the villagers slept. But there was surprisingly little opposition as the first few Nissen huts were erected a couple of weeks ago. Perhaps people were being patriotic; just another sacrifice that had to be made.

Annabel hadn't paid much attention to the chatter, but now she was transfixed.

They were approaching... yes... any second now...

She realised she was holding her breath; they were going to walk right past her front window!

Straining to get a better look, she watched as the blur of their faces gradually hardened into distinct features.

They were passing by now, just feet away from where she hid. The two British officers seemed relaxed, arms swinging at their sides. She wasn't sure what she thought she would find written in the Jerries' expressions, but their faces betrayed no emotion and a couple of them were even chatting nonchalantly. None of them wore handcuffs.

She fancied she would have been able to tell they were European, even if they weren't in uniform. Something about the slant of their jaws, their eyes, their manner, seemed foreign, exotic somehow. Men with strange names from faraway places. Their grey tunic jackets could almost have passed for normal blazers, were it not for the bottle-green shoulder epaulettes, and they wore them open as though they were simply out for a pleasant stroll.

One of the PoWs – taller than the others and with dusky blond hair – happened to glance casually about him, and Annabel darted back behind the wall and flipped around to face the room.

She'd wait for a second or two before resuming her observation. Were the other women watching this, hidden behind their own net curtains?

Her heart was still hammering. She felt strangely unmoored and tried to anchor herself by looking at her very ordinary surroundings, as though her nice sitting room – the sofas, the bureau, the drinks cabinet – could serve as docks that would safely tie her down.

Unable to wait any longer, she turned back to the window. The Germans had passed by. She stared with a sort of repulsed fascination as the men continued to the end of the road, turned the corner, and disappeared from view.

Daniel must have come into the room behind her at some point, and when he spoke he made her jump: 'What are you doing?'

She glanced at him then turned back to the street. The boy was always creeping up on her.

'Nothing. Some PoWs arrived and just walked by. They've gone now.'

He ran to the window with a cry and pulled a net curtain wide. But he could see as well as she could; the street was empty, no sign at all that anything extraordinary had just happened in Bambury. Just innocent little cottages dotting the country lane, pretty and bland as the drawing on a box of fudge.

'There's no one there,' he said, disgusted, dropping the net.

She looked down at the child, his face pale beneath his brown hair, his wide blue eyes staring up at her with accusation in them.

Annabel leaned back against the wall – as shaky as if she'd been running. She realised she was still clutching the magnolia petals, now crushed and sweaty in the palms of her hands.

2

She was beautiful but made of ice . . . neither rest nor
peace was to be found in her gaze.
From *The Snow Queen*

I followed her as she left the sitting room and headed outside to the dustbin. These were the questions that were bouncing around in my head like rubber balls in a box:

What does PoW stand for again? Are they really Nazis? How were they caught? Have they killed people? How long will they stay? Do they know Hitler? Can they speak English? What will they do here? Are they dangerous? Where will they live? When will they be sent back?

'Mother?'

But she snapped, 'Not now, Daniel,' as she scraped a white pulpy mess from her fingers into the bin. Then she went into the kitchen to wash her hands at the sink. So I was left staring at the back of her pretty flowery dress and the brown curls of her hair about her shoulders when she said I had to either (a) go outside into the garden or (b) go upstairs to read a book, but either way I mustn't be (c) getting under her feet.

Normally I'd read a story, but today I went into the back garden so I could climb the big tree in the hope being higher up might let me spot a gang of Jerries heading who knows where. It didn't. I wasn't really all that high to be honest.

She came out after a while and looked up at me and said,

'Don't worry about those PoWs. Because, well, there's nothing to be afraid of. All right? So then, let's hear no more about it.'

I was just going to reply that I was *nine* so was most certainly NOT afraid, when she turned around and went back inside, pulling the door shut behind her.

So I sat there trying to think up a plan for quite a long time until eventually I went inside to tell her I was going to play out. She was sitting on the sofa with a glazed look on her face. The wireless was playing a Tommy Dorsey song and a magazine lay open across her lap. There was a cigarette burning in her hand and a glass with soda water turning oily from one of her special drinks sat on the side table. And enough time must have passed – or she'd completely forgotten about the PoWs – because she didn't even reply.

It was good because, even though it was after school, there was still quite a lot of afternoon and evening daylight left. And we didn't really have mealtimes in my house any more.

I walked in the direction she'd been looking, which must have been the way they'd gone. But the lane was empty so I circled back and headed up to the hill, where I might be able to see more.

On the way, I didn't see anything interesting apart from a soldier trying to fix a broken-down army jeep that must have brought the PoWs to the village. I thought about stopping to ask him where I could find the prisoners, but decided it'd be more fun to find out for myself.

It was cloudier than it had been and a quick spring shower sprinkled some light raindrops down on me, but it wasn't chilly. I just had little pinprick-sized dots of water showing up as dark blue on my light-blue school shirt.

When I was at the top of the hill, I thought I could hunt dragons at the same time as looking for PoWs. So I found a branch that would make a perfect sword. I picked it up from the grass and watched as the wood turned into a sharp piece of silver with a golden handle studded with rubies. No dragons seemed to be around today though, and before long I could tell that my sword had turned back into a stick again. Then I used it to swipe at the long grass growing by the side of the path that led over the little hill above the railway.

It really was rotten luck to have missed the PoWs.

The trains weren't running properly any more, but I'd heard my teacher Mr Finlay say there was a Skeleton Service. I hoped I'd see the skeleton driver and the skeleton conductor through the windows if a train whizzed by.

It would be fun to watch my stick being crushed by the wheels. Maybe I could conduct experiments by placing other objects along the tracks too. A penny, a pebble, a worm. A worm! A worm!

These thoughts cheered me right up.

The grassy verge was steep in places and I had to sort of slide down. I clamped the stick between my teeth and tried to raise myself up on my hands a bit to protect the bottom of my short trousers. Although mealtimes had stopped, and upstairs house-work, Mother *did* still do the laundry – since other people would notice if our clothes were dirty – and she would box my ears if she found grass stains smeared into the fabric.

My stick was now a worm-finder, and I used it to turn over rocks, and leaves, and prod through the grass. I had expected to find dozens of them – rain equals worms – but I couldn't find a single one. Jumping over the metal lines, I walked down the middle of the tracks to continue searching.

I could see the red brick tunnel cutting through the hill up ahead. It was actually also a bridge because a road ran along the top of it. But the street was one of the quieter roads out of the village and didn't lead to London or anywhere exciting like that. Sometimes I liked to look down from there like a king surveying his kingdom.

Perhaps there would be worms on the other side? I would run through it; I'd never done that before.

The ground was gravelly with small pale rocks beneath my

shoes and I watched where I put my feet because it would be bad luck to step on a patch of pebbly ground instead of the wooden sleepers. One foot per sleeper, that was the rule.

Step, sleeper.

Step, sleeper.

When I looked up, the gaping mouth was suddenly in front of me and I noticed how dark it was in there. Maybe I should climb back up the verge, cross the bridge, and scramble down the other side to avoid the tunnel? Wooden stairs had been built into the hill nearby so railway crews could get up to the road, so it would be easy to climb up and over.

But I was right at the entrance now and I didn't want to be a scaredy cat.

'I'm no sissy!' (But I whispered it, so the echo wouldn't steal my words and throw them back at me as if a ghost were repeating what I'd just said.)

Another step, another sleeper.

And I was inside.

I thought the tunnel would suddenly turn pitch black. But it didn't, not yet anyway. I had only just stepped inside, and the day was still strong and bright behind me. Also, I could just about see the hole further down at the other end, opening up to the sunshine outside.

Still, as I took that first step, I knew that I'd crossed over into a different sort of world. It felt a bit colder as I moved into the tunnel, and even the sound changed somehow.

But I'd said aloud that I wasn't a sissy, so what else could I do? I kept walking, forgetting to check my feet only touched the sleepers; forgetting about the bad luck.

I didn't like the sound my footsteps made, and I didn't like the feeling of dark dampness on my skin. I sped up, hurrying to get to the tunnel's exit. It was strange, but I was too nervous to run. It felt like admitting I was frightened would be a big mistake. If I started to run, then something would chase me. That was the reason I couldn't go back the way I'd come in, because if I turned around I'd see what was waiting for me in the dark. I was just approaching the halfway bit of the tunnel now; I was as far as I could be from both ways out.

That was when I saw the nest.

I was so shocked that I actually stopped walking. It was beside the tracks, right up against the curved brick wall. It was dark, but I could see it well enough.

That nest was like the darkest horror from the darkest nightmare. Part of it was made up of human things – a dirty tattered eiderdown, some blankets and pieces of wood, empty bottles, a few scraps of clothes, and greasy newspapers that reeked of food going bad. But the rest of it was all animal. The dirt . . . the smell. Toilet smells. Vomit smells. Rotting smells.

A nest. Half human, half animal. Under a bridge.

Oh! I knew what it was that lived there.

I was standing in a Troll's lair.

The autumn before, not long before I turned nine, I'd come across a dead baby bird. The pink, featherless chick was naked on the cold concrete walkway underneath the church hall's roof, round at the back of the building. It must have fallen from its home in the rafters. It had huge black bulging eyes, this chick, and its tiny yellow beak was open, open, open. Its skin was so thin it was almost see-through and I could see the darker red of its tiny veins and organs packed beneath it. I stared at that little baby bird for a long time. In fact, I squatted down to get a better look at it. I was so disgusted by the sight of it, its obvious deadness, but I couldn't tear myself away.

That was how I felt when I found the Troll's nest. The fear I'd felt since walking into the dark turned solid in my belly as I suddenly realised what it was that lived in there. But I'd stopped walking to study the nest the same way I'd studied every horrid detail of that dead little bird.

My heart thumped faster and my breathing became ragged and uneven. I tried to hold my breath; I didn't want to break any sort of spell, and I didn't want that smell up my nose and in my head. I just wanted to have a look.

Already I was thinking how I'd tell my best friend Harry all about this – even though he lived a long way away and I wasn't sure when I'd see him again. I was pretty sure I'd come off looking amazingly brave, well, a hero really.

With those thoughts making me even braver, and even more hero-like, I stepped away from the tracks, closer to the stinking nest. I pinched my nose between my fingers. If I hadn't been so busy thinking about how far away the exit was, I would probably have smelled the nest before I saw it.

I wondered if any of the train passengers ever looked out of the window at this spot. Or if, as the train exploded into the blackness of the tunnel, they always turned away from the glass thinking there was nothing to see. When they were going through really fast, would they even notice this dark mess of rubbish, pushed up against the walls? And if they did see something, none of them probably realised what it meant. Most grown-ups never thought about Trolls.

Probably, they had enough to worry about, seeing as how they were taking their chances with the Skeleton Service, not to mention the fact there was a war on. I shivered, and remembered again to listen for the tell-tale chugging of the ghost train.

I still had my long stick with me and – with the fingers of my other hand squeezing my nose tightly shut against the stink of the Troll – I began to prod at the nest with a funny mix of delight and horror.

Sliding the tip of the branch underneath the greasy-looking eiderdown that was spread out on the ground, I flipped the corner over, and marvelled at the faded flowery pattern now caked with grime. Using the point of the stick, I scooped up some of the clothes then flung them to one side when I caught the sharp whiff of stale sweat and the tang of whisky, like in the decanter at Grandpa's house.

I jabbed at the pile of blankets and prodded again, much harder. Horrible, dirty things! Finally I raised my stick and hit the pile in disgust.

But the stick snapped into two pieces at precisely the same time as a roar of pain, or surprise, or fury rose up from the mound. The howling bounced off the slick brick walls of the tunnel and filled my head with the terrifying bellows of the beast. It had been hiding beneath those blankets the whole time.

It sat up and its terrible black eyes were swivelling round trying to find what had attacked it. I was standing directly in front of it but it was as though it wasn't able to see me at first. I stumbled backwards in fear, still holding onto the shard of stick I'd hit it with.

It was trying to pull itself into a standing position. I gasped as it began to draw itself up on its hind legs; it was turning into the monster it really was. Surely it would catch me and eat me.

'AAAAAGGHHHHHHHHHHHHH!'

The screaming hadn't stopped. I was whimpering as I tried to back away from it. I could move, but realised I couldn't seem to move *quickly*. It was like the dreams I had where I couldn't run away from danger. But this was real life and I was just shuffling backwards, as slowly as if I were wading through quicksand.

Then I was falling and the stick slipped from my hand as I grasped uselessly at the air. At first I thought it had somehow managed to trip me up, or was even using some kind of evil magic, but then I realised I had tripped over the metal tracks behind me. Now I was lying flat on my back, staring up at it helplessly, as it lurched from side to side. It was holding its head in its hands.

As I began to try to pull myself away, it took its hands down from its hairy face and suddenly seemed to see me for the first time. It took a step towards me and I was flipping over and I was up and I was scrabbling to get away. I was running I was fleeing I was never looking back it was behind me I knew it was behind me it was going to chase me and get me and kill me—

'SODDING KIDS SODDING KIDS SODDING KIDS—'

I could hear the words now, the ones buried in the roaring that had got even louder since it saw me. A new higher-pitched scream joined the furious booming of the Troll and I realised it was me.

But I could see the light ahead; the day was still there outside the tunnel as though nothing had happened. I knew I'd be all right if I could only get out of the dark.

A rock landed in front of me, and shocked me so much I nearly stopped running, but then I understood. The Troll had grabbed a stone from the tracks and thrown it at me.

Another one whizzed past my ear, and another, and another. One bounced off my shoulder and I screamed again – I thought it was the Troll's hand grabbing me. I couldn't hear its footsteps following me any more, but the echoes made it hard to tell how far away it was.

Get to the light, just get to the light. It was all I had to do to be safe.

When I finally burst out into the sunshine, I kept running.

When the burning pain in my lungs became too much, I stopped on the tracks and turned around. I bent over, resting my hands on my knees, and panted. The Troll was there, but it hadn't left the hole of the tunnel's mouth. It had one arm up against the sloping brick wall. I thought it might be afraid of the sun, like Count Dracula. But maybe it was just catching its own breath too. Hadn't I seen it somewhere before? That's it – in the village once – begging for change. How had I never realised it was a Troll?

We stared at one another, assessing each other's power. I'd seen it in daylight before, so it *could* follow me outside if it wanted. But it seemed tired, so I didn't think it would.

After a moment or two, I was able to stand again, and I rested my hands on my hips as my heart and breathing slowed down. I had escaped death by Troll and I began to laugh because I'd outwitted it. I had whacked it with a big stick and now I was safely out of its reach.

It saw me laughing and began roaring again. 'SODDING KIDS!'

It was enough to wipe the grin from my face and I immediately left the tracks to climb up the hill towards the path that would lead me home. I knew its eyes were on my back because of the horrible prickling sensation I felt there, but I kept running and its screams gradually faded to silence behind me.

3

'. . . it shall not be death, but a deep sleep of a hundred
years into which the princess shall fall.'
From *Briar-Rose (Sleeping Beauty)*

'Could the Snow Queen come inside, right into our room?'
asked the little girl.
'Let her come,' said Kai. 'I will put her right on top of the
stove and then she will melt.'
From *The Snow Queen*

Annabel gazed blankly at the sky outside the window as it
gradually turned to navy and made the room blue. The gin was
all gone and inside her head felt smooth.

She was thinking about the PoWs in their Nissen huts. What
were they doing now? It must be strange sleeping in a foreign
country as a prisoner. Were they frightened? Or were they plotting
escape and retribution?

The sound of the front door made her snap to. She hadn't
realised how late it was, or noticed when the sun went down, for
now she found herself sitting in the chair in the dark. She turned
off the wireless on her way to the kitchen where she found the
boy eating pilchards from a tin with a spoon. She pulled down
the blackout blind and they both blinked when she turned on the

light. She wasn't at all sure what time it was. The clock in the kitchen had stopped working long ago.

'Bedtime . . .' she said. Her voice slipped around a little as the word left her mouth.

'Yes.'

She heard the scrape of his chair on the lino and the thump of the tin in the bin.

He followed as she led the way upstairs to his bedroom. The blackout blind was permanently down in here, and she flipped on the yellow tasselled lamp in the corner before scanning the books on his shelves. So many fairy tales.

He climbed into bed – yes, he still had his clothes on, but he could change into pyjamas later when she'd gone; or not, if he wanted to save the effort and wake up to go straight to school already dressed. Was it a school day tomorrow?

She ran her finger along the books and pulled out *Sleeping Beauty*. She sat on her chair, over in the corner.

'Once upon a time—'

'First . . .' the boy interrupted her, shyly.

She looked up.

'First, can you tell me about your Darlings?'

She sighed.

Then she closed the book, folded her hands across it, and leaned back in the wicker seat. He was asking her to tell a story about her childhood – but really he was asking her about the fairy tales.

'When I was a little girl,' she began, 'I had a lovely collection of dollies. Oh, rag dolls and baby dolls and china dolls, which I used to scoop up in my arms and carry about with me. And I called my dollies: my Darlings.'

She heard the boy let out a long breath as he settled back against his pillows.

'Yes,' he said.

'Why, you'd never see me without at least one of my Darlings clutched to my chest!' She smiled at the memory. 'I loved my Darlings so much, you see.'

He pulled the corner of the bedcover up to his cheek and settled his face in the folds as he listened. He was gazing at her, she could tell, but she let her eyes glaze across the distance of time.

'My nanny, Missus Joan, used to read me fairy stories and I knew most of them by heart – and so, even before I could read, I used to whisper the tales into my Darlings' little porcelain ears when I was supposed to be asleep in bed. My Darlings were like my own dear little children.'

She stood up, placing *Sleeping Beauty* onto the cushion, and walked across to the bookshelves to see the titles again.

'These books aren't the ones that I had of course, but I had all the same stories.' She took down an anthology and flicked through the pages to see the drawings. Forests and castles and birds rendered in soothing pastel colours.

'I used to dream of having a child when I was still a child myself, you know. And when I fell pregnant—'

'With me!'

'—I was filled with happiness and the baby inside of me. I'd always wanted to be a mother.'

She shook her head. Looked down at the pictures again.

'When I realised I was going to have a baby, the very first thing I thought of – before the notion of bonnets and rattles and cribs even entered my mind – no, the first thing I thought of was the stories I would read to the child. I was going to be a real mother, and I already knew just how to do it. So I started to frequent bookshops.'

'And you bought all the books they had!' She heard a rustle as he lifted his head slightly, just for a moment, before laying his cheek back against the eiderdown.

Annabel slotted the anthology back in its place, but didn't turn around from the shelves. She bowed her forehead against the wood.

She remembered hoping another customer would catch her browsing the children's section, so she could tell them about the baby she was going to have. It was beyond her now why she thought anyone would be the least bit interested. She cringed to think of herself so puffed up with pride and her own sense of importance.

'I wanted people in the shop to ask me about the baby, I don't know why. But I kept buying more fairy tales and this pile of books grew steadily until Daddy bought the shelves to hold them all.'

She fell silent again, remembering.

But the boy grew impatient and tried to urge her on. 'You couldn't read to me when I was first born, because of your nerves...'

Annabel pushed her head harder against the shelf and closed her eyes.

She'd howled like an animal in that hospital as she was ripped open. Something was bearing down, pushing down through her flesh, tearing its way through her body to get out.

She was barely conscious when she was handed the baby. Before she passed out, she had long enough to note that it was red and wrinkly and was covered in a revolting mucus.

The next day she just stared at it in its cot next to her hospital bed. There was no desire to hold it to her breast or whisper stories into its tiny porcelain-coloured ears. Was this her baby? It screamed so furiously, pummelling its fat little fists in rage.

The exhaustion was even worse when Reggie took her home. She didn't feel able to get out of bed there either. Her hair went unbrushed, her teeth uncleaned, and she could smell herself – a dank, vaguely milky stink – under the covers, but she hadn't the energy to drag herself to the bathroom to wash. And underneath it all was a hot flush of guilt and shame because something was wrong with her and she didn't feel anything like how she'd thought she'd feel.

Both sets of parents told her in various ways to pull herself together, but Reggie tried his best to help her – fetching the baby when it screeched and pushing it onto her to feed. It would suck furiously like an animal, hurting her nipples while she cried, and she always needed to roll over and sleep afterwards to recover.

That first year was so hellish she stayed in bed for most of it – until, about eight months after the boy was born, she overheard furious whispering outside her bedroom door. Reggie was resisting attempts by his parents to have her sent away to an asylum.

After that, she realised she had to perform. Of course, she and Reggie – and almost certainly the child – knew she wasn't really there. Not really Annabel any more. But she would force herself to dress and walk and talk, which was a marked improvement as far as everyone was concerned. Reggie seemed so relieved appearances were being maintained he was happy not to probe too deeply into her emotional state, lest he wake the sleeping beast. Annabel became better at performing and, after a while, she remembered the story books in the child's nursery.

'You couldn't read to me when I was first born, because of your nerves,' the boy prompted again now. 'But then when I was one year old—'

'Yes,' Annabel said, opening her eyes and raising her head. 'For the second time in my life, I began to know the words of all the stories off by heart.'

The boy laughed with delight. 'So do I now!'

It was true. As her son had grown, the words which had seeped into his head before he was even old enough to form his own, were already there, ready to be voiced one day.

Annabel sometimes felt she was invoking the stories, bringing them into the room as she read, and the characters and spells were gradually embedding themselves into the core of the two of them; mother and child.

The months had passed and turned into years, and still Annabel read to the child each night. It turned out she didn't know how to be a real mother, but she knew how to be a pretend one. She had made an excellent pretend-mother as a child after all.

And she loved the stories, too.

She identified with those young lost women, wandering alone in the woods or trapped in their hovels or their castles or their towers.

Annabel never did whisper the tales into Daniel's little ears. That would have been unspeakably intimate. Instead, she sat in a chair in the corner of his bedroom, and he perched at her feet or lay in bed while she folded the edges of the book sharply backwards, making the spine crack, as it had cracked often before.

Not long before the boy had started at the local primary school, she'd come across Reggie in the sitting room gently suggesting to their son that he might be too old for fairy stories now.

'Why, Daniel – soon you'll be able to read your own books all by yourself like a big boy!'

But the child just stared into his father's face, across a sea of tin soldiers that divided them on the sitting-room carpet.

She'd crossed the room to the drinks cabinet and busied herself fixing a gin and tonic to make her head smoother. She felt eyes on her back and turned to see Reggie and the boy both gazing up at her with mute appeal written all over their faces.

She quickly turned back to her task.

Reggie apparently decided to continue trying to talk to Daniel. 'Doesn't that sound fun? Hmm?'

There was no reply from the boy.

'Doesn't it? And you'll be able to read exciting adventure stories in *Boys' Own* magazine about little boys just like you.'

But Daniel's silence – which she guessed would now be accompanied by a look of despair – must have made Reggie's heart hurt and the words fell out of him as he quickly reassured his son that he could have the fairy tales for as long as he wanted.

So the stories continued.

Perhaps Reggie had a point. They were funny crooked little

things, fairy tales. Quite dark, really, some of them. She remembered reading somewhere that in the original folk stories the evil maternal figures were the children's real birth mothers. But over the years – and presumably before publication would be permitted in Victorian times – the stories were changed and the 'wicked stepmother' character was created. It was considered too horrific and unnatural to contemplate that a mother may not love her own child.

At first, Annabel had identified with the sad, lonely young women bearing their burdens in their towers. Now, she identified with the mothers and thought perhaps the stories weren't fair to them; certainly they never took their side into account. She could understand how a sickly mother could give her baby away to a neighbour (*Rapunzel*) or how a desperate mother could be prepared to sell her unborn child (*Rumpelstiltskin*) or how a starving mother could choose to leave her children behind in the woods (*Hansel and Gretel*).

The husbands always endorsed their wives' plans in the stories, but somehow they were not relegated to 'wicked' or even 'stepfathers'. If the mothers were painted as evil, at worst the fathers were painted as weak. She wondered why that was.

Glancing up now, she could see the detritus of household odds and ends placed high up on top of the bookshelves out of the way. Old and worn-out clothes, kept for scraps for the darning she never did, disliked ornaments given as gifts that would never be displayed, and other useless dusty bric-a-brac accumulated over the years. A couple of her tatty old Darlings sat up there, not quite out of sight. Sometimes she felt it was fitting they still listened to her reading the fairy tales each night, but today, suddenly, she felt as though they were up there mocking her. She should have a clear-out and throw it all away. It was all just rubbish.

'Now the story,' the boy said, jolting her out of her reverie.

Annabel returned to her seat and picked up the book lying on the cushion. She sat down and resumed *Sleeping Beauty* where she'd left off. And the story went on.

4

Poor Kai, soon his heart would turn to ice and his eyes
would see nothing but faults in everything.
From *The Snow Queen*

When Mother left after my story, I lay awake in bed for a long
time. But eventually I got up to change into my pyjamas.

Every now and then, I'd hear the clink of glass bottles as she
fumbled around downstairs. I just couldn't sleep. I think it was
because I was still quite shaken up about finding a Troll's lair in
Bambury. But I had been soothed a little bit, because Mother had
told me about her Darlings, who I always liked to hear about. My
favourite part was the bit where she loved them so much because
she wanted a baby. Because she wanted me.

That sort of thing was nice to know. There were some secret
letters kept in the bureau in the sitting room that I took out to
read sometimes. Even though one had something written in it that
was so upsetting that it made my breath stop so that I thought
I might die the first time I read it. Probably I was silly to worry
– I'm sure what the letter said was just a mistake. But if those
words were a poison to me, then the story about her Darlings
was the antidote. In fairy tales, there's always an antidote – it's
just a matter of finding it; like the prince searching for the Water
of Life for his father the king, or the kiss that saved Snow White
after she ate the poisoned apple. The story about the longed-for
baby was like a kiss; a kiss from my mother to me.

But still, I couldn't sleep and I couldn't sleep and I couldn't sleep. My eyes stayed wide open in the dark even though it must have been after midnight. The Troll's stink was still up my nose. And that rock! Hitting me! It could have smashed my head open and killed me.

I got up and crept to the bathroom so Mother wouldn't know I was still up. Slowly, slowly, I shut the bathroom door and turned on the light. I wanted to look at the back of my shoulder in the little mirror above the basin. I unbuttoned my pyjama jacket and climbed up to perch on the pale pink rim so I could see the mark the rock had made when the Troll hurled it at my back.

I was very pleased to see a red mark there, and I knew it would be purple, or maybe even black, tomorrow. My war injury. My badge of honour from my fight with the monster. I wished for the thousandth time I had a best friend in Bambury I could show it to – how impressed he would be at my daring! Of course, I was friends with Harry who lived next door to my grandparents in Great Yarmouth, but I didn't know when we'd next visit. I hadn't even thought of telling Mother earlier; she'd only be frightened of the Troll or angry at me for going down by the tracks. No, she didn't need to know anything about this until I'd figured out a way to make sure she and the village were safe. She'd be happy then. And very proud of me, most likely.

In fact, now that I thought about it, saving Mother from the Troll would basically be just like saving a damsel in distress. That was the best way there was to earn love in stories – a dangerous task like, say, slaying a dragon or something. That made the love even stronger. Love always has to be earned. Everyone knows that.

Poor Mother. She had no idea of the danger she was in, but I'd make sure she didn't come to any harm. Trolls like to eat children best, but they'll snatch and eat anybody if they get the chance. I shuddered to think what I'd do if the Troll snatched Mother away from me. I'd be here completely alone then.

I wondered if I should write to Daddy to tell him about what was going on. But somehow it seemed best to keep this secret even from him; he had his own monsters to fight.

Once again, I thought about the lair hidden in the dark and remembered how the Troll had pounced to attack. I turned those moments in the tunnel over and over in my mind. How it had reared up, and that sick feeling of fear as I ran for my life away from the sharp claws and teeth; its screaming threats. How dare a monster attack me!

It was hard to make that picture of the monster lying in wait in the dark match up with the other time I'd seen it; that time it was pretending to be a beggar, holding out a tin for coins outside the Post Office. But that just made me angrier. How dare it pretend to be something it wasn't? My thoughts turned to vengeance. As I awkwardly craned round to look at my bare back in the mirror, I decided to stalk the beast; like a hunter stalking prey. When I left the bathroom, I found Mother slumped on the floor outside on the landing. I helped her stand up and get to the toilet and closed the door. After a while she came out and I let her lean on me as I led her stumbling to bed.

The next day, which was Saturday, I returned to the railway tracks to set up my official observation of the Troll. On the way, I pulled up a few carrots from a field to munch for breakfast and I watched the monster coming and going all day as I hid up on the hill. And I learned a lot.

I learned that the Troll *did* look a bit like a man. It looked like a man in as much as it had two eyes, two arms, two legs. But it was hideous and very, very clearly, it wasn't human. Coarse black hair sprouted from its terrible face, and thick, wild hair grew in tufts from its head. The hair was shot through with grey. When I'd walked past it in the village that time, I'd seen tiny red broken veins spreading like worms across its cheeks from its turnip-shaped nose. I vaguely wondered why it needed money, but I supposed Trolls were greedy like ogres.

25

I strained to see its face now as it walked by the side of the tracks towards the ladder on the other side from where I hid. Its eyes were red-rimmed and blackly bottomless – this was something I wasn't really able to see from a distance, so it was part guesswork, but that didn't mean it wasn't true. I don't know how I hadn't noticed those terrifying eyes when I saw it begging. It wore tattered clothes, and they were a dirty browny-green colour. Its filthy great claws were huge, with long, blackened fingernails.

And it was big. It was big like a bear.

Over the next couple of weeks, after school each day, I carried on with my observations of the Troll. I went back again and again.

It often wore a woollen hat pulled down over its large ears, despite the coming heat as spring moved towards summer. Once I saw it wearing a ratty tweed jacket with leather patches on the elbows. It must have stolen it from somewhere. It looked ridiculous, like an animal pretending to be a civilised and cultured man.

I watched from behind a tree high up on the hill banking the tracks. Sometimes I stood on the bridge, running back and forth across the road, looking down to see if it was coming into the tunnel or leaving it. I kept a notebook with me at all times, in the pocket of my short trousers. I had a stubby little pencil in there too, and I made careful notes about my sightings.

One day it was gone from the nest and I tasted sweet victory; my stalking must have somehow driven it away from the village. But a couple of days later, I saw it again; it had come back. I didn't know where it had been, but I felt a hot mix of anger and disappointment at its return. I arrived at the hill just in time to see it heading into the tunnel. I leaned back against my tree and looked down over the verge to keep an eye on its lair. I'd have to do better.

The notes in my pocket might contain a clue so I pulled out my book to flick through the pages; perhaps there was something I'd missed. When it first tried to catch me, I'd thought for a moment that it couldn't come out of the tunnel in the daylight, but of course that wasn't true. One of my early entries noted how it had thrown a weapon at me rather than chasing me in the tunnel, which I believed meant it couldn't run very fast. But perhaps I was wrong about that as well.

Although I had managed to get away from it that time in its lair, and it stopped chasing me once I was out of the tunnel, I guessed – despite its shambling, stumbling movements – that it could actually run faster than a leopard if it wanted to. I could imagine its huge, hairy bulk streaming through the forest like an animal, while its dead eyes searched for little children to eat. Now I'd seen that image of supernatural speed in my mind's eye, I knew it was true.

I shuddered. It could run, then. I'd have to be cunning.

I wrote down a note in my little book to record what I'd just discovered.

7th May, 1944: 3.45 p.m. (approx., no watch): Can run as fast (or faster) than a leopard. BE CAREFUL.

I tapped the pencil against my front teeth. Interesting. I'd have to make sure I always kept my distance from it. So I could never go into the tunnel again without being absolutely sure it wouldn't return for a long time. I returned my notebook and pencil to my pocket and leaned forward so I could bring my hand up to feel the area on my shoulder where its rock had struck me. There was nothing there now – the bruise was long gone and it wasn't even sore any more – but we both knew it had injured me. An injury I would nurse for life if I didn't avenge the wrong.

I leaned back against my tree. I was learning its habits. And I would plot its destruction. It was a powerful enemy, but Jack chopped down his beanstalk and slayed the giant, and little Gerda went to war with the Snow Queen and won back Kai.

So yes, it was a tall order, but with Daddy and all the other men away, I was the only one left to do the job; I would be the hero who would rid the village of the Troll.

Imagine how Mother would feel if I saved her! Well, I'd save everybody in the village obviously, but especially her. Think how she would feel then. She would realise that I was brave and strong. She'd hold my hand like Gerda held Kai's hand. She would call me her Darling, over and over again.

5

_____
⚬∞⚬
_____

*She laid her hand in his, and said: 'I'll willingly go away
with you, but I don't know how to get down from here.'*

From *Rapunzel*

$\mathbf{M}$r Dawson wasn't in his farmhouse when Annabel knocked,
so she and Daniel wandered around the grounds for a couple
of minutes until they spotted him in a concrete paved area surrounded by outbuildings and storage sheds. It had rained that
morning and muddy puddles with strands of hay pocked the
surface of the cement.

Annabel waved a hand in greeting as she hurried across the
little courtyard towards the farmer, pulling her trolley behind her
while the boy scuttled to keep up.

Dawson was a ruddy man with a nose that had been broken
long ago. He was either a very old-looking sixty-something or a
very spry-looking eighty-something. The elements had not been
kind to his complexion, and his profession had not been kind
to his body. Various farmyard accidents, with either beasts or
machinery, had claimed, over the years, various lumps of flesh,
and his right index finger. His body looked so battered from years
of work and injuries it was no wonder that he was finally slowing
down, she thought.

'Hello there,' he called out as she drew closer.

'Good morning.' She gave him a polite little smile as she came
to a stop. 'I saw your sign about firewood. Out in the lane.'

She glanced around, hoping to catch sight of some of his PoWs. But the tatty-looking courtyard was deserted.

The place looked shabby and forlorn. The farm he once easily controlled now seemed to overwhelm him – and had, Annabel thought, ever since his wife's death a few years before.

Without Mrs Dawson helping run things, he could no longer afford to employ youths from the village – who had all been sucked up by the war now in any case – and the farm's deterioration accelerated. Most of the fields went untended and the cows had been sold off at auction.

But Annabel thought he looked healthier, somehow, than he had the last time she'd seen him when she came to buy eggs a few weeks ago. The influx of young Germans from the PoW camp down the road seemed to have revitalised him. She hoped she'd pick up some gossip about his new 'employees'.

'Ah, yes, firewood!' The farmer looked almost excited. 'Quite a good idea, that, what with the coal shortages. I thought it was a disaster when the apple trees all got diseased and died. But now we can chop them all down for firewood and the trees will be cleared, leaving me a nice new field to do something with. Just shows you everything happens for a reason.'

'Yes, I suppose it does,' she said, looking into his broken old face.

'Don't worry – I'll make sure you get a good deal on your firewood, love.'

He glanced down at the child standing next to her. 'What with Mr Patterson being away and all that. Can't be easy bringing up a boy without his father.'

Annabel thanked him, but she knew he was lying about a good price on the wood. Nearly all the men of the village were away fighting now. Women and children and old folks were practically the only ones left. There was nothing special about her and the price would be no different simply because she was the one buying it. But summer was coming, and the evenings weren't as cool as they used to be, so hopefully she wouldn't need much wood until the onset of autumn.

'You helping your mother around the house, son?' the farmer asked.

'Yes sir.'

'Good man!'

A fat tabby sauntered over to rub against the farmer's calves and the boy squealed and bent down to pet the animal.

'About the wood . . .' Annabel said.

'Sorry, love! Just go past the house, then walk towards that big barn on your right-hand side. There's a path there you can follow round and that'll take you to the old orchard. There'll be a Jerry there chopping the wood – or he should be at any rate! – and you can get a bundle from him. His English isn't bad, and he knows to keep a record of whatever you take. We can settle up the bill at the end of each week.'

Annabel hesitated. 'I see.'

She glanced in the direction of the orchard. 'But will the Nazi soldier and I be the only ones there?'

Dawson chuckled.

'Oh I see what you mean! Don't worry about him. He's not really a Nazi. Most of them aren't. They're just young lads. Don't give me any trouble.'

Annabel frowned. There was a bit of a pause.

'Tell you what. I'll come down there with you.'

'Oh, thank you, Mr Dawson, I really do think that would be so much better.'

Annabel pretended she didn't notice the farmer suppressing a sigh as he gestured to the path. He was wheezing quite heavily and she tried to work out again how old he was.

'Come along,' Annabel said to the child.

She wondered if Dawson would consider dropping the wood off at her house if she paid a little extra. She had brought her trolley with her, but she didn't much fancy lugging bundles of firewood around and the boy was too small and scrawny to be much help. She envied her parents their reliable electric fires. They'd been the first of all their friends to have them installed, at great expense. She wished she had a neat row of red-hot bars that didn't even need to be cleaned, save for a light dusting now and then.

The unexpected thoughts of her parents annoyed her; she'd had another of her mother's telephone calls today. It was considered a luxury to have her own line – very few people in the village had a telephone – but frankly Annabel could have done without it. Every other week or so, Elizabeth would ring on the pretence of a chat. But the conversation would be a series of humiliating questions: Are you stocking the house? What will you be making for Daniel's dinner? Are you on top of the laundry? She knew the real questions, although unspoken, were: Are you coping? Are you in control? Should you be in an asylum?

The farmer's wheezes suddenly graduated into a coughing fit and Annabel tried to slap him on the back but he waved her off.

'Just need one of my smokes!'

He began to roll himself a cigarette, and offered one to Annabel. But she told him she preferred her own and pulled one from a packet in the handbag perched on top of her trolley. She allowed Dawson to light it for her with a match before he lit his own.

He winked at the boy. 'Not a young man like you any more, am I?'

Daniel smiled shyly but then Annabel saw his eyes widen as he spotted the space where the farmer's index finger should have been. He must have never noticed it before. She watched him staring as the old man smoked with the cigarette clamped between his middle and ring finger instead. She tried to catch the boy's eye to warn him not to be rude, but he wasn't looking at her.

'You know,' Dawson remarked to Annabel after a long, satisfying drag, 'the old orchard is nearer to your place than you coming all the way round the front first. So – after you've met him you'll realise the Kraut's all right – in future you can just cut through the back if you like. You can deal directly with him; Johannes his name is. No need to come and get me.'

Annabel pursed her lips, but remained silent.

Dawson finished smoking and, apparently rejuvenated, began leading them once again along the dirt path. Annabel skirted the puddles, although the farmer marched through them, oblivious in his boots. She shot the boy a warning look in case he decided to splash through the dirty rainwater too. Falling back, she deliberately increased her distance from Dawson because she didn't want mud flicked up onto her bare shins. She eyed the sky as she struggled to pull the trolley behind her, but the sun was elbowing clouds out of the way and it didn't look like it would rain again.

'Here we are then,' Dawson said as they approached a wooden fence.

He unlatched the gate and gestured for Annabel and the boy to enter the dead orchard.

'The lad should be over in the far corner chopping.'

'A real live woodchopper!' Daniel cried. 'I've never met a real woodsman before!'

'Well,' Dawson said, 'good.' He ruffled the boy's hair. 'This one's a German one.'

'Oh they always are,' the child replied. 'Like the father in *Hansel and Gretel*. He was a German woodchopper – that was how he knew where to leave them in the woods.'

'Ah,' Dawson said. 'Is that so?'

'Yes. Isn't that right, Mother?'

Annabel frowned. Maybe Reggie had been right and he really was a little old for fairy stories.

The sun had finally triumphed over the puffy clouds and its golden light wound its way around the fruitless apple trees. It was pleasant to walk under the branches and enjoy the dappled spots of afternoon sun that fell on their shoulders.

Daniel scuttled off deeper into the orchard where she could

see him running his hands along the trees as he wove around the trunks. He seemed to be muttering something to himself, but Annabel was too far away to hear what he was saying.

After a while, they could hear the sound of metal repeatedly striking wood.

'Come back!' she called to the boy.

Presently, they came into a small clearing where a man stood leaning against the wooden stem of his axe. He was panting with exertion and his sweat glistened in the sun. Despite the coolness of the day, and the muddy puddles glinting at his feet, he was naked to the waist. His shirt lay draped over a tree stump nearby. He seemed startled as they entered the clearing and looked as though he might start frantically chopping again, lest his boss think he was being lazy. But he must have thought better of it, deciding the piles of wood spoke for themselves.

'Johannes – your first customers,' declared the farmer by way of greeting.

The German smiled and nodded. He was the one she'd seen looking about him when the first PoWs were escorted into Bambury.

Annabel could tell the man had been blond as a boy, but in adulthood his hair was now a duskier shade that would probably lighten and darken with the seasons. She couldn't tell what colour his eyes were, because the sun was behind her and he was squinting against the glare. He raised a hand to his forehead to shield his face and said, 'How much do you need?'

His accent, while clipped like the mocking Nazi impersonators she had heard on the wireless, had a gentle sing-song lilt to it that gave it a kind of lyrical quality. He hadn't faltered on the words and had spoken quickly and naturally.

She was about to speak to an actual German soldier and even though he was probably not very much older than her, and looked friendly, she swallowed a knot of fear that had risen up in her throat.

She glanced at Mr Dawson, hoping for some kind of assurance, then gestured to her trolley, the tartan material now splattered with dirt from the walk through the orchard.

'I... have this,' she said unnecessarily, since he was already striding forward to take it from her.

She watched his back retreat as he headed past her to a pile of wood further down the way she'd come, and tried to study his appearance some more. But he was already bent over filling up her trolley, and the sun blazed behind him turning him into a sharp silhouette.

6

The young king often went out hunting, for it was a delight to him.
From *The Two Brothers*

On the farm, it was marvellous when I saw the old farmer was missing a finger. I couldn't stop staring at it. But then, I was excited anyway just to be there; I was hoping to see some animals – cows, pigs, horses. But the only thing I saw was a fat old tabby cat. I wished I had a cat of my own to look after.

Mother was disappointed the farmer wouldn't fetch the wood for her. She liked other people to do things for her. That's why it would be so good if I could get rid of the Troll; she'd be so happy when I told her I'd saved her. Why, she'd be overjoyed with me. I tried not to think about the upsetting words I'd read – and then re-read and re-read – in one of Daddy's letters in the bureau.

It had been raining, so it was a bit muddy as I followed her following the farmer on the walk to the orchard. I think that annoyed her too. She was wearing a pretty blue dress with white flowers and a white cardigan and her brown hair was curled. I'd seen the farmer notice how pretty she was when we first arrived. Then he strode off through the puddles as though he didn't know they were there. I was desperate to follow in his path – to jump so I was in his footsteps – and splash through the water. That would have been fun, but I knew better than to try.

'The lad should be over in the far corner chopping,' Farmer Dawson said.

And suddenly it all clicked into place, making me gasp. 'A real live woodchopper! I've never met a real woodsman before!'

It hadn't occurred to me that firewood was made by a wood-chopper. Surely there were machines that did that – but I supposed the war meant there was no spare petrol to run them. The war was why we needed firewood in the first place; we usually used coal.

Woodchoppers were always special and important people in the stories. I thought of the kind axe-man who spared Snow White's life and the heroic woodcutter who saved Little Red Riding Hood by slaying the wolf who'd just eaten her. He slit open the beast's stomach so she could climb out, and then he filled the cavity with stones and stitched it up. The stories sometimes skipped over that part, but I could imagine waiting in the stomach wondering if I'd be rescued. It would be dark and cramped. And then surely there'd be such a gory mess after the wolf was cut open. Marvellous.

I could tell Mother was frightened because the man we were about to meet was a German soldier. But despite all I'd heard on the wireless, and at school from Mr Finlay, and from Daddy's letters about fighting them, I wasn't scared at all because the German was also a woodchopper so he couldn't really be a baddie. I told the farmer about the father in *Hansel and Gretel*.

Although I was impatient to get further into the orchard to find the woodsman, I ran away from the adults into the trees so I could prepare. Taking my cardigan off, I wrapped it around my shoulders to turn it into a cloak and my sensible, brown lace-up shoes transformed into a pair of knee-high leather boots. I was in the forest, when witches and monsters and fairies and talking animals still roamed the earth. As I looked around, I saw the puny, dead apple trees soar towards the sky; they were growing into great, ancient oaks.

I ran my hands along the mystical bark of the trees and watched my fingers following the ridges of the rough wood. These trees knew what had been here before. Branches entwined far above my head acted as a giant sieve and strained the sunbeams through the leaves. Specks of dust danced in the strands of light; they glistened like stars swirling in the Milky Way.

This was a magical place. In the distance – I somehow knew – there was a village nestled in the valley. Little two-room stone cottages, with smoke cheerfully puffing from the chimneys. Horse-drawn carts would be rattling down cobblestone streets and children and barking dogs would scurry out of the way of the hooves. Merchants would be selling their wares, cobblers would be making their shoes, and the womenfolk would be setting pies on the windowsills to cool.

But here, in the ancient forest, it was quiet and still. I fancied I could glimpse a few wooden cabins, spread through the trees, and I knew that hunters or woodsmen lived there.

'Come back!'

The voice was faint; it was coming from very, very far away.

I turned to look over my shoulder. It felt hard to see out through this world I had just created, but I could make out two figures. As though a mist were clearing, I could gradually see the forms take shape. It was my mother and old Farmer Dawson.

I hesitated, reluctant to leave the magic place, which somehow seemed more real, but I ran to join them. Still, I couldn't help looking back. My ancient, magical forest was disappearing now, and I could see more and more of the average English orchard returning as my daydream trickled away. I looked at the sunbeams, hoping to see the constellations inside them, but there was nothing there except dust in the air. A cloud passed over the sun and, in an instant, that effect was gone too. Just the orchard. Just the air. I was back.

But it was then that I heard the sound of an axe hitting wood.

And it was like a miracle. Because I could suddenly feel some of the magic world coming back. In the corners of my eyes, the colours of the ancient forest were blurring back into being. The woodchopper! He was just up ahead, I could tell, and I knew it was going to be special.

I could hear the noise the newly split wood made as it bounced

38

to the ground. Then there was silence, although the air hummed with birdsong and insects.

As we walked into the glade, I saw he was bare-chested. His axe was upside down. The blade, which winked in the sunlight, was on the ground but he was still holding on to its long wooden handle. He was bending over it to stretch out his back.

He stood up straight then, and he was everything I knew he would be. He was tall and handsome, brave and noble. His fair hair was not Brylcreemed into place with a neat side parting like a normal man; it was loose about his face.

The woodcutter took in my mother and me, and smiled when the farmer announced us to be his first customers. He asked my mother a question, and that was when I heard his voice for the first time. He sounded *exactly* like a woodchopper. His voice was low with an accent that immediately placed him back in the magic world I had just left.

It was like I'd been struck dumb and my instinct was to hide myself, so I slipped behind my mother. But then I relaxed, stepped out and slowly made my way to the woodcutter so that I could watch him hurl blocks of wood into the trolley.

His blue eyes flicked up at me and he flashed me a grin as he worked.

'Hello,' he said.

'Hello.'

And I watched him in silence as he finished filling the trolley. A real woodchopper! Just like I'd imagined, but he was *real*.

I wanted to stay and watch him for longer but, when the trolley was full, Farmer Dawson led Mother and me over to a gap in the fence where we could walk through straight into the forest. He told us to walk a little way in and we'd find a path that would lead us out of the woods and on to the road that led to our cottage.

We'd stopped going to church a long time ago, so the next day I was completely free to spend a lot of time thinking. And I climbed the tree in the back garden so I could think about danger. Trolls were bad. And Germans were bad – but the woodchopper was a German and he was obviously good. It was confusing.

But by that night, as I lay in bed after my mother had read me my story, I thought I had come to an understanding of what was going on.

I was in the middle of a secret battle with the Troll and my daddy was battling against the Nazis – and the Fascists, who Mr Finlay said were finally on the run at least. There was danger all around.

The Troll would be prowling at night looking for children to gobble up, even right at that moment while I was tucked up in bed.

I knew my mother, meanwhile, was afraid of the Germans, and for all I knew was wide awake at this very minute – terrified, thinking about them all coming to live in Bambury. And even though the woodchopper we met earlier wasn't a baddie, she probably couldn't tell the difference like I could. There were good Germans, like the woodchopper, and bad Germans, like the Nazi soldiers.

But there *were* real Nazis sleeping not far from our house and that was a fact.

I wondered if I should find out where all the Jerries were living and watch them like I was watching the Troll. But then, I didn't want to divide my resources, because my resources mainly consisted of me. So I decided it was better to focus on the danger that all the other people had missed. All the adults were so obsessed with the Germans it actually got quite boring sometimes, but I bet none of them had even the foggiest idea that there was a dangerous Troll stalking the village. I tried to come up with some plans for how I could drive it out.

It was hard to sleep while I thought about how to make the Troll go away and I was awake for such a long time that I realised my room was getting lighter as the sun came up and pushed through the tiny cracks around the blackout blind. I fell asleep eventually to the sound of the dawn chorus in the front garden outside my window and dreamed dreams of me keeping her safe (and her realising it).

I was sleepy later that day at school. Maybe that was why I didn't have my wits about me.

Mr Finlay had been telling the class about how important it was to read regularly.

'You should all be reading at home,' he said. 'Reading not only provides you with a new way of seeing the world, boys, but it's the best way to improve your grammar and punctuation.'

He then began to question each boy about how often they read, whether they read real books or only comics and things like that.

Unfortunately, he started with the row of desks lining the left-hand side of the classroom. It was unfortunate because that was where I sat. He began with Donald Platt, who was the furthest back, in the corner, and who sat directly behind me.

'Now, Platt,' Mr Finlay began, 'what are your reading habits?'

Like the rest of the boys, I turned around to watch him answer. Donald squirmed in his seat and looked as though he might break his pencil into two pieces he was fiddling with it so much.

'Dunno, sir.'

He looked miserable.

'Come now, Platt, you must read sometimes!'

Donald just shook his head. I didn't know much about him; he was a new boy evacuated from London during the Blitz and was still here almost four years later. In other schools, perhaps, that length of time would make you not a 'new boy' any more, but not here.

'Well, what sort of books do your parents enjoy reading then? What books do you have at home?'

'Ain't got no books!' It was hard to tell if he was angry or ashamed, but I gasped a bit and I wasn't the only one – because he'd just raised his voice to a master.

41

'Platt,' Mr Finlay bellowed, 'you mean to say that you *haven't* any books! Which is almost impossible to believe. Equally impossible to digest is the tone of voice with which you've just addressed me! Now, you come with me; we're going straight to Mr Beecham's office and we'll see just what he has to say about this!'

Mr Finlay stamped down the row and clamped a fist to Donald's shoulder then propelled him from the room. As soon as the master was out of earshot, the others began laughing.

'I knew he was poor, but I didn't know he was that poor!'

'I ain't got no books,' William McCarthy said in a warbling, high-pitched voice. The others laughed louder, and he stood up, clutched his breast, and pretended to cry. 'I ain't got no books . . . at all!'

I laughed along too. Partly because the best thing to do is always fit in with whatever everybody else is doing. And partly because I was quite often their target myself, and any opportunity to be on the other side was definitely well worth taking. But mostly because William McCarthy's impersonations were always spot-on and he really was doing a great job of taking on poor Donald.

McCarthy was sobbing now, while some of the others, giggling, patted him on the back to console him. 'I wish I had just one book!' he wailed. 'But my parents' – he had actually made himself laugh now – 'ain't capable of reading!'

His friends roared at this and he sat back down. He was a new boy too, but despite that – even though it was never quite forgotten – his sense of humour made him one of the popular boys.

I thought of the torture Donald would suffer for weeks now. I could imagine the boys dangling a book in front of his face and asking if he knew what it was. ('Ain't you never seen one before?')

'That was smashing, McCarthy!' Martin Moore told him as the other boys returned to their seats too. His excited face was flushed as red as his hair. 'It was almost like Platt was back in the room!'

William seemed happy with his performance too and he accepted the praise with beaming eyes.

I mustn't let those eyes fall on me, I thought.

The door swung open as Mr Finlay entered and everyone quickly turned to face the front as some of the boys cleared their throats to shake out the last of their laughter. The teacher took up his favourite position, leaning backwards against the large wooden desk that faced the room, and continued with the lesson as though nothing had happened.

'Your turn, Mr Patterson,' he said to me.

'Oh . . .' I said. 'I love reading.'

He nodded for me to go on.

'And my mother and father both love reading too. We have *lots* of books on our shelves at home. In fact, my mother reads me a fairy tale every night before bed.'

I was so pleased I could tell everyone about it without looking like I was bragging. I sat back in my chair, happy with what I'd said. I'd been careful not to make any of Donald's mistakes.

But then I saw the smirks, the rolling eyes. I heard the stifled giggles. I had somehow got it wrong, and I felt a horrible roiling in my stomach and a prickly tingling on my scalp as I thought of what might happen to me at playtime.

When morning lessons were over, I tried to hide in the cloakroom but Mr Finlay poked his head around the door to check for stragglers and shooed me outside. If Donald had come out first I'd have been all right, but he must have still been waiting for Mr Beecham to cane him because I was surrounded almost instantly.

McCarthy and Matthew Lyme twisted my arms behind my back as the others, including a giggling Martin Moore, helped bundle me towards the outhouse at the back of the playground. And they were telling me that I was an odd-bod, that I thought I was cleverer than everyone else, and that I was a sissy. They were telling me that I was stupid for liking stories, and that I was a baby because my mother still read to me. Dozens of hands pushed me inside the little building and then they all leaned against the door so I couldn't get out.

I heard them trying to decide whether to actually hold me upside down and dangle my head into the toilet, but they couldn't seem to agree so decided to leave that for another day when they were more in the mood. But they all agreed to keep me locked in the outhouse until I'd learned my lesson and any boys who wanted to go to the toilet would just have to go in the bushes. They could take it up with me if they had any problems with that.

I didn't want to be outside in the playground with them but I panicked as the darkness and the walls pushed down on me. It felt like I was back in the tunnel and I knew the Troll was in the air around me and could use evil magic to rear up behind me in the dark. I began scrabbling at the door.

'Please! Please!' I tried to push my way out. 'I was just joking about the stories, I'm sorry! Please!' But they were laughing and laughing as they kept me trapped.

Eventually, I realised I had to stop begging because that was making them worse.

'All right,' I called through the door, forcing myself to step back and stand in the dark. 'All right.'

I squeezed my eyes shut and thought of my fairy stories for help. Maybe I could make the magic world surround me in here and keep me safe. But the magic wasn't strong enough that day and I knew if I opened my eyes I'd still be standing in the dirty, smelly outhouse in the playground. I thought of Hansel, who was kept locked in a cage by an evil witch. Gretel used her wits to kill the witch and save her brother, so maybe I could come up with a plan too. As I thought about Hansel and tried to come up with my own ideas for how to escape, my breathing and heartbeat started to slow down and I began to feel calmer.

One by one, they must have grown bored with having to lean against the door and gradually drifted away. After a while, I could tell there was no one there, and I slipped out and went and sat on my own in the corner of the playground where no one would see me.

7

'I forbid you to go into that little room, for if you do,
my anger will know no bounds.'

From *Bluebeard*

The news had thrown her into a panic: Reggie was coming home on leave for a twenty-four-hour visit.

Annabel wished she'd had more than a few days' notice. Weren't these things usually planned some time in advance? She was sure his previous visits were. In any case, there was now a tremendous amount to do and she was desperately trying to prepare the house for his arrival.

The upstairs seemed to have got a bit out of control. There were magazines and newspapers lying slumped where they'd fallen, and piles of laundry and dirty cups and plates on the landing and by the side of her bed.

It wasn't so much what Reggie thought; but his visit meant his parents had booked a room above the Royal Oak in the village so they could see as much of their son as possible – and they could never resist a snoop.

Annabel hadn't gone into Reggie's study even once since his last leave – the room had doubled as his bedroom since the boy was born – so luckily there was no work to do in there apart from a quick dusting. The room smelled a bit stale, and the sheets could probably do with changing, but she opened the window wide to the sunshine, deciding the fresh air would do the job for her just as well.

Heading downstairs, she grabbed a pile of papers in the hall and dumped them by the grate in the sitting room, to burn later in the evening.

My goodness, but all this housework was exhausting. A little rest and pick-me-up was what she needed. She poured herself some gin and sat in her armchair to catch her breath with a soothing cigarette. She inhaled deeply and tried to decide how she felt as she expelled the smoke with a sigh.

The boy was obviously delighted, but it would be strange having Reggie back in the house. While she worked hard to maintain the look of the house outside – diligently picking up stray magnolia petals from the lawn, and keeping the downstairs tidy on the remote off-chance of unexpected visitors – she was able to be much more relaxed in other areas. And she liked that she didn't have to get up and get dressed or clean the house if she didn't feel like it. In some ways, she felt she was finally getting the rest she'd been desperate for ever since the boy was born.

She stood up and crossed to the bureau to pull out a pile of Reggie's letters. The thin envelopes were battered and creased from their journeys, but they were probably no more damaged than when they'd arrived because she didn't tend to look at them again after the first reading.

Settling back in her armchair, with her cigarette still smouldering between the first two fingers of her right hand, she fanned the letters out across her lap. It was hard even to visualise her husband. What had it been – eighteen months since the last visit? Perhaps, if she re-read a few letters while she finished her cigarette, it would help remind her of him.

She selected a letter from the back of the pile, one of the older ones, when he'd still been training at Invicta Lines, the barracks in Maidstone. She noticed there was a note for Daniel tucked inside – she must have forgotten to give it to him.

20th May, 1940

Dear Annabel,
How are you and Daniel? Both well I hope? I'm absolutely fine so you mustn't worry about me. The food isn't very good, but I mustn't grumble!

It's been very busy. Quite tiring – all this physical work is a bit of a shock to the system after the bank!

I hope you're well?

I'm not sure when they'll be shipping us out although there are rumours it'll be next month. They're still training us up. It's strange to know how to use a gun; we've been doing lots of target practice and all that.

Sharing a room with the fellows in my unit almost makes me feel as though I'm at boarding school all over again. Although some of the men here have strong working-class accents so that's a little bit different! They've given me some good-natured ribbing because I pronounce all my Ts and Hs! Ha ha! But they're all very nice chaps, the lot of them. It's been surprisingly fun, considering the seriousness of our occupation.

I received a letter from my parents. They said they've been to see you. Have you sent any letters? I know it hasn't been very long since I left, but I haven't heard from you.

Mother said you seemed well. How's Daniel? I hope you're getting on all right with the cooking. You were always a better cook than me, so I hope you're enjoying it again. Are you still reading to him? I know he likes that. I've enclosed a letter for you to read to him.

Please write back so I know you're well.
Love, Reggie.

20th May, 1940

Dear Daniel,
How have you been, old man? Being good for Mother? It's
very exciting being a soldier – just like the games we play
together. I'm a real soldier now, and I'm officially called
Private Reginald Patterson of the Royal West Kent Regiment.
When I get back – I'm sure I'll have a visit soon – I'll tell you
all about it. I'll teach you the tricks of the trade!
I miss you very much but it's important to be a man and
serve your country. So I want you to be a big boy – after all,
you'll be starting primary school soon – and be a man at
home.
It would be marvellous if you could draw me a nice
picture of you, me and Mother. I'd like that very much.
Love, Daddy.

Annabel replaced the letters in the envelope. There was no point
giving Daniel a letter that was now years out of date. She'd given
him all the others.

She read a couple more letters then pulled another from the
pile. This one had been written a few years after he was first sent
to join the fighting. She remembered reading it and recalled it was
different from the others; the tone had changed, and Reggie had
written in a tiny, cramped hand to use up all the available space
on the paper. She remembered not quite knowing what to make
of it at the time.

8th June, 1943

Dear Annabel,
I don't think all your letters are getting through, because it's
been a while since I heard from you.

48

Things can be hard here and I like to hear about the two of you safe and well in Bambury. I miss it!

I worry when I don't hear from you for so long. I know you've been doing really well without me though, and I'm very proud of you. I was so worried about you when I had to leave that first time to go off for training – you seemed so anxious at the thought of me not being there.

It was terrible when we had to say goodbye at the train station, wasn't it? I think about that day a lot. That was the last time I was an ordinary civilian in ordinary clothes and I still didn't know what being a soldier would really involve.

I'd imagined us saying a quiet goodbye, but instead there were hundreds and hundreds of other soon-to-be soldiers packed on that concourse with their families. It was chaos, and I wonder if you noticed the feeling in the air that I did then – that emotional but somehow festive atmosphere feeding off the crowds of parents, wives and children waving goodbye to the men.

I almost regretted saying goodbye to Mother and Father at our house that morning – it would have been nice to have a little group with me as well. But they were probably right that Daniel might've become too upset when he realised I was leaving. As it was I don't think he realised the signifi-cance at all, do you? He just let me kiss him and cuddle him as normal, as if I were off to work. He was only five though, which is very young, and maybe that's a blessing.

I saw your eyes watering, Annabel, as the train was announced ready to depart – everyone suddenly hugging and crying around us. There was that couple who kissed right on the lips, remember, in front of everybody! You looked so shocked. I don't think either of us quite knew how to say goodbye.

I think about you in your pretty cream hat, clutching your handkerchief in one hand and your handbag in the other. You looked so stricken that day, and so very young.

That was the moment I felt frightened about leaving you. I was suddenly afraid you might not be able to look after yourself and Daniel without me there making sure everything ticked along. I was worried poor Daniel wouldn't understand and he'd keep asking for me and that might upset you even more.

I wanted to say: 'Give him time – he is such a wonderful little boy, you'll see. You two will end up as thick as thieves without me there!' But that busy platform didn't seem the place to say any of this.

I miss him so much though. It's so easy for me to love him and sometimes I wonder if other men feel like this about their children, because the chaps here don't really talk about those sorts of things. I remember you told me once you didn't feel a thing for him. This was when he was just a couple of months old. I'm sure you're horrified now that you could ever think such a thing, but it's the sort of remark you can't forget hearing. And I wonder perhaps if hearing that has made me attempt to make up for it with Daniel somehow.

I'm sorry if this hurts you Annabel, but I panicked at the station because I suddenly thought you could very well fall back into the state you'd been in after you first had him. How could I help, and step in to look after our son, if I was miles away without knowing what was going on?

In the end, I settled for a friendly squeeze of your arm. 'There, there,' I think I told you. 'It'll be all right.'

But your mouth was quivering and your eyes were full.

'I can't do it,' you said, and I remember your voice cracking at the end. 'I won't manage.'

'It'll be fine.' I said that more loudly than I'd intended. I didn't mean to be brusque, Annabel.

They made that final tannoy call just then so I couldn't put things right and then we both looked away, back over to the train, and the crowd was pushing past us as everyone started rushing. Then I squeezed your arm again and had to leave you standing there on the platform and get on the train. I pushed my way over to the window – I wanted to wave to you like all the other men were waving – but I couldn't find you. Maybe you left, maybe it was too upsetting for you – it's all right.

All the men were pushed up against the glass waving and calling out as the train started to move forward, but I went and found a good seat and sat down to have a smoke. I was the only one sitting down at that moment in the whole carriage. It hit me that I was leaving and it's embarrassing to admit it but my own eyes nearly watered. I realised you hadn't told me to be careful or anything like that. You didn't seem very worried about me. But there I was, so afraid about what would happen to you. You and Daniel.

Well, it's been three years and I know you've done a marvellous job so I needn't have worried so. It's just that when so long passes without a letter from you, all those fears I had that day in Waterloo Station come rushing back. Can you understand that, Annabel?

And it's not just that I'm worried about you both – I'm not trying to check up on you as such – your letters help give me a lift too.

Please write to me soon.
Love, Reggie

Annabel stubbed out her cigarette in the ashtray on the table next to her and folded the letter away out of sight in its envelope.

None of his letters before or afterwards were like that. There was something a bit, well, distasteful about it, really – all that emotion laid bare on the page. And the censor would have seen that! She shook her head in embarrassment, on Reggie's behalf and her own.

She was unable to remember how she had responded. Most likely she had, when she got around to it, written some assurances – nothing too emotional – insisting that everything was perfectly all right. It was irritating how Reggie – just like his parents and hers – seemed to assume she was completely incompetent.

In fact, she *had* still been at the station when Reggie's train had left; she'd had to run to compose herself in the ladies' on the concourse before beginning her journey back to Bambury alone.

But she was proud of herself for not openly crying out there in the throng. She had looked quite steadily, she thought, into Reggie's handsome face – his bright blue eyes and neat brown moustache suddenly familiar and reassuring.

When she was on the Tube heading to Victoria, to catch the train to Densford where she'd change again, her eyes began to well up once more so she turned her face to the window and pulled her hat down a little to cover her eyes from the other passengers. She stared at her reflection for a minute or two and then let her eyes unfocus slightly so that she could see through her face in the glass to the black tunnel behind it.

Reggie was the planet she and the child circled around like moons – his orbit the cohesive force binding them into at least a semblance of a family.

When Annabel returned home after seeing him off it was just after half past eleven in the morning. She took a deep breath to compose herself before going inside.

She concentrated on the details of the dark green paint of the front door – it was starting to chip around the little stained-glass window at the top. She would have to arrange for a workman to come and repaint it. She would write the task down on a piece of paper and then accomplish it. She would go around the house checking for anything else that needed to be done. That didn't sound too daunting. Perhaps she needn't have been so worried about Reggie's absence after all. This might actually be a strangely liberating experience.

But as she stepped over the threshold and automatically wiped her feet a couple of times on the rough bristles of the coconut mat, the familiar sights and smells of the house rushed at her to remind her how useless she was. She wouldn't contact a handyman and arrange for him to do odd jobs.

Reggie's parents were waiting for her in the sitting room and she could tell they'd just stopped speaking when they'd heard the door opening.

'Hello, dear,' Moira called.

'I'll be with you in a minute,' she said, as she unpinned her hat in front of the hall mirror.

She smoothed down her hair, took another breath, checked her face again to ensure the ugly red tear stains had disappeared, then hung her hat on the coat stand along with her mac and went to join her parents-in-law.

'Hello, Mother!' Daniel said, looking up from where he sat on the rug pushing some brightly coloured wooden blocks around.

'Here you are!' Moira said, as she and Bill stood up from the sofa to greet her.

Moira strode over to clasp Annabel in an awkward embrace for a second or two before she thought better of it. She took a step back and turned slightly to watch Daniel who had returned to his game.

'Reggie got off all right, then?' Bill asked.

'Yes, yes,' she said. 'He's on his way now.'

'Ah, good. That's that then.'

They all fell silent, and Annabel couldn't think how to break the awkwardness. Reggie had always been there to take charge as a sort of intermediary.

'We were just about to have a cup of tea when you arrived,' Bill said, gesturing down to the tea tray on the coffee table in front of him.

'Oh, lovely . . .'

No one had sat back down and she wasn't sure if they were waiting for her to invite them to, since they were guests in her house. But they'd been here before she even arrived so perhaps she should wait for them to offer her a chair? She remembered hearing the pair of them plotting with Reggie to have her committed to an asylum.

'I'll fetch you a cup, dear,' Moira said, and Annabel stepped further into the room so Moira could get past her to go to the kitchen.

She could smell her overpowering lavender perfume as she passed; her mother-in-law made it herself and was always giving little bottles to Annabel which she threw away.

Tea! That's what Annabel should have done. She should have offered to make them a drink as soon she got in. She'd already let Moira down by failing this small test.

Her father-in-law sat down again while Annabel perched on the armchair, wringing her fingers.

The boy turned to look up at her. 'Look what I made!'

Annabel saw he was pointing to a cube made out of the blocks.

'It's a castle. I made it.'

Having Bill watching the exchange made Annabel feel even more awkward than she usually did around the child.

'Yes,' she tried to say brightly and even attempted a smile.

'It's a castle,' Daniel said again. 'I'm the king.'

'And a very fine one it is too, young man,' said his grandfather. 'Why don't you build something else to show us what you can do? Hmmm, a right little architect, aren't you?'

Daniel nodded and began to scoop up the scattered bricks.

Annabel smiled at Bill, whose moustache and kind-looking face made him look like an older version of Reggie, which she supposed he was. Moira returned with a cup and then poured tea for everybody, including a milky one for the boy.

'You're back earlier than we thought,' she remarked. 'How was it?'

'It was . . .' Annabel trailed off, not sure what the question meant. 'I'll miss him,' she said eventually, although that was not quite true. 'It will be strange without him here,' she added, which was. Her eyes threatened to betray her but she managed to hold her tears in.

'We'll all miss him,' Moira agreed, abruptly. 'The worst thing is the worry, isn't it? I'll be praying every day for his safety.'

Annabel hadn't really thought about that. She'd been so worried about what his absence meant for her that she hadn't really thought about what would happen if he were hurt or even killed. What would she do then?

'You mustn't think about all that – you'll only upset yourself, Moira,' her husband told her.

'Who's upset?' Daniel asked.

'And remember that little pitchers have big ears,' Bill added.

'Nobody's upset, dear,' Moira said. 'That's a good castle.'

They all looked at the boy's design and agreed as they drank their tea.

'Well, we better get a move on after this,' Bill said. 'We've got a long drive ahead of us.'

Annabel nodded. 'Absolutely.'

'Norfolk's lovely this time of the year,' he added.

'Ah, yes, I'm sure.'

Moira fidgeted, placing her cup back on the tray and patting her auburn hair. She seemed more uncomfortable than Annabel with the silences. 'How long have we been there now, Bill? Two years?'

'Um, three, I think.'

Moira laughed. 'Goodness! How time flies!'

'Yes, it does, doesn't it?' Annabel gave a little laugh too.

'Can't say I miss London – especially not now,' Bill continued. 'All those streets reduced to rubble.' He shook his head. 'Moira

55

and I were disappointed when you and Reggie moved out here when you married, and I know your parents were too because we all lived so close to each other before, but now we're glad of it.'

Moira drained her tea. 'Have you finished, Bill? Now then...' She shifted in her seat and looked at Annabel. 'Are you going to be all right, dear?'

Finally.

'Yes... Yes, thank you. I'll be quite all right.' Annabel swallowed and gave a shaky smile. '*We'll* be quite all right, I mean.' They all glanced again at the boy. 'My parents are just a train ride away.'

'Well, you'll let us know too if you need anything,' Bill said.

'Of course, thank you.'

Annabel realised she hadn't drunk any of her tea. It was almost cold now but she took a few gulps.

'I'm sure Bill could do without me for a few days if you want me to stay? Or you could always come up to Norfolk with us.'

'No, no!' Annabel was horrified. 'Really, there's no need to put yourself out. We'll be fine.'

'Or... Well, now I think of it; perhaps we could take Daniel back with us. You know. Just for a little while. Give you a bit of a break? And we'll have such fun, won't we, Daniel? You can play with your friend Harry, remember, who lives next door?'

The boy looked up with sudden interest now he was the topic of conversation.

'No, please – I...' she looked from Moira to Bill. Was this another plot? 'There's really no need for this.'

'Well, if you really think... If you're sure?'

'Yes, quite sure. Thank you for the offer, but honestly, like I said – there's really no need.'

There seemed to be nothing else to say, and Bill and Moira finally put down their cups and stood up.

'Shall I help you clear up then, dear? Before we go?' Moira said.

'Oh no, leave that, please – thank you.'

Bill crouched down beside the boy, wincing as his knee cracked audibly.

'So. Have you finished?'

'Nearly. It's an even bigger castle this time.'

'Very big. Much bigger than the last one. Well done.'

He cuffed the child playfully across his shoulder and heaved himself back up.

'Say goodbye,' Annabel said. 'Granny and Grandpa are going home now.'

Daniel stood, appearing reluctant to be kissed by Moira, but too polite to refuse. She left a smudge of lipstick on his cheek and he wiped at it with his sleeve.

Bill ruffled his hair. 'Bye, Master Daniel.'

Annabel walked Reggie's parents to the front door. 'Thank you for coming.'

'Don't be silly,' Moira said, kissing her cheek.

Annabel resisted the instinct to rub at the spot of saliva and lipstick she could feel there.

'Bear up, old girl,' Bill said, squeezing her arm in a gesture reminiscent of his son's earlier that day.

'We'll visit again in a month or two.'

'Thanks, Moira. Well, goodbye then.'

Daniel had followed Annabel out into the hall and they both waved as the Pattersons drove off. Moira's worried face framed by the passenger window was the last thing Annabel saw before she shut the front door. She didn't look at the peeling paint.

That had been a difficult day, and sitting here now, four years on, Annabel was sure the door must be in even more need of a new coat. She'd check it later to see how bad it was, but first she'd sip her gin and light a fresh cigarette.

One more smoke, and then she'd carry on with the housework. Starting with putting these letters back in the bureau.

Idly, she turned to the most recent, the one on the top of the pile. It had arrived just over a week ago – the morning before she received a scrawled note from Reggie's commanding officer informing her that her husband was due a day's rest and recuperation at home. 'Do him good to see his pretty wife and son!' the man had written.

10th May, 1944

Dear Annabel and Daniel,
Sorry it's been a long time since I wrote. I'm fine apart from the ringing in my ears which stops me sleeping.
Love, Daddy
P.S. Please keep sending letters.
P.P.S. How are you?

'I'm so glad he wrote again! I was worried,' Daniel had said after they'd both read it.

'No need to worry. I told you that.'

'It's . . . not very long, is it?'

'Well, he's very busy.'

But the tone of Reggie's letter *was* a trifle odd. She was surprised the boy had seemed to pick up on it.

'I'm going to write to him straight away!' he had said and charged upstairs.

She'd supposed she should draft her own reply too but hadn't yet started it when she learned of Reggie's upcoming home leave. There was no point now she'd be seeing him so soon.

It was something of a relief; she found it difficult to fill an entire sheet of paper talking about the weather, the food situation, and the boy.

She folded the final letter away and returned the pile to the bureau. Still standing, she finished her second cigarette and her drink, and went back upstairs with some beeswax furniture polish to make everything look nice and shiny.

Reggie's train was due in at 10.12 at Victoria Station.

Moira and Bill had driven Annabel and Daniel down to London to meet him, and the family lined up on the concourse to await his train.

Annabel smoothed down her skirt and straightened her matching green jacket. She had tried to look smart but was now crumpled from the car journey. Moira looked impeccable as usual, in a long-sleeved pink dress that set off her auburn hair nicely. She had doused herself even more liberally than usual with lavender water and Annabel felt nauseous after breathing in the reek of it in the enclosed space of the car.

'Will he definitely remember what we all look like, Grandpa?'

'Yes, yes, of course he will. You can remember what Daddy looks like, can't you?'

'Um . . . yes?'

'Well, there you are!'

'Sometimes I look at the photograph of him and Mother on their wedding day. The one in the sitting room.'

Daniel was standing between his grandparents holding their hands, and when Annabel looked over she saw him scratching his calf with his other foot. He was jiggling up and down slightly. Bill had just taken him to the toilet so she hoped he didn't need to go again.

'But people can look different from photographs,' the boy continued. 'Sometimes they smile so they look happy but they might not be really, and sometimes they look serious, but actually they are very funny.'

'Yes, I suppose you're right.'

'And also, sometimes you might smile and be happy when the photo is taken, but just one minute later you might hurt yourself and be crying and serious.'

'Yes, that's true as well. But Daddy looks just like that

59

photograph in the sitting room, remember? And he'll be very happy to see you.'

At last, the train pulled in and passengers started piling through the doors of the carriages. There were several men in uniform and the family scanned their faces looking for Reggie.

In fact, they nearly didn't recognise him. Bill was wrong; he didn't look like that photograph at all.

Annabel heard Moira gasp next to her and turned to see what she was looking at.

'Oh, goodness,' she said.

Reggie had grown very thin, which made his eyes seem excessively large in his gaunt face. They had a dazed expression and he didn't appear to have seen them at first as he shuffled along with the crowd.

'Christ,' she heard Bill mutter.

'Grandpa, you swore!'

'Sorry, Daniel.'

Annabel realised the boy hadn't spotted him yet; he was still looking around for his daddy.

'Reggie! Reggie! Over here!' Moira called as she marched towards her son.

Annabel could no longer see her mother-in-law's face, but knew she'd have a lovely bright smile plastered there. She tried to rearrange her own expression into something similar while Moira enveloped Reggie in a fierce hug.

She took a couple of steps forward, along with Bill, who led the boy by the hand, as Moira walked Reggie back to them. Perhaps it was just the drab brown-green of his uniform that made his skin look so grey.

'Ah! Hello, Reggie!' With his parents here she felt self-conscious, but reached up to kiss his cheek, which was rough with stubble. His moustache was tatty and almost lost amongst the patchy growth of whiskers.

'Damn ringing in my ears,' he said loudly, waving his hands around his head. 'I can barely hear you.'

Bill stepped forward. 'Wonderful to have you home, son.' He slapped his shoulder and Annabel saw her husband flinch.

Then Reggie realised the boy was there and he seemed to become still as he stared down at him.

'My Daniel.'

The child had been watching Reggie with shock etched across his features and he had huddled against his grandpa's leg. But now he must have seen something he recognised. Because he wordlessly lifted up his arms, and Reggie scooped him up, and they buried their faces in each other's necks.

Moira tried to engage Reggie in conversation in the car during the journey back to Kent, but he was in the front seat and said he couldn't hear her. So she kept up a bright stream of chatter all the way home, which Annabel supposed must have been for everybody else's benefit.

When they arrived at the cottage they all climbed out of the car for a short rest and to drop off Reggie's bag. Moira insisted Reggie shave, so now, to Annabel's relief, he was looking a little more like his old self.

It was clear he'd been left a bit shaken by the fighting. It seemed strange when she compared him to the relaxed-looking Jerry prisoners she'd seen arriving in the village. She thought of the tall one with the fair hair, Johannes, confidently striding down the lane.

And then they were in the car again, heading for Hillwood Grange Hotel in Densford where Bill had booked them in for Sunday lunch. They were given a nice spot by a large window and all ordered the roast beef.

As they waited, Reggie began to fidget, jerking his head and repeatedly scanning the tables.

'They're carrying on as normal.' He tittered, and looked at Moira incredulously.

'Everyone's got to eat, Reggie,' his mother said. 'It doesn't mean they're not as upset about the war as you are.'

There was an uncomfortable pause as Reggie stared at her. *'They're carrying on as normal.'*

In fact, sitting here with Reggie in uniform, Annabel was aware that it did seem somehow foolish to be eating lunch in a restaurant as though people weren't being shot at just over the Channel.

She could see what Reggie was getting at; that this meal, this restaurant, was an absurdity.

But she was surprised Reggie wanted everyone to acknowledge the fact. Apart from the bizarrely emotional letter he'd sent her once dredging up the difficulties with her nerves after Daniel was born, he was usually as much a one for pretending everything was normal as his parents. But after two car journeys featuring Reggie's strange silences and sudden outbursts about the ringing in his ears, Moira's nerves appeared to be ragged. Even Bill seemed a little frustrated with his son. Perhaps they felt as she did and were secretly relieved his visit home would be over by the morning.

The waitress topped up their glasses with vinegary white wine, apologising again that there was no red on the menu today. Annabel took a couple of gulps. She stared at the linen tablecloth, which had been starched so often the fabric was becoming threadbare at the folds. She rubbed it with her finger, feeling where the rough cotton had turned smooth and almost shiny along the crease.

She drank some more of her sharp wine.

Daniel was arranging his cutlery into geometric patterns in front of him. Nobody asked him to behave because at least he was sitting quietly. His smart bow tie was starting to sag. If he was aware of the tension, or his father's distress, he didn't show any sign of it.

The waitress came back with another girl also bearing a tray and their lunches were placed in front of them all with a flourish.

Annabel felt suddenly ravenous; it made a change to have a hot meal. Mostly she and the child ate sandwiches whenever they got hungry, because it was so much easier than thinking about ingredients and cooking.

She idly wondered how the hotel was getting its food.

Opposite her, Reggie was chewing too, but had apparently realised something was wrong with the piece of meat in his mouth.

'I can't eat this bit.'

'Sorry?' Moira asked.

'It's, I don't know, a bit of gristle. It's all bony. They disguised it with all this onion gravy.' He pushed his mouthful into the side of his cheek and looked round at them all.

'I can't swallow it,' he told the table, looking panicky. 'I can't eat it.'

Moira started laughing. 'Spit it out then!'

He shook his head. 'No!'

'You have to! Do it discreetly, in your napkin. No one will notice.'

Reggie started to laugh too, although he had to keep his mouth pinched closed so the food couldn't fall out.

Bill started to chuckle as well, and then the boy joined in. Annabel smiled, relieved the tension had been broken.

Reggie was still laughing, with the meat a tell-tale bulge in his cheek. Finally, he raised his napkin to his lips and spat the offending gristle into the cloth. He folded it over to hide the gravy smears on the white cotton. Everyone was still giggling and Reggie's cheeks were red from trying to compose himself. They were all hunched over, trying not to attract attention, apart from Daniel, who was delighted at the sudden laughter, although Annabel wasn't entirely sure he got the joke.

Reggie laughed so hard, he cried. And then he couldn't stop crying. Tears streamed down his cheeks and Annabel registered with a start that he was suddenly choking back sobs.

It was impossible to tell where the change occurred and there was little to distinguish between the two states at first. Everyone continued laughing for a while before they realised what was going on.

Annabel sobered instantly and saw the stupid grins fade from the faces of her in-laws. Only the boy was still giggling.

Moira cast an anxious glance around the restaurant. Annabel looked around too and saw the diners seated at the tables nearest to them were watching and whispering behind their hands.

'That's enough,' Bill said in a low voice. 'Pull yourself together now, son.'

Reggie turned his face away towards the window and tried to shield his eyes from his horrified family. He gasped as he struggled to regain control.

Annabel was dumbstruck. Was she supposed to say something? Comfort him? She looked to Moira for guidance but saw nothing but mortification in her expression. In truth, Annabel was mortified too, and strangely frightened.

In public! That's what she couldn't believe. She had *never* caused a scene in public – no matter what her own weaknesses, no matter what was going on in her own house; strangers weren't to know.

She noticed even the child was silent now, staring at his father, aware that something was very wrong.

Reggie rubbed his eyes viciously with his palms, to remove any stubborn tears that clung there. He turned back to the table, although he kept his eyes lowered.

'I'm all right now.'

8

*... the youngest son took his cup to the sick king in
order that he might drink out of it, and be cured.*

From *The Water of Life*

'Daniel?'

But I was still staring at Daddy, whose red eyes were staring down at the plate in front of him, so Grandpa shook my shoulder until I looked up at him in the seat next to me.

'Come on Daniel, let's go to the toilet.'

I felt my cheeks blaze red because the other people stared at us as we made our way through the restaurant to the toilets. Grandpa didn't notice because he kept his head down.

'Why is Daddy crying?'

'What? No he isn't.' He held a door open to one of the cubicles. 'Would you rather go in there?'

'He is. I saw him.'

'Oh, that! That's all the onions in his gravy! Haven't you ever heard onions make you cry?'

I nodded uncertainly.

'There you are then. Bit embarrassing, really. Probably best not mention it – you don't want to make him feel bad about it. We'll just give him a moment. With the women. He'll be all right when we get back.'

Poor Daddy! I hoped the onions in my gravy wouldn't make me cry. I'd scrape it off my meat when we got back to the table.

65

I would offer to scrape it off Daddy's as well, but I didn't want to embarrass him for crying. I'd let him scrape his own sauce off.

Back at home, Daddy said he thought he needed a quick nap, so he went upstairs to his bedroom. We had tea in the sitting room but Daddy still didn't come down and, when it started to get dark, Grandpa and Granny said they might as well go and have an early night in their room at the pub.

'But we should wake him up to say goodbye first,' Granny said. 'We've hardly seen him.'

Mother started to stand up from her armchair. 'I can wake him . . . ?'

'No, let him sleep,' Grandpa said. 'That's all he needs. He's exhausted, that's all. Touch of – what do they call it? – battle fatigue. He'll be right as rain after a good sleep.'

When they left, I fiddled with my bow tie until it came off and Mother put the wireless on and made one of her special drinks. I wandered upstairs and listened outside Daddy's door. It was quiet.

I pushed the door open and tiptoed to his bed. He'd put on his pyjamas, which made him look more like Daddy – I didn't really like his green soldier uniform after all, I decided. It was interesting to watch his face as he slept because I could tell he was dreaming – his mouth was open slightly and his eyelids were twitching. His eyes snapped open suddenly and he sat straight up and grabbed me with a gasp, which made us both jump.

'Ah, Daniel!' He laughed a little bit and lay back down. 'It's you. What are you up to?'

I shrugged.

I wondered if I should tell him there was a Troll in Bambury. But then I thought I probably shouldn't worry him when he'd be leaving again first thing in the morning.

'I'm doing a good job looking after Mother,' I said finally.

66

He laughed again. 'I know you are. I can see. You've been a very good boy.'

'Yes.' I lowered my voice. 'I'm doing a lot of hush-hush work around the house to make sure she's protected.'

'Speak up, there's a good boy! There's such a ringing in my ears.'

I repeated what I'd said. He smiled and reached out an arm to ruffle my hair. 'Excellent. Good boy.'

He yawned and pulled back the corner of his eiderdown and I climbed in. It was like climbing into a warm cocoon as he pulled the covers across us and curled up around me. I was wrapped up tight like a butterfly. I still had my clothes on so it was quite hot, but it felt so nice being surrounded by his body. I knew I was probably a bit old to be sleeping in his bed because I was nine – I was very little the last time I remembered doing this, and that was when I'd had a bad dream. But it seemed to me that Daddy had been having a bad dream himself, so I was happy to stay if it stopped him being scared.

His nose was above the top of my head and his breath tickled me as it moved against my hair, but in a nice way. His breathing got deeper and deeper and I could tell he'd fallen asleep again. It was so peaceful lying in his arms I felt myself falling under as well, and although I woke for a minute when I heard Mother going to her own room, I was soon fast asleep again and we stayed wrapped up together all night.

Things were always better when Daddy was at home, and I wished he didn't have to leave so soon. It was early, so I left him sleeping and went to the bathroom. We hadn't done any arm wrestling yet, I thought as I brushed my teeth, and I was sure I'd be able to beat him properly now without him letting me win. Grandpa and Granny hadn't arrived yet to take us to London to see Daddy off, and Mother was still asleep in her room, so we definitely had time for a few matches once he was up.

But he wasn't in his bed when I went back and I couldn't find him anywhere.

I thought he must have gone out somewhere and felt a bit upset because he hadn't told me. But then for some reason I thought I'd just check the garden.

It was then I heard a funny noise in the air-raid shelter. It almost sounded like weeping. I listened for a minute or two, then knocked at the door.

'Daddy?'

The noise stopped immediately, but the door didn't open and after a while I went away.

9

Their world seemed to her much larger than her own;
they could sail across the oceans in their ships and
climb mountains that rose above the clouds . . .
From *The Little Mermaid*

Annabel was exhausted by Reggie's visit – and the close proximity of his parents – and spent almost two days in bed after he left. But on the second day she fancied some fresh air so decided to pop to the High Street to do some shopping that afternoon.

It was lovely and warm and she only needed a thin cardigan over her floral dress. The boy saw her as she was heading out of the front door with her wicker basket and she allowed him to accompany her. She thought perhaps he was a bit sad since his father had left and she felt a little badly for him. She held open the garden gate for him and in a spontaneous rush of feeling placed her hand on the crown of his head as he passed through, making him smile up at her.

She headed to the greengrocer's, Sid Mitchell's shop, for some fruit and vegetables. Occasionally she was able to get gin from under his counter, too. She always told him it was for her father, who liked a tipple. When they entered, Mr Mitchell was discussing the new PoW camp with the pimply adolescent who was his assistant.

Annabel wandered over to the box of carrots and began to select a few; the hotel had inspired her to cook a hot meal.

69

'But who's *in charge* of them, like?' the teenager asked.

'Well,' Mr Mitchell said, 'they all go out to different farms in the day, and then the farmers are in charge of them. But the actual camp itself, which is on a field that used to be part of Ray Dawson's land, is being run by an old boy who was a colonel in the Great War.'

'And that's it?'

'That's it.'

Annabel shifted position so she could watch as the pair talked. Mr Mitchell had grown his thin grey hair long on one side and then combed it over his scalp as though the strands would hide his baldness. He sat on a stool behind the counter, while the youth leaned back against some shelves, intent on his boss's words.

'I forget his name, the colonel,' Mr Mitchell said. 'But he's on to a good little number there – he spends his days inside a hut reading the *Racing Post* and drinking Bovril, from what I've heard. He just has to do a roll-call twice a day and that's a day's work for him.'

This sounded highly unlikely to Annabel. Surely the camp's perimeters would be closely guarded by soldiers or even the Home Guard? The same thought must have occurred to the grocer's assistant, for he sounded nervous when he said it didn't sound as if the camp was 'exactly secure, like'.

Annabel moved towards the potatoes, the boy trailing by her side.

'Oh, don't you fret about that now,' the grocer told his assistant. 'Security's all but unnecessary in a place like that. They don't send us high-level Nazis down here, do they? No, course not. They ship them somewhere top secret, Gawd knows where. Somewhere guarded, somewhere where they can break them down for information. Somewhere up in Scotland more than likely. Or one of those funny little islands off the mainland. Or maybe somewhere abroad.'

Annabel saw the youth's eyes widen as he took this in, but he remained silent.

'This might seem like the whole world to you, lad, but Bambury is just a, you know, just a tiny speck on the map. Mark my words; none of those Jerries in that camp is anything other than a low-level nobody. And because we're so rural, we're so far out of the way that if they ran away from the camp, where could they even run to?'

At this, the grocer's assistant opened his mouth to interject, but the grocer wasn't finished.

'And they don't just ship them here willy-nilly. They classify them first, interrogate them all. You look next time you see one about the village – he'll have a diamond-shaped bit of cloth sewn to the back of his work shirt. They colour-code them all. If they're a high-ranking officer, or have really strong Nazi views, they have to wear a black patch. If they're anti-Nazi they'll wear a white one, and anyone else is put in grey. All the ones I've seen in Bambury are grey, because most people are shades of grey, aren't they, if you think about it? But in any case, they're just the normal Germans. They're not really Nazis at all.'

'But isn't it possible that—'

'No, those PoWs wouldn't even dream of running in the first place, and I'll tell you why.'

He took a slow sip from his mug of tea to allow time for a dramatic pause. Annabel picked up a potato and turned it over in her hands as though looking for blemishes.

'It's because nobody in their right mind would want to leave.' He nodded. 'Just think about it: those young lads can wait out the rest of the war here. Conditions are good, they're safe from the front lines, no one's going to kill them and they won't have to kill anyone else. They're being fed and yes, they might have to do a bit of manual labour or work on the farms around the village, but the rest of the time they can spend playing cards and putting their

71

feet up. Not a bad life if you can get it. There's worse ways to spend a war, if you ask me. Like my boy Teddy on the front line.'

At this, the grocer finished his tea with a gulp and slammed his chipped blue mug down on the counter for emphasis.

He looked across at Annabel. 'Hello, Mrs Patterson. You all right there, love?'

Annabel jumped – she knew she'd been caught eavesdropping – but she gestured to the potatoes and asked what variety they were.

As they headed back through the village, Annabel told the child they were going to walk a little out of their way – in truth go right past their house – in order to have a quick look at the new PoW camp. Apart from the German soldier who chopped the wood, she hadn't seen any of the other prisoners since they'd arrived in Bambury and felt suddenly curious to see where they were living.

They continued down Ivy Lane, not even stopping to drop the shopping off, and turned left. They passed Dawson's farm and walked for another twenty minutes along a road lined with straggly hedgerows and fields on either side, until they came to the site.

Annabel stepped off the asphalt onto the grassy verge to look across the top of the bushes. She shifted her basket against her hip as she took in the camp. The boy ran up and down the hedge, crouching to look through it at various points.

Where, just weeks earlier, sheep had grazed, now stood a holding camp for foreign prisoners. She counted ten pre-fabricated dormitory huts, although there was easily space for another ten and a messy pile of building materials indicated more would indeed be built in due course. Only one had thick black curtains at the windows so she guessed that was the only dormitory occupied so far.

The Nissen huts were basic; just corrugated steel structures with rounded roofs and sides that curved into the ground, as though the building had once been a cylinder or tube that had been sliced in half lengthways. She was too far away to see through the windows but imagined what they might look like inside. She thought each one would probably hold about forty beds or so, and visualised twenty metal cots with thin mattresses lining each side of the building. There were a couple of smaller huts off to one side of the field with water tanks on their roofs and she guessed they must be rudimentary bathrooms, with a toilet and basin and perhaps even a basic shower rigged up.

She gazed around the rest of the camp and noticed a smaller, but slightly sturdier, pre-fab and realised that must be the office and sleeping quarters of the old colonel that Mr Mitchell had mentioned. The lone camp 'guard'.

It still seemed a little strange that an old man was the only defence against roughly forty or so German soldiers, with more to come. It seemed even odder that the men were allowed to walk unescorted to various farms around the village to do their work as though they were leaving for normal jobs in peacetime.

She found it hard to reconcile Bambury's apparently relaxed attitude to the German soldiers with Reggie's shaky distress. It made him seem a bit, well, silly.

There hadn't been reports of any trouble with PoWs in the village and the greengrocer seemed to think they weren't really any different from the Brits. Just unlucky men who happened to be in the wrong army on the wrong side.

She thought of Johannes, the PoW she'd met, and felt a little sorry for him now; he was just an ordinary man being held prisoner in a strange country.

Perhaps she'd return to see him again soon. She would buy more wood – and this time she'd make a point of being friendly.

IO

———⌗———

Before the house, a fire was burning, and round about the fire a man
was dancing — hopping from one foot to the other and howling . . .
From *Rumpelstiltskin*

At first, I couldn't find a gap in the leaves big enough for me
to see through and I had to try several different spots. I ran up
and down impatiently and the tall grass by the side of the road
tickled my legs, but I was desperate to see what the PoW camp
looked like.

I supposed Mother wanted to check for herself that the prison
was secure. She was terribly afraid of the Germans, living alone
and all, now Daddy was back fighting the war again.

When I found a little clearing in the bushes so I could spy on
the camp at last, I felt a strange flash of recognition – as though
I had seen it all once before.

'Oh,' I said, surprised. The strange rounded buildings seemed
like the mystical cabins I'd seen back in the forest nestled amongst
the giant oaks – just before we'd met the woodcutter that time.

Something important was happening; something strange and
magical. Both my worlds were colliding, here, in this place. And
somehow the woodcutter was able to step between the two. He
was the key, I was sure of it.

After a while, Mother turned and set off for home. I stayed
staring for a few moments longer, then rushed to follow her.

I'm not afraid of the Germans, I thought, as we walked down the road leading away from the woodchopper's village, back towards Farmer Dawson's farm and our cottage. I knew what they were like; they lived in a mystical world, which was often dark, but good always, always prevailed. That was just the way it was.

Still, these were dark times, everybody said so, and they didn't even know a Troll was lurking around the village.

I didn't want Mother to worry about all the danger we were in, apart from the war – but there was no need for her to know in any case; I was perfectly prepared to protect her.

I looked at her now, a little way ahead of me, the strong spring breeze threatening to pull her brown hair out into wild tendrils that would whip about her face instead of sitting neatly where it had been set by rollers to fall about her shoulders. I'd taken to watching her lately. Spying on her, in a sense, to make sure she was safe. KEEP MUM, as all the posters said.

I often went round into the front garden and peeked through the sitting-room window to see what she was up to. She mainly sat in the armchair, listening to the wireless and staring into space. Sometimes I secretly trailed her as she went around the village, and watched her queuing for meat at Mr Lupton the butcher's, or patiently waiting in line to use her rations for sugar or tinned fruit.

It was hard to put my finger on, but I felt a bit strange whenever I thought about how things were when it was just the two of us. It was a shame Daddy was away at war. I wished he'd been able to stay longer on his visit home. But like all the hero-soldiers and warriors in my fairy tales, he had to protect our kingdom – which meant fighting battles in foreign lands.

I was frightened something bad would happen to him because I loved him, but I was also frightened something bad would happen to him because then things would always be this way. As it was, my life with Mother was... I didn't know the right word. Confusing? Sometimes almost a bit scary.

Take that letter, for example. The one that made my breath

75

get stuck inside me so that I couldn't breathe when I read it, no matter how much I tried to suck in the air.

I found it about a year ago, when I was searching the bureau in the hope of finding a map that would lead to buried pirate treasure. I recognised Daddy's writing from the letters he sent me. I'd never read hers before and thought they'd be pretty much the same as mine. But they weren't really. I was eight then and couldn't read all the words. His writing was messier in her letters, more joined-up. But I could read that line. The one that said she didn't feel a thing for me. And then my breathing just stopped and I thought it wouldn't start again and I was gasping like a goldfish out of its bowl, drowning in air.

I'm sure now that Daddy must have made a mistake. He must have misheard her – he was having such problems with his ears even now. Look how she liked reading fairy tales to me every night, and how happy she was when she found out she was going to have a baby because I'd be like a real-life Darling.

I just had to be a good boy, that's all. If I always made sure to be a good boy, she couldn't help but love me. She'd love me the way Gerda loved Kai; she went to the ends of the earth, right to the North Pole, to save him from the Snow Queen's clutches.

Sometimes I watched other boys in the village who were out with their mothers. I was careful to watch what they did, how they behaved – how they made their mothers love them. Since I wasn't really friends with anyone at school, I didn't know for sure what it was like at their houses. But I had a funny feeling it wasn't the way things were at mine.

The other boys at school didn't think much of me, but Harry – who lived next door to my grandparents in Norfolk – was my friend. I went into his house one Saturday when it was raining and we couldn't play outside. He was a sporty-looking boy the same age as me. Granny sort of forced us to be friends whenever I went to visit.

And on this rainy day, Harry took me upstairs to his bedroom and we played with his rather impressive train set. His parents had left the door to their bedroom open and I could see it was neat and tidy. Harry's room smelled clean. His parents were downstairs, laughing and joking with each other.

After a while, Harry's mother called us down for tea. I knew it was nice of them to let me stay to eat with them, because people were usually funny about their rations. She'd cooked boiled ham and bubble-and-squeak and she made us both wash our hands with soap in the kitchen before we sat at the table. Harry rolled his eyes at me as we stood next to each other with our hands under the tap, and I rolled my eyes back at him but really I was enjoying myself. They all chatted loudly throughout the dinner and Harry's mother asked me some questions about Bambury. Then Granny came to get me. I was a bit dazed for an hour or so after that visit. I tried to imagine what it would be like if I brought Harry round to my cottage.

Things were a bit messy upstairs and sometimes Mother forgot to get the food in. It was like playing hide-and-seek when I hunted for all the plates and glasses to do the washing-up. Sometimes it seemed like she was very far away, even when she was in the same room. But when I looked to my fairy tales, lots of mothers or stepmothers weren't very nice to children and that was normal in that world, so I should really count myself lucky to be living with my pretty mother in our little cottage in Bambury.

The night after I discovered the PoW camp was really a magical village for woodcutters, my mother read me the story of Rumpelstiltskin. Her words were soothing, like a lullaby, despite the tale of giving away babies and double-crossing, and I felt myself falling into a deep sleep after she left my room.

Perhaps the story had unsettled me more than I realised though, because a sudden noise pierced my dream and I jerked awake with a kick of my leg. My eyes swivelled round the room as I tried to work out what had woken me. But there was nothing, just stillness, darkness, and the normal night-time sounds of the house. I couldn't hear the wireless playing downstairs, so Mother must be tucked up in bed.

Then I heard it again; a sort of rattle. It was hard to make out, but I didn't think it was coming from inside the cottage. I crept over to my window and pulled back my blackout blind so I could look outside. The lane was quiet and still in the moonlight and I looked up and down the street. Perhaps a fox or a cat had knocked something over?

Movement at the corner of my eye made me focus on a cottage a few doors down. A black shape, blacker than the night shadows, was rustling about in the garden. What was it? The shape seemed to be moving and I saw it slowly make its way down the path into the lane and head towards the cottage opposite.

It was when it broke cover by stepping out into the road that the breath caught in my throat. It was the Troll, creeping about on my street in the middle of the night – the witching hour. I leapt back from the window. Was it looking for me? How did it know my father had just left my mother and me alone again? But although I'd begun shaking, I forced myself back to the glass to see what it would do next. This time I pulled back the blind just a tiny bit, so it couldn't see me if it looked up.

It was snuffling about in the front garden directly across from our cottage now, and I watched in horror as it crept down the little side passage where they kept their bins so that I lost sight of it for a few seconds until it came back. It was *smelling* the houses to see who was inside each one. It was trying to find me. Or if not me, then someone else who smelled good enough to eat. Trolls like eating children best, but they also like eating beautiful women. I thought of Mother asleep in her bed. That monster better not try to snatch her away. I swallowed down because it felt like something was lodged in my throat.

There was more movement – it was coming back out! Into the lane! I held my breath as its dark shape rolled back across the road – towards our cottage! I felt sick with fear as it carefully prised open the gate into my own front garden. It was coming into our house! I should scream! Wake Mother! But I couldn't move.

Even my knees were trembling but I was fixed to the spot like a statue as I watched what it was doing below me. I started praying it wouldn't look up and notice my eyes in the crack in the blind, but I could see it was trying not to be seen and was moving slowly and quietly like an animal. It shuffled to the side of our cottage where the dustbin and pig bin were kept. Because of the angle, I couldn't see what it did there. But I heard the metal rattle and knew it must have opened the lids for some reason.

After a few seconds, it reappeared and I watched as it left our garden. It went into another few cottages, on both sides of the street, and spent quite a while in one front garden that had been turned into a vegetable patch before it disappeared around the corner. It had a bag slung over its back. Had it taken something from our bins? It must be collecting ingredients for a spell – that was the only possible explanation. And it had been carefully smelling who was inside each cottage.

Something about its secret creeping around made me see it in its other place for a moment, outside the Post Office holding out its empty tin – but what would the Troll want with coins? Or these ingredients? What was it planning?

I ran back to bed and pulled the covers up over my head, but it took a very long time for me to stop shaking. Things were getting out of hand and Mother and I were in more danger than ever before. Something needed to be done and I knew I'd have to make a stand to save us both.

I spent almost the whole night thinking about what to do, before the idea came to me like a little whisper in my ear.

The next morning, before I went to school, I rummaged through the odds-and-ends drawer in the kitchen. I found the weapon I needed easily enough, and I knew it would never be missed.

There was a thickness in my throat throughout the day whenever I thought about the daring Troll attack I was planning later that afternoon. But a funny tingling in my tummy, like the feeling I always got on Christmas Eve, let me know I was filled with excitement as well, not just nerves. So when I was thrown into the outhouse again at lunchtime, it was almost like I couldn't hear what the others were shouting at me through the cracks of the closed door. And their laughter – this time about how my short trousers were *too* short – floated away over my head.

I leaned against the wall in the dark. Let them shout! These stupid schoolboys had no idea what they were dealing with – who I really was. Their silly name-calling and even their punches meant nothing to me now. I spent the time carefully going over my plot against the Troll. And then a spring thunderstorm burst over their heads like a punishment, so we spent the rest of lunchtime inside the assembly hall, which meant I was free. I'd escaped with just some minor bumps and a tender spot on my eyebrow. Mr Finlay handed out paper and wax crayons so we could draw to pass the time quietly and I drew a picture of me facing the monster, with its arms up in the air in surrender.

After school, McCarthy and his gang jumped on me to get me back for escaping, so it was much later than I'd planned when I was finally able to run down to the railway line to set up watch. But I was in luck because, just as I arrived, I spotted the Troll climbing up the stairs by the tunnel. I crouched down behind a tree and watched as it disappeared into the woods on the other side.

After a few minutes, I judged it was a fair distance away from its lair. I knew it was the right time. It was now or never.

'Now or never,' I said. But I held back.

It could return at any moment. I remembered my suspicion that it could suddenly materialise, like Count Dracula. I wrote another note in my little book:

30th May, approx 5 p.m. (no watch): WARNING: Can possibly appear in thin air? INVESTIGATE.

I stayed down low and prepared to crawl along the hilltop, military-style, to make my way towards the bridge.

But then I realised it was quite a trek and I wouldn't be able to cover all the distance like that, so eventually I stood up and ran along in an almost-crouching position instead. Also, it was much, much muddier than I'd thought and I worried about the dirt on my school clothes.

Once I was at the bridge, I got back on my haunches and raised my head over the brick wall just enough to allow a peek over.

Of course there was nothing to see at the entrance to the tunnel because the Troll was long gone.

'Now or never,' I muttered again.

I stood for a moment, leaning against the wall, and considered my plan.

But I waited. And waited.

I knew what I had to do, but I was frightened. So I waited a bit longer.

In a panic, I realised how much time had passed. It might be on its way back from wherever it had been. Most likely it had gone into the village to steal a child to eat for its dinner. Or, failing that, it would kill some goats and eat those instead.

I had to do it, and quickly, before it returned.

I didn't run to the steps on the other side of the bridge, but instead went back across to where I'd been before and used my usual method of clambering down the steep grassy slope to the tracks below. The ground was still wet and my palms became slick with mud and broken blades of grass.

When I reached the tracks, I looked around and up above me, trying to spot the terrible shape of the Troll appearing at the top of the steps. I waited for a minute or so, but couldn't see anything except the greyish sky turning to dusk.

The moment had come. I had no choice but to enter the tunnel for the second time.

I hesitated before stepping into that dark place, but then I marched right in, as though I was stepping over my fears and leaving them outside as the sun began to set.

I felt braver this time and walked quickly, with a purpose: I was looking for the Troll's nest.

Eventually, I caught the whiff of its stink. The mound of scraps and bits of wood that marked its revolting home was just ahead.

I could feel my heart hammering away beneath my shirt and with some ceremony I reached into the pocket of my shorts and brought out the little box of matches I'd taken from home that morning, a lifetime ago. There was a picture of the hotel in Densford on the front. They'd been in the kitchen drawer for a long time, so weren't from the other day; Daddy had probably taken them after having dinner there one evening years ago.

My fingers fumbled as I tried to pull out a match.

Daddy.

Something scuttled over my foot. I saw a dark blur of motion and realised it was a rat. I screamed, but it was already darting away. I forced myself to calm down. I didn't want the Troll to know I was here. The echo died away and I fumbled again at the box.

The match sparked with a scraping fizz and I held the flame in front of my face to stare into its white heart.

I wasn't allowed to play with matches.

I slid the box back into my pocket. Then I crouched down low, and – like *The Little Match Girl* – marvelled at how much light that tiny flame threw into the darkness of the tunnel. It made a bulb of yellow light around my clenched fingers and lit up the filthy nest. I pinched my nose shut with my other hand because the stench was even worse down here. I think it must have wet its bed like a baby; I hadn't done that for *years*.

I held the match to the corner of a crusty brown blanket. For a second or two I thought it wasn't going to work, and I remembered what had happened when Grandpa threw the dregs of his whisky into the fire to watch the explosion in the grate. I should have brought some of Mother's gin which she used for her special drinks. But then, I could smell a strange, chemical sort of smell, and thought I saw a tuft of smoke. The flame was turning the straight wooden match into a gnarled black flimsy twig. I had to drop it because the burning was almost at my fingertips. And then, with a *pfff* that sounded like a little breath, the corner of the blanket was alive with small flames licking at the wool.

I imagined how I would look to the Troll if it came back now. The blaze would be reflected in my dark eyes and my face would shine with triumph. I'd done it.

Some of the newspaper caught and the fire grew brighter and stronger. I stood up and stepped back. Some scraps of wood were the next to take and they crackled and hissed and sparked. I had to step back again.

The flames grew higher and hungrier as I watched, sick with delight and terror. Not licking now, but roaring, devouring.

Perhaps there had been spilled whisky on those things. I thought I could smell it the first time I found the nest. It would explain the fierceness of the blaze.

I stepped back again and again – I was on the other side of the tracks now – and it was bright enough to read by.

I should probably run now. The Troll . . .

But I stood and watched. The popping and crackling of destruction, the warmth on my face, the fire hurting my eyes . . . I didn't want to run yet.

This was the burning of a monster's nest, it was unstoppable now, and I had unleashed the power of it. I was in control of it because it was mine. I wondered if there was anything else I could burn because oh I loved this feeling. I wanted to watch a building burn – I briefly imagined taking a match to my house – I wanted to watch the village burn. I felt like dancing, like Rumpelstiltskin around his blaze.

The smelly smoke was turning the air grey and thick and it was the coughing and my watering eyes that finally drove me away from the blaze. But I became confused in the smoky gloom and started to panic – I couldn't tell which way was which. I kept running into a wall. It was as though the wall surrounded me, every way I turned, until I thought to bend down and feel for the tracks. I ran like that, in a crouch, the metal line guiding me away until I could see the dim light at the mouth of the tunnel.

I sucked fresh air into my lungs between my retching coughs and rubbed my sore eyes. I looked around frantically for any sign of the Troll. When I was able to climb, I scrambled up the verge, which I was surprised to find was still slippery and cool to the touch. The day looked perfectly normal outside, as though nothing had changed.

When I reached the top of the slope I settled down in my usual hiding spot. I was on my haunches – to stop my bottom getting wet – and I leaned back against a tree to watch and wait for the Troll to return.

I pulled out the hotel matches from my pocket and turned them over and over in my hand. It felt good to hold them. I could see some smoke coming out of the tunnel now, although there wasn't as much as I would have liked. I had wanted to see thick clouds of swirling blackness, billowing – no, bellowing – out as though it were the chimney of a furious coal-burning factory.

'Perhaps you'll think twice now, Troll,' I said aloud. I clamped a blade of grass between my lips as though I was dangling a cigarette, and I narrowed my eyes. 'Won't be messing with *me* again, will you?'

I laughed quietly to myself.

'I know how to deal with Trolls, all right.' I tapped the little packet of matches against my leg. 'I know your game . . . and now you know what happens to Trolls around here.'

Eventually, I spat out the grass because it had gone soggy in my mouth. I stood up to relieve the cramp in my legs and I peed against the tree. It was going to get dark soon and I would have to go home eventually.

I risked a run down to the tunnel to see if my fire was spreading along the tracks. I had begun to worry a bit about what would happen if a train came. But I couldn't see anything in the tunnel. I was frightened of the Troll returning, but curiosity pushed me inside. When I came to the nest there was just a smelly pile of sooty ash and wisps of smoke.

It had burned itself out.

The ground was just gravel and dirt; the fire could never have travelled far from the Troll's nest. I sighed. Never mind. At least the train wouldn't have any trouble now, and the message would still be loud and clear to the Troll; stay away or else.

I ran all the way back up to my place on the verge. I would wait a while. Yes, I was a bit bored now, but it'd be worth it to see the moment the Troll returned to its destroyed nest.

I began to laugh to myself again. Stupid Troll!

Was that . . . ? Was it . . . ?

It was! I could just make out its shambling form as it made its way along the path towards the steps. It was almost dark now, but enough of the sun was above the horizon because I could see a little way ahead.

I clamped my hands over my mouth to muffle my sudden giggles. It was going to find its nest destroyed! And I'd done it! I crouched down again behind my tree, and peeked around the gnarled old bark. The cramps in my legs were bearable now.

It carefully lowered itself down the steep wooden steps, clinging to the metal railing with both hands. It looked old. That only made it look more horrible.

I couldn't see any smoke coming from the tunnel at all now. So it probably wouldn't guess anything had happened from the outside.

At one point it actually stumbled and tripped onto the grassy slope, although it managed to put out a fat sausage-like arm to break its fall. Little mewing, gasping sounds were escaping between the cracks of my fingers.

Must. Be. Quiet. It'll hear me! Oh it was too much!

It seemed I was waiting for ever before it finally disappeared into the mouth of the tunnel. I realised I was hopping from leg to leg and I needed to pee again. This was the most exciting thing I'd ever done.

Now what? I cautiously stepped away from my hiding tree. How would I know what was going on in there? Should I go down and look into the tunnel? What if it didn't even *care* that its nest was burned to ashes?

I had actually taken a couple of steps down the verge when I heard it. A kind of echoing growl came from the tunnel. It was coming out!

I darted back behind the tree.

'Urrrgggghhhhh!'

It was nearly at the exit.

'Urrrgggghhhhh!'

Here it was! It burst outside, staggering crazily and looking around in the gloom. It was clutching charred bits of rubbish.

'Urrrgggghhhhh KIDS!' it screamed in a hoarse voice. Its mouth was a terrible black hole in its black hairy face.

I wasn't laughing any more.

It threw down the sooty rubbish, once part of its nest but now just brittle scraps of black nothings. They lay scattered around its feet on the tracks.

It was wheezing and panting terribly; I could actually hear it from where I hid. I still desperately needed to pee but I didn't move.

'I'LL SODDING... I'LL SODDING... Urrrgggghhhhh!'

It hollered for a long time. I waited for it to stop. To go away.

Lightning made the sky flicker like a dying lightbulb. After a moment, there was an electric crack of thunder and I knew the rain was coming. Fat black clouds sat against the grey-woolly-jumper colour of the sky.

The Troll was still shouting down there on the line.

It would be pouring soon and it didn't have a nest any more.

I felt a bit sick now. I wanted to be able to pee, then I wanted to go home, listen to my story, and forget all about this. I was tired of being out here, and I didn't want to get wet, and I had a horrible heavy feeling in my stomach that I couldn't understand.

II

∞

*'Set out before it gets hot, and when you're on your way walk
nicely and quietly like a good girl and don't leave the path . . .'*
From *Little Redcape (Little Red Riding Hood)*

'I really had much less wood at home than I'd initially thought,'
Annabel told the PoW, before he could express surprise at her
being there again so soon. She had decided to implement her plan
of being friendly to the prisoner. Funnily enough, she'd found
herself thinking of him that morning.

The child was playing out somewhere, and she had done as
old Dawson had suggested: come through the back. It wasn't her
intention that no one should see her – it was the ease of the
shortcut, that was all.

'That's why I'm back,' she said.

She had brought her trolley with her again but now felt stupid
and vulnerable holding it. As a little girl she had once attended a
schoolfriend's birthday party and had found herself to be horribly
overdressed and bearing a hugely ostentatious present compared
to the other children. The sense of shame, and of having done so
obviously the wrong thing, enveloped her now just as it had then.

'Ah, of course, there is no problem.' A sweet smile spread
across his face.

He took her trolley from her and began to fill it. While she
waited, she sat on his chopping block – an oak tree stump – and
watched him work. It was a sunny day, although still not yet warm

enough to go without a cardigan, and it felt nice to be outside. She could feel rough splinters digging through her thin dress into the backs of her thighs, but it wasn't an unpleasant sensation.

She took out her cigarettes and lighter from her handbag. 'Um . . . Would you like one?' She held up the packet.

He turned to look back at her and made her laugh by tipping his head back and folding his hands together as if he was thanking God.

'Thank you,' he said, crossing over to where she sat. 'It's been a long time!'

He took her silver lighter from her hand, and she placed a cigarette between her lips and leaned towards him so he could light it for her. Then he lit his own, making her laugh again by closing his eyes in pleasure as he took in a deep lungful.

'That's really good,' he said.

They smiled at each other.

He was so funny she didn't really feel shy or awkward any more. 'It's Johannes?'

'Hans.'

'Where are you from?'

'Ah, you've never heard of it! It's a little town: Mittenwald. It's in Bavaria.'

'Well, I expect you'd never heard of Bambury!'

He laughed and nodded and she felt pleased with what she'd said.

'That's true!' He took another drag of his cigarette. 'But here we are!'

'Here we are.'

She pulled her legs up so she sat cross-legged on the tree stump. She thought briefly of Reggie – which was silly; she wasn't behaving inappropriately. The skirt of her dress was long and floaty so she wasn't being immodest.

'Your English is very good.'

'Thank you!' He seemed pleased. 'I studied it at university.'

'What's Mittenwald like?'

So he told her a little about the town, describing the pretty pastel-coloured houses, the paintings on the buildings, and how the area was known for making the sweetest-sounding violins.

She smoked as she listened to his soft voice describing his home far away.

'You must miss it dreadfully,' she said. 'It sounds so lovely.'

He smiled and stamped out his cigarette. He'd finished it quickly.

'Would you like another?'

He made another Thank God gesture.

'Help yourself.' She was still smoking her first cigarette so she gestured for him to pull out the packet and lighter from her handbag on the floor beside the stump.

'How did you end up here?' she said. 'If you don't mind me asking?'

He lit his cigarette and returned her lighter to her bag. 'Ah! It's a funny story!'

'Funny?'

'Yes – funny!'

And he told her the story of how he was captured. He made it sound amusing and acted it out. Hans and the rest of the infantrymen in his unit found themselves armed with just bayonets facing British tanks after the other German units nearby had all retreated.

He picked up the axe from the floor to mime holding his useless bayonet against the massive tank, and Annabel laughed as he pulled a funny face, dropped the axe, and stuck his hands in the air.

His jolly version of events made it all sound quite civilised. Not nearly so bad as Reggie made out.

'Then what?' she said.

He laughed, took a final puff of cigarette before stamping it out, and spread his arms wide. He seemed to indicate the whole of himself and everything around him.

'What can I say? This is it! Now I'm here – a prisoner! I spend my days in an orchard cutting the dead trees!'

For some reason that made her giggle, and he caught it too, and then they both laughed and laughed at the ridiculousness of life.

The early June weather suddenly turned into a rainy, cold snap and she was back at the orchard a couple of days later. 'We've had to use much more wood than usual,' she told him.

'Don't apologise! I don't get many customers. In fact, you're already my favourite! It gets lonely out here.'

'Yes, it must. So far from your family.'

'Well, at least I have one friend. I will give you some extra wood!'

And that was how she knew he was kind.

'Oh, hello again Hans – just taking a shortcut because I need to speak to Mr Dawson about something.'

'Nice dress today, Mrs Patterson! You look so pretty.'

'Oh ... I ...'

And that was how she knew he looked at her.

'My goodness, Hans! Look at you lugging all that wood! How strong you've become from all the chopping!'

'Yes, I suppose that's true, Mrs Patterson!'

'Oh, call me Annabel. Mrs Patterson sounds so ... Well, we really have been getting through this wood, haven't we? And it's supposed to be summer now!'

'Annabel.'

'Yes. Or ... or Annie.'

'Annie.'

And that was how she knew it would be all right.

*

91

It was a little unconventional, she supposed, as she made her way home from the orchard one day: becoming friends with a PoW.

But it was just too intriguing to have a foreigner so near to her own little house in Bambury and not want to find out more about him. He was, well, exotic. Seeing him in the glade of the orchard chopping wood made him seem so different from bank clerk Reggie or her accountant father – the only two men she'd ever really known.

And yes – so what? – she sometimes came up with excuses to return to see him, but there was nothing really to fill her days, was there? Or his. Both of them were trapped in Bambury, when she thought about it.

She was going to see him so often – nearly every day – that now she always walked through the woods to get to the orchard from the back, where she was less likely to bump into someone from the village. Dawson had suggested it himself, she remembered gratefully, that first time she went to buy wood. Of course, he'd be aware from her bills how much wood she was buying, but she could explain it away easily to the old man and he wasn't a gossip. It was some of the other villagers she was more wary of bumping into – a couple of people from the Home Guard, some of the women, or the elderly Bishop sisters who loved to spread rumours.

She wondered if she should start taking the boy with her occasionally so it didn't look so unusual. In all likelihood, she didn't really need to be so paranoid – not that she was actually doing anything wrong, really.

She might have considered avoiding the path in the woods entirely, but decided she had no choice but to stick to it because there were some old abandoned mine shafts in the hills of the forest that were said to be dangerous.

It was sometimes better to hide in plain sight, she thought – that is, it would be much harder to explain her presence to somebody if she were found in the middle of the forest – trying not to be spotted – than it would be if she were innocently pulling her trolley on the path on her way to collect some firewood. It was lucky the woods were so quiet though, because if anyone really thought about it, no one would need to buy firewood every day – even if it had been a bit of a chilly June so far.

But, in any case, the only person she saw sometimes on the path that ran through the woods was an old tramp who'd been hanging around the village in recent months. He'd probably lost his home in an air raid somewhere. She had nothing to fear from him – who would he tell, and who would believe him? And whenever she did occasionally see him up ahead on the path, he always veered back into the safety of the trees.

The days were getting warmer and there was little need for a fire these days. But still, Annabel went to see Hans.

There were many more PoWs now, she had heard. The numbers had swelled Bambury's camp to almost full capacity, after a mission dubbed D-Day saw many more Germans captured by the Allies.

While many of the villagers were openly curious about the Germans – most had never met a foreign person before – nearly all were unfailingly polite should they encounter one.

Annabel had even seen the Bishop sisters – who never had a kind word to say about anybody behind their backs – nod their heads with a courteous 'good morning' when they passed a middle-aged German man making his way from one farm to another with a message that he carried purposefully in his hand.

On another occasion, Annabel had been in the Post Office when a German – who, judging by the furious pimples blazing on his face had probably added several years to his age in order to enlist – was running some errands for the old colonel who supervised the PoW camp. The manager had come over to serve the youth himself and asked friendly questions about his name and where he was from. He seemed excited by the boy's halting, broken replies. The manager even tried out a German sentence or two – having learned some phrases in the Great War he explained – but the boy seemed not to understand and repeated 'sorry, sorry' in mortification. The manager, an elderly man with rheumatism beginning to turn the straight bones of his fingers into wavy paths with knobby rocks at the joints, kept trying to be understood. Judging from his conspiratorial air and wide grin, Annabel suspected he was trying to repeat some dirty slang he had picked up. Eventually, disappointed, he allowed the boy to be on his way with the stationery he had been sent in to buy.

Nevertheless, the camp's prisoners didn't enjoy uniform cheerfulness wherever they went. Some of the children – all off for the summer holidays now – would occasionally dare each other to shout abuse at the men. From Hans, Annabel had learned that youngsters from the village would sometimes cycle up to Dawson's farm to yell insults across the fields at the men before riding away. The Germans were using old-fashioned push ploughs because petrol was so scarce, and Hans described what his friends had told him; she could visualise how their faces would simply set, stoical, as they glistened with sweat and pushed the ploughs through the hard earth to the sounds of the children jeering.

Then, one day, Annabel saw one such incident for herself.

She was shopping in the High Street with the boy when she heard a commotion. She was just coming out of the butcher's with her wicker basket and turned to see a red-haired boy screaming with every fibre of his being.

'*I'll fucking kill you!*' he yelled, over and over again.

She gasped as she realised what he was saying, and heard shocked murmurs behind her in the shop. She looked to see who the little boy was shouting at and saw a new group of German prisoners being escorted to the camp in a trailer lashed to a jeep. It was as if the whole High Street was frozen in time; it was eerily quiet apart from the hoarse screams of the child and the rattle of the jeep's engine as it passed by and eventually turned the corner. The Germans remained silent, but stared curiously at the child.

Annabel couldn't remember the boy's name (Mark? Martin?), but she vaguely knew his mother. She was a woman named Evelyn Moore who was friendly enough to Annabel, and had received a telegram a few days ago informing her that her husband Simon had been killed in France.

Evelyn's son had clearly become deranged when he caught sight of the German soldiers in the street as he played out with his friends from school.

Although there were plenty of shocked villagers who saw what happened, no one came forward to tell him to pull himself together, and it was his horrified friends – boys his own age – who tackled him and were now trying to tug him away as the jeep disappeared from view. One hooked his arm around the boy's neck and jerked him backwards, while others latched onto his clothes to help drag him away. But he fought to stand his ground and struggled to fight his way over to where the jeep had gone, with his red hair askew and falling all over his face. But the other boys had him firmly now and managed to lead him away – although his tearful, high-pitched screams echoed down the side streets as his friends tried to pull him home to his broken mother.

Annabel had to step backwards into the shop to avoid them as they passed, and Daniel scrambled behind her as if to hide.

The butcher, Mr Lupton, walked out from behind his counter and came to stand with Annabel and a couple of other customers in the doorway.

'Goodness,' Annabel said.

'Poor lad.' The butcher sighed and returned to his post. 'Got a point though, doesn't he?'

Annabel looked at him strangely – what an odd thing to say. She couldn't think of an appropriate response so remained silent.

'He was a good man, Simon Moore.' He pulled a leg of pork

closer and began to chop into it. 'Some of those Jerries stroll about the village like they own it. They want to be careful.'

She nodded once, politely, and stepped into the street, which had suddenly sprung back to life.

It was hard to comprehend how some villagers could be filled with such anger and fear. Perhaps it wasn't just sympathy for the crying boy, but support for his sentiments, that allowed him to behave the way he did?

Annabel thought how disconcerting it was to come across such hateful views towards the PoWs. After all, they were only grey-patch-wearing normal rank-and-file Jerries, not the high-ranking black-patch Nazis. Some people seemed not to be able to recognise that the prisoners in Bambury were just a collection of ordinary people; individuals. They seemed to have no understanding whatsoever that someone like Hans could be kind and funny and sweet.

She wanted to protect him.

12

─∞∞∞─

'Who's that trip-trapping on my bridge?' roared the troll.
From *The Billy Goats Gruff*

One Saturday, a couple of weeks after chasing the Troll away, I was reading *The Billy Goats Gruff* in the sitting room when I heard Mother rustling about in the hall. She'd not long finished speaking to Grandma on the telephone, which was always quite boring to listen to because all she said was, 'Yes, everything's fine... yes... yes, of course I'm cooking... yes... of course... yes.' I was sitting sideways with my legs dangling over the armrest and now I scrambled to get up to see what she was doing.

I leaned against the door and watched as she put on her head-scarf. She tended not to wear one, so I looked out of the little stained-glass window at the top of the front door to see what the weather was like outside. The branches of the magnolia tree on the front lawn were jiggling. It was breezy then, and she didn't want her hair to be messed up by the wind.

She stood in front of the hall mirror and carefully tied the silk scarf under her chin. It was pretty. Pale lemon with pink roses. She had some beautiful ones with pictures and borders and flowers, but since the war had started she'd only worn her plainer scarves and clothes. People didn't want to look too fancy. Which was silly because they still had all their nice clothes from before – it wasn't as if they'd bought them new. I was happy to see she was wearing her prettier things again. She had a green silk scarf with a pattern of bright red roses and green vines. I loved that one. It made me think of the tangled thicket outside Sleeping Beauty's castle.

She took her lipstick from her handbag on the coat rack and turned her lips red, using her finger to dab it onto her mouth, because it wasted less that way.

'Where are you going?'

She finished applying her make-up, studied herself in the mirror, and dabbed on a little more. She was very beautiful.

'To the High Street, then to buy some more wood so we have some ready for when the summer ends.'

I wondered whether to follow her in secret: that was quite fun. But decided—

'Can I come?'

'May I come, please?' she corrected me.

'May I come, please?'

She turned to look at me for the first time. I stood up straight. I always liked going out with her, and it would be a perfect way to meet the woodcutter again.

'Are you ready to leave?'

'Yes. I just have to put my shoes on.'

She gave a slight nod that meant I was allowed to do just that.

When we were in the village, I trailed behind her as she used her ration book to shop. We'd run out of tea a few days ago and had been using and re-using a tiny amount of tea leaves. I was happy to see that while she was here she was stocking up. We didn't have much food at home. Mother never seemed to worry too much about that. She didn't eat much, but picked at whatever food there was when she was hungry. Her bottle of gin was getting lower and lower though, and I wasn't sure what she'd do when that had gone.

But if there was nothing to eat, Mother didn't seem to mind going without. I'd heard her remark to my grandparents once that I had an abnormally large appetite, and it must be true because I was often quite hungry. We were eating dinner with them at their house at the time – it must have been last summer – and Grandad had laughed as I gobbled up the lamb chops and told her that it was because I was a growing boy. But I felt ashamed because, just a couple of days earlier, I'd eaten a hard piece of cheese – more rind than anything else – that I found on the floor at the back of the larder. And I often filched pears or plums from trees in people's front gardens. I felt my face flush as I thought Mother was probably right and I wasn't normal. My tummy rumbled now as I thought of Grandma's dinners and I offered to hold the ration book as Mother did the shopping – pointing out our allowances for meat and butter as we worked our way along the High Street.

I was excited at the thought of seeing the woodchopper again. I'd secretly followed Mother and watched her as she gradually became friends with him, but it would only be the second time I'd actually met him myself. She kept telling him she needed more wood, although I knew we had mounds and mounds in the coal cellar now.

The visit was good, although I didn't learn much more about him. He and Mother chatted about boring things like what she had heard politicians saying about the war on the wireless. Although I didn't speak to the woodcutter myself, at one point he winked at me as I watched him work. That made me think it'd be fun to come back and talk to him by myself one day, without Mother.

After he'd loaded the wood into our trolley, Mother told him she was going back to the farm to settle up with Farmer Dawson. But he wasn't at the farmhouse when we knocked, and she said she didn't want to traipse around trying to find him while she was dragging the trolley, so we turned back to the orchard. I was glad we'd get to see the woodchopper again for the second time that day.

As we walked back through the apple trees I saw two old women further up, some way ahead of us. They must have come from the road, and were making their own way to the glade to buy some wood.

'Look, Mother,' I said.

'Oh,' she muttered, and stopped. 'It's the Bishop sisters.'

She seemed to hesitate, and looked around. 'Let's not walk all the way back into the orchard; there must be another way to get into the woods from here.'

I followed her to the fence that marked the farm's border with the forest, but it was unbroken here and there wasn't a gate. Mother seemed annoyed, and tutted, but then pulled up her skirt and climbed over it like a tomboy, which made me laugh.

'You'll have to lift up the trolley from your side to help me,' she said.

It was heavy with wood and I struggled to push it up as she pulled it over the fence. Once she'd heaved it onto the ground she said, 'All right, come along then, hurry up.'

I clambered over the fence. 'Why are we going home this way?'

'Please stop pestering me with questions!'

But I didn't mind taking this way home. I almost wanted to giggle – what a funny adventure we were going on together.

Now we were in the forest, Mother set off at a brisk march and I hurried to follow her. I realised we were cutting across the woods so we'd find the path that would lead us home further down – away from the woodchopper's clearing. She seemed to be struggling as she pulled the trolley along the forest floor. Leaves and small twigs kept jamming the wheels. She had to drag it behind her after they stopped turning altogether. She got redder and redder in the face and looked more and more annoyed, but I was enjoying our adventure.

I was still trying to hide my wide smile when my mother suddenly let out what was almost a yelp. She stopped short and I almost went straight into the back of the trolley. I looked around to see what she was staring at, and was struck dumb when I saw the Troll looming up about ten feet ahead, blocking our way.

I was too frightened even to scream. But the terror had me in its tight, sweaty grip. I felt as though I might be physically sick, just vomit right there on the forest floor, and I began to tremble.

Mother's voice, when she spoke to it, sounded strangely high-pitched so I knew she was frightened too. But to my amazement she greeted it politely.

'Er, hello there,' she said.

I remembered dully how sure I'd been that I would be able to protect her against danger. But danger was here, in this forest, standing right in front of us, and I realised that I was just a child. A little boy. I was helpless against it. And worse, so was she.

I began to really shake. How could she protect me from the Troll? She wasn't brave at all.

I wished Daddy was there.

Then I thought of the strong woodchopper with his axe that had glinted in the sun. Him, I thought, let it be him. Please let him come to save us.

The Troll slowly turned its eyes upon me. It opened its revolting hairy mouth and a tongue slithered out. It looked at me and licked its lips like it was hungry.

To my left, I saw the monster had lit a fire. It was burning just for me.

I knew it as surely as I knew my own name that there was a huge cast-iron pot somewhere nearby. It had made its spells in that pot and now I knew it wanted to boil me up, eat me and chew on my bones.

I saw other things too. I saw that it had set up a new nest in the woods and strung a sheet across its lair to protect it from the rain. There was broken-down furniture it had found or stolen. It had made itself comfortable. It had been biding its time, patiently waiting for me to arrive.

How did it know I would be coming by here? I hadn't even known myself. It had evil powers, I realised, and could see the future. That must be why it had stolen scraps from our street – to cast a spell that would bring Mother and me to its lair.

It was holding something in one of its great fists. Something round and shiny, that almost looked like a can of food but was more likely some kind of weapon. A cutting, eating tool.

I felt a flash of heat in my underpants, and realised I'd wet myself slightly before I clamped down to stop the flow. The warmth spread and then cooled so that the wet was cold against my skin.

But my mother was still shrilly chattering to the Troll as if we had just bumped into a neighbour on the High Street. 'We, er, seem to have got off the path somehow. We're just on our way home. Excuse us.'

Suddenly, she was off, pulling the trolley behind her so fast it was bouncing up in the air as it hit rocks, despite the weight from the wood inside.

My fear was so total, so all-consuming, that it took me a second to understand that she was leaving.

I can't walk, I thought. My legs won't work. I can't follow her and she's leaving me here on my own with the monster. That letter! That letter said she didn't feel a thing for me. Could that be true? God, she's leaving me. She's—

Don't think about it. Focus on the monster.

It was still looking at me with its dead eyes. It hadn't said a word to my mother. It was like it didn't even see her. I was the only one it had eyes for. It hadn't moved, but I knew it was thinking quickly behind that expressionless, hideously hairy face. It was deciding whether to strike.

I realised I was moving. My legs were working after all and I was running to follow my mother as she scuttled like a frightened deer through the forest.

She was going to leave me, I thought. She was going to leave me behind.

She didn't stop until we found the main path that we could follow back to the village. My lungs felt tight and I couldn't breathe, and she was panting from the effort of pulling the trolley. We both stopped to rest for moment now we were standing within the safe lines of the path, laid out beautifully clear and man-made before us.

'He's a nobody, harmless,' she said, so quietly it was almost like she was saying it to herself.

Was it a lie to reassure me? She was already pretending what happened hadn't been important. But she'd been frightened; I could tell.

I tried to nod to make her feel better. She didn't notice I'd wet myself.

A day or two later, when I could think of the experience without feeling sick, I decided that – if I played by the rules – it would be safe enough for me to go back to the forest. Of course, now I knew the Troll had made a new lair in the woods, I'd have to be careful. But I still wanted to get to know the woodcutter for myself. It was dangerous, but I would simply have to brave the black magic in the forest in order to find the good. I thought as long as I stayed on the path, the monster wouldn't be able to get me any more than the wolf would have been able to get Little Red Riding Hood if she'd actually followed the sensible advice.

Either way, I kept a careful lookout for signs of the Troll but didn't see anything and before too long I arrived at the orchard safely. Once there, I straddled the fence, which I turned into a chestnut-coloured mare as soon as I had a leg either side of it. I was in a jousting tournament, so I leaned forward with my eyes narrowed and managed to lance my opponent and race to victory at the other end of the arena. I laughed as I conjured up King Arthur, who nodded at me to signal his approval, and the Lady Guinevere waved her handkerchief in delight. One of the ladies of the court went so far as to blow me a kiss. I saluted to the monarch, then allowed myself to pump my fist in triumph to the roar of the crowd. I would, no doubt, be invited to sit at the Round Table now.

'Thank you! Thank you so much!' I called to the rabble. I

glanced back to see the nobleman's aides lift him up from the grass where my joust had pushed him, and help him into the castle. He would be all right; I had bruised his pride and his chest, but the damage went no further than that.

I directed my mount to leave the city walls, and allowed her to carry me where she would. I looked around. Apple trees. But as we rode further into the woods, the fruit trees gradually gave way to oaks and I recognised the magic forest I'd discovered here the other day. I jumped down from my steed.

'Wait here.' I patted the side of her neck, which felt as muscled and hard as a plank of wood on a fence.

I wandered deeper into the trees. The mud from a few weeks ago had all dried up and we were in the heat of summer now. I listened for the secret sounds of the forest.

Sure enough, soon I could hear the unmistakable sounds of a woodcutter and I stopped to watch him work. I wrapped myself in a cloak of invisibility and stood behind a tree at the edge of the glade.

'Does your mother know you're here?' He seemed amused to see me.

I stepped out so he could see me better but I just shook my head. Mother probably hadn't noticed I'd left the house.

'Are you here to help me cut apple wood?'

I laughed as I eyed his heavy axe. 'It's as big as I am!'

He feigned surprise. 'You can speak!'

I edged closer to the tree to hide my face. I could feel my cheeks turning pink. He shrugged and returned to his work.

I watched him for a few minutes before creeping closer. He grinned at me as he wielded the axe. He was so powerful he had turned a whole tree into nothing more interesting than logs for the fire. He'd worked hard, and most of the apple trees in this part of the orchard were cleared now.

A pale blue cotton shirt with a grey patch sewn on the back was lying across a tree stump, but I thought his grey trousers may have been part of his soldier uniform once. Eventually, he stopped working and sat down with his back against a tree at the edge of the glade. He poured steaming tea into a mug from a flask that looked like one we had at home. He was out of breath.

'Is your name Hansel?'

'No.' He was surprised. 'Just Hans.'

'Oh.'

I scuffed at the ground with the toe of my shoe. I let out a sigh and looked around as though I really should be leaving.

'Hans comes from my name: Johannes. Have you heard of that name?'

I shook my head, but moved a little closer to him.

'Johannes means John.'

'John?!'

'Yes.'

I laughed uncertainly. Surely he was teasing me? A man like him would never be called something so boring and ordinary as John.

'Hansel just means Little Hans. My grandmother called me that sometimes when I was a little boy. When she was feeling kind.'

I knew it. He *was* Hansel! 'Like in *Hansel and Gretel*! You know that story?'

He smiled and shrugged which meant I wasn't sure if he was answering yes or no and he leaned his head back against the tree. 'Sit down,' he said.

I climbed up on the chopping stump opposite where he sat and crossed my legs. The rough scars from the axe's blade poked splinters up against my bare shins and through the material of my short trousers. I gazed down at him, just across the way.

'Why aren't you away at war?'

'I'm nine!'

'Oh! I thought you were much older! Maybe fifteen or sixteen.' I was delighted.

'What's your name?'

'Daniel.'

'Dan-sel?'

I laughed. 'No! Daniel! Daniel!'

'You have been here twice with your mother to buy the wood, yes?'

'Yes. That was me.' I chewed my lip. 'Please don't tell her I came. I'd get in trouble.'

'All right,' he said. 'I promise. Where is your father?'

'Oh, he's fighting. He's very brave. He's—'

Oh dear.

'He's . . .'

'It's all right, Daniel. I understand.'

But suddenly, I realised I didn't understand. Would my father kill Hansel if he were here right now? I looked at him lying there, the axe casually next to him, and I remembered the tight muscles in his arms that I'd seen that first time, which were even bigger and stronger now. I tried to remember what Daddy looked like. It had been weeks and weeks since I'd seen him. All I could think of was the sound of muffled weeping in the shelter and all I could picture clearly was the photograph in the silver frame in the sitting room. He was standing next to Mother on their wedding day. He was skinny and shy and was wearing a suit with a stiff tie.

Maybe Hansel would win. Maybe Hansel would kill my father.

I found now that I couldn't even hold the image of the photograph very clearly in my mind. Mostly, when I looked at that picture – careful not to let my fingerprints mark the glass – I looked at Mother. She looked so young. She was laughing at whoever was holding the camera. I would try to match up the two images; the Mother in the photograph (before she had me) and the Mother I shared the house with.

Suddenly, I didn't want to think about either one of my parents. I jumped down from my perch. Embarrassingly, I felt as though I might cry.

'Don't go! There is no need for you to go. I'm sorry. I didn't mean to upset you.'

He was standing up.

106

I turned away to leave, but something made me hesitate. Something about his apology – so kind, as if I were an adult – made me want to stay. I bent to untie and retie my shoelace for something to do. I blinked a few times and my annoying eyes, although they burned from the effort of holding back tears, seemed to settle down.

I turned my attention to my other shoelace.

'No, it's just that Mother is waiting, I have to go.'

'Ah. Well, if you have chores or . . .'

'Well. No. I mean, I do, but . . . maybe I can stay out a little bit longer.'

'All is good!' He stretched and picked up his axe. I moved from the stump and placed a block of wood there for him to chop.

'Thank you,' he said. 'What is this story you said? About *Hansel and Gretel*?'

So I told him everything I knew about the story while he worked, and I saw him smile with recognition, and I knew I was telling him the story of his own childhood.

On the way home, I kept a careful lookout for the Troll, but didn't see it. I thought it had probably moved to the woods permanently now its tunnel-home had been destroyed, but decided I'd better keep a close eye on its burned-out lair by the tracks too. Just in case.

I made my way to the tunnel and watched the entrance for a while before going down. I looked inside and even shouted 'Troll!' a couple of times to make sure it wasn't inside. When I went in I saw at once I was right to be careful – it had gradually been repairing its nest. Everyone knows Trolls love living underneath bridges and now it seemed it was moving back.

That powerful heat I'd felt inside my own body when I burned its lair tempted me, and I wondered whether to destroy this one too. But then I remembered that funny feeling I'd had afterwards, and decided I'd let the Troll think it was safe to return. It'd be easier to keep an eye on it in the tunnel as well, rather than if it was living loose in the forest.

The summer holidays meant I had plenty of time, so I decided to go back to the railway line the next day to watch for it and work out what it was up to.

I had a messy jam sandwich wrapped in paper with me because I thought it'd be fun to have a nice little picnic by myself up on the hill while I waited for the monster to show itself. But when I arrived at my observation post, I was just in time to see the Troll leaving the mouth of the tunnel.

It lumbered from the exit over to the wooden stairs that had been built into the verge. Once up on the path it turned left and began to walk, heading away from the village.

Ah! No time to have my lunch now; I had to follow the monster.

I squished my sandwich down into my pocket and slithered down the verge. But before I was even at the bottom, a train was roaring its way around the bend. Annoyed, I began doing impatient little jumps as I waited for the carriages to whizz by. The wind of it slicked my hair back and fluttered through my shirt, as a blur of heads looked down on me from just a couple of feet away. I didn't see the skeleton crew. Then it was gone just as suddenly as it came and the hunt was back on.

I flew across the tracks and clambered up the steps as fast as I could. I couldn't see the Troll, so I began to run in the direction it had taken. I was breathless from the steep climb and the excitement. I was stalking my prey, I thought, like the wolf tracked Red Riding Hood through the forest – always keeping sight of her through the trees.

Except I couldn't see the Troll at the moment. Hopefully I wouldn't lose it. I had no way of knowing whether it had turned off into the straggly forest to my right. For now, the path was still following the line of the train tracks, but further ahead it would veer away and leave the railway behind.

Just as I rounded the bend that took the path in its new direction I saw I'd caught up with the Troll, which was only a short way ahead of me now. I darted into the cover of the woods to my right. There were just some overgrown fields to the left now, and the path was gently sloping down towards the countryside. I wasn't even sure where it led. I had never been this far away from the village by myself before.

I stood still for a moment to think. Where was it going? How far should I follow it? As long as I stayed on the path I would be able to find my way back to the railway bridge, but I didn't really know where I was any more.

Then I remembered its dirty nest under the bridge and how it had tried to catch me, chasing me through the dark with its nightmarish roar. And the other time, when I had seen it trying to smell me out in the witching hour, and the third time, when it nearly caught me for its cooking pot.

No. I needed to find out where it was going. Besides, I was a wolf.

'The hunter becomes the hunted,' I muttered.

I went on tracking it but kept to the safety of the ever-thickening forest. The fields on the other side of the path were falling away, melting into scrubland, which melted into forest. The path was narrower now and overgrown.

How long was it going to keep walking? I was getting tired and it was very hot. My stomach was growling at me, and I remembered my sandwich. The raspberry jam had bled through the bread but it was delicious. I'd had enough of tracking the Troll and was about to turn towards home when it did something interesting: it headed into the forest.

What was this?

I hurried to catch up and realised that it hadn't turned at a random point, but was following a narrow trail, which snaked its way through the woods.

I felt a bit sick; something was happening now. I tried to keep myself hidden – if it turned to see me on the trail, which was only wide enough to allow single file, I would be done for and I knew it would easily catch me amongst the trees.

Once again, the ground was sloping downwards and I suddenly realised where we were and where it was going. It had come to the so-called Densford River, which wasn't really a river at all, but a small stream. We were further up than the place Daddy used to take me to swim on hot days.

I hid behind a tree to allow the distance between us to build up.

It shuffled along, its tatty boots stumbling through the matted floor of leaves, and I thought it was going to make its way down to the water. But instead, it ducked behind a large tree.

It was facing the tree and its claws were flat against the trunk.

What on earth was it doing now?

It looked strange. It looked like . . . me. I realised my position almost exactly mirrored the Troll's. Every so often, it would cautiously peer around the trunk to see what was in front of it.

It's looking for something, I thought. No. Wait. It's looking *at* something. And it doesn't want to be seen. It's hiding!

What was it hiding from?

I couldn't see.

After a few minutes, the Troll slowly sank down to a crouching squat. In its new position it seemed to feel braver, and it shifted slightly to the left-hand side, so that while most of its body remained in the shelter of the tree, its head and shoulders were bent outwards.

I craned my neck to look, but I still couldn't see what it was staring at. I couldn't even see the stream from where I was, although I guessed the Troll was probably looking down at it.

I backed off into the forest. I tried not to make any noise, but I wasn't too worried about rustling leaves or breaking twigs as I walked; I was still some way away from the monster. And the woods were far from silent, with the breeze and the birds.

When I felt I was a safe distance away, I circled back. I wanted to approach from a different direction. I wanted to place myself further forward, to see what the Troll was looking at.

I wasn't frightened. Anything that frightened the evil Troll must surely be safe for me. The enemy of my enemy is my friend. Mr Finlay taught us that phrase at school.

I looped back eventually, and when I felt I was getting closer, I slowed down so I could approach carefully. But something was wrong. I couldn't see the Troll ahead of me.

I glanced around to see if it had decided to walk back the way it had come, and I gasped. I had come too far; I was now in front of the Troll. I could see its hairy head still poking out from behind its tree.

I wasn't directly in front of it, otherwise it would have spotted me. I was to its right, while it was still staring to the left. I quickly backed up, and hid again.

I leaned back against the smooth tree trunk. The bark was hung with silver strips, ready to be peeled away like onion-skin. The tender new bark underneath was pinkish. Knots in the wood looked like eyes, and I knew they were looking down on me in disapproval.

'Sorry,' I whispered to the tree. 'Sorry.'

'Well,' said the tree, 'at least it didn't see you.'

I realised how stupid I'd been. I'd been so intent on my task, I hadn't really paid attention to where I was. I was practically at the stream. Had I just listened, I would have been able to hear the water.

Now that I was more alert, I could hear shouts too. Who was there?

I edged around my tree, and looked down at the river.

Nobody interesting. Just two boys. Older than me by the looks of it. Perhaps eleven, twelve. They had left their clothes and underwear on the banks and were splashing about in the water, which was only a few feet deep.

I turned my attention back to the Troll. I still needed to work out what it was doing here.

I looked at the side profile of its head, at its blotchy red cheeks and its filthy, black beard, and then I looked at the boys in the river. It was watching *them*.

Right now, they were making a game of trying to push each other under the surface. One of the boys was bigger, so he was winning. He stood up to crow about his victory and the water streamed down his back over his buttocks. His skin was very pale, which combined with his nakedness made him look a bit like a white sculpture of a nymph or an angel.

The second boy leapt out of the stream and jumped at the first. He wrapped his arms around his shoulders and managed to push him backwards. The nymph-looking boy shrieked as he went down, but he was laughing when he came back up.

I was too far away to see their faces clearly, but I didn't think I knew them. They probably went to the secondary school over in Densford.

The expression on the Troll's face changed now. Its black, beady eyes were fixed on the boys as they wetly wrestled and played. It wanted to eat them, I could tell.

I thought about running down to the river, screaming at the boys to escape, but I didn't because the Troll didn't make any move to catch them. Maybe it had already eaten that day?

I just watched it, watching them, for a long time.

After a while, they'd had enough and climbed the bank to throw their clothes on and make their way home. When they'd gone, the Troll clambered down and pulled off its filthy rags. Strangely, that made it look more human. Its face and claws were blackened, but its body was white. It didn't look so very different from the boys, just older, saggier, wrinklier. It carefully picked its way into the stream and sat down, drank some water from cupped claws, then rubbed at its arms like a human would in a bath.

It was funny, really. Those boys had had no idea they were being watched by a monster. But then, the monster had no idea it was being watched by me.

13

Little Gerda's heart beat with both fear and with longing . . .
From *The Snow Queen*

The outside of the apple was very pretty, with a white-
and-red cheek, so that anyone who saw it longed for it.
But whoever took a bite from it would surely die.
From *Snow White*

'All these apple trees and no apples,' she said with a nervous laugh. 'I thought you might like to eat one.'

She passed him the fruit and flushed as he brought it to his mouth and bit into the flesh.

He wiped juice from his lips with the back of his hand. 'It's good.' Then he smiled at her. 'Thank you.'

He offered the apple back to her, inviting her to taste it. And she took it from him and brought her mouth to where his wet mouth had just been.

This then.

They both knew what it meant, of course they did. She hadn't planned this when she bought the fruit that morning, but . . . did she? The apple was always the fruit of knowledge and the fruit of sin – and they both had new knowledge now; she couldn't pretend they didn't.

He took her into the little wooden shed that housed seeds, tools and some rusting machinery. He closed the door. It was hot and sticky outside and she was uncomfortably warm because she'd worn the long-sleeved dress that Reggie always said she looked pretty in.

Hans had said it might be cooler and that they should shelter from the burning sun in there while they finished the apple. But when they were inside he laid the apple on a shelf and didn't touch it again.

The shed was so small, more like a lean-to, so that they were standing very, very close together. They were facing each other. She had been physically closer to strangers than this; when visiting her parents in London a few months ago they'd had to run to a Tube station after hearing the terrifying howl of an air-raid siren. People were packed on the platforms, and eventually lay down as the hours passed and they waited for the all-clear. They lay together on the tiles like rows of sardines. But somehow, just standing a foot or so away from this man, in a small, dark space, felt disturbingly intimate. The sky seemed to darken somewhat, or perhaps it was just that the small windowpane in the shed was smeared with years' worth of grime and cobwebs. Very little light could penetrate.

There was silence for a beat. Or two.

Something had changed now in the air, and they were both breathing shallowly, quietly, so as not to break the spell. He was facing her, but she had turned her head so she was staring at the door – she might bolt at any minute; she was trying to make a decision. She could tell he was looking at her – he was much braver than she was. Her shallow breathing and abnormally strong heartbeats made her feel faint. Her hands were gripping a shelf behind her.

She felt, rather than saw, him turn his own head slightly away from hers. He must have been looking at a point just over her shoulder. Had the moment passed? Maybe nothing would happen. Her stomach threatened to lurch and she wasn't sure if it was intense relief or fiery disappointment. Was it possible to feel both at the same time?

But then she felt his fingers lightly touching her right hand. It might have been a mistake – did he know he was touching her? If it was possible for things to become any more still inside that little old wooden shed, they did so. After a hesitation, he slid his fingers along her hand. Still she kept her gaze averted and said nothing. There was no doubt now though, that he knew what he was doing.

Was it too late to stop it? Not really. What would he do next? She hadn't really given him any sort of encouragement. She thought she might be holding her breath. Was she shaking?

His fingers pushed up the long sleeve of her dress and he caressed the softness he found there, stroking the underside of her wrist. She had never noticed how sensitive that area was. The motion gave her goosebumps and it felt almost erotic, but she forced herself to remember it was just his fingers, just a sleeve, just her wrist. Nothing at all.

She was still holding her breath but heard a faint ragged quality affect his breathing. Her head was still averted.

Was it still possible to pretend nothing had happened? Probably – neither had acknowledged that he had touched her. What was he going to do next? What would happen when they had to leave the shed?

He must have turned his face back towards her again, because she could feel his breath moving her hair and against the side of her throat. She seemed suddenly very aware of her own body. But she still hadn't given him any encouragement. Did his shaky breaths indicate fear – she was certainly frightened – or arousal?

She felt a shifting; he seemed somehow to be directly opposite her now. She might have turned her face further away. She might have closed her eyes. She felt his fingers on her other hand, and it was almost unbearable.

He was leaning over her now, breathing into her neck, and

lacing his fingers between hers. She must have moved towards him – how else could he have found her lips? But a second or two after it had started, she realised that they were kissing, softly and rhythmically, and then he pulled her arms up so that they were around his neck and pushed against her with his body so that she was crushed between him and the wall of the hut. But the pressure felt good, and comforting, and she felt weak as though she might cry, and she couldn't deny this, this was too far, this was too far, and she pulled away from him, stumbled from the shed and ran home without looking back.

14

There she lay; so beautiful that he could not turn his eyes away and he slowly stooped down to kiss her. But as soon as his lips touched her mouth, she opened her eyes and awoke and smiled sweetly at him.

From *Briar-Rose (Sleeping Beauty)*

Like most woodcutters, Hansel had his own little wooden cabin. It was just off to one side of the glade. So when I went looking for him, and he wasn't splitting apple trees into logs I would usually find him inside his hut. He'd be sitting on an upturned crate drinking tea from a mug with his flask nearby or he'd be rummaging about on the shelves looking for something.

The first couple of times, I knocked at his front door, and he came outside to greet me. Once, he invited me in, and I sat on the floor chatting to him while he finished his drink. He let me have a sip of his tea, and I gripped the mug tightly in my hands as I drank. I thought of the Red Indians, who share a peace pipe during their powwows, and I knew this was a similar sign of friendship from him to me.

Sometimes we played games together. I taught him hopscotch, and we used thin branches of the apple trees to mark out the grid. Perhaps other adults, like my mother, would think it was strange that a grown-up enjoyed playing children's games. He wasn't my father, after all. In some ways, he was better than my father, because I never forgot he was the woodcutter from my stories. He was a mythical creature almost, conjured by magic into Bambury.

One day, we were playing hide-and-seek. It was Hansel's turn to count and I ran off into the orchard as usual. But this time, I'd decided to make it more difficult, and I carefully circled back so I was in the glade. Hansel was sitting on the chopping block with his hands over his eyes.

'. . . . thirty-two . . . thirty-three . . . thirty-four . . .'

I tried not to laugh. I had planned to hide inside his cabin, but now I remembered the rusty hinges would make the door squeak if I opened it. Hansel would know where I was before he even finished counting to sixty. I decided to hide behind the cabin instead.

When he finished calling out the minute, he shouted, 'I'm coming! Are you ready?'

I had to bite my tongue. No matter how many times I told him the right thing to shout before he came to find me, he never seemed to remember it correctly. 'You have to say, "Here I come – ready or not!"'

I couldn't see Hansel from my hiding spot, but I heard him run into the orchard in the direction I'd first taken. My plan had worked, so I leaned against the back of the cabin to wait.

After a while, I picked up a jagged stone from the ground and turned to idly scratch on the wooden wall of the cabin. The edge of small rock perfectly gouged out a line from the dark wood, and revealed a paler, cleaner strip of wood beneath. I considered carving my name, but then everyone would know who had done it, so I just scratched a small pattern instead.

That was how I found the knot hole. It was at my eye level, and although the hole was small, when I pressed my face against the wall just so, I could see clearly into the cabin. The cabin had two counters running its length, and where I was at the back, I could see straight down the gangway. Things were slightly blurry around the edges, and I had to wait for a second or two to allow my eye to adjust to the dark inside, but I had found a perfect spy hole.

Just then, I heard Hansel crashing through the orchard. 'I'm coming! Are you ready?' he was shouting. Infuriating.

I didn't want him to see what I'd carved on the back of his cabin, and I didn't want to chance him finding out about my spy hole either, so I slipped around to the side, and allowed him to find me there.

After that, whenever I went to the glade and couldn't see Hansel, I went behind his cabin to find my little knot in the wood. I'd watch him for a while, before walking around to knock on his door. It made me feel powerful, watching him without him knowing it. I'd become a government spy. Sometimes I radioed back details to HQ about what I'd seen. I had to whisper, otherwise the target might have heard me.

So that morning, when I came into the glade, I was excited that Hansel was nowhere to be seen. Time to engage in a little reconnaissance mission. I ran back into the orchard, and approached the wood cabin on my belly, shuffling forward with my elbows. I didn't want to be spotted on enemy radar.

When I reached the back wall, my fingers curled into my palm to create my special spy telescope and I stood up to position it against the hole. It made it harder to see, so I put it away and put my naked eye before the knot. My eyelashes fluttered against the wood like butterfly wings, and the light pressure on them from the wall felt ticklish.

They were standing so close.

I didn't know why they were both standing so unnaturally close together. They weren't talking. I didn't know what they were doing, what they were waiting for.

And then he kissed her.

And it was so quiet, even though their mouths were moving.

I had never seen a man kiss a woman like that. I couldn't remember ever seeing Daddy kiss Mother that way, although I had seen pecks on the cheek between them, and between people in train stations.

After she ran away, I walked the long way around so I could approach the glade from a different point, a safer angle.

I called out so he knew I would be with him soon.

(*I'm coming . . . Are you ready?*)

15

⬥

He kissed her rosy lips and played with her long hair, and took her in
his arms, so that her heart began to dream of human happiness . . .
From *The Little Mermaid*

When her hair was being combed, Gerda began to forget her
playmate Kai more and more.
From *The Snow Queen*

It happened again. In the end.

She went back.

She had thought of little else since. A few days after the kiss
– a kiss, was that all it was? – a sudden summer rain arrived
to puncture the humidity. She had been restless all day and in
boredom went to her bedroom to try to nap.

She managed to sleep for a couple of hours and when she woke
up it was after four o'clock.

In the late-afternoon light, sharp from the whitish-grey sky, she
watched fat droplets of rain sliding down the windowpane. They
were reflected as shadow raindrops on her bedcovers.

She lifted her bare arm and twisted her wrist this way and that
to watch the shadows of water appear to slide over the smooth
skin there. He'd stroked her wrist.

She enjoyed watching the shadows play across her skin, and
the movement made it look as though the shadow water was

dripping down her arm. Her skin looked so white compared to the reflected dark grey of the raindrops. She felt as though she was in a film at the cinema; life reduced to black, white and grey. She lazily watched the fake display of water on her exposed arm and imagined him licking the raindrops from her skin.

She furiously leapt up from her bed, closed the curtains, pulled on her dressing gown and marched out of her room, but jumped as she almost ran into the boy who had been loitering on the landing by her open bedroom door. She skirted him and went downstairs into the kitchen where she put the kettle on the hob to boil.

But there were only so many times she could put it out of her mind. Was he thinking of it too?

She had to go back; it would look strange to Dawson if she suddenly went elsewhere after telling him of her plan to stock up her supply of wood before winter.

And somehow, she had decided she didn't want that kiss to be all there was. She had been so lonely for so long.

She pulled back a chair and smoked a cigarette from the packet lying on the table as she waited for the kettle to screech.

She was thinking, thinking.

The boy had trailed her downstairs and started scratching around to pull a meal together.

He fried eggs and bread together in a pan and she thanked him as he put a plate in front of her. She ate distractedly, then led him upstairs for his story. It was very early still, she supposed, probably only a little after five o'clock, but an early night would be good for everyone.

Her mind was made up; after the child went out to play in the morning, she would return to the orchard in the woods.

The next day, she bathed and dressed with care. It was still too early, so she gazed out of the window in the sitting room, smoking a cigarette to kill some time. It was here she'd watched as he and the first PoWs came into Bambury.

Yesterday's summer storm seemed as though it were about to return to battle with the season's stickiness. The clouds in the sky were rumbling like a stomach, but not because they were empty – they were full of thunder.

Despite this, it wasn't dark. A dirty yellow light was somehow penetrating through the clouds, filtering through the net curtains, so that the day itself seemed jaundiced. She stubbed out her cigarette and began to pace the room. The lace doilies on the dresser had taken on an unpleasant, sickly hue, like the wallpaper in her parents' house, stained from her father's cigars. The sky was swollen; a boil that needed to be lanced. The earth seemed expectant. She felt jittery, could feel the energy in the air. She wanted lightning to burst the storm open. She wanted the rain to come now. It would be a relief. She couldn't bear the waiting of it.

Annabel was still pacing a circle. She was a caged animal. She understood the electric charge in the air – her own body crackled with it.

She had never felt so trapped or so alive.

Even during her courting days with Reggie, she had never felt like this. This was different. This must be love. She stopped pacing. Of course! She was desperately in love with him.

Really, the impending thunderstorm meant that she should stay inside, but they had gone too far now and she had to go. She needed to go. It was all she could do to stop herself from charging through the front door and tearing down the street to find him.

Annabel noticed the boy watching her from the doorway. He drove her mad with his constant creeping. She told him to go out and play because she had lots of chores to do. If he seemed surprised to be sent out when a storm was brewing, he didn't show it.

She managed to wait until ten o'clock.

Then she made some tea and put it into a flask which she threw into her handbag. She had already given him the other flask from this matching set. Hurriedly, she pulled on her mac, put on a little lipstick at the mirror in the hallway – not too much, she didn't want it smeared across her cheeks or chin when he kissed her – and she pulled the front door shut behind her. Her heels clipped on the pavement like she was a trotting horse, but she couldn't bear to slow down. She hoped the rain held off until she was there; she had an umbrella but didn't want the humidity frizzing her hair and causing the curls to drop out.

She had agonised over what to wear – too dressy and she would look silly standing in the rural mess of the orchard – but too drab and she would feel dowdy and plain. She had settled on a summer dress that was perhaps a little light given the ominous sky, but wasn't inappropriate because it was now July after all. The colours were bright daubs of dye and she hoped it would make him think of her as a flower – perhaps he would call her his English rose – or maybe a butterfly. She was exhilarated in a fraught sort of way.

Thunder could bellow and lightning could split the sky wide open and the rain could lash down – but they would be safe under the little wooden roof. The friendly storm would keep customers and Dawson away, and the sweet noise would muffle their sounds.

And she knew he would love her today. There, in the shed, on the rough wooden boards, while soldiers of garden equipment stood sentinel and with the smell of the earth and growing things around them.

Later, he stroked her hair, running his fingers through the strands like a comb. They were naked and their legs were still entwined.

He propped himself up on one arm, cupping his head in his palm as he looked down at her.

She asked him questions about his life in Germany, before the war. He told her he didn't have a sweetheart, which was what she really wanted to know. He began to play with the silver locket around her neck and the tiny chain tickled her throat as he ran the charm along the links. She told him the heart was empty – no photographs or hair or keepsakes inside – it was just a gift from her parents years ago. She showed him her name and birthday engraved on the back; she didn't want him to think it was from her husband.

He asked her questions, too. Away from her house, and the boy, and memories of Reggie, she found herself able to view her life quite objectively. She was honest. Or mostly honest. She told him she had been unhappy for a long time, and had struggled after the boy was born.

She didn't mention the horror of the first year, the whispered threats of the asylum that finally forced her to realise she had to get up and pretend to be a functioning woman. But she told him the story of the time she had once almost run away.

'Once upon a time,' she said, with a little laugh and a shrug. 'It was a long time ago.'

'Really? You were going to run away?'

'Well, I didn't get very far.'

'What happened?'

She sat up to fumble for a cigarette in her handbag and lit it for them to share. They listened to the sound of the summer rain battering the little shed. It made the temperature pleasantly cool after the fierce heat of their bodies, cool enough to cuddle, and she lay back down, her head in the crook of his shoulder as they smoked.

'The boy was about three, I suppose. It was spring, before the war started. And I just woke up that day and wanted to go away. So a bit later, that morning, when my husband had left for work, I just thought . . . I'd go.'

She flipped over onto her stomach so she could see his face.

'Is that . . . Do you think that's just absolutely . . . terrible?'

'No, no,' he said and lifted up a little to kiss her. 'I think it was actually very brave to leave.'

She gave a slight nod, unable to speak for a moment. He really understood.

'I walked to the end of the road,' she said with a sudden hoarse laugh. 'And that was as far as I got!'

She took the cigarette from him and took a deep drag.

'It was my only serious attempt to run away, but I didn't get any further than the end of the lane that led away from Bambury. Isn't that funny? I just stood there, for quite some time actually, wondering whether to walk for another twenty minutes or so until I got to the station. It was the train I'd been thinking of when I woke up, you see. I'd woken with an almost unbearable desire to get on a train.'

He nodded up at her and she held the cigarette to his lips, making them both smile as she helped him smoke.

'I wanted to sit on that train for hours,' she said, 'seeing all the fields and towns blurring as they sped past. The images beyond the window would just swim by as though I were underwater. It was such a strong fantasy; can you imagine that? The urge took me by complete surprise because I'd been fine for a couple of years by that point.'

She fell silent as she remembered trying to decide what to do on that street corner. Trying to decide whether to go back to her crafted façade or whether to escape.

But of course, reality had leached into her dream as she stood on the pavement. Besides a few shillings in her purse, she had nothing.

'I didn't know where to go,' she said. 'The train's destination was never actually part of the fantasy. I hadn't taken any clothes with me and I don't know how to type or do anything like that so a job was out of the question. No; I realised I would have to turn back. And I thought, "Oh! This can't have been a serious attempt to run away after all." But still, I lingered.'

She gave another almost-laugh as she sat all the way up and

wrapped her arms around her knees, which she pulled tight to her chest.

'It was funny really. I was probably standing on that corner for, goodness, fifteen minutes or so! Still as a statue. Cherry blossom had fallen all over me while I stood there.

'I must have looked a picture – you know, a bit strange – because an old lady stopped to ask me if I was all right! I didn't know her, luckily, and I mumbled a silly excuse about waiting for a bus and thanked her for pointing out there was no bus stop on that stretch of road – I'd have to walk a bit further down.

'Then I turned around and walked home. Reggie was at the bank so no one knew what I'd nearly done.'

Hans sat up and wrapped his arms around her. She leaned back into his chest, so she was enclosed by him. She was still curled up in her tight little ball.

'Poor Annie . . .'

She had brushed the fallen petals from her hair and clothes as she made her way home down the tree-lined lane that warm spring day. But she'd hesitated, just for a moment, before lifting her key to the lock.

The child would still be upstairs, where she'd left him.

'When I closed the front door behind me, I perched on the step at the foot of the stairs for a while, just, you know, sort of willing myself into action. Eventually, I went up and opened the door of the nursery.'

She'd kept her hand on the cool, brass doorknob, which was greasy from the sweat of other people's hands. Reggie's mainly, she'd supposed, and both their mothers'.

'The child was in his cot – he was much too big for a cot, really, but we hadn't got around to . . . Anyway, he was standing up, clinging to the wooden bars like an animal. He stared at me very solemnly, but didn't make a sound. The two of us just looked at each other across the room. "I ran away today," I told him.'

Annabel swivelled round now, and wrapped her arms around

Hans's neck so she could cling on there, and he took the cigarette from her fingers and finished it, smoking over the top of her head.

The following Sunday, a little over a week since she and Hans had become lovers, her parents came up for tea. It was her father's birthday.

Annabel had made some sandwiches and her mother brought her sugar rations so they could pool them to bake a cake, but something wasn't right with it. The sponge was flat and dense but they all ate it anyway and pretended to enjoy it so as not to waste the sugar, although her father wasn't particularly successful at hiding his disappointment.

They were sitting around the wrought-iron table in the back garden, occasionally batting at a wasp or insect hovering over the crumbs. The summer storms from the week before had long since been beaten back by the sun, and the smell of hot earth rose up from the ground. Annabel was enjoying the warm prickly feeling on her bare arms as her flesh started to cook. Her skin had already taken on a honeyed hue from sitting outside in the orchard with Hans, chatting to him or just watching him while he worked.

After tea and cake, and a half-hearted attempt to sing Happy Birthday which trailed off because it felt so silly with just three adults and a child in the garden, Annabel told the boy to go and play in the woods. But he said he was too hot and lay down on the lawn in the shade and closed his eyes.

'Hasn't he got any friends in the street to play with?' her mother asked in a low voice.

'Oh, not today.'

'But . . . usually then?'

'Yes. Usually,' Annabel said.

'I had too many chums to count at that age,' her father told them both. The thought seemed to cheer him up and he pulled a handkerchief from his pocket and set about tying a knot into each corner so he could wear it as a hat to protect his bald head from the glare of the sun.

Annabel suppressed a sigh. He was going to reminisce about his boyhood.

'What fun we'd have. Why, my parents wouldn't see me until supper time. Got into some trouble, mind you.' He chuckled. 'Best years of my life.'

'Do you think it's safe, though?' Elizabeth broke in. Annabel suspected she was trying to avert an anecdote.

'What do you mean?'

'Well, supposing there's an air-raid siren and he doesn't hear it all the way out there? And I don't like how close you are to all those Germans.'

Annabel smiled openly at this, and secretly inside.

'This isn't London, Mother. And we're not in a "Bomb Alley" town or on the coast. I've hardly even been in the shelter since Reggie built it!'

They all looked at the eyesore at the end of the garden, a messy patchwork of corrugated iron and turf.

'And as for the Germans . . .' her words drifted away and she felt a flush beginning to bloom on her cheeks that felt like glowing, scarlet roses. She felt a strange, secret pleasure to be almost speaking about her lover openly.

'Yes?'

'Well, some of the ones in the village are really very nice. They're safe enough, aren't they?'

'Safe?!' her father bellowed.

'You know what I mean. They have to be accounted for all the time. They can't really roam freely or anything. I think it's quite secure. And besides,' she had remembered the grocer's words, 'where would they go, anyway? They're better off here. Not to mention they're watched over by a colonel.'

Her pleasure was quite gone now. She felt irritable and defensive. She busied herself clearing the table – standing up to pile plates and cups on the tray. Worse than her anger was the shame. For the first time she seriously considered what her parents, in fact, what *anybody* would think of her if they knew her secret.

Affairs were sinful, dirty, and wicked. But for a woman – a mother – to have an affair with a prisoner, a German soldier, in a sordid little shed? It was obscene, and she was disgusting. Sweaty bodies writhing together like snakes against the earthy floor amongst spades and ploughs while his kind slaughtered young British men, some still in their teens. She closed her eyes. People would think she was depraved. They'd call her a traitor.

Annabel carried the tray through to the kitchen and set it down on the sideboard with a bang. She leaned against the work surface for a moment to compose herself, but jumped as her mother walked into the kitchen with the milk jug.

'Forgot this,' her mother said and set it down next to the tea tray before heading upstairs to the toilet.

Annabel filled the sink with scalding water and mercilessly plunged her hands into it again and again as she rinsed the china. Thank goodness no one had ever seen her with Hans, apart from that first time she met him, when Mr Dawson and the boy were there. And of course she and Hans had sworn each other to secrecy.

Her mother had come back down and she could hear her affectionately berating her father in the garden through the open door. She'd caught him napping in the sun and was now making him come inside so he didn't get burnt. They came through the kitchen as they made their way to the sitting room, the boy following them as he laughed at his grandad getting in trouble.

When Annabel finished washing up, her hands were red and puffy-looking, steam rising from them before she enclosed them in a clean dishtowel.

She went through to find her father dozing. Since she couldn't put the wireless on and risk waking him in a bad temper, there was nothing else for her and her mother to do but sit in silence.

She had thrown out the papers and magazines when she tidied the house before they arrived, so in the absence of any activity, her mother settled back against the sofa and went to sleep too.

Daniel approached Annabel's armchair.

'I'm going to play out now,' he whispered, lightly touching her bare arm.

He left the house and she saw his dark head through the window as he walked up the garden path to turn right towards the woods.

Annabel sat there for a long time, thinking, looking at the net curtains as they danced listlessly against the open window, undulating when they caught a breeze. And the three of them were still sitting like that, perhaps an hour or two later, when Daniel returned home. He called out as he opened the door, waking his grandparents, and came in flushed from the heat.

'Time for another cup of tea,' Annabel's father said as he opened his eyes.

'I'll do it,' her mother replied, stretching as she stood.

'And what have you been up to, young man?'

'I was in the woods, Grandad. Just playing.'

He'd returned earlier than Annabel would have liked and it made her feel tired. She always felt the need to perform at being a mother in front of her parents, because they'd been so horrified at the state of her after the boy's birth.

'How wonderful,' she said. 'Well, I hope you had a nice time.'

He nodded vigorously and came to hover by her armchair.

'Well, I'm still not sure I like it.' Annabel's mother had returned from putting the kettle on the stove and she leaned now against the doorframe. 'It sounds dangerous to me. It's not like playing out on the streets in London where everyone watches out for everyone else's children. I don't like the look of those woods.'

'Don't talk nonsense, Elizabeth,' her husband said. 'Just because you've been in the city all your life, you're frightened of the country. Daniel's lucky to have all this on his doorstep. I'd have loved playing there with my friends when I was his age. We had a whale of a time whenever we managed to get someone to take us out to Epping Forest.'

'I was only saying—'

'I know, Mother.' Annabel had decided to try to prevent both an argument between her parents and any anecdotes from her father. 'But I really do think it's all right. Children have been playing in those woods for ever. It's practically what they were designed for – isn't that right, Daniel?'

'I'm a big boy now, anyway,' the boy told the room, pushing back his hair, which was damp with sweat. 'Mother knows I'm safe in the woods even when I stay out till it's dark. Even when I stay out till it's after ten o'clock at night!'

'Well, that's a bit of an exaggeration.' She laughed nervously, but relaxed when her parents laughed too.

'His shirt seems a bit tight, Annabel,' her mother said, into the brief silence that followed. 'Under the arms. Don't you think?'

Annabel looked across at the boy. 'Well,' she said. 'He grows so quickly.' His clothes did look a bit on the small side, now she thought of it. And his hair was too long. She'd been taking her eye off the ball. It was so important to keep everything looking right.

'Shooting up, aren't you?' her father said. 'Like a beanpole.'

'I've already spoken to a woman in the village, *actually*,' Annabel said, thinking fast. 'She's going to give me some of her boy's hand-me-downs that'll fit him better.'

'All right, I know when to mind my own business,' Annabel's mother said and went back to the kitchen to make the tea. Annabel followed her, and began transferring the now dry saucers and cups from the dish rack back to the tray.

'Heard from Reggie lately?' her mother asked behind her as they both returned to the sitting room.

Annabel laid down the tea tray and self-consciously smoothed down her hair. She tried not to think about her husband too much. It was too confusing.

'He writes when he can,' she said noncommittally. 'I don't get all of his letters by the sounds of it, but I think most get through.'

She poured milk into all of their cups and then the tea through its little strainer. Daniel was kneeling at the coffee table waiting for his own cup.

'I don't think he gets all of mine, either,' she continued, 'but it's better than nothing, isn't it?'

'Sometimes they cut holes in Daddy's letters when he says something like where he is or where he's going.'

'That's the censor stopping information from falling into the wrong hands, young man.'

'I know, Grandad.'

'Goddamned Huns would stoop to anything.'

'Father, please!' Annabel said, sharply.

Her father looked surprised at her tone, then shocked them all by apologising for his language in front of the boy.

After a pause, Annabel's mother continued with her questions.

'But he's doing all right, is he? Conditions aren't too bad out there? Getting enough to eat and all that?'

'Yes, yes, fine.'

In truth, it had been quite a while since Reggie's last letter. She sometimes wondered if something had happened to him, but there was no telegram. And his letters had become much shorter with longer gaps in between, so that she couldn't quite summon up genuine fear that he had been killed or gone missing in action.

'I think the food's not too bad, actually,' she said as she passed round the tea. 'That's about all he can tell us. That and his problems with his ears. Sometimes the letters have had so many holes cut through them they look like paper snowflakes!'

That night, long after her parents had left, Annabel lay in bed and tried to sort through her jumbled thoughts.

There was a streetlight, now defunct, outside her window, and she had always enjoyed the warm, orange glow that beamed around the thin paisley curtains. She missed it terribly now all the lights had been shut down for the blackout. Her own blackout precautions, thick black cloth taped over the windows, sealed her in and wouldn't allow even a chink of the cold blue light of the moon inside. The eerie darkness of the village unsettled her.

Annabel had never been in an aeroplane, but she had once seen aerial photographs of British cities in a magazine long before the war. She imagined how Bambury would have looked from the air. She imagined the photograph would have shown the village blazing with the whitish lights of indoor electricity, and yellower tones from the few houses that still used gas lamps and candles, and the orange lights she loved so much that delineated some of its streets. But tonight, from above, little Bambury would be as black as the surrounding woods, and even London and Cambridge and Manchester and Liverpool – and all the other big cities that *were* photographed – would be dark tonight too. England and the rest of the British Isles were now as black as the night sea. It would be like looking at a dark hole where the country used to be.

The bright lights had all been snuffed out in a bid to blind the German pilots hunting for targets below.

She remembered, with something akin to nausea, the churning, sickening swirl of her emotions in the kitchen earlier that day after discussing the Nazis with her father.

But it was too hard to associate Hans with the Germans she heard about on the wireless. He was nothing like shouty Hitler and the frightening men of his government, and he was nothing like the stories of cruelty attributed to faceless German soldiers in the news.

How could he be evil? How could he be everything they said he was?

Then she considered what they might say about *her*. She had to admit to herself now that she was an adulteress. Poor Reggie seemed to be losing himself – but here she was, not only fraternising with the enemy, but loving him.

She threw herself over onto her stomach with a soft moan and buried her face in the pillow, then restlessly flipped over again. But no matter her position, she couldn't stop the feelings that made her so uncomfortable. She remembered the hot flush of shame she had tried to scald away at the sink that afternoon. She couldn't shake the images of her parents finding out about their filthy daughter. She would have to put a stop to this. She would tell Hans that it had to end. But he would try to convince her to carry on, so perhaps she should simply stop going to see him and leave him to work out that she was never going back.

No!

No. She couldn't just abandon him like that. Whatever anybody else thought about the German soldiers, she was the only person in Bambury – maybe even in the country – who actually knew one of them properly and knew what he was really like. He was in all honesty the kindest, most understanding person she'd ever met. How could she even think of leaving him? She was in love with him.

She wished he were lying in bed next to her. He would make her see things the right way again. They would face each other, and whisper like children telling their secrets to one another in the dark. They would have the luxury of time, which would give them the luxury of lazy intimacy, not tempered by fear or the hands of her watch. And if they lived together they could make a real home, a place that would be a comfort and a salve. Then she imagined him in the camp barracks. Was he awake? Was he in bed, thinking of her before drifting off to sleep? Maybe he was dreaming about her. Or perhaps he was sitting on the floor, with the other PoWs, playing cards or dominoes.

She pulled the pillow over her face and wept.

16

'But beware that you do not say anything about this to anyone. Keep your silence.'
From *The Water of Life*

After reading to me as usual, Mother went to her own room. I could hear her crying, which used to be quite normal but it had been a while since she'd done that.

When she left, I removed the blackout curtain so that the moonlight could fall across my bed, held back only by the branches of the magnolia tree in the front garden. I understood that we weren't allowed to let any light seep *out* from our windows, but surely there was no harm in letting the light come in?

Grown-ups couldn't sling a black cloth across the moon, much as they might like to.

I couldn't think when it was too dark. I couldn't see the edges of my room to tell if something was lurking in the inky black.

The silvery light coating my eiderdown and showing me what was there – just the bookshelves, just the Darlings sitting on top – reassured me and allowed me to concentrate. I climbed back into bed and turned my face to the moonbeams.

My shock at seeing my mother with Hansel inside the woodchopper's cabin was starting to wear off now. Until I saw that shed-kiss, that shared kiss, I had no idea that was going to happen. I wondered what secret, adult signs I must have missed somehow, despite all my spying on them. Now, suddenly, things had changed.

I thought of my Daddy and knew she shouldn't be kissing Hansel. But Daddy seemed so far away again; I was struggling to remember his face. And I loved Hansel too. And I loved her. I understood it. This was the magic world – this was happening in the ancient forest; this wasn't even vaguely connected to 'real' life with houses and banks and rules and schools.

I often went to watch them after that first kiss. Hansel kept his promise to me; he never told her that he knew me too, and he never spoke to me about my mother. He didn't want to get either of us in trouble with the other, and that made me like him more.

And the moment I saw their lips touch, I knew I'd never speak about it to them. Not to mention all that came afterwards, all the things they did and said, not knowing I was just the other side of the wooden boards of the walls. They thought it was their secret, but I knew it too, and that was *my* secret.

17

'I'll huff, and I'll puff, and I'll blow your house in.'
From *The Three Little Pigs*

There weren't very many men left in Bambury any more, just the old, the lame, the feeble-minded. They were the ones who weren't any good to the armed forces for one reason or another, and Annabel thought perhaps that was why some of them seemed so angry.

Their frustrations needed to be vented and, though there were not so many of them, these disparate men had banded together. They made much of being the 'Home Guard', which in theory meant they were another line of defence, but in practice meant harassing housewives about their blackout curtains, or the poor quality of their air-raid shelters. She'd read that some Home Guards in other parts of the country had been issued revolvers left over from the Great War, but none of these weapons seemed to have filtered through to the men in Bambury.

Naturally, these guards hated the Germans for turning them into impotent stay-at-home men without any sort of useful role to play. And, conveniently, there were quite a lot of Germans staying nearby for them to focus on.

Annabel was a little afraid of them.

They came round one day in mid-August, about six weeks after she and Hans had begun their affair, demanding an inspection of her garden. She recognised their leader, a man named Bernard Higgins.

'Here about the regulations,' Higgins said, without any pre-amble, as she opened the door.

'I – I beg your pardon?'

She felt a stab of nauseating fear that they were there to arrest her or some such. How did they know? Had someone seen them?

'Regulations. Your garden. If you don't mind.'

'Now?'

'If you'd be so kind.' He smiled. Higgins was in his late fifties. He was a powerfully built, stocky man, and Annabel saw that he was quite drunk with the petty power the Home Guard mandate had provided him.

The others – four of them – were peering at her behind him.

She opened the door to let them inside.

'Just through here, is it?' he gestured with his clipboard. Various forms peppered with tick-boxes were held in place by the rusty clip.

Annabel pushed back against the wall as they filed in. It was beyond her why they all needed to be here for this. A man she didn't recognise brushed against the hall mirror, almost knocking it off its hook. He caught it in time and had the grace to give her a sheepish look.

'Oopsie daisy,' he said, pushing his black-rimmed spectacles further up on his nose.

Annabel glanced into the street as she closed the door behind them. She caught sight of one of her neighbours on the other side of the road, leaning against her own doorframe with her arms crossed. Annabel couldn't remember her name, but they were nodding acquaintances. The woman was staring at her with narrowed eyes. She wasn't sure if she too had just received a visit from the Home Guard, and was offering grim solidarity, or whether she had, in fact, suggested they visit Annabel's house because she believed there had been some kind of infraction.

Annabel raised a hand uncertainly.

The woman nodded, just once, adjusted the patterned scarf tied around her head, and went back inside. Annabel hurried after the men, who were already opening the back door and making their way into the garden.

They looked ridiculous as they prowled around the lawn in their shabby suits with their proprietorial air.

Higgins had taken one member of the group straight across to the air-raid shelter and they made a great show of inspecting it with expressions that demonstrated just how serious their job was. The others, including the mirror man, were ambling around the perimeter of the wooden fence. They stopped at the far corner, murmuring in low voices.

Higgins's companion was an extremely fat man who walked with a cane, despite only being in his late thirties or so. Annabel knew his name was Richard something-or-other and that he'd had several of his toes amputated as a result of diabetes complications. Reggie had pointed him out to her one day.

'Did you know you can't walk properly if you lose just one big toe?' he'd whispered at the time. 'You can't balance.'

As she looked at the man now, she supposed that his disability was what prevented him joining up. He hobbled around after Higgins, struggling with the cane on the grass. He was sweating heavily but seemed to be taking his role very seriously. He was putting everything he had into examining the shelter.

Annabel hovered at the back door, watching the men go about their business. She hoped they wouldn't need to go upstairs to check the blackout blinds. It was a bit messy up there.

'Can I make any of you some tea?' she called.

There were a couple of 'no's and a couple waved their hands dismissively. Higgins was evidently much too busy to reply.

She turned her attention to the three men at the far end of her garden. None of them was very old. She recognised Jimmy Dockett, who was about twenty-two or twenty-three. Although he looked big and strong and healthy, she knew he was epileptic. It was hard to believe that with no warning he could have a fit. She wondered how she would react, and what the others would do now, if he fell down in convulsions with froth bubbling from his mouth as he writhed on the lawn. She had once seen that happen in a doctor's waiting room when she was a little girl. She remembered screaming and her nanny Missus Joan had rushed her outside the surgery immediately, so she never saw what they did to the man to make him stop. It was one of the most frightening things Annabel had ever witnessed and she began to wish fervently that Jimmy wouldn't have a fit in her garden.

Strangely, considering his illness, Jimmy had a reputation for being a bit of a bully. He'd probably become that way to avoid being bullied himself. He was big though, strong-looking, so that probably helped. She had heard that he'd even been arrested a couple of times for fighting.

She didn't know the mirror man or the other fellow at all. They both looked as though they were in their early forties. The mirror man had thinning brown hair and an open, kind-looking face. She wondered what was wrong with them. Perhaps they had been soldiers but had been sent home injured.

What with Jimmy's mean streak, Higgins's puritanical air, and Richard's sheer size as he lumbered around, she felt uncomfortable.

Eventually, Higgins motioned for the others to join him. There was some more quiet discussion and then Higgins strode towards her with the others in his wake.

'Well,' he said as he consulted his forms, rifling through the pages as though to remind himself of his findings, which he had, in fact, only just found. 'You'll be relieved to hear your bomb shelter's all right.'

He peered at her over his reading glasses, then glanced back at his clipboard when she simply said, 'Oh. Good.'

'However,' rustle, rustle went the pages, 'we have ascertained that you do not appear to have a vegetable patch.'

141

There was another pause.

'Ah. Well, no . . . That is, not yet.'

'And may I ask why, Mrs Patterson?'

'Well, I . . . I . . .' she glanced around the garden and at the five men staring at her. 'I certainly have every intention of digging one. It's just . . . the time . . .'

'We must all *make* time, don't you think so, Mrs Patterson? I'm sure I don't need to remind you of the "Dig for Victory" campaign.'

'No, no thank you. I'm perfectly aware of it. As I said, I've been busy, but I most certainly intend to plant some things. Over there!' She pointed at the end of the garden.

'And, were we to visit you again, say, Thursday week, there would be some improvement in that direction?'

'Next Thursday? Why yes, I suppose I could—'

'Glad to hear it. Right, chaps?'

They nodded.

'Excellent,' somebody said.

'We're about to put these up – show her the posters, Albert.'

One of the men held up a cartoon image of Hitler doing his bizarre and simultaneously sinister salute. He had a stash of them and was obviously intending to put them up around the village. Underneath the picture, the words read: WASTE THE FOOD AND HELP THE HUN.

'Ah, yes. It's . . . very true,' she said in response.

'Show ourselves out then, shall we?' Higgins said.

'Oh, please, let me just . . .' She gestured them back into the house and they trundled back through the way they'd come.

'I'll be careful this time,' the mirror man joked, and exaggerated his careful movements as he walked past the frame.

She could tell he was trying to be nice to her, so she laughed a little.

'Yes please – I could do without the seven years' bad luck!'

He smiled. 'Couldn't we all?'

'Don't mind Mr Higgins,' he told her, once the others were outside. 'He's just trying to make sure you ladies are all right, that's all. All these women living by themselves, it doesn't seem right. That's why it's our job to see that you're looking after yourselves properly during this blasted war.'

'I understand. It's perfectly all right. I'll work on the vegetable patch.'

'It makes my blood boil to think that this is the fault of those Jerries living the life of riley just over yonder, while here you are, doing your best.'

His face, so well-meaning and earnest just a moment before, had taken on an edge.

She didn't know how to respond, so she thanked him for coming and forced a smile as he left. She waited politely with the door open until he was on the other side of the gate at the end of the path where the others waited. He struggled to close the latch behind him.

'Oh, you can leave that!' she called. 'Well, thanks again! Good-bye.'

She automatically checked there were no new magnolia petals on the front lawn as they walked away down the lane; she'd forgotten the tree had already finished its short season and she'd binned the last handful of petals weeks ago. The front of her home looked spotless and not having a vegetable patch was only a minor misdemeanour.

She closed the front door, leaned against it for a second or two, and then hurried into the sitting room to look out of the window. She wanted to see who they would visit next. There they were; going down the front path of a cottage a few doors down. She felt vulnerable. These men had power and if they ever found out how she was breaking all the rules – the most important ones of all – they were like wolves who could bring her house crashing down about her.

*

When she heard about the beating, it was the mirror man's genial face suddenly turning to something edgy and hard that she pictured first in her mind's eye. And then she remembered the vague threat in the butcher's words as he paid tribute to poor, dead Simon Moore.

It was Hans who first told her what had happened, although she knew she would hear more – the gossip and rumours from various villagers – within a day or two.

One of the PoWs was walking alone when he got into some kind of altercation.

'He's very badly hurt, very badly. Some men began . . . teasing him,' Hans said, 'is that the right word?'

'Taunting?'

'Yes. Taunting. But Erik can speak fluent English – better than me, maybe – and he began to argue with them.'

Annabel didn't really want to hear the rest, but she didn't stop him.

They were sitting outside, leaning against the shed. They'd hear if anyone came, she reasoned, and they could both jump up and pretend she was there to buy some wood. Her trolley was standing nearby. It was a dangerous game though, she knew, because if they didn't hear someone approaching, that person would know in an instant everything there was between them. A man and woman, sitting so close, side by side with their legs stretched out in front of them as they leaned against the rough beams and chatted in the warm sunshine. That's what intimacy looked like, and any fool would recognise it. Even before they stopped to wonder why she needed firewood in this heat.

'Erik has a temper, everybody here knows that. It was bad luck that it was him they met, perhaps. But . . . Well, Erik says they would have beaten any of us, even if we were calm and said sorry and agreed with everything they said. He says the only reason they didn't manage to kill him is because he was fighting back.'

'Who were they?'

'I don't know that! Neither does Erik.'

'But what did they look like? Were they old, young, tall, short, what colour hair did they have?' Perhaps because the Home Guard visit had made such an impact on her, she found herself wondering whether any of those men had been involved. Jimmy Dockett, perhaps.

'I don't know. What does it matter anyway?'

She supposed he was right.

'It's like the perfect crime,' she said. 'A victim nobody cares about; and one that a lot of people would like to rough up.'

Hans was silent.

'Oh, I'm sorry, dear!' she gasped. 'I didn't mean that. Please forget I said it.'

'Don't worry. I was thinking the same thing.'

'It was just a one-off, a horrible attack. Please let's not think any more about it!'

Hans picked up a small stick and began to scrape at the ground.

'It feels like something's changing,' he said. 'It feels like people are getting more angry here.'

Annabel didn't know what to say, so she said nothing.

'A lot of people know that I work in this orchard every day. I'm alone. Nobody can see or hear me from the road.'

'People are friendly too! Most people don't have anything against any of you!' She reminded him of Dawson, and the Post Office manager. Then the Bishop sisters. 'And they don't like anybody!'

Hans had scratched a groove an inch or two deep in the earth with the twig.

'I'm not trying to frighten you, Annie,' he said. 'But you are saying these things as though people are happy we are here in their village. You must know that isn't true. How could that possibly be true?'

Annabel felt close to tears. They'd been having such a nice time, soaking up the sun. She didn't understand why he had to tell her

145

that ugly news about Erik. And she didn't understand why they now seemed to be having some kind of argument.

'Nobody would hurt you, Hans! Please don't say such a thing.'

He stopped staring at his stick-plough and turned to face her. 'Don't cry, please.'

'I'm not!'

'I'm just saying that somebody *could* hurt me. You need to be prepared for that. If it happens—'

'Stop it!' She stood up, and furiously brushed down the seat of her skirt. 'I'll have to leave if you're going to continue to talk this way!'

'Annie!' he laughed. 'Pull me up!'

She reached for his hands.

'Oof!' he said as he stood. 'I thought my arms would stop being pain, by now. Sore, I mean. But chopping wood is such hard work.' He put his hand to her cheek for a moment and smiled.

She hesitated. He was obviously trying to change the subject, but she didn't feel mollified. She wouldn't be able to bear it if something happened to him.

'I wish this stupid war had never happened!' she cried. 'I wish we could live together normally.'

'We wouldn't have met if this stupid war never happened, remember?'

She tried to smile. 'I'd better get back.'

'Let's go in the shed so I can kiss you goodbye.'

But when they were inside, she didn't want to kiss; she clung to him and started crying.

'I'm sorry,' he said. 'I'll be fine. Nobody will try to beat me. I'm sorry.'

Over the next couple of days, Annabel heard more fragments of the story. She bumped into Jean Bainbridge, a wife of one of Reggie's former colleagues, who told her that a PoW had been sent to hospital.

'Nasty incident,' Jean added, 'there's no need to resort to common violence. That's what makes us better than them, isn't it?'

The boy must have eavesdropped on the gossip around the village. He found her in the sitting room where she was soothing her head by sipping from a glass of the port left over from her parents' visit. He wittered on about broken ribs, punctured lungs and fractured cheekbones until she shouted at him to leave her alone.

'Wouldn't it be nice if this was our little house?'

She laughed at his words and looked around at the walls of the dusty old shed. 'Perhaps it would be nicer to live somewhere a bit more comfortable, Hans!'

She looked down at his hands, which she was massaging with a little Vaseline. He'd mentioned they were often sore and his palms were rough and calloused. When they were softer, she would dig out the worst of his splinters with the pin on her brooch.

The muscles in his arms and shoulders often ached too, she knew, and she wished she could take him home with her to let him soak in a hot bath. But it was stuffy and close in the shed, which had grown uncomfortably warm in the sunshine, so maybe the summer heat in here would do him good.

Hans looked down at his hands in her lap. 'I worked very hard this morning,' he said. 'It felt like if I could chop enough wood there would be a prize for me.'

She smiled in sympathy. Only a fraction of the trees had been cut down and there were many, many more he would have to fell in order to clear the dead orchard.

'I chopped and chopped,' he said. 'But when I am chopping, I am thinking of you.' She stopped massaging his hands and just held them. 'And it seems like you are the prize I am working for.'

She looked up into his eyes, shaken into silence. He clearly felt as much for her as she felt for him. She blinked away the tears that threatened to come.

He must have seen them though, because he said: 'Life is very sad and very hard for both of us now.'

'Yes,' she whispered.

'But knowing you gives me happiness.'

'It's the same for me!'

'I think even if life wasn't hard and the war wasn't here, I would still be feeling that you are my happiness.'

She nodded. 'Yes.'

'I wish there was a way we could be together like life was normal,' he said.

But the next time Annabel went to the orchard, he was angry.

'Good morning, darling,' she chirped like a fool, 'I've brought you some nice tea,' she indicated the flask she was pulling from her shopping cart, 'and some bread and jam for a snack!'

'Hello,' he replied, glancing at her, and swung the axe down from above his head to split the wood balanced precariously before him.

'Well, would you like to have it now?'

'No thanks. Maybe later.'

He bent to retrieve one of the fallen logs and stood it on the stump to split again.

Thwack.

She flinched. And couldn't help thinking of those long-ago queens losing their heads to the executioner.

He bent down to grab another chunk of wood.

What have I done? she thought. She put the flask back in the trolley.

'Aren't you going to stop working?'

'I'm busy.'

'You usually stop what you're doing—'

'Damn it, Annabel!'

'Hans!' She was shocked.

'I have to get this done, you know.' *Thwack*. 'I do actually have a job to do here. Other people come and want to buy wood sometimes, can you believe it? Dawson comes to see if I'm working.' *Thwack*. 'We aren't a normal couple.'

He threw his axe across the glen, and the blade cleaved the grass open and lodged there. She gasped. She had never seen him behave this way.

He covered his face with his hands. There was a pause that lasted a moment or two. 'I'm sorry,' he said, dropping his arms to his sides.

She was frightened. She was frightened he was going to end it. 'Darling, I don't like it any more than you do. It's beastly to behave like we're doing something wrong. But please...'

She found she was unable to finish her sentence.

Please what? What promise could she possibly make him? How would things be different in the future? One side would win the war, one would lose. They would still be on different sides of the line. Her husband would come home. Probably. Hans would be sent back to Germany.

'Erik died, did you hear?'

'What? No! I had no idea!'

Hans crossed the clearing and pulled his axe from the ground. He stamped the grassy wound down with his heel.

'I'm so sorry.' She took an uncertain step towards him. 'I know he was your very dear friend.'

'Well. He's dead anyway.'

'You told me you'd talked to him after they – well, after he was hurt. It sounded like he was all right.'

He placed more wood on the block. He stared at it but made no move; the axe handle remained limp in his hand.

'I thought he would be all right. He walked back to the camp. He was talking. He was talking all the big talk. How well he was fighting them, you know?'

She nodded.

'And then he was in the hospital.'

'What happened?'

'The doctors told the colonel he had bleeding in his brain. He was fine, then suddenly . . .' He made a gesture with his hand.

She watched his face, unsure how to comfort him. She saw his expression harden after a moment and knew he was thinking of the men who had attacked his friend.

'They killed him,' he said. 'They murdered him.'

He smacked the wood off the stump with his palm and sat down. She stared at him mutely. She wondered if she should offer him the tea again. It might make him feel better.

'They're going to catch us, Annie.'

'No.'

'They're going to catch us.'

'No one knows!'

'They're going to catch us, and they're going to kill me. Or they won't catch us, but they might kill me anyway. Or they won't catch us, they won't kill me, but we will never see each other again when the war ends.'

He smiled at her and shrugged. 'Lots of possibilities. But none of them is good.'

She felt her face collapsing and allowed the tears to fall. He stayed where he sat.

'You're in danger too, you know. You should know that. And I don't want you to be in danger because of me.'

'Please, Hans!' She hated how she sounded like a child whining, or worse, begging. 'Please don't say such things!'

'We have to stop now, I think.'

She began to sob harder, rubbing furiously at her eyes. Her face felt hot and blotchy, her eyelids swollen.

'Please! Please!'

'Annabel! Be quiet! Somebody might hear!'

That made her wail. He rushed over to her and bundled her

into the shed, pulling her trolley in behind them. 'Stop it!' He looked out of the dirty little window even as he was feeling in his pockets for his handkerchief. That reaction was a force of habit; he was a wood-chopping prisoner; he no longer carried a handkerchief in his pocket. He used his fingers, instead, to wipe her eyes.

'What else can I say to you?' he asked, his voice somewhere between angry and helpless. 'What do you want us to do? Do you want me to say yes, all is good! Let's leave here now together – why not?'

Annabel came to her senses and pulled out her own hanky from her handbag. She cleaned herself up without looking at him. And with as much dignity as she could muster, she reached for her trolley and left the shed without another word.

18

But the Big Billy Goat Gruff charged at the troll and poked his eyes
out with his horns, and tossed him off the bridge into the stream.
From *The Billy Goats Gruff*

Ever since I'd first spotted the Troll silently snuffling at the pig
bins and the neighbour's vegetable patch on our lane, I made sure
to watch for it most nights. It was hard work staying awake after
story-time, standing by the window when I wanted to be curled up
in bed. But at night, with the cottages sealed up by their blackout
blinds, no one apart from me knew a monster came to roam
up and down the lane during the witching hour. It didn't always
come, but when it did I wanted to make sure I saw it.

I'd worked out it was definitely taking things from the bins
– scraps of food – like the dirty animal it was. It was collecting
special ingredients for its spells. And it was working out who lived
where, I was sure of it. I could almost see it using its massive nose
to sniff me out. It was hunting for me the way I was hunting for
it. And one day it would work out which cottage Mother and I
lived in.

Tonight, I was at the window earlier than usual because there'd
been no story-time. Mother had been a bit forgetful lately, and
there had been a few times I'd had to remind her to read to me.
This evening when I went down to the sitting room to ask her,
though, she said she was too tired and would read to me for
longer tomorrow instead. So I used the extra time to keep watch

for the Troll. But as I gazed out into the dark street, there was no sign of it.

Soon though, I knew, watching out for it wasn't going to be enough. The creature was building up to something, and it was hatching its plans for when it finally found me. One day, it would make its move – and when that day came it would try to get into the house. I strained my eyes as I looked for it in the dark. How could I protect Mother and me and our cottage? I had to be prepared for when it decided to pounce and gobble me up, or steal Mother away to eat her in the woods.

Booby traps! That was what I needed. Why didn't I think of it before?

Tomorrow I'd smash some glass bottles from the bin and sprinkle them along the top of the wooden fence around our garden so it'd cut its claws if it tried to scrabble over. I would get some glue from Daddy's shed and start sticking a hair from my head across the front and back doors so I could tell if it broke in while Mother and I were out. I'd read spies used that trick and had always wanted to try it. I wasn't sure how I would distract Mother while I was fiddling with the hair and the glue, but I'd just have to find a way.

I'd try to think up other Troll traps too – perhaps digging holes outside the back of the fence, the bit that led to the forest, so it would be harder for it to climb over into our back garden. Then I started thinking about what plans I could put into place tonight – no time like the present.

I crept downstairs and when I got to the bottom I could hear the wireless and smell my mother's cigarettes so I knew she was sitting in her armchair.

I tiptoed to the kitchen and set about making a magic potion of *poison*. I'd leave the mixture out in my room and if the Troll came in, it would see it and gulp it down mistaking it for a refreshing drink. Really of course, it would make it drop down dead on the spot.

I climbed up onto the sideboard and got a large glass from the cupboard. Quietly, I opened the back door and went into the garden, where I used a stick to push dirt and mud into the cup. Back inside, I mixed in some horrible-smelling cleaning chemicals which Mother kept under the sink.

Stirring it all together turned it into a smooth brown paste. It didn't really look very nice but the Troll would be in my room in the dark and wouldn't be able to see it properly. Also, it'd be thirsty from the effort of breaking into the house, so I was sure it would gulp it down as soon as it saw it. Probably it'd laugh and think how clever it was to be drinking a nice cup of coffee before it carried on with its evil plans.

Carefully, I carried the cup back up to my room and put it on my bedside table. I'd leave it there, but would hide it from Mother before the next story-time so she didn't drink it by mistake. I'd keep it under my bed. She didn't come in my room at any other time and now that she'd stopped cleaning upstairs she wouldn't find it by accident.

Another idea came to me then. And I went back downstairs to fetch a knife from the kitchen. I'd keep that underneath my bed too. I might need a weapon.

I climbed back into bed finally, but the sight of the cup of poison next to me kept me awake with excitement. I almost hoped the Troll *would* break in, just so it would drink the potion and die and then Mother and the police would congratulate me for killing it.

She'd had a row I didn't really understand with Hansel and seemed sad. It would be wonderful if I managed to kill the monster. I could show her how useful and brave I was, and that she didn't need Hansel. It was *me* who would protect her and make her happy. She would smile at me the way she smiled at him. First, I just needed to rescue her. I smiled as I thought how she'd tell me what a clever Darling I was.

19

The prince was carried into the house and did not look back for her. The little mermaid felt so sad that she plunged beneath the waves and miserably swam home to her father's castle.

From *The Little Mermaid*

'Ohh, what I wouldn't do to get my hands on one of them,' Jean Bainbridge said.

'Go on, Jean!' One of the other women laughed. 'What would you do then?'

'I'm perfectly serious, I'll have you know.' Jean delicately sipped her dry sherry. Then she looked around the table at all their faces. 'Well, not really – you know I disapprove of how that Jerry was attacked. But, honestly. I feel so angry! You should have seen her. She's in a terrible state.'

Annabel shifted uncomfortably in her seat. She hadn't wanted to come. It made a nice change to be in the pub, but she didn't feel she had much in common with these women, even though they were mostly the same age as her.

She'd run into Jean earlier that day. Annabel vaguely knew several people in the village because it was such a small place, but she wasn't close with anyone in particular. However, Jean's husband used to work with Reggie at the bank, and the two women were the same age, so they felt obliged to be friendly when they saw one another. Jean had just turned twenty-nine and had invited Annabel to her 'little birthday bash' at the Royal Oak.

Annabel wished she'd been quick enough to think of an excuse to decline.

Now they were discussing Evelyn Moore, whose husband Simon had been killed in France.

'She's in a dreadful state,' Jean said again. 'Poor thing. You can't do anything for her. I don't think she'd be eating at all if I wasn't taking her round some bits and pieces.'

'I'll make her a casserole,' a woman named Marjorie said. 'Everyone likes my casserole.'

The others murmured that it was indeed very tasty. Several of them suggested other dishes they could bring the grieving widow and her son.

Annabel's mind started to drift away and she wondered how she could tell Hans about her night out. She liked the idea of casually mentioning it to him, perhaps by simply passing through the orchard as a shortcut to settle a bill with Dawson. She enjoyed the thought of him imagining her having fun without him. She hoped he'd worry that other men would be circling her; he needn't know there were no decent ones left in the village. She wanted to punish him.

Also, she hoped that a night out would make her seem more alluring. She didn't want him to know how bored, boring and unhappy she felt most of the time.

But her plot to either spite or inspire Hans felt pointless now – she wasn't having a nice time at all. She wished she were with him in his shed. Failing that, she'd have preferred to be at home, alone, where she wouldn't have to make conversation with these exhausting women.

All they wanted to talk about was how much they hated the murderous Germans.

Annabel wondered if Hans had ever killed anyone. She had never asked him. She wondered if Reggie had; but that was somehow harder to imagine. She wanted to ask Jean how the British were different when they were pulling their triggers, and dropping their bombs, but it would be like uttering a treasonous question to the king. What was the point? The king wouldn't answer and it could only end badly for the questioner.

She wished they would change the subject. Nobody talked about anything but the war these days. What on earth had people discussed before? She couldn't remember.

'I was frightened when I first heard about the PoW camp,' she said finally. The others looked at her, a little surprised. She hadn't said much all evening and she might have spoken a bit louder than she'd meant to, but she continued anyway. 'But you see them out and about sometimes in the village and they don't seem to mean us any harm. It's a relief because I live so near the camp.'

Once again she trotted out her story about how polite even the Bishop spinsters had been to one of the German men.

'Frankly,' one of the older ladies replied sternly, 'I'm quite shocked at how friendly some people are behaving towards them. I always avert my face if I see one in the street.'

'Oh, me too!' Jean said. 'It's appalling how some of the villagers are acting as if there's nothing going on. Personally, I think it's dangerous that some of them are allowed outside the camp during the day to work and so on. They can come into contact with normal people and who knows what they might do? Supposing one decides to escape and attacks somebody? Or worse, what if they turn somebody into a spy or something.'

Annabel thought Jean had become a little unhinged by all the 'keep mum' posters, 'careless talk costs lives' and all that, but it wasn't the first time she had heard the sentiment.

'Germans have got no compassion whatsoever,' said the other woman.

'That's right. I'll never get over my brother's death,' Audrey Meade said shakily. 'Henry never got to experience life – he will never get married now, never have children...'

Jean put her arm around Audrey's shoulders. Annabel wondered if she was regretting her decision to organise this evening. What a birthday.

'It's a tragedy,' someone else agreed. 'But Mr and Mrs Ferris have lost both their sons. Both of them! Can you imagine?'

'It's the children I feel sorry for.' This was said quietly, and Annabel looked at the young mousey woman who had spoken.

Nobody said anything. They all knew she had been looking after her three young nieces who had been evacuated from the East End of London. One night, during the Blitz, their former home had been blown to smithereens and the maelstrom of rubble and fire had consumed their parents, who'd both stayed in town working for the civil service. This woman, who was not long married, had lost her sister and her brother-in-law and then had to tell the girls they were orphans and would never go home again.

'If I could get my hands on one of them . . .' Jean said again. But this time there was no jokey riposte. The mood had soured irrevocably.

Annabel walked home slowly. It was very warm, but it had rained lightly while they were in the pub and now the wet paving stones shone in the moonlight. She was glad of it, because it seemed less dark than it would have done otherwise. How she missed the street lamps, she thought for the thousandth time. Funny the things she'd taken for granted. She listened to the sound her heels made on the concrete, bits of gravel grinding wetly beneath the soles of her shoes. Her footsteps were not a uniform sound; sometimes she slipped a little and her heels scraped along the pavement. She had, perhaps, drunk rather more than she'd intended, but at home the port had gone and the gin was running low, so it was nice to be able to drink freely. She had ordered one gin and bitter lemon after the other, drinking for something to do to avoid conversation.

They thought she was one of them, with a young child and a husband away fighting, but she wasn't. Not really.

Jean had hugged her as they said goodbye at the door of the pub. The others all needed to go in the opposite direction, towards the centre of Bambury.

'Thanks for coming,' Jean said. 'I do appreciate it. You're sure you'll be all right getting off on your own?'

'Yes, yes, of course I will. Thank you for inviting me, it was . . . lovely. Happy birthday!'

Annabel felt stupid now about her plan to show off to Hans and make him think she had friends. She'd felt so lonely sitting in the midst of those women and she felt terribly low now. She wished he lived in the orchard as well as worked there. She would have gone to him right at that moment and woken him up. But he was imprisoned in a Nissen hut, while an old man nearby drank Bovril and kept watch.

Once home, she considered her options: bed, a nightcap, a cup of tea. She wasn't sleepy in the least.

While she was in the kitchen boiling water for the pot, she wished she had some biscuits or something sweet. She was peckish; a lot of alcohol always did that to her.

I'll bake him a cake, she thought. I'll bake him a cake and see him tomorrow and say sorry and make things right again.

She cursed the war and rationing, for it was hard to bake without plenty of butter and sugar and eggs. But her mother had recently given her a recipe for a cake made out of carrots. It sounded odd to Annabel, but her mother had tried somebody else's at a church fete and insisted it was really quite nice. 'Carrots *are* sweet when you think about it,' she'd said.

Annabel hoped she hadn't thrown the recipe away and was relieved when she found it stuffed into a drawer in the sitting room. She realised she still had her mac on and threw it over the banisters on her way to the kitchen. She was quite excited.

She turned on the oven and made a mess as she stirred the ingredients together with a wooden spoon. Eggs from Dawson's farm meant she didn't even need to make do with the powdered kind. The batter tasted surprisingly good, so hopefully the cake wouldn't turn out too badly after all. She hadn't realised how much noise she was making as she pulled out pots and pans from the cupboards to find her rarely used cake tin, until the boy came downstairs to see what was going on.

'What are you doing?'

He was bleary-eyed and she saw him check the time on the clock on the wall, even though it had stopped long ago.

'I'm baking a cake.' She noticed she was slurring a little as she spoke.

'Now?'

'Yes, now.' She scraped the thick mixture into the round cake tin she'd found. She stepped over the pans on the floor and nudged a large pie dish out of the way with her foot so she could get to the oven. A blast of fierce heat hit her full in the face as she pulled open the door and she recoiled slightly before pushing the cake inside. She slammed the door closed and stood, satisfied.

'Here.' She handed the bowl to the boy, who was standing watching her on the other side of the table. 'You can lick it out if you like.' She smiled magnanimously and the boy used his finger to scoop up the batter.

Hans was good for her, she thought. He made her feel things. She looked at the boy and felt an unexpected rush of emotion.

She made another cup of tea and the boy began to put the pans away. He washed out the bowl and stacked it on the rack to dry, then he poured himself some tea and joined her at the table.

He seemed excited to be up so late, and Annabel didn't want to send him back to bed. She rather wanted somebody to bear witness to the triumph of her cake. Warmth and sweet smells were emanating from the oven and although it was a little hot, the kitchen felt pleasantly cosy.

The boy was wisely keeping quiet; had he started jabbering away he'd have ruined the moment and she would have sent him upstairs.

After a while, she took out the cake and carefully turned it onto a wire rack to cool. She prodded the sponge gently with her finger; it had a lovely consistency. It was darker than a Victoria sponge cake, but the russet colour and the smell made her mouth water. It was much better than the one she and her mother had made for her father's birthday.

'Well done, Mother!' the boy cried.

'Yes! It does look rather nice, doesn't it?'

She didn't have any icing sugar, so wasn't able to make a topping, but she didn't think that would matter too much.

She wanted to try the thing before she gave any to Hans, so she carefully cut two slices and handed one to the boy. It was warm and delicious. It had been a long time since she'd had something so sweet and so good.

'It's got carrots in it,' she said.

'Carrots?' he laughed, incredulous.

'It's an old medieval recipe. They used to use carrots as sweeteners when sugar was rare and expensive.'

'Well, it's jolly nice.'

She wished Hans could see what a good mother she was being to the boy.

'Isn't it funny how nothing changes?' she said through a mouthful of cake. 'Sugar's rare and expensive again now. Sometimes, it feels to me as though we've reverted to medieval times. Kingdoms of Europe bickering and wars and dark streets and food shortages...'

The boy was silent. She realised it was pointless speaking to him. She'd have to tell Hans her theory tomorrow when she told him about the origin of the cake.

'Right. Bed.'

'Yes.'

She yawned as she stood up. She'd go to bed too.

'I'd better clean my teeth again now I've eaten a midnight feast,' the boy said.

'All right.'

She covered the cake with a clean tea towel and followed him upstairs. She really was quite sozzled.

Annabel awoke with a dull headache and her mouth so dry it tasted bad. She had some water beside her bed that she'd brought up with her a night or two before. It had an unpleasant taste, but she gulped it down gratefully.

At least she didn't feel too sick.

She sat up and looked at her alarm clock, which was never used for its true purpose, and saw it was eleven o'clock. Her resolve last night to make things up with Hans suddenly materialised again in her head, and she remembered the cake she'd made him.

She hurried downstairs to have some tea to wake herself up properly; she usually visited him in the mornings and left him later on in the day, when Dawson or other customers were more likely to show up. There had only been a couple of times when they'd heard someone coming towards the glade from the farm-yard side, and she'd had to hurry off towards the woods.

Upstairs, she bathed and held two dresses against herself in front of the mirror to see what colour suited her that day. Her pretty yellow dress made her look sallow, so she picked the pink one instead.

She hadn't bought or made any new clothes, but she was wearing dresses she hadn't tried on for years. She was choosing brighter colours and more daring styles. During her worst times, that first year after the boy's birth, she had gone for days without getting dressed if she had no reason to leave the house.

But all that was behind her now.

She put on a pair of pearl earrings and the silver heart locket. Her perfume was running dangerously low, but she sprayed a generous squirt of Vol de Nuit across her neck anyway. He had told her he loved the scent.

In the kitchen, she wrapped some slices of cake in a tea towel, placed them at the bottom of her trolley and then left for the orchard.

But on the walk, she began to feel afraid. What if he didn't want her back?

'Forgive me,' she said simply, when she came upon him in the glen. Her voice was hoarse. She noticed her hands were shaking so gripped the handle of her trolley.

'No. It was me – I'm sorry.'

She shook her head, relieved.

'Really, Annie. I'm sorry. I am. I don't want to stop things.'

'You don't?'

They were facing each other, a few feet apart.

'No. But . . .'

He crossed the distance between them and put his hands on her shoulders to look at her. But she stepped into him and he wrapped his arms around her instead. She remembered the cake in the trolley and was about to suggest they eat it to celebrate when he interrupted her thoughts.

'I'm thinking . . .' he said into her hair.

'What?'

'You said it yourself. You want us to be together. I'm thinking . . . I'm thinking we have to go away.'

She was so startled she laughed and stepped out of his embrace. 'Go away? You mean run away?'

'Yes.'

She stared at him and couldn't think what to say.

'Remember I gave you our possibilities once, and said none of them was good? Well, there is another possibility that I have thought of.'

'But Hans! Where would we go?'

She couldn't pretend she hadn't dreamed about running away with him. Running-away fantasies had been a part of her adult life for as long as she could remember. But unlike her earlier fantasies, which had started around the time the child was born, it was not the act of running that fascinated her. No, her recent daydreams involving Hans skipped over the actual running, and revolved instead around setting up home together.

'Where would we go?' she asked again. Horrified, hopeful.

He didn't reply; he seemed to be thinking. She thought about Reggie. The boy. Maybe they'd be better off without her?

She waited for his answer. His English was excellent, but he was undeniably German and anyone would know it as soon as he opened his mouth. They couldn't run away and pass for a normal couple.

'I might be able to find some of my father's friends in Liverpool. I think I know someone who would help us get away. Maybe we could get to Switzerland after that.'

'Switzerland!'

'It's our only good possibility!'

'But Switzerland!'

'Just think about it. Just think! We love each other. We can be together, we can be happy! I know you haven't been happy for a very long time.'

'I know, but... Hans!' She let out a strangled little laugh again, but he didn't laugh along with her. 'But... how could we?'

'There's things you'd have to do. Plans. You'd have to—'

'Wait, wait a minute! I can't talk about that yet, let me just think for a minute.' She took another step back and began fiddling with the handle of her trolley. 'Tell me... tell me how it would be.'

Finally, he smiled at her. He stepped forward and gathered up her hands in his.

'We would have our own house, not pretend like over there!' He gestured with his head back towards the little shed. 'We would be together, we would have a normal life.'

'Yes...'

'We can walk away from the war and leave everything behind us. I know I will make you happy.'

164

'Happy?'

'Yes. And I can teach you German or we can both learn French and we can live wherever we like. Together. We can have a home and it will be just you and me. Think how nice it is when we are together in a dirty old shed; now imagine we have a real home together.'

'It does sound so...'

'I know you don't like talking about bad things, Annie, but I think we have to make this decision soon. I am very frightened something will happen, like what happened to Erik.'

She looked away. 'Don't say that.'

'If you want, I could go first to make sure you are not in any danger. If you could just help me get to Liverpool I think I could get to Switzerland by myself. Then I could write to you and you could come when everything is ready and perfect.'

'I... I... do wish we could be together.'

He squeezed her hands and waited for her to look back into his handsome face.

'I know you think this is a difficult decision. But we keep saying our problem is difficult, oh, it's so difficult... But, when I think about it – then actually... No. It's not so difficult at all, Annie. The answer is very simple.'

20

*'I will set you three tasks, and if you can perform them all,
you shall become my daughter's husband and master . . .'*
From *The Six Servants*

I was the keeper of a powerful secret. I knew about their kisses and what they did inside the cabin and what they talked about when they thought they were alone.

But I had another secret as well; Hansel wasn't really a wood-cutter. I knew that now. It had gradually become clear to me that he was far too special for that. Not *just* a magical woodcutter; he was also a prince. Yes. An enchanted prince under a spell. He was trapped – that much was obvious – condemned to hack away at apple trees all day and spend his nights locked up under guard and key.

I didn't want my mother to be the one who broke the spell. I wanted to be the one who would help him escape. And if I helped him get away, then he'd leave her behind.

Ever since she'd met him, it was like she was disappearing in front of my eyes. Sometimes she didn't even want to read to me, and I knew how much she loved that.

I'd heard him speak to her of Liverpool and Switzerland, and I couldn't let him take her away. She mustn't be allowed to try to leave me. Not again.

There had been a terrible moment, several weeks ago, when I was watching them through my spyhole. They were naked on the floor and what they'd done had been frightening to watch because it wasn't soft like that first kiss. They made sounds like they were in pain and I was just thinking about running in through the door at the front to make them stop hurting each other when they stopped. But the really terrible moment happened when they were just lying there, smoking and talking. She told him how she nearly ran away from me. When I was three. And my breathing stopped, just like that, and it was like the time I found that letter from Daddy.

So, no. Much as I loved him, I couldn't let my woodchopper-prince take her away with him back to his kingdom. He'd have to go by himself.

And really, it would be for the best. It would be the best thing for Hansel to return home, and it would be the best thing for my mother, even if she was sad at first. She wouldn't know what part I'd played. And she would turn to me for comfort. She would call me her Darling.

I wasn't a watcher, a listener, of the story any more. I had my own role, and it was a very important part to play.

So while Hansel never said the words *as such* to me, I knew what it was he needed.

He needed to escape, and it would be me – not her – who would help him.

We were lying down. We'd just been chatting in a lazy sort of way about this and that – my life in the village, what people were saying about the PoWs, what I'd heard on the wireless about how the war would soon be over, my best subjects at school, my favourite fairy stories. We hadn't played any games that day. It was very hot and Hansel said he was too tired.

He was chewing a blade of grass, and the end shot forward into the air like a beanstalk trying to grow into the sky. My head was resting on my bent arm, and I was curled towards him, watching his eyes. They were closed, but still I looked for a clue as to what he could be thinking about.

'I think . . .' I began, 'you're going need some money, aren't you? To . . . get away.'

Hansel didn't open his eyes and didn't say anything.

'Some money. And, maybe, some food for the, er . . . the journey.'

I didn't want him to open his eyes now. This made things easier. I felt very awkward.

I tried to slowly turn my body away so I was lying on my back beside him, mirroring his position. I didn't want to be caught staring at him as I revealed my role as saviour to him. I copied the shape of his body so I looked as casual as he did.

'And . . . maps.' I stopped for the first time. Why wasn't he saying anything? 'I – I'll try my best,' I finished with a strange sort of nervous gulp, so that the last word was swallowed up by my throat.

He started to sit up so I quickly closed my eyes. I wished I'd thought to put a piece of grass into my mouth too.

'Did your mother tell you to speak to me of this?'

My eyes snapped open as I laughed in disbelief. '*She* won't help you escape! She doesn't want you to go away! And, and, well, she definitely doesn't want to go away either.' I closed my eyes again and tried to look relaxed. 'No, no, my Daddy's coming home. What would he do if he came back and she was gone?' I laughed again, although it sounded a bit shakier this time. 'He's coming back here. And Mother and I live here. Together. *Here.*'

I heard him sigh.

'I'm very, very tired,' he said. 'Maybe work and playtime is over for today. Mr Dawson asked me to help him on the farm this afternoon. Yes, I will finish here now.'

I felt a crumpled breeze as he stood up and his shadow made the red light behind my eyelids turn to black. 'I think you should go home.'

I sink you shud go hom.

Then I was up and brushing down my short trousers as I made for the fence without looking at him.

'Daniel!'

I wasn't going to turn around, even though I had stopped walking. I wanted him to say it to my back. But I did turn round. Of course I did. I wanted to see his face.

'You don't understand. What you are saying . . .'

I nodded. My throat was tight and I knew I wouldn't be able to speak any more. He looked serious, with a tight little frown.

'What you are saying – about getting me maps, and food and money . . . These three tasks are very dangerous.'

Three tasks.

I hadn't even thought about it like that, but of course it all made perfect sense.

There were always three tasks, and they were always dangerous.

I fought the urge to run over to hug him. He had given me the gift of his permission. I wanted to thank him, but I could sense that wouldn't be quite the right thing to do. Instead, I simply nodded a manly, knowing kind of nod, and turned and walked towards the forest.

I spent a lot of time in the woods over the next couple of weeks, trying to find the best escape route during a series of secret missions. I kept half an eye out for the Troll all the while as I experimented with different trails. Hansel wanted me to take him to the train station in Densford. When we got there, he'd stay hidden in the woods while I went to buy a ticket from the station master, which he'd then use to make his way to Liverpool.

So I had a lot of work to do to find the best way through the forest to the station. When I returned home from one such scouting mission, I took the county maps that Daddy kept in the bureau in the dining room up to my bedroom, spread them out across my bed and lay face-down, almost on top of them, so I could pore over the legends.

I turned over onto my back and pulled the maps onto my chest, willing them to give up their secrets to me.

Today was a glorious day and it was a shame to be inside, but this was important work and had to be done. I hadn't seen or heard Mother in the house so she must be out, with him in the orchard, or perhaps just running errands in the village.

I felt a shiver as I realised they could escape now – right this minute – and I'd be none the wiser. She'd just be gone, as though she'd never existed. But she was terrible at making decisions, and I'd heard her telling him she was still thinking about the best course of action to take. She kept telling him she needed more time, just a little more time. I was glad about that. Clearly it showed she didn't want to leave me. Because I was her Darling.

I let the maps fall on the floor and got up to open my window. Leaning out into the summer sun, I looked out across our front garden and turned to look down the lane. The other cottages were all peaceful, no sign of anyone about.

The petals had long gone from our magnolia tree and something about the burnt orangey glow to the early-afternoon light reminded me that autumn was on its way.

Buying a train ticket at Densford seemed like it might be a bit difficult, now I thought about it. I'd never bought a train ticket before. I didn't even know where Liverpool was. And despite all my time in the woods, I still hadn't found the trail that led to the station. Maybe I should forget about that part of the plan for now. I should probably just concentrate on finding a place where Hansel could hide for a while first. Maybe we could make a secret camp in the woods that only the two of us would know about.

He could build a little one-room wooden cabin there, a new woodchopper's hut, and I could bring him food and blankets. This solution fixed another problem too; I'd been worried about missing Hansel once he'd gone away, but this plan gave me the excitement of pulling off a daring escape mission *and* all the time I'd want with him. I'd have him – and Mother – all to myself.

I smiled as I turned my face up to the almost cloudless sky. I hoped he'd stay there for a long time. It would be like having a secret pet to look after, and it was the excitement of the secret, rather than the glare of the sun, that made my eyes water.

I thought I'd really hit on something there. After all, my plan to build escape funds for the train ticket wasn't really working. I had gathered a few shillings found hidden in cluttered drawers, or under the furniture, and had once taken some from Mother's purse. I scanned the streets for dropped change, but people picked up their pennies when they fell, or picked up somebody else's, so I never found any.

Pulling myself out of my daydreams, I ducked back inside my bedroom and returned the maps to the bureau downstairs.

I thought of what else I had to do as I left the house, heading to the orchard to spy on them if they were together, or play with Hansel if he was alone.

Gradually, I would start pilfering food from the larder and cupboards, and make a secret stash of cans of soup or tins of pilchards or vegetables. It wouldn't be the first time I'd given food to Hansel. I wanted to show him how important to him I was, and prove I was just as capable as Mother at providing what he needed.

Of course, I wanted to help Hansel because I loved him and wanted him to be free. But, well, it wouldn't be a bad thing if he was out of the way so Mother could get back to thinking about me a bit more.

I couldn't remember a time when she'd seemed more cheerful – and she was terribly keen to make sure that I was having a nice time. Why, she was always sending me out to play – not in an irritated way, liked she used to do, but in a happy carefree way. Now she was bright and gay – we'd even made a cake together that time – and it would be good to have life be about just the two of us now she was so jolly.

As I headed into the woods, steering clear of the path in case I ran into my Mother but watching out for the Troll, I thought perhaps it wouldn't be a good idea to tell Hansel about my plan for setting up a hideout camp just yet.

I knew he'd want to catch a train straight away, so he could travel to wherever Liverpool was. It would mean he'd have to take his chances on the Skeleton Service, but Hansel was brave and strong and that wouldn't frighten him. He wouldn't realise he'd be much better off living in the forest – with me to help him and visit him. I thought again about how wonderful it would be for him to a build a new woodchopper's hut that only I knew about. He didn't need to go to Liverpool. I'd go along with the idea of helping him get to Densford Station for now, and then – when we were in the woods – I could show him the beginnings of our camp in the forest. I was sure he'd come round once I explained.

Plotting this escape was the most marvellous game I'd ever played, and now I could see the game didn't have to end. And my head filled with pictures of us together in the magic forest, until there was no room for anything else. The dreams were like spun candyfloss clouds hung across the sky; and I was just as unable to catch hold of them.

21

'It is the prince whom I love. More than anyone.
He is always in my thoughts and it's to him I would
willingly pin all my hopes of happiness . . .'
From *The Little Mermaid*

'Oh but Grandmother, what terrible big teeth you have!'
From *Little Redcape (Little Red Riding Hood)*

Reggie's parents, Bill and Moira, had organised what they called a 'Grandparents' Saturday' with Annabel's mother and father, who had driven up to Great Yarmouth for the occasion in their Austin 7 Ruby. Annabel and the boy had travelled by train that morning, in a carriage filled with purposeful-looking men and women in all sorts of uniform.

Her parents planned to stay overnight – at a bed and breakfast, rather than put Reggie's parents to any trouble – but Annabel would catch the train back to Bambury in the evening. She'd told everyone she didn't like to be away from home too long in case there should be any word of Reggie.

Of course she'd apologised profusely to Hans, telling him there was no way she could wriggle out of the occasion. She'd taken off her necklace and given it to him to keep hidden in his pocket until the next time they met.

'Look – I'm giving you my heart!' she'd said, and he'd laughed and kissed the silver pendant and wrapped it up in a piece of paper so he wouldn't lose it. He was never searched at the farm or the camp, so she wasn't worried anybody would find it.

So now here they were, both sets of grandparents and Annabel and the boy, finishing lunch at a smart restaurant in the town. They'd all take a walk along the seafront afterwards. The Pattersons' neighbours were going to join them on the beach because Daniel was friendly with their son, Harry or Henry or something.

Bill had brought along a bag containing a cricket ball and a bat and, as the coffee was served, said 'all the boys' would have a bit of a game while the ladies sunned themselves on deck chairs.

Annabel stifled a sigh as her father spoilt the festive atmosphere by grumbling about the poor quality of the coffee. 'It's like drinking muddy water,' he said, making a big show of putting his cup back on the table in disgust.

Annabel suspected since he'd offered to pay, after a tussle over the bill, he felt he could moan without being rude. Her parents were better off than Reggie's and her father often came up with an excuse about why the Pattersons should let him foot the bill.

'Ah, you can't get good coffee for love nor money *anywhere* nowadays, David,' Bill replied.

'Well, I think it's all been lovely,' Moira said. She seemed a little tipsy from the wine.

'Bloody Krauts have got a lot to answer for, depriving a man of decent coffee!' Her father shook his fist in mock rage – a strange attempt to cover up his genuine annoyance.

The others laughed and the situation seemed to defuse.

'I feel that way about my nylons!' Moira said. 'I do miss my nylons!'

Annabel's mother nodded vigorously. 'I know, I know.'

'I've been thinking about doing what these young girls are doing; drawing a line up my bare leg with a bit of eyeliner!'

'You wouldn't!'

'I might!'

They laughed again and Annabel found herself smiling along with them. That was actually quite a good idea. She imagined how her legs would look from behind if Hans were watching her.

She laughed as she pictured him finding out the lines rising up under her skirt were not real stockings, but were just painted on her skin and would rub off under his warm hands and lips.

The incongruity of that image in this setting made her laugh all the harder.

'Dear oh dear!' Annabel's father shook his head, but Bill just chuckled.

Annabel tried to control her giggles by clamping her fingers across her mouth, but then she got the hiccups. She almost laughed again as she watched her father manage a thin smile so he didn't look like a bad sport in front of Reggie's father, but she guessed the women's cheerfulness was irritating him.

As the laughter died down, Moira sighed loudly.

'Oh, it's nice to laugh for a change,' she said. 'I feel as though I'm on edge all the time, worrying about Reggie and the war. I don't know about the rest of you, but the letters I'm getting from him seem increasingly . . . fraught.'

Then she leaned forward over the table, and said: 'It's lovely to see *you* looking so well, Annabel, dear.'

Annabel hadn't seen the Pattersons for months, not since that day back in May when Reggie had been home on leave and there had been that horrible scene at the restaurant.

She imagined the difference between who she was then and who she was now must be striking. She felt happier, more confident.

She'd needed Reggie's mollycoddling protection in the past, but not any more. In all honesty, she couldn't say that she was no longer a needy person, but she needed a different person now. A secret person.

'Um, thank you,' she replied.

Of course, she'd been turning thoughts of running away with

175

Hans over and over in her mind. It was easy to get lost in the romance of it; the joy of being together, the joy of escape. But as soon as she opened a little door in her head to let in the day-dreams of a life with Hans, other thoughts flooded in to drown out the pleasant ones – thoughts of organising logistics, leaving the boy and Reggie and her family, figuring out where to go, and how on earth they could possibly hope to avoid capture. Wouldn't running away together be hurtling headlong into trouble rather than the best way of escaping it? She tried to clear her head and concentrate on what her mother-in-law was saying.

'Honestly,' Moira insisted, 'you look really – I don't know how to describe it – you just look really well in yourself.'

Annabel wondered if it was as obvious to the others as it was to her that Moira was being pointed. She seemed to be annoyed, not pleased, that Annabel wasn't as broken as she used to be. And she seemed to be implying Annabel wasn't as worried about Reggie as her.

'Thanks, Moira. That's nice of you to say so.'

The others were looking at her across the table now to see what Annabel's mother-in-law was noticing. They nodded and murmured similar sentiments. Annabel's face was hot. She was embarrassed to find herself the centre of attention so suddenly, and felt resentful that Moira had thrust her into that position. She also felt something else. Something more confusing.

They think I'm perfectly fine, she thought. Besides Moira, some of them are sitting here admiring me; they think: isn't she coping admirably despite the absence of her husband? They're shocked that little Annabel is doing all right by herself.

Annabel was irritated that Reggie's parents, and her own, all assumed she was incompetent. But now she was surprised to find she didn't like being thought of as strong either.

She liked being someone who had to be looked after, and was comfortable drifting along in life's current. She didn't want to have to make decisions, and then act on them, come what may.

'It was nice to see Moira and Bill again,' Elizabeth said later, as they walked along the street in the summer evening. It was after eight o'clock but the leafy streets were still bathed in sunshine. They'd left the Pattersons and their neighbours at the beach and were now strolling towards the station, where her parents would see her and the boy off before going to their bed and breakfast.

'I used to really enjoy having tea with them after church while you and Reggie were courting,' she added.

'Mmm. It's a shame they had to move here for Bill's job.'

Annabel's father and the boy had fallen behind, and when she glanced back she saw they were both ambling along with their hands clasped behind their backs, although they didn't appear to be talking.

'Moira certainly seemed to think you're looking well.'

'Yes. I didn't really know how to respond to that. I felt all shy.'

'It's funny, Annabel, but as soon as Moira said it I knew exactly what she meant.'

'Oh?'

They paused and turned to face each other as they drew level with the station entrance, and stood for a moment to wait for the others to catch up. So it *wasn't* just Annabel who'd felt the undercurrent beneath Moira's words at lunch.

Elizabeth leaned back against the wall and watched her daughter.

'You do seem a bit different somehow.'

Annabel felt a horrible tingling sensation, as though a big spider had just crawled into her chest to lie across her heart. She felt suddenly breathless.

'Different? How?'

She turned to look for her father and the boy, but they'd stopped to examine something on the ground and were still some way away. She had no choice but to face her mother.

'It's hard to put my finger on, but ...'

The spider shifted; raised its spindly legs, revealed its beady eyes, its fangs.

'Well . . . ?'

'Well, look at what you're wearing!'

'What?!' She looked down at her pink blouse.

'It's a bit low cut, isn't it? You're a respectable married woman, Annabel, not . . . And what Moira was saying – well, you *do* look good in yourself. You seem, almost . . . happy.'

'Ha! You want me to be unhappy?'

'Stop it. I'm trying to explain. I haven't seen you happy for a long time. Not since you and Reggie were courting, and then when you were carrying Daniel. Of course I want you to be happy. But . . .'

'But what?'

'It's just not *seemly* for you to be so carefree. There, I've said it!' She shook her head as if she were relieved the words had left her mouth, but she continued talking: 'Your husband's away fighting, he's in terrible danger, you're having to raise that child all by yourself, and we're in the middle of a war, in case you hadn't noticed.'

A sick sense of shame – always close to the surface – flared inside Annabel and the spider rubbed its legs together deliciously. Annabel's voice was wobbly when she spoke and her eyes were very full. She felt defensive.

'I'm not happy about any of that! I'm just trying to make the best of things, that's all! Isn't that what I'm supposed to do?'

A movement at the corner of her eye alerted her to the fact that the boy had crept up on them.

She whirled to face him. 'Do you mind?'

He looked up at her in surprise.

'Shoo! Haven't you ever heard that curiosity killed the cat? Besides, it's rude to eavesdrop!'

'Come along, Daniel,' her father said as he walked up, and led him into the station.

'Of course you're supposed to make the best of things, dear. But the way you've been acting lately, it's not like that. It's as if you're enjoying yourself. And that's not right at all.'

Annabel rubbed along her lower lashes with the tips of her fingers to remove the tears already pooling there.

'I'm not,' was all she could manage.

'I thought it when I saw you for Father's birthday, and the last few times I've spoken to you on the telephone . . . You've got responsibilities, Annabel. You've got Daniel. And frankly, he seems a bit distracted himself – daydreaming all the time. You paid no attention to him at lunch – but his table manners were atrocious. And I can't help thinking he's starting to look a bit . . . well, almost unkempt. But it's as if you're just oblivious to all of it—'

'Please!'

Her mother sighed. 'What is it, dear? I know Reggie's good to you. But you never talk about wanting him home. Anyone would think you're pleased to be living by yourself.'

'I'm not! I'm not!'

'Well. All right then. There's no need to get upset. Just think about it. Acting as though everything's fine is just . . . It's not the done thing. All right?'

'All right.'

Annabel's mother nodded, satisfied. 'Good. Then let's say no more about it.'

And the spider in her chest settled back down and her heart slowly began to return to a normal rhythm as they walked inside the station to wait for their train. But Annabel's mind was still whirring, whirring, whirring.

By the next morning, she realised she was being silly to put so much stock into what Reggie's emotional mother – and her own – had said. Why, all she'd done was giggle at one of *their* jokes at lunch and now she was being lambasted for it. What was 'unseemly' about laughing? Or about wearing a pretty top? The cheek of it!

She was determined to push such trivial complaints to one side as she hurried through the woods, lest it spoil her mood before she reached Hans.

She broke into a little run as she entered the orchard, while the rational part of her scanned the trees for strangers before calling out his name.

He scooped her up as she jumped into him, almost knocking him over, and they were both laughing even as they tried to kiss.

Later, they lay on the grass outside the shed. He was on his back while her head rested on his bare chest. He'd pulled on trousers and boots and she was back in her skirt and blouse.

'How did you learn to speak English so well?'

She glanced up to see his crooked smile, but she knew he enjoyed the questions.

'You know this! I studied it at university. But first I learned it at school when I was a little boy in Mittenwald. Then when I was about thirteen to maybe sixteen, my father's job – he was the boss of a big company that made shoes – made us move around. We spent some time in England, in Liverpool, where his company had a factory. When we went to other places in Europe the common language was always English when I needed to speak to someone in a shop or something like that. Actually, I used to think I might like to be an English teacher, so I went university, but then the war . . .'

'Did you go to school when you lived in Liverpool?'

'No, no. While we were moving a lot, my father gave me schoolbooks to read.'

'I've never been up north.'

Hans shifted and they both sat up. He tried to smooth his unruly fair hair back into a neat side parting, then pulled a crumpled pack of cigarettes from his pocket. He offered her one, but she shook her head. He was a frantic smoker; he sucked furiously and his cigarette was reduced to a column of ash in just a few puffs.

'I used to think about being an architect too,' he said. 'I wanted to design great buildings.' He laughed.

Annabel laughed with him. She was having a wonderful day.

'In the summers I worked for my father's shoe company, and travelled a lot, all over Europe. I loved looking at all the buildings in the different cities.'

'How exciting!' But she was also thinking about how easy things sounded for him. All those options. He knew what he wanted to do and could simply set about doing it.

She smiled at him. 'Now, you're here. And I'm so glad!'

He didn't say anything, but looked away as he finished his cigarette. The sun had lightened his hair since she'd first met him, and now his face and chest were a warm copper colour.

His mood seemed to have shifted and she didn't ask any more questions. An awkward silence invaded the little glen; all roads lead to things we can't talk about, she thought.

He jumped up and stamped on the tip of the cigarette with the heavy tread of his work boot.

'We have to leave here, Annie – you must know that.'

'It's difficult, Hans. Just let me think! Everyone says the war will be over soon, maybe we should just wait a bit longer and see how—'

'No, we have to talk about this! This is not a game, a fairy-tale romance, what we are doing; it's dangerous. Why won't you talk about us leaving? You have to—'

'Oh!' Annabel cried, as an old collie dog bounded into the clearing and jumped up at Hans. He bent quickly to rub the dog's ears and flanks before it could bark for attention.

'Quick! Quick! It's Dawson! He's coming!' he hissed.

And sure enough, Annabel thought she could hear the old man's wheezing and lumbering footfalls. She bolted like a rabbit running for its burrow and hoped Mr Dawson wouldn't hear her or see the bright yellow of her skirt darting through the trees. She forced herself to slow down when she came to the forest path.

She'd been careless – she should have taken her trolley today as she usually did, then she could have pretended she had just arrived to buy some wood.

She managed to make it back to the lane without meeting anyone, but it had been a close call, she had to admit.

It was only as she approached her front gate that she saw the Home Guard man, Mr Higgins, leaning against her front door waiting for her.

'Ah, is this about my vegetable patch?' she said, desperately trying to think of excuses.

'No, no. A different matter altogether, Mrs Patterson.'

She swallowed nervously. He couldn't possibly know. Could he?

'Where have you been?'

She closed the gate behind her and stood looking at him at the other end of her path. 'Sorry? Oh – I was just out for a walk.'

'I see.' He looked at her hard.

'I . . . fancied some fresh air.'

'You've been gone a long time. You were one of the first houses I knocked at this afternoon, and I've visited every house on this street and *still* been here ten minutes waiting for you to come back.'

'Oh dear, I am sorry. Would you like to come in?'

'No, thank you. I've got more houses to visit after this.'

'Well, how can I help?

'Did you know Simon Moore?'

'Evelyn's husband? Yes, I met him a few times. Such sad news.'

'He was my cousin,' Higgins said. 'By way of marriage.'

'Oh, I had no idea . . . I'm so sorry.'

'Well, that's by the by. Since he was killed by the Hun, people have naturally been talking. It seems to have opened people's eyes finally.'

'Um, yes of course,' Annabel said, although she didn't really understand what he was getting at.

'There's a petition going round. About getting more restraints on the PoWs.'

'Restraints?'

'Of course. I know some bleeding hearts in this village think they're no different from us, but we mustn't forget they're the enemy. It's ridiculous they're allowed to walk around unescorted, and work without supervision and the like.'

'Oh.'

'Wouldn't you agree, Mrs Patterson? Here you are.' He walked forward to hand her his clipboard, and she looked through the list of signatures already there.

'Well, I . . . I don't know. They're supervised by their employers, aren't they? And a colonel?'

'Him! He's so old he's half-demented. Even a woman like you could probably do a better job. Just sign there.' A chunky finger pointed at the bottom of the list.

Annabel hesitated. 'Well . . . I'd like to think about it first, if that's all right?'

'I beg your pardon? What's there to think about?'

'Well—'

'Do you think German prisoners should be *welcomed* with open arms, Mrs Patterson? Do you *want* them swanning around free as they like?'

'No, of course not, I—'

'Because it sounds like it. It sounds like you think—'

'No, I don't. I understand what you mean now. You're quite right. Here!' She scrawled her name on his list.

22

... the thorns held fast together, as if they had hands, and the
young men were caught in them and died miserable deaths.

From *Briar-Rose (Sleeping Beauty)*

Of course, my time scouting for shelter and hatching plans in the woods took me away from Hansel a bit. But I knew he understood; I was very busy.

Sometimes, when I did go to the forest to watch them secretly in the wood cabin, I still heard him trying to get Mother to agree to leave with him. But she kept saying she needed more time.

She didn't tell him about the petition, the one I saw her sign from my open bedroom window. I'd ignored Mr Higgins ringing the doorbell because I'd been too busy looking at my maps upstairs.

I really was a very good spy. I knew all sorts of things now.

But hearing Hansel trying to get Mother to help him escape just made me more determined to help him by myself.

In a way, not visiting him as often made it even more exciting when I did see him – there was always so much to talk about. I'd tell him all about the plans I'd been making.

In the beginning, he didn't say much, he'd just smile and nod along when I talked of how I could help him. But then he started asking me questions and I knew he was taking me seriously. He'd ask me what people in the village were saying about the PoWs, and what I heard on the wireless about the war, and how I thought the escape would work. So I was glad it was me who told him about the petition, not Mother, although I didn't say she had signed it. I made him promise not to tell her how he knew about it. And then I think he started to realise that, actually, I could do the things I promised I would. And I was his best chance after all.

One day, as I sat cross-legged on the ground a little way away from him as he chopped the wood, he said: 'Tell me again. How exactly will we get to Densford Station?'

'Oh, it's just through the woods,' I said, vaguely waving with my hand when he glanced over at me.

The truth was I'd never actually managed to find my way there, but I felt sure it'd all work out once I had Hansel with me. Surely he would be able to read maps better than me. In any case, once we were in the forest together, I would explain my plan of how Hansel could set up a secret hideout and I could come and visit him so he wouldn't be lonely. I was sure he'd agree to it.

'And what will we take?'

I began to reel off my list. I'd gradually been packing supplies – food and maps and the few coins I'd scavenged – into a dusty old haversack I'd pulled out from the cupboard under the stairs. I kept the bag under my bed, next to the Troll poison and my knife.

'You haven't spoken to anyone about this? Not even your mother?'

'Of course not! It's *our* secret.'

He sighed and rested the blade of the axe on the ground and sat on the stump. He didn't say anything for quite a long time.

'All right,' he said, eventually. 'All right, Daniel. We'll do it.'

Once Hansel agreed that I was going to be the one to save him, he suddenly wanted to run away as soon as possible. And a couple of days later he told me he was ready, and that we'd leave the very next day.

The night before the escape mission, I took down my black-out blind and let the moonlight into my room. I didn't bother watching for the Troll because I had more important things to think about. I lay in bed, staring out at the moon, which shone through the branches of the magnolia tree.

My arm dangled over the side of my bed and my fingers trailed across the beige canvas and leather buckles of Daddy's old pack, now lumpy with tinned foods pilfered from the larder and dusty glass bottles of Daddy's ginger beer that I knew Mother wouldn't miss. My fingers traced the landscape of the hills and valleys of the bag.

Nearly time.

But it wasn't; the sky stayed the deepest, darkest black and the moon seemed fixed in place. Only the tick-tocking of the clock on the bedside table assured me that the seconds were counting down, and dawn was coming after all.

I left before she woke up.

She'd just think I'd gone to play out as usual. The knapsack slung over my shoulders bumped hard against my back as I jogged to the orchard. It was a nice day, a bit chilly I suppose, but then it was still early. It was September now, the beginning of autumn, and it was just starting to feel like it. Already, some of the trees were starting to shed their leaves onto the forest floor.

I was there before Hansel arrived for work. I stayed out of sight in the woods in case Farmer Dawson was with him.

Even as I saw him enter the glen alone, perhaps at a slightly faster pace than usual, and glance about him, I held back. I watched him head into his cabin and come out with his axe and a small bag.

I'd always enjoyed watching him secretly, but today would be the last time. I felt a sort of tearing inside me as two different wishes fought against each other – one to help him escape, and the other to make him stay here for ever.

But then I thought of Mother turning to me when he was gone. I would be her only Darling then.

186

It was clear to me that Hansel was rushing. Usually, he would chop down a tree, which didn't take long because the trunks of the apple trees were not large, and then chop that trunk into large chunks, ready to be chopped on the block into smaller logs for the fire.

'I like to do it one tree at a time,' he'd told me once, 'because it breaks my boredom. When I get bored of one task, it is soon time to do another one. And I like a job to be finished altogether. One tree finished is one tree finished. Then I can start again.'

But this morning, not long after dawn, and earlier than usual – he must have run from the camp – he was hacking at the trees with the axe. He made several fall, and let them lie where they fell.

He was almost frenzied, and my gentle happy-sad thoughts of losing my wonderful woodchopper-prince began to turn into something hard to describe. Something that felt a bit like fear.

'Help me,' he said, as I finally approached.

I was a bit taken aback. I was the rescuer, clearly there to help him escape, so where was the smile, the friendly man-to-man greeting?

'There's a pile of wood in the shed from yesterday – carry it out here and put it next to the block.'

I hesitated, then put down the knapsack where I stood.

'No! Take it with you, in case someone comes.'

He was probably just nervous. I was sure he didn't mean to snap at me.

I went into the cabin and hid the bag behind some kind of farm machinery. I couldn't find the wood he was talking about, but I didn't want to go back out to ask what he meant. I didn't understand what he was doing.

Why was he working so hard when he knew he was going to be leaving today? Perhaps it was like he'd told me once; he enjoyed seeing a job finished. Did he want to finish clearing the orchard before he left? There'd never be time!

But then I saw he'd emptied some old boxes, and filled them with firewood he'd made.

I understood then what he'd done, and was glad I hadn't asked.

It was a good idea; something I hadn't thought of in all my careful planning. It shocked me a bit, that he'd obviously been thinking about this too. I don't know why it shocked me, but it did. I thought I'd been in control, but he'd been making plans too.

He was making the glen look like he'd been working there all day. If someone arrived and found him gone, they'd see evidence of his hard work. Trees lying ready to be chopped, and a pile of firewood he'd already made.

I dumped some wood on the ground and he whacked the axe into the block and came to help me, throwing armfuls carelessly onto the pile I was building there.

At the end of each day, Hansel had to take the wood he'd chopped to a storage shed on the farm in wheelbarrows to keep it dry. So this wood here was more than he could have put by yesterday. He must have been keeping back firewood for several days, at least.

He looked around with his eyes narrowed.

Then he took a newspaper-wrapped sandwich from his small bag. I didn't know what else was in there. It was only half a sandwich and there was a bite mark in it. I could tell from the way he was holding it that the bread was hard. It must've been part of his lunch from yesterday or even the day before.

He laid it on the ground next to the chopping block, along with a flask of water. I had another flask for him in my bag, because he'd asked me to bring him one for his journey.

Now it was my turn to look at the glen around us. It would look like he'd stopped for lunch, or a snack, and would return any minute. Maybe he'd gone back to the farm for something or had just popped into the woods to pee.

Something twisted in my belly, but he seemed to catch sight

of me for the first time then. He cuffed my head playfully. He winked.

It was all I needed.

My fear was gone, and it was Hansel and I working together again as part of our daring escape mission. I tried not to smile too much, because this was a serious business, but actually I almost wanted to giggle.

'All right,' he said, with a final glance around. 'Let's go.'

So we did.

I had to run to keep up with him. He was probably not running at full speed – because I never would've been able to keep up with that – but he was definitely moving at a quick jog.

I wondered if now was the right time to share my plan about the hideout. But he kept asking questions about Densford Station, and checking I'd packed the maps, and it was obvious he wanted to get as far away from Bambury as quickly as possible.

I felt a little bit hurt. Was it so easy to leave me – and my mother – behind?

I supposed it made sense now I really thought about it, though. Of course he needed to put as much distance as possible between himself and the people who would catch him. My plans for a new, secret wood cabin suddenly felt silly; a bit childish.

'Which way do we go? This way?' he said, as we hurried along. 'At the train station, I will stand outside, and you can buy my ticket so I don't have to speak to anyone.' He stopped and thought for a moment. 'I better put the clothes on now.'

I watched as Hansel pulled my father's old things from the bag I'd packed, which he was now carrying. He started to undo the shirt of his PoW uniform, with its tell-tale grey patch. But then he hesitated.

'No, better to wait,' he said. 'We might see someone who knows me while we're still near Bambury. Better I look the same as always.'

189

He'd given me his smaller pack, which was stuffed with a pair of boots he said had belonged to his friend Erik and a couple of packets of cigarettes. To make my load lighter, he now put the boots in his bag, and gave me Daddy's clothes to carry instead. The bag was smaller than his backpack, but it was still too big for me. It hit the backs of my legs as I ran.

I tripped and fell, and the twigs and dry ground of the forest scraped my knees and the palms of my hands. My eyes welled up with a sharp sting at the shock and sudden stab of unexpected pain. Bits of dirt and gravel were ground deep into the cuts and I tried to brush them out.

He ran back a few steps to pull me up.

'All is good? Come on!'

And he was off again. I tried to catch up, but he was starting to get too far ahead. I felt the panic of the lame boy being left behind by the Pied Piper. But my knees hurt and I didn't want to run any more. My palms pulsed with pain. They were badly grazed and little strips of skin were ruched up where I'd slid along the ground as I fell. Despite trying to wipe them clean, bits of earth were still packed into the cuts along the edges.

'Hansel! Wait!' I called.

He spun around and slapped his finger to his lips. He looked impatient and a little bit angry. He gestured for me to catch up.

So I stumbled on.

23

⚬‒⚬

'I wonder if you are worth going to the end of the world for?'
From *The Snow Queen*

Annabel woke late. It was slightly chillier than it had been and she chose a cream dress with long sleeves and a lattice detail across the chest.

She rarely bothered with breakfast. It was her habit to sleep in, but she'd slept for longer than usual and it was already long past midday. The boy had busied himself being useful for a change the evening before; she had a new bottle of gin and he had refilled her glass of gin several times, which had made her rather tipsy. But she only had a slight headache, which was already dissipating.

Normally, she headed out to see Hans straight away so she could spend as much time at the orchard as possible. But today she planned to pop into the village first to buy some treats for him.

The larder and cupboards were bare. She must admonish the boy for eating so much. Didn't he understand there were food shortages? She would go shopping. She'd buy Hans some fruit perhaps – they always both laughed now when she arrived with a gift of an apple. She idly wondered whether she had enough ingredients to have a go at making something sweet for them both to share. Stewed apple, perhaps? Or a rudimentary crumble, using sweetened breadcrumbs maybe, in the absence of flour and butter?

As she ambled down the lane towards the village, enjoying

the sunshine, she allowed her mind to drift away from her with thoughts of kisses on lips dusted with sugar and spices. Her mouth watered at the thought of all the sweet things to come.

24

Gretel began to cry and said: 'How are we to get out of the forest now?' But Hansel comforted her and said: 'Just wait a little, until the moon has risen, and then we will soon find the way.'

From *Hansel and Gretel*

'You have to run fast, yes?' He almost hissed the words. 'This isn't a game now. This is dangerous.'

His eyes were hard.

'I *know*!' I was panting.

He had a couple of scratches on his face. A low branch must have swiped at him as he ran. I wondered if I had similar cuts on my own face, but it was hard to feel anything apart from the heat in my burning palms and scraped knees.

'I have to go to the toilet,' I said.

He clenched his lips together into a tight little line. 'Quickly. But we must run faster after that.'

I walked off into the woods. I just wanted to stand still and rest. I scrabbled with the buttons on my trousers and watched my pee make a pond which turned into a muddy river, pushing little bits of leaves and twigs out of its way as it rolled on away from the trunk.

I had a quick, sneaky drink of water from the flask I'd brought him. I shouldn't have really; it was meant for him, but ... well. I didn't drink all of it, and I could refill it when we came to the river. With that thought, I splashed some of it onto my palms and

193

knees and winced as I washed away the worst of the earth packed into my grazed skin.

I took my time heading back to him. I thought he could've been a bit more sympathetic about my injuries. I didn't *have* to help him.

'We must go now,' he said. His eyes seemed to be stretched wide in his face.

'That way.' I pointed in front of us. 'The path is over there, behind us, but we can stay away from it. I know the direction we need to go.'

He took off again, jogging away before I'd even finished speaking, and the wind whistled past my ears as I ran after him. I started to feel a pain in my side, bending me double as I tried to run, as though a piece of twine was pulling me inwards by stitching my guts together.

Shouldn't have drunk that water.

'Can't . . . can't . . .' I panted.

Hansel ran back to me and grabbed my arm, then pulled me along behind him for a few paces. I heard the arm of my shirt-sleeve rip before he let me go.

'We have to keep going!' His voice was like a bark. 'Hurry up! I need you to show me where to go! You have to run fast!'

'Stitch!' I cried. But he didn't seem to understand. Despite the cramp in my side, I tried to keep my legs pumping because I was frightened of falling again.

Hansel pushed past a low branch and I knew what would happen a second before it struck me. Long enough to expect the impact, but not long enough to do anything about it.

The branch snapped back and caught me square in the face, although I'd already started to turn my head and bring my arm up to ward off the blow.

'Oh! Oh!'

There was blood. Lots of it. I could feel its warmth flooding down through my nostrils and then, a moment later, the taste of tin in my mouth. Hot metallic sharpness on my tongue and in my throat. I nearly gagged.

My eyes began to stream from the blow. Through blurred tears I could see he looked horrified. He muttered something in German. He put out his hands to touch my face.

'Don't!' I screamed, crying, with my hands curled in front of my face to make a cage to protect it. 'Don't touch! It hurts!'

'Ah,' he said. 'Ah, God, God. Your nose!'

'Is it broken?'

'Let me see!'

But I wouldn't let him touch me. The pain was in my nose, between my eyes, in my whole head. I couldn't see for the pain.

I kept my hands held out in front of me, to make sure he wouldn't touch my face.

I sensed rather than saw him moving around, changing his angle to get a look at my nose.

'It's not broken... Daniel? It's not broken, yes? It only hurts. I'm sorry.'

'Just a nosebleed?' I asked incredulously. The pain was unbearable. 'You *hit* me.'

'No, I'm sorry. The tree – it was an accident. We were running so fast. I'm sorry. All is good, all is good – it's not broken.'

But I didn't want to run any more. I sat down, and the dry little leaves and twigs on the earthy floor dug into my thighs as my short trousers rode up. I tipped my head back, because I'd heard that's what you were supposed to do to stop the blood. But it felt better to tip my head forward, over my crossed knees, and let the blood drain out onto the forest floor and wait for it to stop.

I felt a mean sense of satisfaction at the amount of blood dripping to the earth. That would show him, I thought.

And it did.

He held his warm hand on my back, just above the bag, as he bent over me.

'I'm sorry.'

I said nothing. But tears now fell onto the leaves along with the drops of blood and I fought to stop them. Nobody likes a crybaby.

'Sorry, Daniel,' he said. 'I'm sorry. I know it hurts like hell.' He patted my back.

I sniffed, and wiped blood away from my lips. I stared at the back of my hand, smeared with red.

How had everything gone so wrong, so quickly? We'd only left the orchard about an hour ago.

Gently, I used my fingertips to touch my nose. The slightest pressure made me wince and brought tears to my eyes again, but Hansel was right. My nose felt normal. No bones poking out.

I shrugged the bag off my shoulders to rest for a moment. It was a relief to have the weight removed. It left behind a sweaty patch on my shirt – like the patch of a PoW – and the air was nice and cool on the wetness.

He moved over to a tree and leaned against it. I sniffed and stood up to face him.

He looked at me hard.

'You can't buy me a train ticket now,' he said, eventually. 'Your face...'

I gaped at him, hurt. That was all he cared about!

'Sorry, Daniel,' he said quickly. 'Are you all right? I didn't mean to hurt your nose.'

I nodded.

'Can you continue?'

'I can't run so fast,' I said. 'Everything hurts.' There was a bit of a wobble in my voice.

'I know,' he said, a bit too eagerly – he was pleased I hadn't refused to carry on helping him. 'We'll go slower. We'll go slower this time, yes? I promise.'

'All right.'

'All right then.' He patted my back.

I tried to smile.

'We just need to ... we do need to hurry. Probably no one

knows I'm gone yet, but this afternoon they will, and they will look for me. Do you understand?'

'Yes; we have to run while we can.'

'That's right.'

I felt like crying again, but I picked up my bag and began to move again, past Hansel, ducking beneath the branch that had so brutally smashed my face. And a second or two later, I heard him following me. Gradually, I picked up the pace, but I didn't run, because I no longer felt like it. I just walked as quickly as I could.

He must have been impatient, but he didn't try to rush me any more. We stopped a couple of times to have a drink of water. If he noticed I'd already drunk from the canteen, he didn't say anything.

After a while, we heard the river. We were not far from the spot where I'd seen the Troll watching the boys playing.

A breeze ruffled my shirt and I shuddered. I didn't want to cross the river at that spot, so I led us further on. I spotted a fallen tree that we could use as a bridge to avoid getting wet.

We made it across then scrambled down the bank and filled the flask by letting the river flow into its open mouth. The water looked clean enough, but it wasn't the same as tap water so I thought I'd try not to drink any more until I was back home again.

My thoughts began to turn towards saying goodbye to Hansel. I was feeling more and more relieved that I hadn't mentioned my plans for a hideout camp to him. I was glad I was leaving him at the train station; this had been enough for me.

We kept on for what felt like hours, and the afternoon began to drag. We were deep in the woods by now and I was tired. I hadn't thought to bring any food for myself but I didn't like to ask if we could stop for a snack. My whole body felt heavy and it was an effort to keep moving, but he showed no sign of slowing down.

Sweat mingled with the dried blood on my face and stung my eyes.

Hansel kept switching between manly 'you can do its' to friendly 'come ons' to sharp digs like 'hurry, hurry', that did nothing to hide his frustration at being stuck with me. He wasn't making me feel like his brother-prince; he was making me feel like a little boy who was slowing him down. Even though *I* was supposed to be the one in charge.

'How much further until Densford Station?' he asked.

'Er,' I looked around and realised I had absolutely no idea where we were any more. 'Not much further.'

It had been a terrible mistake to leave the path, but I was too frightened to tell him I'd got us both lost. I had never been this far into the forest before – why would I? For all I knew we were walking in circles; everything certainly looked the same. I hoped we'd stumble back upon a trail or path so I could pretend everything was going perfectly to plan.

The problem was, ever since having my silly idea about a hideout camp, I hadn't really thought about how to lead him *out* of the woods.

Dreading his discovery of my confusion, I kept my lips sealed and stopped begging for rest stops and toilet breaks. I hadn't a clue whether we were anywhere near Densford or not, and I began to worry he'd ask to check the maps; he'd know how to read them and might discover I'd got it all wrong. He'd be so angry. No, the best thing I could do was to keep acting with confidence and hopefully we'd end up in the right place eventually.

I desperately scanned all the stories I knew for help. Children were always getting lost in the woods. Hansel and Gretel had left a trail of breadcrumbs – but that was so they could find their way back to where they'd come from (which didn't work anyway).

Then I remembered.

The greatest story of all.

The wise men found the baby Jesus by following a star and the sun was a star, so as long as I kept that directly in front of us, we must be following a straight path at least, and if we kept walking in a straight line for long enough that was bound to take us somewhere. Hansel had no idea, but now all we were doing was following the sun.

That was my plan and for a good part of the afternoon we followed it.

I began to regret my decision to help Hansel escape. To think I'd been so excited about this just last night! I couldn't sleep with excitement as I watched the moon gradually glide across the window, shining on me through the magnolia tree.

With a sickening lurch in my gut I suddenly thought: hang on a minute, no, that can't be right! Because the moon was moving... and the sun is always moving too, isn't it? We're following a moving target. We really *are* walking in circles.

Desperately, I tried to think of a way to rescue the situation. Hansel was getting impatient and kept asking me where we were, and how soon we'd be out of the woods.

Surely he was going to suspect I didn't know as much as I'd made out. I was just pretending. I'd been pretending the whole time. That was the whole point of the game. From the day we met. It was all just a game.

I felt a bit angry. What sort of adult would believe a small boy?

The answer popped into my head the same moment the question was formed: a desperate one.

Why, though? Why was he so desperate to escape? His life was wonderful in Bambury – working in the sunshine, and with my mother and me for friends.

It was when I heard the sound of running water up quite far ahead that I began to run.

'Ah, yes,' I called behind me, 'the river does a big loop so this is, er, very good! We're nearly there!'

In truth, I was trying to get as far ahead of him as possible in case we had somehow come out at the part of the river we'd been at earlier, where we'd used the tree as a bridge. Then the game really would be up. He'd recognise the place and know I'd been leading him nowhere all this time.

I charged forward, crashing through the forest, to find the source of the running water before he did.

'Stay back!' I shouted. 'I'll just make sure it's safe.'

He was quite far behind me – my sudden burst of speed must have taken him by surprise.

But he didn't stay where he was; he was running too. He was following me. I wasn't sure why; my shouted warning about possible danger was a good point. Why wasn't he listening to me? Why wasn't he staying back? I wondered if he thought I was running away from him? Perhaps he thought I was leaving him to fend for himself.

Actually, I had thought about telling him I wanted to go home and that he'd just have to figure out how to get to Densford Station by himself. I'd thought that when the game stopped being fun, and when I was hurt, and when he was shouting at me, and when I realised I was the leader of a journey – a leader who didn't know the way.

'It's all right!' I shouted, 'I'm just checking the river's safe!'

I kept running, but he was running full force too now, and was catching up.

'Stay *back*!' I called over my shoulder, and it was in that tiny moment, just as I was turning away, that I saw it happen.

Of course, the whole thing took just a second or two and it was done. I was running, he was running, and I only saw it out of the corner of my eye, in the length of time it took to turn my head. Everything was happening so fast. But with a horrible snag, time suddenly slowed down as though split seconds were full minutes. So I saw every terrible detail. It looked as though Hansel was performing a curious dance.

First his arms flew up, then his eyes widened and his mouth opened in surprise.

He was suspended like that for a second. And then it seemed

his knees buckled, and his arms circled as though trying to grab hold of the air itself. But it wasn't his knees; it was his feet that were disappearing. Down, down.

They fell through the forest floor, which furiously sucked in the rest of him. His whole body was snatched down and those circling arms, and those scrabbling fingers, were the last I saw of him.

25

⚬⚬⚬

The poor girl thought: 'I can no longer stay here! I will
go and search for my brothers.' And when night came,
she ran away and went straight into the forest.

From *The Six Swans*

The wicker basket slung in the crook of Annabel's elbow gently batted at her hip as she strolled along. The air was alive with birdsong and butterflies. It had been a glorious summer. Her thigh muscles ached pleasantly.

She went straight to the greengrocer's and meticulously checked each Granny Smith for blemishes before placing half a dozen in her basket. Some blackberries laid out in simple wooden bowls caught her eye and she took a punnet.

She smiled as she watched the elderly grocer, Sid Mitchell, put three apples into a brown paper bag and hold the corners before expertly spinning it over a couple of times, sealing it closed.

It was as he repeated the process with the remaining three apples, and just as she was about to dig out her purse from her basket, that he said: 'Terrible news.'

She glanced behind her, but there was no one else in the shop. 'I . . . I beg your pardon?'

'I said, "terrible news". Isn't it? About the missing Kraut?'

A prickle of fear, but still just a prickle. 'What missing—? A PoW?'

'Oh, you haven't heard then?' He passed her the bag of apples. 'Yes, yes, it's the talk of the village.'

'What PoW?'

'They're all out looking for the bugger now. Excuse my French.'

'But, I mean, what happened?'

'One of the prisoners has upped and gone. Vanished.'

'Vanished?'

'Into thin air.'

She was stunned into silence and realised she was just standing there gawping at the grocer, the apples still in her hand. She dropped the bag into her basket and scrabbled once more for her purse so she could get out of there and find Hans to speak to him about it.

Her fingers shook slightly as she handed over the coins. Mr Mitchell must have noticed because he said: 'Nothing to worry about, dear. He'll be long gone by now.'

'Oh, yes, I'm sure you're right.'

Either a PoW had run away, as Mr Mitchell seemed to think, or something had been done to him.

The till's bell rang out as Mr Mitchell slid the money drawer shut with a flourish, but he still had her change in his hand.

'Dreadful business.'

'Yes.'

'It was the fella who worked for Ray Dawson clearing the orchard.'

Annabel felt as if she'd been punched in the stomach and she suddenly thought she might be sick. She rushed from the shop and was on the pavement beneath the striped awning outside when an arm pulled her back.

She cried out as she spun around.

'You forgot your blackberries – and your change, Mrs Patterson! You'll be needing that! Look after the pennies, as they say.'

'Oh, my, yes. Thank you.'

She threw everything into the basket and tried to pull away from his grasp. But he had more he wanted to say.

'Look, you mustn't be worried. I'm sorry I was the one to tell you now! He'll either be long gone, or the Home Guard will catch him and stick him in prison, a proper military prison, so there's really no need for you to be frightened.'

'No.' Her voice was just a whisper. 'Thank you, I—'

'The word went out some time ago, so they might even have him by now. Ray Dawson went to speak to him and he wasn't there, and he waited and waited – he always gives everyone the benefit of the doubt, that one – but he never came back. So he went to the camp to see if he was there, or if the colonel knew anything about it, and that's when they raised the alarm. Like I said, for all we know, they've already got him as we speak!'

She wriggled out of his grip, which was like a vice around her upper arm.

'Thank you,' she said again, as she backed away from him.

She turned and began marching down the High Street, desperate to break into a run, but managed to restrain herself until she'd turned the corner.

Then she was bolting towards her lane, towards the orchard. Her hair streamed out behind her as she ran, her white sandals slapping on the paving stones. She wished she could let her basket fall to the ground, but it would raise suspicion should somebody find it, so she held on to it as she ran, holding back tears.

He had spoken of leaving, but only so they could be together; he wouldn't leave her, surely? Maybe he was trying to get to her somehow. Perhaps something had happened, some sort of emergency, and he was looking for her, or waiting for her somewhere. But he didn't know where she lived; the two of them had never left the orchard and all he knew of Bambury was his route from the PoW camp to Dawson's orchard and back again.

Oh God, what if he hadn't run away at all but had been hurt? The same men who beat Erik so savagely that they killed him could have attacked him as he worked. Everyone knew he was there alone.

No – surely not – there must be some other explanation.

There might be a clue nobody else would be able to interpret at the orchard. A note for her perhaps, hidden in their shed? The orchard first then, and she'd decide what to do from there.

Annabel was forced to slow down to a brisk walk as the country road became her lane, dotted with cottages. She hurried as much as she dared and simply dumped her basket inside her front garden as she rushed past.

Once she was out of sight of the last house in the street, she broke into a run.

26

He might scream as much as he liked; it was of no use.

From *Hansel and Gretel*

The way Hansel was suddenly gobbled up by the woods was like a series of strange events caught up in one dramatic movement. One minute he was there, running towards me on solid ground – and the next he wasn't.

His helpless arms thrown up; his buckling knees; his feet plummeting down followed by the rest of him; his splayed fingers clawing at the air in a pointless attempt to save himself.

It was like that, and it happened silently. Because it seemed to me that the noise came a second later.

A sort of crashing, tearing sound, and his shocked cry as he disappeared. Then his scream as he hit the bottom. Followed by the screams of pain as things fell on top of him where he lay.

I stood for a moment trying to make sense of what I'd seen.

I had just run across that same part of the forest myself – Hansel was practically in my footsteps as he tried to catch up with me.

I wanted to run over to look down into the gaping hole that had just opened up in the earth. But I was frightened. I was afraid the forest would eat me up too.

I could hear his groans. He was calling my name.

I wasn't sure how long it took for me to pick my way to where he'd fallen. The hole wasn't very big. Maybe I wasn't heavy enough to break it open, or maybe I'd just dodged the danger zone.

I could see bits of rotting wood ripped clean through, pointing with jagged teeth down into the dark cave that now held Hansel.

It was an old mine shaft. I'd heard rumours of them – and of a network of tunnels underground – but never paid much attention because I'd never been this deep into the woods before.

I bent down carefully.

The hole was so dark and deep I couldn't see him clearly. It was more like a suggestion of him, a smudge of his white face at the bottom of the gloom. There was a wet earthy smell of rotting timber and a nasty damp feel to the thick air slowly leaking out of the hole for the first time in a long time.

He was still calling my name.

'Hansel?' It was a whisper.

'*Ah, mein Gott!*'

My mouth was so dry I found I couldn't swallow properly.

'My legs! My legs! I can't move!'

There was another crash from inside the hole and a roar from Hansel. A loose plank of wood must have clattered down from the crumbling wall, or else he'd grabbed a piece of debris as the pain turned into a hot frustrated rage and he either threw it or smashed it against the side of the tunnel.

I thought I had also heard, not a splash exactly, but a squelching sound. He might not have landed in a pool of water but he definitely wasn't on dry ground.

I scooted back on my heels, pulling away from that terrible hole.

My heart was beating so hard it was painful, and my breathing was ragged and shaky.

I was trying to think. He had fallen a long, long way. Maybe twenty feet or more. I thought of broken bones snapping like dry twigs inside his skin. I thought of the wood and rusty nails gouging him as he fell and spearing him as he landed. I thought of blood. I squeezed my eyes closed and turned my face away from the sudden slit, carved like a scar into the forest floor.

Think. Just think.

With a sickening jolt of fear I realised the hole could be a trap. Lying in wait to catch us. But no. No, that couldn't be right. It was ancient. Just part of an old, crumbling, flooded mine.

I had to try to get him out. But how?

I couldn't go to anyone for help. Or could I? I couldn't tell Mother without also revealing that I'd tried to help Hansel leave her. She'd hate me. And I didn't think she'd know how to get Hansel out of the hole and help him either.

He needed rope and big men, maybe even some kind of machinery to bring him to the surface. I could tell them, these men I'd bring, that I'd just happened to stumble across Hansel, after hearing his shouts in the forest. But I was so far away from Bambury, would they really believe I was just playing by myself out there? And look at me – I was a mess, covered in blood. They'd know I'd helped him. They'd think Hansel was a German outlaw. And they'd make me an outlaw too.

I squeezed my eyes tightly shut, but burning tears managed to push through anyway.

And supposing I did run to the farm to tell Farmer Dawson, or into the village to tell the first man I came across, about my 'discovery' of a PoW in a hole in the woods and they believed my story . . . What would happen next?

Yes, they might figure out a way to haul him up out of the mine shaft, but then what? He'd be in so much trouble, maybe even more trouble than he was in right now. He'd be a PoW who tried to escape. They'd punish him, take him away.

Another thought occurred to me now. Supposing I did fetch someone who managed to get Hansel out and take him to hospital? In his anger and pain, Hansel might tell them what I'd done. That the whole thing was my fault. And then Mother would find out about me anyway.

He was calling my name again.

'Are you still there?'

I opened my eyes and looked across at the hole. It was still there, a mouth ripped in the ground.

'Daniel? Are you there?'

He sounded frightened now. Not just hurt or angry.

I thought about this. He seemed to think I might have run away. He had no way of knowing I was here, backed up against a nearby tree. Crying like a baby, with snot streaming down over my lips. I wiped underneath my nose with my hand; it was still too sore to touch.

He was crying out in German again.

My heart had slowed to a dull thudding that beat in time with the seconds as they pounded by.

Think!

Beat.

Think!

Beat.

I took my backpack off and crawled over to the hole, as quietly as I could, not wanting even the leaves to rustle. I started to peer down inside, but held back.

'I know you're there!'

I stayed very, very still.

'Daniel!'

I heard crashing down there again.

'Daniel? Daniel, I'm hurt! DANIEL!'

Carefully and quietly, I backed away from the hole. When I bumped into a tree I stood up slowly and leaned against the trunk, never taking my eyes off the tear in the ground.

'Are you still there?'

More crashing. Then a furious roar: 'DANIEL!'

I stumbled away, staggering like the Troll, falling over my feet until I was running.

I was dimly aware that I could be at risk of falling down

another mine shaft myself, and I was glad I'd left my bag behind so I was lighter, but my fear about Hansel and what to do next was so overpowering that the threat of it didn't really register.

It dawned on me that I could come back later that day with supplies, medicine and water, while I worked out what to do. Hansel would be calmer by then; he could help me decide the best course of action to take.

Tears streamed down my cheeks as I ran. I knew I hadn't seen his face that final time as I almost, but not quite, looked down into the hole. But it didn't matter, because I *had* seen it. My imagination had reached down into the dark and made a picture, and I knew the picture was true.

He was on his back, staring up at me, his eyes wide, stunned with pain and fear, begging for help.

But still I kept running, whimpering with my own pain and fear, and the shame came then. I was trying to outrun my guilt more than I was trying to outrun the echo of his screams.

And the echoes of his screams were gradually muffled as I increased the distance between us, then became silent as they were swallowed up by the great forest, whose branches stooped low to conceal the hole and whose leaves dimmed the sound of the man trapped inside it.

I was sobbing now, and that made it hard to run, but still I pushed on, doing my best to retrace our footsteps. Howling and choking and snotting.

My heart had sped up again, and now it was telling me what to do: run-run, run-run, run-run.

So I did. And I ran and I ran and I ran.

27

'I would risk it all to win him.'
From *The Little Mermaid*

'I must find little Kai. Do you know where he is?'
Gerda asked the roses.
From *The Snow Queen*

Annabel hurtled towards the entrance of the woods. Nearly there, she told herself. There was bound to be some rational explanation once she got to the orchard. Why, Hans might even be there himself. Some sort of misunderstanding – and it wasn't him who was the missing PoW after all. Or else it was him, but just a case of crossed wires; he'd been sent on an errand by the old colonel, who'd forgotten all about it when later questioned by Dawson.

As she ran, she replayed the greengrocer's comments in her head, looking for words in his statement that led to Hans and words that led away from him.

Finally, she saw the little entrance to the forest; the two wooden posts that delineated a gap in the foliage and marked the start of the beaten path through the trees.

She was nearly upon it when a group of men emerged from the woods.

'Oh!' She stumbled to a stop.

It was the Home Guard, nine of them, led by Higgins, who carried a long wooden truncheon. The others had weapons too, she saw now, but none was carrying a gun. One man was ludicrously armed with a rake. She recognised Dawson, the thug Jimmy Dockett, as well as the nice bespectacled man who'd nearly knocked her hall mirror off the wall.

With a sickening twist in her gut she knew they were hunting for Hans. Or perhaps she was too late and they'd already found him?

Higgins stepped forward. 'Where are you going in such a hurry?'

'I . . .' She glanced at the entrance to the woods. What could she tell them? And how could she find out what they knew about Hans? What had happened to him?

'I . . .' she said again, bringing a hand to her chest to indicate she was out of breath and needed a moment.

Some of the officers behind Higgins shifted from leg to leg – they were impatient to move on. But Higgins stood firm, his feet planted apart as he squared up to her. He was waiting for an answer.

'It's . . . Daniel,' she said finally.

'Your son?'

'Yes, I . . . I'm looking for him. I can't find him anywhere.' She looked at Higgins to see if he believed her. And decided to risk a question. 'Why? I mean, what are you doing here?'

'Haven't you heard? One of the PoWs escaped.' Now he was looking hard at her. 'You shouldn't be out here – it's dangerous.'

They hadn't found him then. Where was he?

'Oh! Goodness! But . . . Daniel. There's a place he likes to play. I'll just go a little way in, I'm sure I'll find him.'

'No, Mrs Patterson, we can't allow that.'

Farmer Dawson spoke up now. 'The PoW who got away was the one who worked in my orchard.' He seemed embarrassed.

'And that's right by the forest,' Higgins pointed out. 'Like I said, it's dangerous.'

'Oh, but – that's all the more reason I need to find Daniel immediately!'

'We'll keep an eye out for your lad. But this is no place for a woman. You need to go home. He'll probably turn up there soon enough anyway, come dinnertime.'

She looked at Dawson and the other men to see if she could find an ally. But they stood behind Higgins like his own personal army.

'Go home,' he repeated.

But she hesitated – wondering if she was strong enough to stand them down.

Just then, she heard a cry from inside the forest. She and the men turned as one to face the woods. From the corner of her eye, she saw one or two of them clutch their weapons as though preparing for a fight. Now she could hear running – the unmistakable sounds of shoes hitting the beaten earth as someone headed towards them.

Annabel took a couple of steps back and noticed she wasn't the only one who did so.

Hans?

They faced the opening in the canopy of trees, which still gave nothing away – although the sound of running feet was growing louder and closer.

She tried to swallow down a knot of fear that had lodged in her throat.

Hans?

But with a noisy crash of sprayed-up pebbles and a jagged scream and flailing limbs, a battered and bloody child burst out of the woods.

It was as though he hadn't seen them at first, but with another cry he skittered to a halt a few feet from them.

He was almost unrecognisable, but with a jangling incomprehension at how it could be so, she saw through the mess that the child was a boy, and that the boy was Daniel.

28

---✺---

*He pulled at his left leg so hard with both
hands that he tore himself in two.*
From *Rumpelstiltskin*

They saw me first, before I saw them.

They were standing in a group looking right at me as I crashed out of the woods. Some of them were holding truncheons and one held what looked like a torture tool; a spiky spear with metal teeth that loomed above me.

They were all crouched slightly, like animals ready to pounce.

They know, I thought. They've been looking for us.

I gasped, and shrank back. Then I tried to run away.

'Good God!' one cried. Wildly, I looked over and saw it was Farmer Dawson.

Then another man, standing closer to where I was, reached out and grabbed me as I stumbled away. He held on even tighter as I shrieked in terror and struggled to get free.

'It's all right sonny, it's all right!' he shouted. 'We won't hurt you!' He shook me slightly and forced me to look into his face. 'Nobody's going to hurt you!'

I stopped thrashing, but I was still crying uncontrollably and I began shaking.

'Jesus!' He looked at the others, who seemed to be stunned into silence.

Then a woman spoke. '. . . Daniel?'

My cries stopped in shock as I looked round for the voice, because I couldn't place it out here amongst these men. Then they parted like a sea in front of me and I saw her. She was wearing a pretty cream dress that made her look like an angel, just when I needed her most.

I stared at her. Then I was dimly aware of the iron grip on my upper arms relaxing as my mother and I faced each other across the divide.

'Is that you?' she said.

I wanted to run to her, to burrow my head into her cool, clean skirts, feel her fingers stroking my hair. *It's all right now*, I wanted her to say, *I'm here, I'm here, my Darling.*

I was still mute. Because, really, what could I say?

'This is your son?' said the man who was now loosely resting his hands on my shoulders. He released me completely. 'What in God's name happened to you? Who did this?'

I saw myself as they saw me then. My clothes were ripped and dirty, my eyes felt almost swollen shut from crying, there was my smashed nose, my hair must be sweaty and wild, and I was caked in blood. I looked down to see it had dried on my hands and my shirt in brown and red stains.

'N-nobody, sir.' My teeth were chattering.

There was a silence and some of the men glanced at Mother, perhaps to see if she would take charge now. Maybe they thought she would come to me. But she looked stunned, and just stared at me along with them as though she didn't know me any better than they did.

I looked around at the men. The only one I recognised apart from Farmer Dawson was the Home Guard man Mr Higgins.

It was clear to me they'd all been after Hansel. And I felt sick at the thought they'd find out what I'd done. I was a traitor to the country, to the King.

An icy shard of thought poked my brain, which told me: Save yourself . . . you could tell them he kidnapped you.

I thought they'd probably believe my word over a PoW's. I could tell them I'd managed to escape and had cleverly thrown him into a hole. Then I'd be a hero – and they'd rescue the woodchopper, so it wouldn't really be like I'd betrayed him. Although he *would* be in terrible trouble. And he might tell them how I'd helped him, and how it was all my idea.

No.

I was torn in two – half of me down the hole with poor Hansel and the other half here, facing my mother.

'It's all right, lad,' another man told me. 'You're safe now.' He came over to me and the man who had grabbed me backed away to give him room.

He crouched down so he could look into my face. He wore black-rimmed spectacles.

His kindly expression made me bite my lips in an attempt not to start crying again. Something about him reminded me of my daddy.

'What's your name?'

'Daniel Patterson.'

'Well, Daniel. It's lucky you found us. And lucky your mum was here with us looking for you. You're going to be all right now.' He smiled. 'Why don't you tell me who did this to you?'

I could only shake my head.

'This boy needs to be taken home,' Mr Higgins said, with a nod towards Mother, 'if he's not going to talk. I'd like to hear what he's got to say because it might be important – but the rest of us have got a job to do regardless.'

The kind man looked annoyed with Mr Higgins because I saw his lips go tight for a second, but then he spoke to me again.

'It's good you found us, Daniel, because it's obvious something bad happened to you today. We're all out here because we're looking for a bad man. A German. Is he the one who did this to you? Did you see him?'

I couldn't do it. I couldn't let them think Hansel had hurt me.

That would make them even angrier at him than they already were, and they'd hunt him down – sure to find him now, trapped in his wet hole like a frightened fox against a pack of dogs.

'No!' I cried, perhaps a little too quickly, perhaps a little too sharply. 'I didn't see any Germans. It ... it wasn't ...'

'All right, all right, Daniel, just take your time. But you must tell us who hurt you.' The afternoon sun glinted on his spectacles as he leaned forward, eager now I seemed ready to talk. 'Who are you frightened of?'

I think it was those words that did it. Who was I frightened of?

Its horrible image reared up in my mind. It had haunted me, and yes, I was frightened of it.

'It was ...'

Now all the men were leaning forward, because my voice had dropped to a shaky whisper.

'It was ...'

'Who?' Mr Higgins whispered.

'It was ... the Troll.'

I saw the kind man blink behind his spectacles. 'Who?'

'For God's sake,' Mr Higgins muttered.

But the kind man wouldn't give up. 'Who's the Troll?'

'It used to live by the railway tracks, under the bridge, but now it lives in the forest.'

The light was still reflecting on the man's spectacles, but suddenly it seemed as though a light came on inside his eyes as well.

He turned to face the others. 'He's talking about that tramp. The one who's been about the village.'

There was a murmuring, but I couldn't catch the words. My mother stood as still as a statue of an angel on a church. My heart was thudding again, and my face felt very, very hot. But still the man wanted more from me.

'What did he do to you, son?'

Ah, there. The 'son'. I wanted to be comforted so badly. I hoped he'd put his strong arms around me and squeeze me tight.

I thought I might tell him anything now. It seemed as though he was ready to believe me.

'It's all right. You can tell me.'

The others stood very still and were very quiet. I looked over at Mother. She nodded her head slightly. 'Tell him, Daniel,' she said, with a strange croaky voice.

It felt like it was just the two of us. I thought: Oh, she wants me to tell this story. The Story of the Troll.

I turned back to the man crouching in front of me. I couldn't quite bring myself to look into his eyes, so I stared at his white cotton shirt instead. His sleeves were rolled up, and I noticed the sweat patches under his arms.

'What did he do to you?' he said again.

'It was awful!'

'Yes?' He reached out and patted my shoulder.

'It wanted to . . .'

'Yes?'

'It tried to . . . eat me . . .'

I glanced up at him to see if he'd believe me. Understanding seemed to fill his face, which changed his features; he looked disgusted.

'It's all right, son,' he told me. 'You don't have to worry about him hurting you any more.'

His expression confused me because I'd never seen anything like it before – it was kind and furious at the same time.

I looked away from him into the faces of the other men. One by one their expressions changed and I saw the same hot light come into their eyes.

'Jesus Christ,' one murmured.

My mother's face was a mirror of theirs and I heard her whisper, 'No!'

I wasn't entirely sure they'd believe me about the Troll so I was a bit surprised by their reactions. Obviously, I thought they'd be angry when I told them the Troll had nearly caught me, but I hadn't expected their fiery eyes.

All day I'd been very frightened – but the sudden change in the men scared me even more. I looked at Mother but her eyes were closed now and it seemed she was further away than ever.

'He's shaking like a leaf,' Mr Higgins said. His voice was ragged with emotion. 'Argh, God, that revolting tramp should never have been allowed to stay around here. Filthy, dirty ...'

The nice man took his hand off my shoulder and was now avoiding my eyes. He stood up.

'Where is he, boy?' Mr Higgins growled, and pointed towards the forest. 'Up there?'

'No, no! No, I—' I was desperate to keep them away from the woods; the further away from Hansel the better.

'Tell them, Daniel!' Mother burst out. It was like she'd suddenly come to life. 'You have to tell them, so they can find him.' She looked at the men. 'You must see this man is more dangerous than the PoW. You have to look for him first, surely? He has to be arrested.'

She wanted them to catch the monster for me! The men exchanged glances.

'Don't be frightened,' the nice man said to me. 'He's never going to hurt you again. But you have to tell us where it happened. We know you were in the woods when he ... attacked you. Your mum told us you'd been playing. He lives in there, isn't that what you said?'

I stared at Mother then stared up at him. How could I stop the Home Guard traipsing around the forest? I didn't see how it could be avoided now.

'Well, yes,' I looked down at my dirty, bloodstained hands as I wrung my fingers. 'It happened in there. But not very far from here. It was where it lives.'

'You need to take the boy home,' Mr Higgins said to my mother, even as he was already moving – striding towards the forest entrance.

A couple started to follow him but the nice man said, 'Wait, wait!'

Mr Higgins turned to look back at him and the others stopped walking too.

'We need him to show us where this tramp lives; we can't just hope we bump into him. That hasn't worked out very well for us so far today, has it? I didn't see any tramp in there. Did any of you?'

There was a beat as Mr Higgins appeared to consider this. I looked at Mother but she was watching Mr Higgins.

'All right,' he said, and he looked at me and added: 'You'll have to show us where the tramp is.'

'I want to go home,' I said. 'Mother?'

'Go with the men, Daniel. Show them where . . . it happened.'

She didn't want to take me back with her.

'Go home, Mrs Patterson,' Mr Higgins said. 'Wait there for us. We won't be long.'

She nodded and walked away. She avoided my eyes as she left.

'Come on then, lad,' Mr Higgins said to me and led the way into the forest.

I was at the back with the nice man. Ahead, one of the others was slapping his truncheon against his open palm as he strode along.

Once inside the forest, they all turned to me.

'Now you have to show us the way,' Mr Higgins said.

So I went to the front of the group and was the leader of my second mission that day. At least I actually knew where I was going this time – and, luckily, taking them to the Troll's dirty lair in the forest was taking them in the opposite direction from Hansel.

As we walked, the men seemed to swell with energy. They were muttering amongst themselves, using swearwords.

I was so exhausted I wanted to lie down right there on the forest floor and go to sleep. It must be very late in the afternoon by now, I thought. I hadn't eaten or drunk anything for hours. My body was so tired I wasn't even shaking any more. I felt like I was past fear, past anything.

But I stumbled on, taking the men to where Mother and I had seen the Troll in the woods.

I didn't really think about what would happen when we got there. I didn't really care. It probably wasn't there anyway – it was more likely to be under the bridge in the tunnel.

The one thing that spurred me on was the thought of what a good job I had done leading these men away from Hansel.

After a while, I saw the tattered sheets and tarpaulin up ahead.

'This way!' someone shouted from behind and rushed past me. 'Let's get the bastard!'

We were closer to its lair than I'd realised. The men started running towards the nest and one tripped over a tangled tree root in his hurry to get there. I ran after them. I didn't feel tired any more; my blood was rushing around my veins now.

That was when I knew what was going to happen. But I wasn't sure how it made me feel. I was still scared, but now I was excited too. I did hate and fear the Troll, and I did want to protect Hansel. It was like that expression Daddy used sometimes; I was killing two birds with one stone.

I wanted the men to frighten it. And yes, I wanted them to hurt it and drive it out. I strained to see up ahead. Maybe it wasn't even there – but before the thought was formed, I saw them dragging it out from its broken-down home into the light.

I ran forward to see a couple of them grabbing onto its filthy clothes and arms.

The Troll's dirty black beard and straggly hair made it look even more animal-like as it turned its head about wildly. It struggled as they shouted at it, but mostly it seemed stunned. These weren't boys from the village tormenting it for fun.

'Up there!' Higgins roared, jabbing his truncheon up at a

thicker part of the woods over a little verge. The men pushed and pulled the Troll up into the cover of the trees.

Their truncheons began to batter it before it had even reached the top of the small hill. That was when it found its voice. 'Wha . . . What?' But the words turned to screams and then to grunts while it tried to protect itself.

The Troll fell onto its knees and was dragged even deeper into the woods by its arms. Farmer Dawson was wheezing and had fallen behind the others but now he was scrambling up the verge ahead of me.

The men seemed to have forgotten I was even there. I followed, making my own way up the verge, where I hid behind a tree to watch. My hands were shaking, so I gripped the bark to make them stop.

It was curled into a ball and its arms covered its head.

'Eugh, he stinks!' one of the men cried, as he swung his foot into the Troll's side. 'He stinks of piss!'

The truncheons were flying and the noise sounded like somebody was whacking a stiff sofa, except each whack was met with a grunt or cry from the Troll. The only time the blows didn't make that whacking sound was when the wood connected with bone, and then I knew one had struck its head.

'Argh! Stop! Stop! Help!' it managed to scream.

The man with a rake was using it, sharp claw end down, to beat at the Troll's back, tearing the fabric of its coat and carving up strips of flesh like a fork through butter.

'DIRTY – STINKING – POOFTER – PERVERT—' the nice man bellowed as he raised a truncheon again and again.

After a while, the others stopped and fell back, and just Mr Higgins and the nice man carried on with their truncheons.

I saw the blood colouring their weapons as they were raised, ready to rain down on the Troll once more. I couldn't take my eyes off the attack. It was fast, and clumsy. Not like a fight at the pictures at all. I could smell blood in the air, and a strong stink of urine.

I thought I might vomit, but I couldn't look away.

Some of the men had hung back on the edges from the very beginning. The others who had peeled off from the beating now stood panting, watching as Mr Higgins and the nice man continued.

Farmer Dawson, who was one of the men who hadn't laid a finger on the Troll, cried out 'Higgins!' at one point, but Mr Higgins didn't stop and nobody said anything else.

None of the men stopped it, and to me it seemed they were looking on as though an unpleasant job, one that had to be done, was being carried out.

I felt so sick I wanted to stop it myself, but I thought of Hansel in his hole and I knew that this had been meant for him. This would have been his fate.

There was a sickening crack and I knew it was the Troll's head breaking open.

The nice man didn't look nice any more. His spectacles had flown off and landed nearby, but he didn't even seem to notice he was blind. He and Mr Higgins were sweaty and their hair fell about their faces. Their teeth were bared and their eyes were glassy. With a retch I realised they looked like Trolls too.

The crack and crunch of head bone gave way under the pounding to a wet squelching noise and then I saw globs of shiny white goo mixed with blood flying into the air with every whack.

The others backed further away, and at last Mr Higgins stopped, dropping his truncheon and resting his hands on his hips as he panted.

But the nice man was still there, standing over the Troll's mashed and mangled head, pumping and pumping, raising his arms and bringing the truncheon down over and over again.

'Joe,' Farmer Dawson said.

But the nice man couldn't stop. His fleshy face was red but he carried on.

'FILTHY ... PERVERT!'

It was brains. Bits of brain that were spattering his clothes and face. He didn't seem to notice. Strands of matted hair streamed from the bloody end of his weapon each time he raised it.

Eventually, Farmer Dawson rushed forward and grabbed his raised arm. The nice man looked around, startled, like someone who'd been shaken awake while sleepwalking.

And then there was silence.

The silence seemed to last for a long time.

'... We were just meant to teach him a lesson!' a shaken-looking, stocky man said finally. He said it as though they had all discussed the matter beforehand and that the plan had somehow gone wrong. But I knew there had never been a plan.

'Christ, Higgins!' Farmer Dawson said.

The other men, who held their own bloody weapons by their sides, said nothing.

'He deserved it!' Mr Higgins said, eventually. He looked defiant. 'Some men are too cowardly to do what needs to be done, but not me! And what's more, I'd do it again!'

Some of them looked down.

I thought they'd forgotten I was with them, but then Mr Higgins said: 'Have you all forgotten what that pervert just did to that boy over there?'

He pointed his bloodied truncheon in my direction and they all turned to look at me, where I held onto the tree to keep myself from falling down.

That truncheon, pointing like a finger, sent the blame of the Troll's killing over to me. The Troll's blood was on their hands. But now it was on mine, too.

29

There stood poor Gerda, barefooted . . . A whole regiment
of snowflakes advanced against her.

From *The Snow Queen*

Annabel made herself a stiff drink of gin when she got back
home, to settle her nerves and still her shaking hands.

She knew the Home Guard would come here. It was very
important that the house looked presentable. Normal. Above
reproach.

So she cleaned.

She remembered her shopping basket in the front garden and
went to retrieve it. The apples had crushed the blackberries and
their juice had bled through the brown paper. She dumped the
whole lot in the outside bin, basket and all.

It was early evening now – it had been more than two hours
since she'd left the men and the boy in the woods – but her head
was still reeling. Everything was spinning so horribly out of
control.

And to think: everything had been perfect when she'd woken
up that morning. She'd been going to buy treats!

First Hans's disappearance, and now . . . whatever it was that
the tramp had done to Daniel. She couldn't bear to think about
that and pushed unwanted images from her mind as she scrubbed
at the kitchen floor with a damp rag.

Nothing I can do about that, she thought as she worked on

the stained linoleum; the Home Guard will take charge of the situation.

She felt guilty for thinking it, but at least it had distracted them from hunting Hans and she had encouraged them in this. If Hans really had escaped – left of his own free will – then it could only be connected to her. He'd surely find a way to get a message to her, so she could join him later.

After the men had taken the boy back into the forest, Annabel had considered trying to run the long way round to Hans's orchard, to search the shed as she'd initially planned. But all her energy had ebbed away when Daniel told them about the disgusting tramp. Again, she quickly clamped down on that train of thought.

Even if she did still have enough fight in her to go to the orchard, she didn't think she'd be able to get there and back in time before the Home Guard came to return the boy to her. And what if somebody – Dawson, or the old colonel – should find her? There might be a guard stationed there even, searching the place for clues just as she'd intended to do. How would she explain her presence? So she thought it was safer if she did what Higgins had told her to do. And she'd gone straight home.

She scrubbed harder and harder at the floor with her rag; the frenzied activity was helping her avoid thinking of Daniel and was warding off the fear for Hans wringing out her insides.

Another worry began to gnaw at her now . . . Could she be in danger herself? Had somebody found out about their relationship? Or if Hans really had run away before attempting to contact her – what if they caught him and made him talk, so that he was forced to reveal the affair himself?

Oh God, the whole village would know what she'd done. She might be arrested. Reggie's parents, her parents . . .

The stains were long gone and Annabel slowly leaned forward and lay her hot forehead on the cool, damp lino.

After a moment or two she shook herself into action and stood to rinse out her rag at the sink; the sitting room still needed doing. She went through and decided to start with the windows.

A moth was sitting on one of the windowsills, as though he were gazing out at the front garden. She wondered if he really was looking out there or if he was asleep – weren't moths nocturnal?

Before she killed it, she leaned forward to have a closer look. Its furry head and wings looked dusty, as though they would feel chalky to the touch. When she was a child she had thought that moths were just decrepit butterflies. Their wings were so drab and featureless, and she had thought that their beautiful colours had faded the same way a person's hair would fade, becoming duller and duller until it was grey. The moth looked like an ancient butterfly, too tired even to hold up its wings behind its back.

She pressed her cloth down hard on its still body and when she looked at the cloth afterwards, there was just a smudge of grey-brown dust left behind. It was as though the creature had never even existed.

She jumped when the doorbell rang. She had been so distracted by the insect, the cleaning, and her own churning thoughts that she hadn't noticed the group of men walking up her garden path.

She looked out of the bay window then to see them gathering at her doorstep. They must have seen her, framed in the window, inspecting her cleaning cloth. They stared at her. How? Fearfully? Angrily? She was suddenly reminded of a picture from one of Daniel's books – the terrified villagers marching with fire and pitchforks to the monster's castle in *Beauty and the Beast*.

In front of them, borne forward, was the child. She was shocked all over again by his appearance. He was dirty, scratched, bloody. His clothes were torn. His eyes, his eyes though... They were huge and wild and frightened and frightening.

She stood, frozen, like Lot's wife, who was turned into a pillar of salt when she looked at something she should never have seen. She stood there so long, Higgins had to ring the bell a second time.

She opened the door and the men – some of them were bloody too, she noticed now – tumbled into her narrow hall. She was propelled backwards, as though she were nothing more than a piece of seaweed adrift in the onslaught of the tides.

In the sitting room, she faced the dishevelled men. The boy was shaking violently, his teeth chattering audibly.

'What was your lad doing in the woods anyway?' Higgins began, and his sudden bark of words was too loud in the quiet of the house. He was furious with her. 'What was he doing in the woods, for God's sake?'

'Higgins,' Dawson said to him, 'don't...'

Annabel felt herself begin to tremble again. She would have spoken, asked them what had happened, but her mouth was so dry all she could do was swallow. Maybe she wouldn't have asked anyway; she was afraid to know the answers.

Some of the men seemed jittery, shifting from one foot to the other. It felt as though everyone was in motion in that little room; nothing was still.

The mirror man, who seemed to have lost his glasses, stepped forward. He put a hand on the boy's shoulder. Daniel jumped and spun around as though he had been branded with a hot iron. The man's hand recoiled, hovered in the air. He raised his other hand too, open-palmed, to show he was not a threat.

'Why don't you go upstairs, sonny?' he said. 'Maybe you'd like to... have a wash. Clean yourself up a bit. We'll sort things out with your mum here.'

The boy left the room and one of the men gently pushed the sitting-room door so it almost closed behind him. After he'd gone, Annabel realised she hadn't spoken to him. Something terrible had happened, but she had made no attempt to question him, or comfort him. She was thrown; her role as a pretend-mother hadn't kicked in this time, when she most needed it. She didn't know what to do.

A richer, deeper silence enveloped the room now. A couple of the men shuffled their feet, cleared their throats. They seemed reluctant to speak, and still, she trembled. She ached to sit down. She was worried her knees wouldn't support her while she listened to whatever these frightening men had come to say. She was still holding her cleaning rag.

'We went into the woods to look for him,' Higgins said eventually, and the strange relief of everyone in the room that he'd finally begun the story – and the horror – was palpable.

Annabel groped for the armchair behind her. She thought of how Higgins had seemed to her that day when he came to check up on her back garden. He was powerful and people listened to him. He was a leader. But something was strange about the way the others were behaving with him now. Higgins seemed unnerved, but in truth, all the men seemed unnerved, jumpy.

Annabel was nodding mechanically. Her eyes were fixed on Higgins and she kept nodding, nodding. Somehow she knew that despite whatever he was working his way up to, he was enjoying telling the story. He was enjoying his part in it.

'We were . . .' He hesitated for the first time. 'Angry.'

She became aware again of the other men. There had been a shifting within them, like a collective sigh released.

'We were already angry with that damned PoW. Some of us had weapons, as you know, from the Home Guard's office, truncheons and the like.'

Was she still nodding? She wasn't sure. She was imagining the pulp of Hans's head stuck to a wooden bat.

'We were already angry . . .'

God, what had they done? What was he trying to say?

She realised it was now dark outside when one of them switched on the light. Neither Higgins, nor any of the others, pointed out that her blackout curtains were not in place yet. So the lights from the room beamed out into the black street for any German bomber to see.

'And the state of your boy—' An edge had come back into

his voice and he looked at her disapprovingly. 'I've never seen anything like it. Well, you saw him.' He shook his head. 'Bleeding – clothes half ripped off of him.'

Several of the men looked away. Annabel had definitely stopped nodding now. Her heart was thumping so loudly she actually had to concentrate on Higgins's mouth forming the words so she could make out what he was saying.

'That disgusting loner should never have been allowed to stay around the village. People felt sorry for him; thinking he'd been bombed out of his house in one of the cities, but all along...'

She was perched forward, gripping the arms of the chair so tightly it hurt her hands.

'He obviously...' He made a sort of rolling gesture with his meaty palm. 'Disgusting... you know.' He hesitated again and looked at one of the other men, who shook his head almost imperceptibly. So he changed tack, and continued with the story he'd come to tell.

'We found him, though. To teach him a lesson... to punish him.'

She pictured a truncheon again, thick with matted hair and blood.

'Anyway, you and the boy won't have to worry about him any more.'

Annabel's throat made a strange, strangled sound.

In the silence that followed – the men seemed to be waiting for her to speak – Higgins's posture changed. His anger seemed to return to him and he became more belligerent, the way he'd been when he first entered the house. He seemed frustrated that she wasn't saying anything, hadn't, in fact, uttered a word since they had arrived.

'No one's sorrier than I am that the child had to witness that – but maybe it's for the best.' He paused. 'We did what needed to be done; nothing more, nothing less. What's done is done – there's no need to tell the authorities. Well, we *are* the authorities, but I mean the police, other people . . .'

She still couldn't bring herself to say anything. What was the appropriate response?

'What the hell was he doing out there alone in the forest, at any rate?' he snapped eventually. 'Why wasn't he home with you?'

Annabel stood. Her voice, when it finally came, was thin and cracked. 'I'd like you to leave now.'

'Hang on a minute! We just saved your son!'

'Let's go, Higgins,' Dawson said, turning to the door. 'It's a lot to take in. Let's leave her be.'

'Not a word of thanks!' He turned to the others. 'D'you know she's not said one word since we found that boy? What kind of mother is so . . . so *cold*, after something like this?'

'Higgins!' The mirror man put a hand on his arm.

Higgins allowed himself to be diverted, and turned to follow the men who were making their way into the hallway and out of the front door. A receding tide.

But then he stopped and turned. 'If you'd been looking after him properly like a normal mother, none of this would have happened.'

He must have relished the spite of his words, and Annabel's gasp seemed to satisfy him.

'Let's go,' he called out to the men ahead of him as he stepped through her front door into the garden. 'It may be dark now, but we've still got a German bastard to catch, in case you've forgotten!'

None of the men responded with any enthusiasm – the fight seemed to have gone out of them – but most gave half-hearted nods as they left the house and made their way down the street.

Annabel closed the door and leaned against it for a moment, before heading to the stairs and sitting on the bottom step.

She sat that way for a long time and tried to figure out how everything could have imploded so spectacularly while she had been looking in the other direction.

Hans was in terrible trouble, wherever he was. The child had been hurt. A man had been killed. The village knew she was only a pretend-mother.

It was all her fault. There was no one else she could blame.

She had convinced herself that being a pretend-mother was good enough, but that had never been true. There was something wrong with her, and she had failed in her only duty on earth: to protect the boy.

But still – Annabel couldn't help it – she wondered whether Hans would come for her. It was true he knew nothing of the village, of life outside the glade – but she had described her house to him, and he knew she lived on Ivy Lane. He could find her if he tried. It was just that she needed so badly to be comforted now, and Hans was the only one who could soothe her.

Perhaps she would hear a quiet tap on the back door, or clumps of earth being thrown at an upstairs window. Or perhaps she could expect a carefully coded letter from him telling her what to do next. How to find him, where to go.

She couldn't leave with him now, of course.

She thought of Higgins and his men and their weapons. They might still catch him, despite his head start. That would be her fault, too. Why had he done it? The answer was simple; he would never have tried to run if it weren't for her. His dreams of their life together had taken over and he was running away to try to turn them into reality. That was the only possible explanation.

Her thoughts turned to Reggie. Should she write to tell him what had happened to the boy? Perhaps she should wait and tell him next time he was on leave. She didn't like to upset him so terribly when there was nothing he could do about the situation. And he was so odd in himself on his last visit home, she wasn't sure how he would take the news. She wondered whether, in fact, she needed to tell him at all. He'd feel badly for not being here to prevent it, and he might think badly of her for allowing it to happen. He'd tell both their parents. They'd decide she was an unfit mother again and might try to send her away.

At last, she allowed herself to think of the boy.

What did that tramp do to him, out there in the woods? She didn't want to go upstairs to find him. She didn't know what to say to him. She had no way to comfort him. She had let him down. She had let him down more than she had let anyone down, and she knew she had let down everyone that mattered.

What had happened to the child was her fault, no one else's. She always knew he played in the woods, and she knew of the tramp; she didn't think anything of it. And she never noticed what time he came home, or asked him where he went or what he did.

Annabel wasn't sure when she would be able to get up off the step. She didn't want to see the boy. She didn't want to look at him. She couldn't bear how the sight of him would make her feel. She didn't want to hear what he had to say. She didn't want to see his eyes.

So she sat on the stairs all night, silent and static. And the night got darker and darker until it got lighter and lighter. She had once gone away in her head before, and she could feel it happening again now; she was going for good.

30

⸺

The old king said to his people: 'I wish he were still alive!
How it grieves me now that I had him killed.'
From *The Water of Life*

At first, I'd been watching her from a crack in the bathroom door, but now I came out onto the landing and sank down against the wall at the top of the stairs – never taking my eyes off her. I wrapped my arms tight around my knees as if I could hold myself together in one piece.

I looked down the stairs at her stooped back. I could tell a lot by the way she was sitting. She sat there for such a long time. She'd been sitting like that since the men had left.

It had been a long night and now it was dawn. Hansel must be frightened, alone in his hole. I'd planned to head back to him, but that wouldn't happen tonight. And it was hard to even imagine how I could help him, now this terrible thing had happened. How could I tell Mother what I'd done to Hansel? She didn't know I'd lied about the Troll trying to eat me, but she knew I was responsible for its brutal death. She was horrified by it; who wouldn't be? How could I have her hate me even more by telling her I'd helped Hansel escape? And how could I tell her it was my fault he'd fallen through the forest floor? After all, I'd taken him deep into the woods and he was following *me* when I led him across the top of a dangerous, rotted mine.

It occurred to me that when I was helping Hansel leave, I was actually stealing him from her. Didn't I want her to be upset when he ran away? So upset, she might turn to me for comfort?

Could that still happen? It didn't feel like it.

I ached inside as I stared down at her. I wanted her to pull me onto her lap and fold herself around me.

The men would be back in the forest by now, I knew. Despite what they'd said to Mother, thoughts of catching the woodcutter would be put to one side for now. They needed to get back to the mess of flesh and bones that once had been a Troll.

After the beating was over, they'd left the weapons lying next to it in the woods. Mr Higgins and the nice man had to take their shirts off because of the gore smeared across their clothes. They wiped their faces. You could still see splatters of blood on their trousers, though, if you looked, and marks like rust stains on their white vests.

There was a strange ringing in my ears so that I could barely hear their murmured conversations as we made our way towards the village, but I knew they'd decided to return to the forest afterwards. Snatches of sentences made it through the clanging in my head and I understood that it would be buried somewhere, deeper in the woods, and tidied away.

One of the men wanted to make it all official; the police could be told he'd put up a fight and they had bravely stopped a dirty criminal resisting a Home Guard citizens' arrest. But the idea fizzled away. The mess of pulp made things 'problematic', he admitted. Even I could see that.

Time seemed to be behaving strangely because no sooner had we left the forest than suddenly we were turning onto Ivy Lane.

I saw her standing in the window, holding a cloth in her hand. The men would tell her what I'd made them do. I knew it would never be the same afterwards.

I stared at her – although she didn't see me at first – while one of the men fiddled with the latch on the gate. The bare branches of the magnolia looped gracefully towards him and almost touched his shoulders.

I could see only the men's backs, not the expressions on their faces. Arms reached for me and I was pushed forward. Pushed up in front of them and through the gate. Hands on my shoulders guided me to the front door and that's when I began to shake and shake.

She jumped when Mr Higgins rang the doorbell and I saw her see me through the pane of glass separating us. I knew that my eyes must be mirror images of her own. We were both of us filled with horror.

Mr Higgins had to ring the bell again before she could move.

I wanted her to make them leave the house. I wanted them out. I didn't want them to tell her I was responsible for splitting a Troll into meat and blood and bone up in the woods.

But it was me that left; the nice man made me go out of the room and she didn't even look at me as I went. None of them did.

I knew they were all desperate to get away; the blood was drying on their clothes and they wanted the day finished.

The sitting-room door wasn't closed completely, so I stood outside – watching them through the small gap.

I couldn't see Mr Higgins's face from where I hid, but I could see hers. She was crumpled in the armchair and kept nodding and nodding, but I could see her knuckles straining against her skin as her hands gripped the armrests. It made them look like desperate claws clinging on there.

Somebody flicked the light switch. Whoever it was must have regretted doing it because they were all suddenly lit up under the bright glare and her face was terrible to see. I closed my eyes and leaned my head against the doorframe. Little ridges dug into my forehead and I was glad of the pain.

Finally she told them to go, but Mr Higgins got angry. He said she was too cold, too calm. But he didn't know her; she was *always* calm. I looked at her again. That's how she was. I never saw her any other way, apart from the times in the cabin with Hansel.

When the men turned towards the door, I ran up the stairs two at a time. But I watched from the landing as they went off into the night.

Mr Higgins was the last to go and he said it quietly, but I heard him say it: 'If you'd been looking after him properly like a normal mother, none of this would have happened.'

She cried out, and I choked back the sob in my own throat in case they heard me. Hot tears stung my eyes and I rushed into the bathroom and curled up on the floor. Then I pressed my hot face to the cool stand of the basin and clung on to it as though it could save me from drowning.

The bathroom window was open and the voices of the men floated up to me as they left to return to the forest to get rid of the Troll and find Hansel. I cried harder as I tried to convince myself they wouldn't stay out all out night looking for him. He was a sitting target now; he couldn't run and there was nowhere to hide. The voices faded away and then they were gone.

I clamped my hands over my mouth, trying to keep quiet so she couldn't hear me downstairs. It was a long time before the tears finally stopped coming, and my rib muscles ached from holding back the sobs my body was trying to make. I didn't sleep, but it was as though I wasn't quite awake either and I lay there for a long time.

Eventually, I dragged myself across the floor and reached up to grasp the door handle to pull myself up. I quietly opened the door. My face felt sore and swollen.

That was when I saw her sitting on the bottom step. She had been there the whole time, I realised, as if Mr Higgins had punched her and knocked her out.

Her shoulders were slumped and her head was bowed as it rested on her hands propped up by her elbows on her knees. But she was perfectly still. I couldn't see her face, but somehow I knew if I was standing right in front of her I would see she was dry-eyed.

I watched her hunched back for a long, long time.

More time must have passed, because the house began to fill with a pretty pinkish glow as the dawn came. She didn't show any awareness that we were breaking into a new day, but I went back into the bathroom and quietly closed the door.

The water ran red into the basin as I washed the dried blood and crusty tears from my face. I pulled the twigs and leaves from my hair. But before I threw them in the bin, I wrapped them in toilet tissue so she wouldn't see them and know where they came from.

Carefully, I eased the door open and crept to my room, where I bundled my ripped and bloodied rags under my bed – in the spot where Hansel's pack had been just the night before. I'd throw them away, somewhere she wouldn't find them. I put on my pyjamas and climbed under the eiderdown.

A feeling that I couldn't quite put my finger on made me want to be in the right place, and look the right way, the next time she came across me.

Of course, there was no fairy tale that night. I wondered if that would ever happen again. I must have drifted off to sleep at some point though, because I found myself inside a nightmare.

Its eyes were looking right at me as its head exploded under a wooden bat that splattered it to pieces again and again and again. And I looked down at the bat, and it was in my hand, and it was me who was pounding that head and grinding it into the ground. I sat up in bed with a gasp and a thudding heart, and the sheets were wet with my sweat.

The real world had smashed up against the magic in my forest – Hansel was broken at the bottom of a hole, and the Troll was battered to pieces – and the magic had lost the battle. If it had ever been there at all.

I lay back trembling in my sticky and cold bed. I didn't sleep again but stayed there until it was time to get up.

That morning, I thought I'd find her at the bottom of the stairs, but she wasn't there. At some point, she'd gone up to her own room. She must have come to the same decision as me about the best way to carry on.

She came down when I was in the kitchen making porridge. She smoked a cigarette at the table while I stood on a small stool and stirred the mixture in the pan. Something about the look and texture of it – those white globs – made me feel sick.

But I scooped it into two bowls and carried them over to the table. We both acted as though we were eating, by stirring the food and managing to push a spoon into our mouths now and then. We didn't mention the day before because we didn't speak at all.

She drifted away to the sitting room and I did the washing-up, then went upstairs to get ready. I'd head out, and so far that would be like a normal day. But I still felt sick as I got dressed, with a painful tummy ache that had suddenly clamped my insides. The truth was I still hadn't managed to come up with a plan to help Hansel. I still didn't know how I could get him out of that hole. And even if I could, what then? What about his injuries? And where could he go?

I started to dawdle. I went to the toilet. I investigated my face in the mirror and found it was still tender with a blue-grey bruise starting beneath my right eye. I changed my clothes to something a little warmer because it was autumn now and there was a chill in the air. I stuffed yesterday's tattered outfit into my school satchel to throw away somewhere later, or maybe even burn. I still had the matches from when I—

Don't think about it.

I flung the bag over my shoulder and went to the kitchen to get something for Hansel's breakfast. Or lunch now. There wasn't much in the larder; Mother had been supposed to go out to buy the rations yesterday before—

Don't think about it.

I grabbed the last tin of sardines off the shelf. That would have to do. The can went into my satchel along with a flask of barley water. And I set off.

As I headed to the woods, my tummy started to feel a bit better. At least I was doing something. Perhaps an idea would come to me on the way. It was a long walk, after all. And at the very least, Hansel would be grateful for the food and drink and company while we tried to figure things out. Maybe he'd have a plan. A tingle of excitement now fluttered in my tummy instead of the cramps. I couldn't help it. As long as I didn't think about yesterday it seemed to me that I might be able to rescue something good from this.

And it was nice to be out of the house, away from the memories of the men in the sitting room and Mother's face and her silent collapse at the bottom of the stairs.

The satchel swung as I made my way along the lane towards the forest and the breeze ran through my hair and calmed my thoughts. It was a cool day but the sun was poking through the clouds at the moment and it was quite pleasant to march along.

Stepping into the shade of the woods caused a brief moment of sickly panic because—

Don't think about it.

I'd been in the forest a million times so I didn't have to let *those* memories ruin the woods for me. I forced myself on. But a cloud must have covered the sun, and the trees blocked a lot of the light, so that the darkness seemed to settle on my mood as well.

I headed to the river crossing and made my way across the fallen-tree bridge, trying not to remember how I'd stalked the Troll near there once in what felt like another life.

On the other side of the bank I scooped out some dirt at the base of a trunk and buried the clothes I'd worn the day before.

I covered them over with the earth and rocks and branches and then washed the dirt from my hands in the cold water. I tried not to think of how the men must have done a similar thing last night with the remains of what used to be the Troll.

It was a moment or two before I could carry on, but then I was off again.

I did my best to retrace our steps from yesterday, but the problem was I'd been horribly lost when Hansel fell. How could I hope to find that same spot again now, when I didn't even know where I'd been? It occurred to me I might get so lost I wouldn't even be able to find my way home. I wasn't sure how I felt about that.

I trekked for a long time and got annoyed and sweaty and was forced to drink a bit of the barley water.

It was a long way away, I knew that much, but even so it took me hours to find the old mineshaft. I felt a jab of hot relief when I finally came upon the hole, followed by another jab almost immediately of regret at finding it at all.

I had nearly missed it, but then I saw a shard of ripped and rotten wood poking up from the forest floor. It was a piece of the mine, the old ceiling that had rotted and collapsed under the weight of Hansel running across it. It stuck up like a tombstone, looming over the tear in the ground that had swallowed up my woodchopper.

Quietly, carefully, I made my way closer. I felt suddenly nervous – and jumped as the hole seemed to come alive with noise.

'Hello? Hello? Help! I'm down here! Help!'

I hesitated and stood still.

'Daniel? Daniel, is that you?'

I bit my bottom lip hard.

'DANIEL! I know you're there! Goddamn it!'

His bellowing echoed around the hole and it sounded like an angry monster in the labyrinth.

But then the echoes died away and the forest was silent once more, apart from the muted sound of birdsong and rustling leaves.

Still, I held back. If I were to call down to him, what could I say? I had no way to help him. And he just sounded so *angry*. Did he blame me for his fall? I'd forgotten the rumours about the dangers of old mines and so hadn't ever thought to warn him.

I didn't have any way to get him out and I didn't have any rope. I wasn't even sure how I could get hold of some – and how I would manage to pull him out by myself if I did.

Suddenly, I remembered the tin of sardines and the barley water in my satchel. Surely he'd be glad of those, while we tried to work out where to go from here.

'Hansel?' My voice sounded hoarse and unused and I realised it was the first time I'd spoken since telling the story of the Troll to Mother and the men yesterday.

'Daniel? Daniel? Oh, thank God!' There was a sound from the hole that might have been him crying something in German but it was not loud enough for me to tell.

'Yes, it's me,' I called out. 'I'm here now. I'm back.'

'Good, good, that is good—' His voice sounded hoarse, too, and broke off with a ragged gasp. It was a second or two before he tried again. 'That's very good.'

I took a step closer to the split-open mine. But not too close – I didn't want to fall down myself.

'Daniel – I need help. I'm really hurt. My legs are broken, maybe my back . . .'

I winced, but he hadn't finished.

'I need help, do you understand?'

'Yes, I know!' I called back, hoping he wouldn't ask me about the plan.

That was bad news about his legs. They must be very sore. William McCarthy from school broke his arm in the playground playing rugger last year and he cried and cried. And every time he let one of the others sign his plaster-of-Paris cast he told them the story about how he thought he might die because the pain was so bad.

I thought my nose was broken yesterday – and that hurt badly enough even though it was just a bang.

I needed to take his mind off things and distract him while I tried to think of what to do now I knew how badly he was injured.

'I've brought you lunch,' I shouted. 'That'll make you feel better, you'll see!'

'*Mein Gott!* No, Daniel, listen to me – I need help! You have to tell someone! Tell your mother. She will need to tell others. But I have to get out, Daniel, I can't stay here. I can't. You must fetch help!'

I chewed my lip again and glanced around.

I couldn't possibly tell my mother. Think how hurt and angry she'd be to find out I'd tried to help him leave her. And if I told anyone else in the village, she'd simply find out that way instead. Also, I'd be in terrible trouble with those frightening men. They might put me in prison as a traitor or even do to me what they'd done to the Troll. Hansel was in danger too, although he didn't yet know what I knew about the men with their rage and their weapons. I'd have to think of another way to help him.

'I'm going to throw your lunch and drink down to you, all right?'

'What? All right, but then run to fetch somebody.'

I'd have to throw the tin and flask down the hole and hope that they didn't hit him and that he could reach them where they fell. The open mouth in the ground looked scary, like it could easily get bigger, and I didn't want to get too close to it.

Pulling the supplies out of my bag, I decided to wriggle to the hole on my front. It felt like it would be less dangerous for me that way.

When I was still a couple of yards away from the opening, I shouted a jolly 'Watch out down below' and half rolled and half threw the tin and then the flask towards the hole.

I was relieved when I heard them hit the bottom without a yelp of pain from Hansel.

'I know you've got some supplies in your bag down there, but I just thought—'

'Good, thank you,' he called up. 'Now run to get someone. Please, Daniel!'

'Um ... all right then. I'll be off now.'

'Yes, tell them to hurry.'

'I will.'

I wriggled backwards and stood up when I felt I was a safe distance away. I walked away into the woods, so he couldn't hear me. Then I sat down against a tree to think.

I scrubbed at my eyes but no ideas came to me, perhaps because I was so tired. After a while, I decided I might as well go home to eat something, check on Mother, and get some rest. I picked up my satchel, and the bag containing Daddy's clothes that I'd abandoned here yesterday, and began to make my way home. I'd come back tomorrow when I was bound to have worked out what to do next.

But the next day – after another silent evening with mother and a nightmare-filled night – I still hadn't managed to come up with a plan.

And I felt sick again as I dragged myself back to Hansel's hole. I was able to find it straight away this time.

We didn't have another flask at home so I couldn't bring him a drink today – hopefully he'd kept some back – and our larder was practically bare so there was no lunch either. He'd be all right for a day; I'd bring more supplies tomorrow. I'd take the ration book and go shopping myself if necessary.

But when I got to the mine, I didn't like to announce I was there only to explain I didn't have anything for him. And what would I say when he asked me why no one had come for him? He'd have been waiting for men with ropes and a stretcher. All day and all night. He'd know I hadn't done what he told me to do.

Instead, I sat cross-legged on the ground and picked at the earth with a sharp stick. I kept an ear out for Hansel calling for me, but he didn't, so he must have been all right. He was probably having a nap. The rest would be good for him – his legs were probably starting to heal already. McCarthy had told everyone how his bone was actually repairing itself under the cast, so it wasn't as if you needed any medicine as such.

After about fifteen minutes or so, I got cold just sitting there – the weather had been so much cooler lately – and I walked home quickly to warm up.

The next morning I went to the village first and bought some bread and two bottles of ginger beer.

The problem was, when I arrived at the mine I knew he'd be even angrier than the day before. I remembered how angry he'd become in the forest when we were running; I'd ended up with my face bashed in.

Woodchoppers can be nice, like the hero with the axe who saves Red Riding Hood, but sometimes their feelings about children aren't very nice, like the woodchopper who abandons his children, Hansel and Gretel, in the forest.

Now it felt too awkward to call out to him and throw him the shopping in my string bag. I'd torn off a couple of chunks from the loaf to nibble on during the long walk, and they suddenly felt like stones sitting in my stomach.

I dithered at the surface.

'Hello?' His voice sounded raspy and thin and I froze so he wouldn't hear me. 'Can anybody . . .'

I felt a hot, almost feverish prickling at my scalp and a cramping sensation in my tummy. Hansel had been down at the bottom of the mine with broken legs for four days now.

'Daniel . . . ?'

My eyes filled with sudden tears and I blinked as the forest went blurry and I couldn't see the hole any more.

I just didn't know what to do. I couldn't do what he wanted – no one, especially Mother, could find out what I'd done. And I was terrified that someone would somehow stumble across his hole and get him out, because I knew then he'd be interrogated and would tell them everything.

As quietly as I could, but rushing to escape the thoughts trying to follow me, I left the shopping by a tree and made my way back the way I'd come. When I got home, later that afternoon, Mother was upstairs. Lately, she'd been spending all day in bed and when she was up she just floated around like a ghost. She'd taken her gin up to her bedroom and now kept it on her nightstand.

On the fifth day I heard him calling my name again. It was mixed in with some German words and he wasn't making much sense. His voice sounded so much weaker. I clung to a tree trunk nearby and wept – stuffing my fist into my mouth so he couldn't hear my crying.

At one point he bellowed for help at the top of his lungs with a cracked scream, obviously not caring who found him. I sank down and doubled over, pushing my face into my knees to stifle my cries and clamping my hands over my ears so I couldn't hear him.

When I returned on the sixth day, the hole in the ground was silent so I knew he must be sleeping. He didn't make a sound all day, even though I stayed for hours. Hansel was silent the next day too, and the next. And all the days after that.

And then I stopped going.

Kent, 1945–7

⊸∞⊷

31

She could not forget the handsome prince,
and she grieved for him . . .
From *The Little Mermaid*

Little Gerda stopped and said her prayers . . .
From *The Snow Queen*

Annabel was on her way to the grocer's. It was the only one in the village or she'd have gone elsewhere. But she wanted some gin and the little shelf behind Sid Mitchell's counter was the only way she knew to access the black market. He always made sure to ask if her father was ready for him to get hold of another bottle.

It was a warm day in May; just over a year since Hans had arrived in Bambury with the first of the PoWs. She remembered seeing him that first time as he walked down the lane.

It was silly, but she always felt slightly on edge in the grocer's, remembering how it was there she'd first learned of Hans's disappearance. That was just the start of the horror, which was compounded when something awful happened to the boy. She quickly pushed those thoughts away, and thought of Hans again.

It'd been months now and there was still no word from him.

But he had managed to escape capture by Bambury's Home Guard, at least. She scoured the papers now, for news of a German PoW picked up elsewhere in the country. Sometimes she prayed to find his name so it would end the not knowing, and other times she prayed not to see it, so there was still the possibility of hope. There was nothing though, so perhaps he really had managed to make it abroad. It would be hard for him to travel freely, so it was possible he was still trying to make his way to Switzerland. She didn't think he could be there yet, or he'd have sent some kind of message, a coded way of letting her know he'd made it and wanted her to join him. She was still trying to make up her mind whether she would. Certainly she wasn't happy here; she was bereft without him – and constantly tortured herself about the boy – but the thought of fleeing overseas still scared her.

She simply couldn't work out why he'd run without telling her first, without saying goodbye. Perhaps he was trying to protect her. Spare her the grief of knowing he was leaving, or perhaps he was making sure she knew nothing about any of it so she couldn't be implicated later if something went wrong?

But as the months had passed, she'd found it harder to cope. The fear had gradually ebbed away and left a searing loneliness in its place. Wherever Hans was, she had to accept he could never return to Bambury. She'd been frightened to think of the future when she was with him, but at least she had the possibility of one. Now, on the bad days – the days she became convinced he'd been caught – she feared she had no future at all. And on those days, the exhaustion that had smothered her after Daniel's birth seemed to return.

And it would be like that for a time, until she told herself she must accept her lot and get up and pretend to function again. Or it might be a visit from her parents-in-law that forced her from her bed to do her best to clean, to stock the house, to buy the boy new clothes as he outgrew his old ones. But all she did was never enough; her mother telephoned every other week, and now even Moira was regularly ringing, to check up on her. They seemed to think she was pining for Reggie; the interminable war was now in its sixth year.

Annabel braced herself and entered the shop. She was just greeting the grocer when a crying Mrs Mitchell suddenly burst through from the back room behind the counter, shouting she'd heard it on the wireless.

Her husband couldn't understand her at first. 'Slow down, Ma, for God's sake. Slow down,' he said.

But she kept shouting; she'd just heard the Prime Minister making an announcement – Germany had surrendered and the war in Europe was finally over. Her husband started crying too, and they hugged each other – laughing through their tears – and then embraced Annabel between them.

'Teddy will come home now,' Mrs Mitchell cried. 'He made it through all right! Teddy will come home!'

But all Annabel could think was: 'What was the point? What was the point of it all? All those years of fighting and death?'

And the victory itself seemed doubly pointless now that Hans had gone.

Reggie would come back, she supposed. And their life would carry on just as it had been before the war. She tried to force a smile onto her face as the Mitchells started jumping up and down on either side of her, before ushering her into the street so they could share the news with the other villagers, and celebrate with those who'd already heard.

'I can't believe it – my Teddy's coming home,' Mrs Mitchell was telling the small crowd gathering in the High Street.

'Three cheers for the King!' her husband cried. 'Hip hip—'

'Hooray!'

'Hip hip—'

'Hooray!'

'Hip hip—'

'Hooray!'

Mrs Mitchell still had her arm around Annabel. She suddenly vigorously rubbed her back. 'I don't think you've quite taken it in, dear! But your Reggie's coming home now, you'll see. He's coming home!'

But a couple of weeks later Annabel received a letter from the army. Reggie wasn't *quite* going to make it home to Bambury, after all.

She found the envelope sitting on the kitchen table where the boy had left it for her before school. She read it standing up.

Reggie had been shipped back to England before Victory in Europe Day, it said – and she could only assume the slow military machine was why she hadn't been informed sooner.

He'd been diagnosed with shell shock and sent to a 'clinic' in Sussex. She took the letter through to the sitting room and sat down in her armchair to read it again.

Poor Reggie.

Eventually she forced herself to ring his parents to break the bad news. Ha! It was almost funny to think he was the one – not his poor, strange, weak wife – who ended up in an asylum in the end.

They were shocked at first, but then Moira rallied.

'He'll be all right, my Reggie,' her voice told Annabel through the receiver. 'What that poor boy has been through out there, I don't even like to think about, but he's home now. That's the main thing. He'll be all right now he's home. Those army doctors will sort him out in no time. And we can help him.'

'Of course, nobody is to know about this,' Annabel heard her father-in-law say; he must have been standing next to his wife, crouched down with his ear pressed to the telephone between them. 'We'll just put it about that Reggie's still in France, working with the army, helping sort out administration issues and rebuilding Europe and all of that.'

'All right,' Annabel agreed slowly. She heard muffled mumbles. And then Bill spoke again.

'That's what we'll tell Daniel too, in case he accidentally blurts out the truth to somebody. We can't risk people finding out. Reggie would be ashamed. And he might not be able to get his job back at the bank otherwise. And there's no need for Daniel to know, anyway. No point upsetting him.'

'Fine.'

She heard Moira take a deep breath. 'Hopefully some rest on the south coast will do Reggie the world of good – and now the war's over he'll never have to fight again. He'll be better soon and can come home and nobody will ever have to know about . . . well, whatever this is.'

32

'I dare not tell my sorrows to anyone ...'
From *The Goosegirl*

'Are you excited about going down to Sussex, Daniel?'

I'd been watching the countryside glide past the car window, but saw now my grandmother had turned around in her front seat to look back at me.

'Yes, Granny.' I'd just been wishing the summer holidays would never end – it was September now and soon I'd be starting my final year at primary school. It was hard to believe a whole year had passed since ... that thing. I didn't know how I'd managed to get through it now. I'd started my fifth year just a week or so after ... it all happened.

'And a lovely day for a drive, isn't it?' Grandpa said.

'Yes.'

'Lovely day,' Granny repeated. She bit her lip and looked at Mother, who was sitting on the back seat next to me. But Mother was staring out of the window, just as I had been. Then my grandmother looked at Grandpa, who kept his eyes fixed on the road, but nodded slightly, even though she hadn't asked him a question.

'Now,' Granny said. 'We've got a wonderful surprise for you! I know your tenth birthday was a while ago, but think of this as a belated present! It's a secret though, so you mustn't tell anyone about it.'

It was my turn to look across at Mother, but she still had her face turned to the window.

'We're not *just* going to the beach today. We're going to visit Daddy!'

'Daddy?'

'Yes, he's . . .' she looked at Grandpa again. 'He's home from France. Isn't that marvellous?'

'We're going to see Daddy? Today?'

'Yes! Isn't that exciting?'

I was so shocked I could only nod. I hadn't seen Daddy for a very long time. 'Is he coming home with us now?'

'Ah, well. No. No, not just yet, dear.' She glanced across at Grandpa again. 'Now, there's something we need to tell you. Daddy isn't quite his usual self at the moment. That's why he's having a little holiday in Sussex.'

Excitement began bubbling up in my stomach. I was going to see Daddy! I let out a little laugh and tried to concentrate on what Granny was saying.

'He's been there for a little while already. Grandpa and I have already visited him with Mother – several times, actually. While you've been at school. But we thought as the school holidays'll soon be over—'

'Why didn't you tell me?'

'Well, it's what I was saying about him not quite being his usual self. He's staying in a sort of . . . clinic. Remember that trouble he was having with his ears? Anyway, we thought it'd be best if we went to see him first. To try to cheer him up—'

'Why is he sad?' I had a sudden awful feeling Daddy was sad because he somehow knew about what I'd done in the woods.

'Well, you know, he's much better than he was and we thought it might do him good to see you.'

'Why is he sad?' I asked again, although I was dreading the answer.

'Oh, he's just sad about the war.'

'But it's over now!'

'He's just sad it happened.' She turned back in her seat and faced forward again. 'We all are.'

I looked around the car and could only see the backs of three heads.

Daddy was sitting on a wicker chair in the gardens with a blanket on his lap even though it was hot. As we approached him I could see his hands were shaking violently.

'Don't worry about that,' Grandpa bent down to say low in my ear. 'He always does that. He'll get better and grow out of it.' I felt Granny squeeze my shoulder as we walked towards him.

But it was horrible to look at his hands shaking and shaking like an old man's.

'Hello Reggie,' they all said in bright voices when we came up to him, and after a moment Mother bent down to kiss his cheek. I could see his face was rough with stubble like sandpaper.

'Look who's come to see you today,' Grandpa said.

And, though he had been expressionless until now, I saw him try to smile at me. It was almost worse than the shaking, because I could tell that the smile had been a big effort for him.

I couldn't smile back though, because clearly this man was not my daddy.

During the war, and after that thing, I'd always been hoping he'd come home. But now I didn't want him there; this crumpled-looking man who didn't look anything like Daddy. As I thought that, a sickly trickle of guilt ran down into my tummy.

Granny began talking about the squirrels she'd spotted over in the far trees, and was saying how relaxing it must be to enjoy the sun and watch the animals. It suddenly dawned on me that Daddy was ill. They were speaking to him like a child.

How could he come home to our silent house in Bambury where he'd realise I was now just as far away as Mother? It wasn't like it was before. She didn't even read to me any more. We barely looked at each other, but we'd found a way of living that was working. We acted as though everything was normal when we were in the village and we kept the act up at home too. But I didn't know how I could pretend with him there.

I looked at this strange person who used to be Daddy and knew at once our strange house had no place for him. I thought of the monsters who came to visit me at night while I was asleep, like demons from a story. And it was like Mother was haunted too. So she and I both had our own demons; we couldn't help Daddy with his.

I glanced up at Mother, who had turned as though she was watching the squirrels, but I could see her eyes. She was hating this as much as I was. She wanted to be gone, too.

That helped me somehow. We were sharing the same feelings at that moment. It was almost like we were together. I wasn't quite there myself any more – that's how I knew how it was for her when *she* disappeared, even though she was still standing right there.

I don't think my visit to the clinic had the effect Granny and Grandpa had been hoping for. I think they thought Daddy would jump up cured at the sight of me, like a miracle. And my horrified reaction to the whole thing probably wasn't what they'd wanted either. So they didn't offer to take me again and I never asked to join them.

And time passed and passed and went on and went on.

And still, Mother and I didn't speak of it – that terrible day.

Instead, we pretended nothing had changed for either of us. In fact, we helped each other, in a strange sort of way, if either of us looked as though we were about to wander away from safe empty words. And sometimes I thought that she was a pretend-mother and I was a pretend-child and we were both pretend-people silently going about our business.

On the surface, nothing had changed at all. We still lived

together in our little cottage in Ivy Lane and the men from the Home Guard still lived in the village. But it was easy enough to avoid people's eyes if Mother and I happened to find ourselves in a shop queue or in the Post Office or on the bus with someone who knew part of what had gone on. Either she'd steer us away, or they'd suddenly appear to remember they had somewhere else to be and would hurry off.

One chilly day, not long after I turned twelve, we'd returned home to hear the telephone shrieking as we walked through the front door.

'It'll be Grandma,' Mother said. 'I've got a headache. Tell her I've gone to bed.'

I went into the sitting room and picked up the receiver.

'She's always got a headache when I telephone,' Grandma grumbled when I explained. 'Strange how it comes on every other week, on my day to speak to her.'

I said nothing, but listened to the crackles on the line.

'Are you still there? Hello? Operator?'

'I'm still here, Grandma.'

'How are you, dear? Has your mother been... What did you have for dinner last night?'

And I described a stew with dumplings.

'Hmm,' she said. And was quiet for a while. 'Has she been busy? With the housework?'

I looked around. The secret rooms of the house had always contained little patches of chaos. But the chaos had bred, and multiplied, and stretched. It began to trickle down the stairs. Papers and books and bottles began growing on each step. And then the sea of chaos spread into the not-secret rooms, bringing a tide of dirty cups and dishes. Sometimes I would attack the mess, and sometimes I couldn't see the point. Once, when I was tidying my room, I found a glass filled with crusty brown gloop and a knife under my bed. With a shudder of shame, and embarrassment, and guilt, I wrapped them in an old pillowcase and threw them into the dustbin outside. It might have been after that I stopped trying to clean. Mother found ways to stop both sets of grandparents from coming to see us.

'Yes,' I said. 'She's always doing lots of housework.'

'And how's your father?'

'He's . . . getting better.' I thought about it and realised it was true. 'Mother went to see him again the other day. They let him use the telephone in the office sometimes. I speak to him. He's, I don't know, he's cheering up.'

'Yes, I heard he's been using the telephone. That's wonderful!'

'Yes.' He really did sound more and more like Daddy each time I spoke to him now. I had to try not to remember those horrible shaking hands and that horrible shaky smile and if I could forget that and just listen to his voice it was like he was normal again. But I still couldn't decide if I wanted him to come home. Would it make things better, or worse?

'It'll be Christmas soon. You'll have to make him a nice card. Grandad and I are so looking forward to you and your mother coming to stay with us. You haven't forgotten it's our turn, have you? You were with your father's parents last year.'

I'd been trying not to think about it. Christmas was usually difficult.

It was Christmas-time just a few months after that terrible day, and it was strange and awkward at Grandma and Grandad's house that year.

I think they knew something was wrong, but Mother had suffered with nerves when I was born, so maybe they thought it was that again. I'm not sure what they thought was wrong with *me*. Grandma tried to ask once but I pretended I didn't know what she was talking about. Over Christmas lunch, Grandad kept making jokes to try to make us snap out of it.

As I said goodbye to Grandma now on the telephone, I hoped this year would be easier. Mother and I were better now at behaving normally.

*

So the winter came, and Christmas, and it turned into a new year: 1947. And then the winter seemed to change; it became a strange winter that didn't know when to stop.

At first, when I looked out of the sitting-room window at the bare magnolia tree stooped over the lawn, it looked pretty. The straggly garden looked as though it had been sugared – shimmering flecks of crispy white crystals coated branches and blades of grass.

But after the frost, the snow came. Layers upon layers of it kept falling and didn't stop. Broadcasters on the wireless said it was the longest period of snow ever recorded in Britain; the coldest winter; the worst for three centuries. Snow was seven yards deep in the highlands of Scotland, but every city, every village, every town in the country was suffering. It was treacherous, they said. People would likely die.

It was the third winter since that terrible autumn day. And I tried not to think of him being covered by snow out in his hole.

33

The walls of the palace were made of snow, and the
windows and doors of sharp winds . . .
From *The Snow Queen*

Annabel looked out of the sitting-room window and thought:
It will be horrific.

She knew that. But what else could she do? They'd be trapped
by tonight.

Outside was an alien landscape. The lane didn't exist any more;
instead, peaks and valleys of solid white almost completely hid
the other cottages from sight. She might have been looking out
of an Alpine hut.

She felt like she had spent most of her life gazing out of this
window. It was an effort to suppress the memory of watching Hans
arrive that sunny spring day nearly three years ago, and of looking
out at the men on her doorstep who brought her a bloodied and
brutalised boy while she'd been worrying over her missing lover.

She watched as the window briefly clouded from her breath.
There were flecks of icy stars on the wooden rim of the sill and
they looked like crystal spiders gathering there.

She'd just spoken to Moira, who had telephoned to tell her the
doctors were discharging Reggie. He was ready to come home.
Annabel no longer minded that the staff deferred to Moira; keeping
Reggie's mother informed of his progress rather than her, his wife.

The roads were impassable of course, at the moment, but after the thaw he would come back to Bambury. Moira said she and Bill would stay in their usual room above the pub to help welcome Reggie home and settle him in. When they left, Annabel supposed life would be the same for her as it had been before the war. It would be as though Hans never happened.

She brought a cigarette to her lips to draw the smoke deep into her lungs, enjoying the crackle as the tip burned towards her. She tapped it over the ashtray she was holding in her other hand, letting the column of ash float down like confetti. One by one, people had stopped coming out of their houses. She'd heard that the RAF were having to drop food parcels in some parts of the country, whereas just a couple of years ago it was bombs that were dropping from the sky.

There was nothing to do but wait for the whole damned thing to pass. It had been snowing for weeks and it felt like the world was ending – being buried deeper and deeper, one day at a time.

She'd be shut up in this house as though trapped in a coffin. With Daniel. He'd trail round after her, following her movements with his doleful eyes. Wanting to talk to her. So desperate for something she couldn't give him. Sometimes she shouted at him to leave her alone. He drove her to it. He made her feel uncomfortable. And he was getting so tall; he was twelve now. Impossible to imagine he lived inside her once.

It seemed to her as though the boy was constantly trying to create happy memories, which she found disturbing; disturbing and exhausting.

'Do you remember that time Daddy opened the larder and all those tins fell out?'

'Do you remember the time we helped Mr Finlay look for his dog?'

'Do you remember the time we baked a cake in the middle of the night?'

Do you remember? Do you remember? Do you remember?

She wasn't stupid. He was trying to take her back to the time before; before what she'd begun to think of as 'The Incident' –

neutral calm words that could be used as shorthand in her own mind for the events of that awful day.

But she couldn't go back. And frankly, things hadn't exactly been perfect even before the war, and Hans, and that revolting tramp. No, she couldn't go back. But equally, she felt just as unable to go forward. She was stuck in a day, in a moment, in a nightmare.

She felt a fierce flush of guilt whenever she thought this; but the truth was that the boy – and his serious, solemn face – reminded her of everything she'd prefer to forget.

The snow wouldn't be so bad if he weren't shut up in here with her. She could go to bed and stay there and never have to talk to anyone. Talking was such an effort now. She felt exhausted all the time, although she slept deeply at night and napped during the day.

Of course, it was an effort to get dressed and go to the shops on the High Street, but at least she could walk around hoping to bump into someone who might distract her for a while. She also hoped for news of Hans, in truth, stupid as that was. Was he really out there somewhere, still on the run, or perhaps safely back home in Germany? It was so hard to believe he wouldn't send word. Or had he been caught somewhere or attacked, and that was the real reason he'd never tried to contact her?

These were questions she had asked herself thousands of times.

Another drag of the cigarette, while looking at the blank sheet of nothingness outside, was like a salve to her restless mind.

She had tried to believe the snow would soon melt away, leaving black tarry sludge behind, until that melted too. But by Monday she finally accepted that it was getting worse and now they would have to stay inside until the thaw.

Annabel wrenched herself from the window, stubbed out her cigarette, and put down her ashtray amongst some of the clutter on the sideboard. She went through to the hall to wrap up before braving the cold. Not all of the shops would be open but she'd have to venture out with her ration book for provisions before they were sealed in.

The boy was upstairs, reading in his room most likely, and she called out to him as she left to tell him to bring as much coal from the cellar as he could manage into the sitting room. All of it, ideally. God knew how long they'd be trapped.

Snow crunched beneath her feet with the same sound as gravel as she carefully made her way down the lane. The icy wetness of it seeped through her shoes. The leather would be stained and she could tell her toes must be white and shrivelled from the water pooling in each sole. Although she soon lost sensation in her feet apart from the burn of the cold, she could feel an unpleasant squelching with every step. She knew she'd be left with red welts on her cheeks where the frigid wind slapped her face as it screamed past her ears.

She pulled her scarf up over the back of her head and trudged on to the High Street to gather supplies from the few shops that had fought to stay open. She'd buy meat and bread, but also things that wouldn't go off while they were trapped: powdered eggs and condensed milk and tinned food.

The greengrocer's was closed. Old Sid Mitchell and his wife must have battened down the hatches to hole up in the back flat. It was in their shop that she first learned about Hans's disappearance, and there too when she heard that the war had finally ended. Annabel shook her head to try to clear it of the past as she walked by. Too many memories in this village, but she had to stay, because how else could Hans find her?

A light flurry of snow began to dance in the air around her and she hurried into the butcher's. The sawdust scattered on the red concrete floor was doing little to soak up the snowy footprints left by his customers.

Jean Bainbridge was at the counter when she went in and there was an awkward greeting; Annabel had gradually stopped pretending to be friendly, although she continued to maintain normal social etiquette.

'I was just saying it's definitely worse today than it was yesterday,' Jean said, nodding at Mr Lupton carving the carcass on his block. 'Much colder.'

The butcher chuckled. 'If you say so. Snow's snow, isn't it?'

Jean glanced at Annabel, inviting her to join in. Her hair was red against her white mohair hat. 'Bitterly cold.'

'Bitter,' Annabel murmured. The word itself sounded as though she was spitting it out of her mouth. Yes, she was bitter.

After buying some pork she finished the rest of her shopping and made her way back to the cottage. Just before she reached Ivy Lane, she slipped on some ice, falling backwards onto the pavement. But the snow softened her landing and the sound of her cry felt as though it had come from far away.

She lay still for a moment, surrendering to the snowdrift cradling her. It was so quiet. The landscape was not just featureless; it was obliterated.

After a while, she picked up her shopping bag from the pavement, brushed snow off the seat of her coat, and trudged onwards. The cold wind made her eyes water and before long they were streaming.

She would change into dry clothes when she got home. Perhaps she would have another gin or two before lunch. Just to warm up.

Once home, she took her string bag through to the kitchen and called for the boy to put everything away in the larder. He came running down the stairs and set about the shopping.

Leaving the room, she headed to the sitting room to make herself a drink.

She could feel the boy gazing after her, no doubt looking infuriatingly sad. She thought he had started to say something, but she was gone before he could even form the words.

Upstairs, she shrugged off her wet clothes and sat down heavily at her dressing table. She was wearing just her slip.

It was too chilly for this. To conserve coal she should really only heat the sitting room and stay down there, but these days she spent more time in her bedroom, so she kept a small fire going.

The wood she'd bought from Hans had run out long ago, and she never could bring herself to return to the orchard to buy more from a different PoW. She'd started buying coal from the coalman instead – never mind the expense and the shortages, despite the best efforts of the Bevin Boys conscripted to work in the mines. Many of the PoWs had been sent home now, although she'd heard some had chosen to stay.

The blaze in her grate was too paltry to warm the whole room; she could only feel the heat if she stood directly in front of it and then it burned her shins while the back of her body felt colder than ever.

Still, she sat in her slip and studied herself in the mirror. She hadn't the energy to pull on her nightdress and dressing gown yet. Although she would get up eventually to do that, so she could climb underneath the eiderdowns and counterpanes piled up on top of her bed. A reversal of the princess and the pea – she'd be buried by the soft mountain instead of sleeping on top of it.

She sipped her gin – was this her fourth or fifth? – and studied her face. She was thirty-one. She still looked young; she could easily be mistaken for a girl in her early twenties. She could see small lines at the corners of her eyes. She was pale from the winter – and looked more so with the shock of red lipstick she'd applied before going out – but her face wasn't unattractive. She was quite pretty still, really. She tried to think of Reggie, who'd be home soon, but she felt nothing.

The cold had leached into her bones and she shivered. She'd have a bath before climbing into bed, she decided, and crossed the landing to run the tub.

Naked, lying in the shallow water as it slowly filled, she continued to assess herself as she drank more gin. Her body was fine, although she would need to be a little bit curvier to have the hourglass shape she'd always strived for. Her breasts and stomach showed only minimum damage from the baby that claimed them once, and the stretch marks on her flat belly had faded to nearly invisible white lines; tiny folds in her skin like a secret.

If there was no one to *see* her, to speak to her, and to love her, did she really exist?

34

There was a whirling, rushing sound; and on the wall were
strange shadows of horses with flying manes . . .
'Oh, they are only dreams,' said the crow.
From *The Snow Queen*

I heard her go from the bathroom to her bedroom. She'd have a nap. It wasn't yet midday but Mother often slept during the daytime. I was jealous of the way she could sleep – so deeply, so untroubled by monsters. But it was nice to think of her sleeping peacefully upstairs.

I turned back to my *Boy's Own* comic on the kitchen table. I didn't read fairy tales any more. I blamed them, somehow, for the lies that came so easily to me when I was younger. Stuff about Trolls and woodcutters and other nonsense. I felt embarrassed, ashamed about all of it. Lies were like stories; and both were dangerous.

But maybe the stories in those old books weren't *all* lies. Maybe monsters did exist. I'd seen them. I'd seen them in real life. And I was being haunted by them in my dreams, too.

The nightmares took over from the stories in a strange way.

When Gerda in *The Snow Queen* was trying to find Kai, she spoke to the roses to find out if he was lying dead in the earth where their roots were. I didn't need to speak to the roses; I knew exactly what was down there. Those cold bodies rotting in the ground were monsters who wanted me down there with them.

The man in the mine would whimper for me, calling my name. His hand bursting up through a muddy marsh, blades of grass stuck to his grimy skeletal fingers, clutching at my feet as I tried to walk over where he lay.

Or else it was another beast, with matted black hair, looking into my soul with its red eyes as its head exploded under the impact of a wooden bat. Its eyes remained fixed on me, even as the flesh was beaten away from around the sockets. Sometimes, as it died, it looked at me as though *I* was the monster, and that was the worst of all.

I liked it when I cried out, because that woke me up.

She must have heard me, but she never came. Never mentioned it.

Did she pull the covers over her ears? Burrow down into her bed to drown me out?

That night, watching her curved back as she sat hunched over on the stairs; that was another nightmare that tormented me sometimes. She just sat there, silent, unseeing, even when I stood in front of her. And when I tried to touch her, to make her see me, my hands floated through her because she didn't exist any more – or was it just that I didn't exist to her?

The terrors in my own mind were punishing me because I deserved it. I deserved sometimes to wake up screaming and covered in hot stinking urine because of that hand coming for me out of the ground.

I jumped up from the table now and ran upstairs as though I could escape my own thoughts.

Her door wasn't shut because of the mess on the floor, so I crept in to look at her sleeping. She looked so peaceful. I quite liked the idea of being snowed in together. We could make the cottage cosy and warm inside. I thought maybe we might be able to begin again in our little house buried beneath the whiteness. Everything looked like a fairy tale in the snow, didn't it?

I couldn't bear to think of the stories themselves, but I still missed our story-times. I couldn't ask her to begin reading to me again, but I wondered if there was another way I could bring her back to me. Maybe I should remind her of those evenings; I knew she'd enjoyed them too. Then I remembered her Darlings, and how much she'd loved them. If I reminded her of that, perhaps she'd remember how she only felt that way about them because she'd wanted a real-life Darling. She'd wanted *me*.

A couple of the dolls were on top of the bookshelves in my bedroom. Maybe I should bring them down? She'd be so happy to see them – it was bound to cheer her up. I rushed across the hall into my room and dragged the wicker chair over to the shelves so I could stand on it. One of the Darlings was too far back for me to reach, but I was able to grab hold of the dusty skirt of a porcelain doll. I pulled it down and sat on my bed to clean it up a bit. It must have been up there for years. Dust and cobwebs had knotted together to form thin strands of grey that fell like hair across the doll's pale pink face. I licked my thumb and then rubbed at the porcelain to reveal blue glass eyes looking up at me, and a tiny painted rosebud mouth. I brushed the worst of the dust from the doll's blonde ringlets and faded pink pinafore dress. Then I took it into Mother's room.

She was still sleeping, beneath a pile of blankets and clothes. Part of the pile had slipped off to one corner of the bed, and I propped the Darling up there so she'd see it when she woke.

I'd go back downstairs in a minute and make a pot of tea, but I'd just stay and watch her for a moment longer. Her dark hair was spilling across the white pillow, and her face was closed and beautiful.

Sometimes, I felt as though I'd spent my entire life waiting for her to open her eyes and see me.

35

*In the middle of that enormous snow hall was a frozen lake.
It had cracked into thousands of pieces and every one of
them was shaped exactly like all the others. In the middle
of the lake was the throne of the Snow Queen.*

From *The Snow Queen*

The snow was burying the house. The snow was burying her. It
would keep climbing higher and higher up the walls, the windows,
silently packing the cottage away. It would be dark. Would air be
able to get in, through the sealed windows and doors? She cried
out as she sat up in bed. After her bath she'd pulled on layers
of clothes that almost at once felt suffocating. She pulled at the
scratchy woollen neck of her jumper.

Air! She needed air.

She struggled against the blankets, fighting them as they tied
her down like ropes. The gin sloshed in her belly, her head was
heavy, and she felt sick. As she fought to get out of bed she saw
something from the corner of her eye and screamed. The unblink-
ing face of a Darling was staring back at her. Annabel couldn't
understand. She reached over to grab her dolly. Her Darling's
ice-blue eyes seemed to sear into her soul; and the lack of love
inside her was laid bare. Her Darling knew who she was beneath
all the pretending: an unfaithful wife, a traitor, a bad and neglect-
ful mother. But she'd have to go on pretending for ever, because
Reggie was coming home. There'd be no end to it.

The walls closed in around her and she fell out of bed onto the cluttered carpet. She flung the Darling aside and pushed the empty glasses and dirty plates out of her way as she crawled to the door. She was suffocating. The room was getting smaller. She needed to get outside – she needed to breathe fresh, cold air – because now her lungs were constricting too.

She gripped the banisters as she staggered, panting, down the stairs. Couldn't breathe.

Something was wrong with the front door; it wouldn't open. She pulled and tugged at the latch but it wouldn't budge. The doorframe had swollen from the onslaught of snow or else ice had frozen the lock solid. With a frustrated cry she ran to the back door in the kitchen; it might be easier to *push* a door open.

But the snow had already piled up against it and she couldn't force that one open either. She slammed into it again and again as she tried to escape.

'Let me out!' she cried. 'Let me out!'

'Mother?'

She spun around. The boy was standing in the kitchen doorway, looking at her across the room. His eyes were wide and he looked frightened.

'Help me! I have to get out. Help me.' And she turned back to use her whole body to fight the snow again, ramming her shoulder into the door. 'Can't breathe.'

The boy didn't move at first, but then he was next to her and began to help her push. The snow was more than a yard high from the wind-drift but at last it began to give a little. He pushed his small arm through the gap they'd made and scooped snow away from the door. When he brought his arm back inside, his jumper was crusted with ice and his hand blazed red with cold. She threw herself against the door with renewed panic and he stepped away.

Finally there was a gap big enough for her to wriggle through. She started to squeeze outside.

'Your feet!'

She looked down and saw her stockinged toes at the bottom of her thick trousers. Clumsily, still only just managing to keep her panic at bay, she pushed past him into the hall and rammed her feet into the shoes she'd left lying there earlier, then lunged to grab a coat from the stand.

'Where are you going?'

His voice sounded strange, she thought, as though a hand was around his throat squeezing it tightly. But she turned her attention back to the buttons on her coat.

'Need . . . air.'

She stumbled back towards the door.

'Going to walk. Need to move around.'

'But it's going to snow again!'

'I have to— Got to get some air. I'll be all right after a walk. Got to get out.'

She twisted her head as she slipped sideways through the crack, and found herself looking at her son as he watched her go. His face slipped from view as she escaped from the dark stuffy house into the clean white snow.

The sharp air cut her throat and lungs and she began to cry. As she wept, she felt her teardrops turning to ice.

36

The Snow Queen flew away and Kai was left alone
in the endless hall.
From *The Snow Queen*

It was very quiet when she was gone. The snow didn't just look like cotton wool – it seemed to work like it too, because it made it hard for me to hear anything. I thought I should probably leave the door open for Mother, so she could get back in again. But it was so cold. My arm hurt from when I'd pushed it into the snow and I rubbed at my hand to help the feeling come back into my frozen fingers. The cold was streaming in through the gap in the door like an icy river that would flood the house. So I pulled it closed and then it became even quieter.

I backed away from the slushy puddle on the kitchen floor. I was shivering.

Where was she going? I ran into the sitting room and climbed up onto the windowsill to see out above the line of snow. She'd already made it through the gate onto the lane. I took down the net curtain so I could see more clearly. She was stumbling like she was ill, but I guessed it was just that she was struggling to keep upright on the mounds of snow and ice. She was heading towards the forest. I watched until I couldn't see her any more. The sky was grey; the shade of dirty snow, hovering between light and dark, even though it was only early afternoon. Nights ate up winter days though; it'd be pitch black by tea time.

I went upstairs to peel off my wet clothes and gasped as the air hit my bare chest. My teeth were chattering as I pulled two jumpers over my head. They were too small for me so I had to wrestle with them to get dressed. Then I wrapped my eiderdown around me like a cloak and went down to the sitting room to build up the fire and wait for her. She'd need my help to get back in.

I was too restless to read or even to listen to the wireless. So I just waited in the silence for her muffled footsteps. I dozed, now and then. After a while, I crossed to the window to see if I could see her coming. But there was just a vast, empty white world. So I went back to my eiderdown nest in the armchair.

Snowflakes began to fall again. They weren't delicate flecks but big and solid – each piece a cluster of several flakes frozen together – and they stormed down furiously.

The thick flurries meant I could barely see to the end of the garden gate when I climbed up to look out of the window now. But I knew that the endless whiteness I'd seen earlier was steadily growing and spreading. I sat down again. I'd just have to wait until I heard her banging at the door. She'd be home from her walk soon; nobody would stay out in that.

I stoked the fire, and watched the flickering flames.

After a while, it became too dark to see the snow falling. I switched on the side table light and suddenly I could only see myself and the room reflected in the black glass. It was odd, this mirror image; like looking into another world with another me in it. It looked the same, but different. It looked warm and cosy because of the fire, and the yellowy light of the lamp.

If she'd turned back as soon as the snow started, then surely she should be home by now. Was that right? I tried to work out the timing in my head. How long had she been gone before the snow fell? I wasn't sure, but that amount of time must have passed already, so if she walked in a line then turned around when the snow came, then . . . Ah, but I hadn't calculated for the deeper drifts she'd be walking through, and the thick snow cluttering up the air, which would make it harder to see. And then, I hadn't thought about where she'd have ended up. Maybe she was still there. She'd gone towards the forest. Perhaps she was sheltering under some evergreens until the blizzard passed. Or – unlikely; I never wanted to go there again – but maybe she'd gone to the cabin, the shed, to think about . . . him. Perhaps she was waiting inside, and would set off when the snow stopped. Maybe she'd even gone to Farmer Dawson's house – overcoming her usual pains to avoid him, so she could wait in the warm? That made sense. That's what she must have done. I leaned back in the chair, the eiderdown around my shoulders.

But I couldn't settle. I was ready to jump up as soon as I heard her. But the snow didn't stop and she didn't come.

I waited and waited. Something was gnawing at my insides now. This waiting, these feelings . . . I was waiting for her to come back, just like Hansel had once waited for me. I couldn't bear to think about that so I got up again, climbing onto the windowsill to look outside. I squinted, trying to spot her white face in the dark of the night, or her dark coat against the white of the snow. But I couldn't see either of these things.

I went to the kitchen to check I hadn't somehow missed her going around to the back garden. She wasn't there either. I returned to my post at the armchair.

Oh! What I was thinking? What if she was hurt? Lying somewhere with a sprained ankle? I remembered how she'd stumbled and how slippery the snow was. And all the while, I was just sitting here in an armchair in front of the fire. I had to get outside; I had to look for her. An old thought – the sort of thought I hadn't had since I was nine – jumped into my head: I could save her!

It was an effort to get last year's winter coat over my layers of clothes, and my boots felt too small as well, but I tugged them on impatiently. I pulled on my woolly hat and gloves. I'd find her! I'd help her home.

I struggled with the front door until I realised it wouldn't open, then ran to the kitchen. But I slammed into the back door as I pushed down the handle, expecting to run straight through into the garden; the old snow we'd managed to push back slightly had collapsed and fallen back against the door, and mounds and mounds of new snow on top of that now held it closed like a vice.

Using the weight of my whole body, I threw myself against it, as if I were a ball bouncing against a brick wall, but that's just what it felt like; like I was slamming against bricks and concrete. I started to panic and shoved, using all my strength, groaning as I strained to make it move. I thought of how I'd found Mother doing this, just hours earlier. I began to cry as I remembered how it had taken two of us to get the door open just a little way. Now there was only me.

I cursed myself for being so small and scrawny, and I cursed myself for all that wasted time when I'd just sat there and allowed the snow to shut me in. Then I remembered the windows – but the downstairs ones opened outwards and were almost completely covered by snow too. I ran from room to room upstairs – thinking I could jump out, since my landing would be cushioned – but the same thing that stopped the front door from working must have happened to them, too. They were frozen shut. Should I smash one? Mother would be very angry when she found out. And it would let in the cold and snow and the house would be freezing, and we wouldn't be able to get it fixed until the snow disappeared and the village went back to normal. In any case, if I jumped onto the snow, wouldn't I be heavy enough to sink down into it? It would be up over my head – how could I walk around in that and hope to bump into Mother? No. I wouldn't be able to get out and find her. She'd have to make her own way home, because it would certainly take the two of us – one pushing, one pulling at a door or window – to get her inside.

*

I didn't mean to sleep – I didn't think I'd be able to – but I must have drifted off. When I woke up, my neck hurt from where my head had laid awkwardly against the armrest. It was dark, apart from the lamp next to me. It was still night then, and Mother had still not come home. I looked at the window. The snow now completely covered the glass and was a lighter colour at the top, with an almost blue-ish tinge to it. Why was that? I didn't realise until I went to the toilet upstairs. It wasn't dark outside at all. It was a new day.

It was cold in the house; the fire in the sitting room was just embers. But I shivered because of the feeling inside me, which was colder than the icy air in the bathroom. She'd been gone all night.

As I watched, it began to snow again. I pictured Mother in Farmer Dawson's house, or in a cottage on the lane, after she'd reluctantly agreed to spend the night. She might be looking at the weather herself somewhere right now, and saying to somebody, 'Well, I can't set out just yet, I'll wait until later – I'm sure it'll clear up soon.' Not everyone in the village had a telephone, so probably she had no way to let me know she was safe. I thought of the telephone as I trudged back downstairs, trailing my eiderdown cloak behind me. I didn't want to worry any of my grandparents, but ... She'd been gone all night. A sudden urge gripped me to hear Granny's comforting voice. She wouldn't be able to help really, all that way away in Norfolk, but she might know what I should do. And she would be someone to talk to, while I waited for Mother to arrive.

I'd never actually placed a call on the telephone, but I knew how to do it. I started to feel better now I had some sort of plan. I'd telephone Granny, build up the sitting-room fire, then eat breakfast. I picked up the receiver.

'Hello, operator?'

The line was dead. I pumped the buttons a couple of times, making the tinny bell ring inside it, then tried again. 'Operator? ... Operator? Are you there?'

Nothing. Just static that crackled and sounded like a storm.

'Hello? Can you hear me? Operator?'

That was that, then. The snow must've brought the telephone lines down. How could the flimsy wires, the frail wooden posts, survive it? Even if they could, how could the telephone operators get to the telephone exchange when the roads were blocked, and the trains couldn't run, and the whole country was shutting down?

I stayed looking at the useless telephone for a while. I didn't want to turn back to the gloomy room and think about what I had to do – make the fire, and get some food, and wait for Mother. She thought she could slip out and get home in time, but she'd misjudged it, and now it might be a few days before I saw her again. My teeth began chattering and I wasn't really sure if it was because I was frightened, or because I was cold.

I'd be here alone, without her. That was something I'd been terrified of my whole life. Everything I'd done, all those terrible things when I was nine, all of it was for her; I just wanted to stop her leaving me.

37

❦

He sat pondering his patterns of ice, thinking and thinking . . .
From *The Snow Queen*

The first few days I fell into a sort of routine. I'd get up to make the fire, eat bread and butter for breakfast – which I kept on the sideboard so I didn't have to go to the freezing kitchen – and would then pass the rest of the day trying to entertain myself, stopping for lunch and dinner when I got too bored, or too hungry. I made powdered eggs, nibbled on sandwiches and crackers, or would heat tinned tomatoes on the fire and eat them straight from the can.

I wandered aimlessly around the house. In Daddy's room, I remembered all the clothes he had in his wardrobe and pulled on some of his trousers, his jumpers – rolling up the legs and arms. They were more comfortable and I felt warmer. They didn't smell like him – they smelled of mothballs – but it was like being surrounded by him anyway. I wore his winter coat, and wrapped the eiderdown cloak around me.

I read. I listened to the wireless – singing along to big-band songs, and listening to the broadcasters talk about the snow, and how several programmes would have to be cancelled because nobody could get in to perform them. As the weather worsened, the wireless gradually stopped working. Occasionally, the lights went out and I remembered newscasters saying power stations were struggling to get enough coal to create electricity. That was all; nothing to be scared of, sitting there in a buried house alone in the dark. There was just one candle in the kitchen drawer, and it didn't last long. I hated the dark, the waiting, because I couldn't help thinking – was this how Hansel felt? Before he— Was this my punishment? Every now and then I checked the telephone, but it just crackled and hissed at me.

Once I ran up and down the stairs to keep warm. It worked, but then I got sweaty, which made my clothes feel cold against my skin as soon as I cooled down. There was still a fair bit of coal left, and I was glad Mother had thought to make me fill not just the three large scuttles, but several buckets next to the fire in case we weren't able to get outside to the coal cellar.

It wasn't long before I realised I should be rationing my food. I started skipping lunch. When the last of the bread turned mouldy I toasted it all on the fire and ate it in one go, with globs of icy butter on it to take away the rank taste. The meat was long gone, and only a few tins remained in the larder. I started skipping dinner.

Gradually, I stopped leaving the sitting room unless I really had to. It was too cold in the rest of the house; I might as well have been outside. It was better to stay down here, even though it was dark. I started peeing into a metal bucket that had once held coal, although I'd go up to use the toilet if I needed to do more than pee. But I didn't need to very often. My tummy was hard and swollen; nothing would come out. I wasn't eating enough, I suppose.

Sometimes I cried. Hating myself all the while; I was twelve, after all. It wasn't like I was a little boy.

If the cottages next door had been closer, I might have banged on the walls in the hope of hearing a comforting knock in reply. But no one would hear, so I didn't bother. The snowdrifts almost hid the houses opposite from view and I never saw anyone at the windows when I looked outside.

I slept a lot, curled up in the armchair. I dragged down

bedcovers from my mother's room as well as my own and slept beneath all of them. I stuffed towels against the bottom of the sitting-room door to stop the draught getting in through the crack. I did the same to the front door and the one into the back garden. I always slept all night and again for hours during the day. Whenever I woke up, I could feel the cold had somehow seeped inside my cocoon. The covers were so cold, they felt wet. I would squeeze them in my hands to try to tell if there was water in them. There was ice inside the windows in the mornings, and all day throughout the rest of the house. A large crack appeared in the pane of glass in the bathroom. I started skipping breakfast every other day. I thought about food a lot. Sometimes my tummy hurt and made strange noises.

It started to feel like hard work to get up for any reason, and it seemed to take longer and longer to get the fire started. My mind felt slow, foggy. I couldn't imagine how I'd had the energy to run up the stairs once, let alone several times in a row for no reason. When was that? A week ago? Two? I started to count the days in my head but got muddled and gave up. Of all the food we'd had in the house, only a small knob of butter was left now. It froze solid each night after the fire died as I slept. Every other day I chipped at it in the mornings and ate the pieces that flaked off. I sucked them so they'd melt, and the taste would make my mouth water even though I was eating.

It was strange, but I didn't really feel the cold any more. My fingers looked almost blue whenever I took my gloves off, but I couldn't feel them at all. I might have taken some of my layers off, if only I had the energy.

One day, I forced myself to the kitchen to fill my jugs with water to take back to the sitting room. I was so tired that day, it seemed easier to crawl rather than walk, although it was difficult with the eiderdown around my shoulders and my baggy clothes, and with two jugs hooked over the fingers of one hand. When I finally reached the sink and stood up to turn on the tap, nothing came out. I stared at it. Turned it off, then on again – all the way round, as far as it would go. The pipes had frozen. Of course they had. It was a wonder they hadn't before.

I felt so tired I couldn't even force myself back to the relative warmth of the sitting room. I sat down on the floor and watched my white breath as it puffed in front of my face, like tiny clouds. I wondered if I would die. I wondered how that made me feel.

After a while I dragged myself back to my chair in front of the fire. There didn't seem anything else to do. Should I write Mother a note? Explain I'd tried my best. That I didn't blame her. That I hoped she was getting on all right at whoever's house she was staying in. I could write to Daddy, too, and Granny and Grandpa and my other grandparents. I could leave the letters out on the sideboard, just in case. But I was so sleepy. I'd have a little nap first.

. . . Snow is just frozen water, isn't it? I thought when I woke up. The house was surrounded by water. There was water everywhere.

I fetched a rolling pin from the kitchen and climbed the stairs. Dragging myself up as if it were a mountain. I didn't have much energy, and I was slow – but I was thirsty. Thirst was more powerful than hunger, I discovered. Snow hadn't quite covered the whole cottage and there was still some natural light upstairs. I gripped the rolling pin in my gloved hands and banged the end of it against the crack in the bathroom window. Thoughts of Mother being angry about the broken glass didn't worry me now.

I felt dizzy and had to rest by sitting on the side of the bath for a minute. It was all right; I just hadn't recovered from climbing the stairs, that was all. This plan would let more cold in, but it was a plan and it was good. I'd pile snow up high onto a tray and carry it downstairs to put in jugs and bowls and saucepans. I hadn't thought to bring a tray up with me. No matter, I'd use a picture frame that was hanging up on the landing. After a while I attacked the window again and the glass finally broke after a few more tries. I punched a hole through it with the baton, and the glass was mashed into the snow behind the pane. I pulled the shards out and dropped them into the sink. Then I scooped a handful of snow into my mouth. I took another handful, and another. It took a long time to quench my thirst; a mouthful of snow did not turn into a mouthful of water. But it meant I probably wouldn't die. Not yet, anyway. I wondered how that made me feel. It was cold and I felt ice coating my throat as I swallowed. And I did it again, and again, drinking the snow until I felt like I was made of it.

38

She was the Snow Queen! . . . 'Are you still cold?' she asked, and kissed his forehead. Her kiss was colder than ice. It went right to his heart . . . He felt as though he were about to die.

From *The Snow Queen*

The snow was melting. I supposed that was good. The wireless started playing again, but the serious-sounding announcers in London spoke of terrible flooding across the country as yards of snow turned to water in the roads and snowmelt ran into rivers that burst their banks. They described cars floating down the streets like boats, while houses lost their ground floors to the rising floods. Entire herds of sheep and cattle were dead, as the animals froze or starved or drowned. Quite a lot of people had probably died the same way, I thought, but I switched the wireless off because I didn't want to hear about that. Densford River was not far away, but Bambury was high up with old mines beneath it and I didn't think flooding would be a problem here.

I was tired all the time. I didn't know why I was so exhausted when I was barely doing anything. Clearing out the ashes and making a new fire each morning seemed harder and took longer each new day. I decided to leave the wireless on all the time, so I didn't have to get up to turn it on or off – even if they did say things I didn't want to hear. Voices came and went as the announcers made it into the studios or they didn't, and as the electricity worked or it didn't. When the voices weren't there, I listened to the static that sounded like a storm.

The butter was gone.

I had to use a ladle now to reach down to the snow as it sank away from the bathroom window. I was worried about what to do when I could no longer reach it. I knew I wouldn't have the strength to smash a downstairs window. Idly, I thought about using string to lash the ladle to a broom handle but it seemed complicated. My dreams were strange and dark and the monsters were there and I woke up thirsty.

Noises and banging. Silence. Noises and banging.

I pulled down the covers of my cocoon and listened. They were the noises of my dream; I snuggled back down. Rustling and shuffling sounds. Again, I pulled off the eiderdowns and blankets that covered my face so I could hear better. It seemed too much effort to sit up but I turned slightly so I could look towards the window.

Something black slammed into the glass through the snow, making me jump. The black thing moved from side to side in a big arc. Some light came in. The black thing was a gloved hand. The snow muffled the words, but I could hear voices. Suddenly I was looking across the room, through the window, into somebody's eyes. A pulled-up collar, and a pulled-down hat, meant that was all I could see of their face. The first face I'd seen for weeks.

The gloved hand knocked on the glass. The face shouted something. I thought I should say something back, but the shock of it, the tiredness, the cold – all of it seemed to weigh down heavy on me, making it hard to move.

Then there was a crashing noise. Smashing at the front door. So loud. I knew that sound: metal on wood. An axe. Chopping. Hansel?

It wasn't Hansel. It was a group of bundled-up men who forced open the sitting-room door when the towel twisted on the carpet briefly stopped its path.

'Not another one?' someone said, as they came in.

A sad sigh. 'Looks like it.' A man walked over to me and our eyes locked as he crossed the room. 'Christ, he's alive – check the rest of the house!' He rushed towards me. 'All right there, son? You all right?' His arm lifted me up. 'Easy does it. You're all right now.' He looked around and saw a bowl with a little water in it, and brought it to my mouth so I could drink.

'Who else is here, son?' he said.

I tried to shake my head.

The others filed back into the room as the man slid his other arm beneath my legs and picked me up. 'Easy does it,' he said again.

'Empty,' a voice said. I recognised the voice as Mr Higgins and I shuddered. This was the old Home Guard. 'No one else here. Place looks like a bomb's gone off in every room.'

'Christ. Have you been on your own this whole time, lad? How old are you?' I wanted to ask where my mother was, but had to close my eyes. He gave me a sort of squeeze. 'You'll be in a nice warm bed soon – in hospital. They've been out ploughing the roads so we'll get there all right.'

My eyes fluttered open again as he carried me through the hall, past the jagged shards of the front door, and out into the street. The bright white light bouncing off the snow and sky hurt my eyes.

Some other people were standing around. I recognised a couple of neighbours, who came to stare at me as I was helped into the passenger seat of a car. An old lady was lying in the back. I couldn't tell if she was dead.

'We've just a few more houses to check on this street and then I can take you both to Densford Hospital,' the man said, and shut the door.

I closed my eyes again.

'People have died,' the old lady said. 'The Home Guard told me. They've found them. Dead, in some of the houses.'

She started to cry. I didn't open my eyes.

'Goodness, you're so *thin*!' Granny said when she saw me. I'd forgotten a nurse had asked me for my grandparents' telephone number and hadn't realised they'd be coming until I saw them marching up the ward.

She sat on the starched white bed and I could smell lavender as she pulled me close. I tried to pull back, but she wouldn't let me, and then I stopped trying because it felt so nice to be squeezed by a warm person.

'You need fattening up,' she said softly, into my hair. Another hand began rhythmically tapping at my back and it was Grandpa, standing by the side of us.

'Brave lad,' he said. 'You're a good boy.'

I'd been asking all the doctors and nurses about Mother, but somebody must have already explained to my grandparents that she hadn't come home after her walk and there was still no news of her, because they didn't ask me any questions about where she was, even when they drove me back to the cottage to pack some things. They said I'd be staying with them in Great Yarmouth for a while.

The front door was boarded up with wood, so we walked around to get in at the back. The snow was still deep, but nowhere near as bad as it had been.

Granny gasped as I led them through the house on the way to my room. But she just smiled at me when I turned to look back at her, although Grandpa was pressing his lips together.

'It's a bit messy,' I said.

'Can't be helped,' Granny replied. 'Now, you get your clothes together. Grandpa will help you. I'm just going to check all the rooms and, er, see what needs doing.'

When she came back, she told Grandpa he'd probably want to have a look around because there were some odd jobs that he'd need to do.

'I had to break the bathroom window,' I said.

'I'll have a look,' he said.

Granny came over to look at the pile of clothes on my bed.

'Don't forget to look in Annabel's bedroom,' she said to Grandpa as he went out onto the landing, 'and the sitting room. There's, er, something you should take outside.'

I remembered the bucket filled with pee, and felt my face burning red with shame.

'Oh, I need to—'

'It's all right, Daniel, let Grandpa do it.' She sat down on my bed and began to fold my clothes. She looked at me but I went over to the window so I didn't have to see her face. 'You were a very clever boy,' she said. 'Very clever.'

Then I heard her tut.

'Daniel, these jumpers are far too small for you – even skinny as you are. And these trousers are no good either.' I heard her stand up. 'Come on, let's just go. Let's go and have lunch in the pub. We'll get you some new things in Great Yarmouth.'

So we went to the Royal Oak and all ordered shepherd's pie and, while we were waiting for it to come, it suddenly occurred to me that if Mother hadn't left when she did, there probably wouldn't have been enough food for us both to survive. I decided to ask about her.

'Have they checked all the houses yet? You know, for Mother?'

'Um, I'm not sure, dear,' Granny said. 'I know everyone is looking for her, though.'

'I'm sure they'll find her soon,' Grandpa said. 'But . . . you might need to prepare yourself—'

'Grandpa's right. They'll find her. So there's no point worrying about any of that yet. Let's just concentrate on feeding you up, shall we?'

'All right.'

'Good. Because Daddy won't want to see you looking skinny as a rake! Not long now until the roads will be clear enough to go and get him. Won't it be wonderful to have him home?'

She looked at me strangely when I didn't answer.

'Daniel? You knew about that, didn't you? Did Mother get a chance to tell you before she... Anyway, Daddy's well enough to come home now.'

'I knew he was getting better.'

'Yes, he's much, much better. And as soon as the roads are clear enough, we'll all go and fetch him from the clinic. Isn't that wonderful?' She seemed to think for a moment. 'You and Daddy can both stay with us in Great Yarmouth for a little while. Then Grandpa and I can get your cottage shipshape for you, and you can both go home when it's ready.'

Was he really better? I wanted to ask if it was my daddy who was coming home, or the man with the shaking hands. But then the food came and I forgot to worry about it.

Daddy was like Daddy, in the end. But a sort of thinner, quieter version. I realised he might be thinking the same thing about me. We were both different now.

But he'd laughed and picked me up – right in the clinic foyer – when we walked in, even though I was furious and embarrassed and hissed 'I'm twelve!' at him. Secretly though, I liked it. Because I knew it meant he was back. When he shook Grandpa's hand, I noticed his own didn't tremble any more, and he kissed Granny's cheek and gave her a long hug and said he couldn't wait to come home.

We stayed with them for weeks. Daddy began to seem more and more like himself and I remembered more about him the longer he was back. It was funny how I'd forgotten little things, like how much we enjoyed arm wrestling together. We were both getting stronger in those games now, as Granny fed us up. Once, as I watched him across the dinner table, I realised he wasn't really a warrior, like I used to believe – at least, not in the way I used to think – he was just a man. He was my father. And I was so glad I was his son.

Harry, the boy who lived next door, came to knock for me after his mother bumped into Grandpa, who told her I was visiting. Granny sent him away, telling him I'd nearly died after fending for myself in the snow. After that he knocked every day, and when Granny finally decided I was well enough to play out, Harry kept telling me I was a hero.

Eventually, Daddy said it was time for us to go back to Bambury. Harry and I swapped addresses so we could be pen-pals. I felt sad to be leaving, but thought we should probably get back to the village, so Mother knew where to find us.

There was a new red front door on the cottage, and the inside was clean and tidy. It was strange to be returning home, to be walking into a house without Mother, but with Daddy instead.

He said I still wasn't quite strong enough to go back to school yet, even though it was March and the snow had nearly all gone.

'Another couple of days,' he said. 'Get your strength back.'

I was relieved because I thought I needed quite a lot of strength before I could face the boys at school.

So I was home when there was a knock on the new door, and when I opened it there was a policeman standing on the step. Horrifying images of the dead Troll and poor dead Hansel reared up in my mind, and with a sick lurch of guilt and shame I wondered if I was about to be arrested.

But he smiled at me politely and said: 'Hello, son. I think I'm after your father – Mr Patterson?'

Daddy came out into the hall. He looked at the bobby and then at me.

'Daniel, why don't you go and put the kettle on and make us all a nice cup of tea?' He turned back to the policeman, who was taking off his tall helmet, and showed him into the sitting room, shutting the door behind them.

I always listened at doors, always. But just then, I realised, I didn't want to. I'd make the tea, like Daddy asked. Because I thought I probably didn't want to know what the policeman had come to say. And if I made the tea, that was another five minutes, ten maybe, that I could not know.

And things would be the same in the world for that five minutes, or ten maybe, and Mother was in someone's house, but had broken her leg, and that person didn't have a telephone, and Mother had forgotten our number, and had lost her memory but it was just starting to come back, because she'd banged her head in the snow and—

No more stories. Make the tea. Take it through. Listen to the truth.

We already knew she had never gone to Farmer Dawson's. He'd been found alive, but weak, in his farmhouse after the snow started to thaw and he was taken to hospital the day after me. There was no sign of Mother anywhere on the farm or out in the orchard. Farmer Dawson had pneumonia and he died. One of the nurses had told me, when I asked about him. It made me feel guilty to think it, but I felt a horrid flash of relief; one less person who knew what happened that I'd have to see around the village.

I called out at the sitting-room door so Daddy could open it and let me in. I put down the tray and poured three cups. I forgot to ask the policeman how much milk he liked, and if he took sugar. It didn't matter because the cups sat untouched, steaming, on the table.

'It's not good news, I'm afraid, Daniel,' Daddy said. 'It's Mother.'

He looked at me to make sure I understood what he was saying. He looked sad and tired.

I wondered if I was supposed to say something, but I didn't know what to say so I stayed quiet.

He glanced across at the policeman, who looked down at a small black pad he had clasped in his hands. I think Daddy hoped the policeman would start talking to me instead, but he didn't, so Daddy cleared his throat and carried on.

'She was . . . Somebody found her. In the woods.'

I remembered the magic, the golden light and the fairy dust that I'd once daydreamed into the forest. And then I thought of the darkness in there; the darkness that was real, because I'd really seen it. When Mother disappeared, the woods weren't magical. They were cold and dark and filled with the dead.

'A man found her. She was lying down. She looked very peaceful.' He cleared his throat again and looked at the policeman. 'That's right, isn't it?'

'Oh yes. Yes. Very peaceful. Frozen in the snow, just like she was asleep.' He half lifted his pad, as if to show me. As if that was written down in there.

'She was quite a long way from home,' Daddy said, after a while. 'She was very deep in the forest. I suppose she went for a walk, maybe she got lost and sat down – maybe she got tired or confused – but that was the worst thing she could do, of course, because . . .'

I nodded. My eyes were dry. Inside my head though, there was a loud, screaming noise, like the kettle boiling.

I thought of ice crystals forming along her eyelashes. I thought of her lips turning blue. I remembered how I watched Hans kiss those lips for the first time. It was so beautiful.

'Where was she?' It was hard to believe she hadn't been found in the orchard. It seemed as though that would make sense.

'Oh, a long way away.' Daddy sighed, looking at the policeman, who nodded. 'She was almost on the other side of the woods. Almost at Densford.'

'Oh.'

I remembered the story she'd told Hansel once. About the time she wanted to get on a train more than anything else in the world. How she'd run away from me when I was a baby in the cottage and begun to make her way to Bambury Station. Well, Bambury's tiny station had already been closed for days when she left during the snow, but trains were still running from Densford Station then.

292

Was she trying to get there? She might have had some money in her coat pockets. Was she trying to find a train to take her away? Was she going to disappear somewhere, or perhaps head to Liverpool to try to find Hansel? Or was it just meaningless chance she'd been found at that particular spot? Perhaps she'd just been walking mindlessly, not caring where she ended up, because she was planning to head back home. Or was lying down in the snow always part of the plan?

'Do you ... do you want to ask anything else, Daniel?'

I shook my head. I would never know what I wanted to know.

'All right. Well then, the constable's here from Densford Police Station. He very kindly came to tell us about Mother. It's nothing to worry about – just a formality – but you were the last person to see her, so he just wants to ask you a couple of questions.'

Daddy must have seen something wild in my eyes. Because he rushed to reassure me again and the policeman joined in; it was just because he needed to write it in his pad to show the sergeant, that was all. I didn't want to get him in trouble with his boss, did I?

But I was thinking how I'd killed Hansel, and how I'd killed the Troll, and now I was wondering if I'd killed Mother, too.

He asked me about the moments before she left the house, and I told him how I'd helped her open the door; I'd helped her get out. It was a relief to say the words to him.

The policeman didn't seem particularly angry about that though, and he peeled back the black elastic strip that held his pad closed and wrote something down and then thanked me and stood up to leave.

Daddy followed him into the hall to see him out and I stayed in the armchair I'd once lived in and looked at the three cold cups of tea on the table. I wasn't sure how I felt. Sad, of course, but no sadder than I'd been before, really.

'Thank you, sir,' I heard the policeman say out in the hallway. 'I'm, er, so sorry for your loss.'

293

'Thank you. It is a bit of a shock, but well – I think we were sort of expecting it, to be honest. After all this time.' I heard the sound of the front door opening. 'Can I ask? Where is she now?'

'Oh, she's at the funeral home in Densford, sir. The dog-walker found her early this morning and reported it straight away, so we sent some officers to get her immediately.'

'Ah, I see. Thank you.'

'They got more than they bargained for, actually. Because as they walked through the woods – they were coming from the Densford side – they found a, well, a sort of sinkhole.'

'A sinkhole?'

'Yes, you know, down into one of the old mines, I suppose. You know how people always say it's dangerous around there? Seems there was something in it, after all. This was about a fifteen-minute, twenty-minute walk from where we found your wife. They had to go all the way back with the stretcher and come back again with ropes so they were all tied together for safety.'

'Oh. Goodness.'

'Yes. They've cordoned that whole area off now. To be honest—' he dropped his voice, 'it was too late for somebody.'

'What do you mean?'

'They looked down into the hole and saw, well, bones. From years ago. You know: a skeleton.'

My whole body began shaking, as though the winter had returned. I closed my eyes. They'd found him.

'Good lord!' Daddy said. 'Well, thanks again for—'

'They reckon they know who it is, too. Or was, I should say.'

'Who?'

'That PoW they never found.' There was a moment of silence. Perhaps Daddy just looked at the constable blankly, or maybe he shook his head to show he didn't know what the policeman was talking about. 'There was a PoW who ran away during the war. They looked for him everywhere. Had the Home Guard and us lot out looking for him, out at the stations, checking cars on the roads and all sorts. This explains it. There'll be a proper investigation – they went back and brought him up earlier this afternoon – but he was wearing a PoW shirt, and no one else has been reported missing in these parts so it must be him.'

I wondered if Mother had seen the hole too, and finally realised what had happened to Hansel. Was that why she lay down in the snow? But that didn't quite make sense. Because she'd have wanted to lie closer to him, wouldn't she? And that thick snow would have probably made it hard to see the mineshaft, unless she'd been right on top of it – and then she'd have fallen down herself.

Daddy made a couple more mild noises of surprise, then thanked the constable again and said goodbye.

From the window I watched the policeman walk down the path, get into his car and drive away. Daddy came to stand behind me and I felt his hands on my shoulders. He probably felt me shaking.

'There was nothing you could have done. It was nobody's fault. Not even Mother's.'

I nodded, but couldn't stop looking at the empty road that led towards the forest. She nearly found the woodcutter. She nearly found her prince again.

39

Little Kai was blue — indeed, almost black — from the cold; but he did not feel it, for the Snow Queen had kissed all feeling of coldness out of him, and his heart had almost turned into a lump of ice.

From *The Snow Queen*

Not long before Mother's funeral – which had been delayed for weeks so the ground could thaw – there was another knock at the door. Two policemen stood on our doorstep. Both wore similar brown suits and trilby hats.

I wouldn't have known they were policemen, but Daddy could tell, because he told me who they were when he looked out of the window after hearing the knock. I came to look and saw something in their faces that made me think Daddy was probably right.

I felt very, very calm.

Daddy went to open the door and they came into the sitting room, holding their hats in their hands.

'Am I being arrested?' I asked.

'What?' One of the men, the older of the two, laughed. 'Arrested? No, son, you're not being arrested.'

He looked at Daddy, who smiled and shook his head. 'I'm sorry. It's been a difficult time. The last time a policeman came here, he told us about my wife . . .' Both the men nodded at this; yes, they knew all about it. 'And I'm afraid Daniel seems to be blaming himself.'

'Oh!' The policemen said together as they both looked over at me.

'No, no, no,' the older the one said.

'You mustn't,' the younger one said.

'Look,' said the one with grey hair. 'My name's DDI Stephen Taylor. DDI means I'm the divisional detective inspector. It's true I'm here because I have to ask you a couple of questions, but you haven't done anything wrong!' He gave a little laugh. The other one nodded.

'Is it about my wife?' Daddy asked. 'Why do you need to speak to Daniel?'

'Perhaps we could have a word with you first, sir? In private?'

'Of course. Daniel, will you—'

'No – do you know what?' the detective said. 'I've had a better idea. Let's all go and have a chat somewhere else. Would that be better? I don't want to bring back memories of the last visit. Would you like to go to see the police station, son? See the cells? Oh dear! Your face! No, no, we don't have to. Not at all. Is there a little cafe round here? We could go and have a ginger beer? Or a hot drink?'

Daddy nodded uncertainly. 'Um, there's the pub.'

'Even better! Why don't you go and sit in the police car, son, and we'll all come out in a minute and go to the pub. See? Nothing to worry about. Nothing whatsoever.'

I pulled on my coat and went outside like I was told and then after a few minutes Daddy and the policemen walked to the car and we drove down the High Street to the Royal Oak.

'A beer garden, fantastic,' Detective Taylor said when he saw the sign outside. 'I know it's a bit chilly, but let's sit in the fresh air, shall we? I expect we'll have it all to ourselves as well which will be a bonus.'

We were well into spring now, but there were still traces of that strange, terrible winter in the air. A breeze on my face felt like it could have tiny specks of ice in it, and the sky was grey and gloomy.

297

He wasn't how I would have imagined a detective to be. I'd probably have pictured a smooth private eye like Sam Spade. But this man was jokey and chunky, his grey hair thin and wispy. And he had an accent, northern or Welsh, I wasn't sure.

He and Daddy had been talking about PoWs in the car, and as we walked around the back of the pub to the beer garden, he said: 'It's amazing how many of them are still here – they don't want to leave! It's the same up and down the country. They made friends while they were here. I know a chap – not from these parts – whose family had two of them round for Christmas Day. During the war this was! Everyone in his village all had one or two prisoners for the day so the PoWs could have a proper family Christmas! Have you ever heard the like?!'

My eyes watered. If Hansel hadn't escaped, would that idea have been floated in Bambury, too? Would we have been able to have him spend the day with us, me and Mother, in our little cottage? It seemed unlikely, now I thought about it; many of the villagers were already turning against the PoWs, even before Hansel ran away.

We sat down at a wrought-iron table and Detective Taylor sent the other policeman inside to order our drinks.

'All right,' the policeman said, finally. 'I expect you're wondering what all of this is about.'

He folded his hands on the table and leaned towards me, looking serious all of a sudden.

'Now, I don't know if you know about this, but a PoW escaped a few years ago. Not long before the end of the war – about eight months before VE Day.'

'Yes,' I said. I meant: Yes, it was me. Yes, I helped him escape. Yes, I killed him. But my throat strangled my words before they could come out.

He nodded. 'Good. Now . . .' He pulled out a large rolled-up envelope from his jacket pocket and smoothed it flat on the table.

'I want to show you a photograph of this PoW. His name was

298

Johannes Müller. I want you to tell me if you've ever seen him before.'

The policeman started to fiddle with the envelope, which I could see was filled with some papers. He glanced up at Daddy. 'They went to all the camps and took lots of photographs of the PoWs,' he said. 'Documenting it all. Magazines and newspapers, but government and Red Cross photographers too. They keep everything in the archives at the Imperial War Museum – it's not just about the Great War any more – so I went there and found this. It's fascinating really – photographs of PoWs watching concerts in barns, and working in factories, the men in their camps and—'

'There's a photograph? Of Hans?'

Daddy and the policeman both looked at me in surprise.

'Sounds like you did know him then,' the detective said, and he pulled out a stiff piece of paper from his envelope. 'See for yourself.'

The sheet began trembling as soon as it passed from his hand to mine across the iron table top. Perhaps he thought I was just shaking because of the cold.

I gazed down at the blurry black-and-white image. Two men stood side by side. A little hut just visible behind them.

'One's the PoW, but I'm not sure who the other—'

'It's Farmer Dawson!' I let out a funny little noise not unlike a laugh. I hadn't seen Hans's face for years, and of course the farmer was dead too now, but here they both were.

Neither was smiling, because of the formality of having their photograph taken. But Farmer Dawson looked relaxed, as though he'd been laughing just before the shutter snapped. And Hans. My woodchopper-prince. His handsome face was stiff, turned slightly away from the camera's eye.

They were standing quite close to each other, their hands by their sides. Hans's hands were tight little fists. He hadn't wanted his photograph taken. Perhaps that was why Farmer Dawson had been laughing. Perhaps he and the photographer had been teasing him.

They were both in short-sleeved shirts, so it must have been a warm day. I never heard Hans mention that a photographer had come, so perhaps it was not long after he arrived in Bambury, before his life became tangled with mine and my mother's.

'Thank you,' I said, as though he had given me the photograph to keep. It felt like a gift.

I felt a strange pang that I couldn't show the photograph to Mother.

I ran my finger over his stern-looking expression.

'Ah, yes, I thought that might be the farmer. He's passed away now, hasn't he? The prisoner's name and his PoW number were in the caption, although Mr Dawson didn't get a mention!' He looked at Daddy and chuckled. 'Shame, really. I could've done with speaking to him.'

He turned to me. 'So I take it you knew this PoW? Hans, you called him?'

I looked back down at his face in the photograph. 'Yes.'

'Daniel,' Daddy nudged me slightly in the shoulder, 'tell the detective how you knew him; where you met him.'

Just then, the younger policeman came out with a tray. He had a cup of cocoa for me, and beers for everyone else.

Daddy nudged me again.

'Mother and I . . . We . . . Hans was a woodchopper. He sold wood for Farmer Dawson.'

'Ah, yes, we knew he sold wood. But we didn't know your mother was one of his customers. Were you always with your mother, or did she sometimes go alone?'

I nodded.

'Sometimes alone?'

I nodded again. I couldn't look Daddy in the eye. It felt terrible to be speaking about Mother and Hans with him right next to me. But I wouldn't tell any more lies. I wouldn't tell any more stories. That's what I'd just decided. If someone asked me for the truth, I'd tell it to them.

'Was she frightened of him, son? Did she ever say anything about it? Did she suddenly stop going? Did she make a complaint against him to the farmer? Or maybe she saw him the day he disappeared – do you remember?'

I looked up in shock. 'Frightened?'

'I'm sorry to upset you, son. I think your mum must've not mentioned it so as not to worry you.' He gave me a funny, sad little smile and then gave the same look to Daddy, who patted my back. 'We think he robbed your mother. Grabbed a necklace from around her neck. Maybe he stole it before he ran away – he was probably going to sell it. We found it on him, you see. A necklace, a silver locket, with your mum's name and birthday engraved on the back.'

'Oh, no!' I shook my head.

'I'm sorry to have to tell you this. Did he seem dangerous, violent? Were you frightened of him?'

'No! No!' I was aware I was almost shouting.

'All right, Daniel,' Daddy said. 'We'll get all this straightened out, and they're going to give us Mother's necklace back. No need to get upset. Look, calm down. Why don't you have some of your drink before it gets cold?'

So I sipped from my cup, careful not to spill any on the photograph I was still holding in my other hand, and the chocolate was dark and bitter and scalded my tongue.

'You've got him all wrong,' I said.

'Maybe she lost the necklace?' the younger policeman said. 'It could have fallen off when she was in the orchard, and the PoW saw it come off, or maybe he just found it afterwards, and stole it then?'

I looked away.

'Did she lose the necklace?' the older man asked. 'Do you remember? Did she ever mention it?'

I looked down into the cup as if there were answers in the thick brown drink. I didn't want to lie any more. But I didn't want to hurt Daddy.

'He was . . . Hansel – I mean Hans – Hans was our friend.' It was the best I could do. 'He would never hurt her.' I stopped because I realised that wasn't quite true. He was going to hurt her by leaving.

'Ah, well then,' said the detective. 'That clears that up. We didn't know she was one of his customers – the farmer's office is a bit of a tip and we haven't gone through all his records yet. She must have dropped the necklace there.' He took a long, satisfied drink from his beer. 'Good lad.'

'Well done, Daniel,' Daddy said. 'We'll finish our drinks and walk home.' He looked at the policeman. 'I'm relieved she wasn't robbed. You worried me when you said that!'

And they all carried on, drinking and chatting, because they thought everything was fine. All the answers added up.

'As I said, she never mentioned this prisoner in her letters,' Daddy said.

'Well, she wouldn't, would she? If he was just some PoW she bought wood from every now and then.'

I was glad they didn't think Hans was a violent robber. But they still thought he was a thief. And hearing them talk about him now, as if he was nobody to her, to *us*, was almost worse.

Like all adults did sooner or later, they began chatting about how they'd spent the war. I looked at Daddy. He was trying so hard to be *well*. He managed a joke about his service. 'Not a scratch on me!' he said. 'I was one of the lucky ones.' But it wasn't true. Not really. He did get hurt in the war. Only no one could see it now because he knew how to hide it. I knew Daddy didn't like talking about the war, and it seemed Detective Taylor realised that too because he started talking about his investigation again.

'Knew we'd find out where the bugger went in the end. It was one of those cases that everyone kept thinking about, you know? It was as if he'd just disappeared into thin air.'

'Well, case solved!' Daddy said.

'I'll drink to that!' the younger policeman said, and took a glug of his beer.

'There was still quite a bit of work to do, though. Even when we established it was definitely him that had fallen down the mine – it's not an easy business tracing PoWs. The German army is obviously dismantled now, so we had to find his family, to inform them what happened. On a form he filled out when he got here, he said he was from a place called Mittenwald. But we couldn't find an address and the records on PoWs are sporadic, to say the least, and files sometimes got lost and so on.'

Daddy nodded.

'Not sure if I should show you this, but . . . well, it'll be common knowledge soon enough.' And he picked up the manila envelope again.

My heart began to thump at the sight of it in his hands. He'd found out something else! Something about Hans. He'd tracked down his family.

'The Red Cross was in charge of, sort of, overseeing PoWs were treated all right. And each country compiled their own records of the PoWs they held, and those records are now all held centrally by a department at the Red Cross in Switzerland. On index cards, would you believe – millions and millions and millions of index cards.'

Daddy was just nodding politely, but I was hanging on every word; and I wanted him to get to the point. I wanted to grab the envelope.

'Well, they're obviously sensitive and personal documents and so they're not available to Joe Public. Not yet, anyway; might be one day, I suppose.'

'But you managed to access them?'

'Yes. We got one of their archivists to do a search for us. What with all those index cards you can imagine how long it takes. They have all the Great War prisoners' files there too.'

I couldn't stop staring at the envelope. Information about Hans's family, his life before Bambury, must be lying just beneath the brown paper.

'I also had a look at the local records in Densford and contacted the 'Deutsche Dienststelle' – if I'm saying that right – which has records on German PoWs and—'

'What did you find?'

'Daniel!' Daddy looked shocked at my interruption.

'Sorry,' I said immediately to the policeman.

'Oh that's all right. Young boys love all the investigation stuff, I know! It's exciting to them, isn't it? And your lad had met this PoW, so it's only natural he wants to know more about him.' He shifted in his seat. 'Well,' he said, addressing me now, 'I found a couple of references to the fact Johannes Müller was indeed a PoW held in England from April 1944, but of course I couldn't find a record of him ever being released or returning home to Germany.'

I nodded.

'But what about his family? Did you find them?'

'Well, I'm sorry to break it to you, son. But the long and the short of it is this: I hit a bit of a dead end. I couldn't find any records relating to your Hans Müller who was born in Mittenwald.'

'So there's nothing?'

'A-ha! I didn't say that now, did I?' He gave me a grin and I could tell I was supposed to be enjoying the game. Probably, he was used to telling stories about his investigations, and people loved the slow revealing of facts, like watching individual brush-strokes painted on a piece of paper until at last a whole picture suddenly jumped out at them. But I had to stop myself from screaming at him to stop speaking in riddles.

'I was at a complete dead end trying to find out more about

our Herr Müller, but I didn't let that stop me! I had more than I usually have to go on because I had a photograph of him.'

He pointed at the picture I was still holding in my hand.

'I had an idea. Well, not so much an idea, more what we call in the trade "a hunch".'

I laid the picture down flat on the table, and placed my hand on top of it so it couldn't flutter away.

'I got my superiors to agree to me contacting the British army, well the military police to be precise, in Germany. That was no easy task, I tell you. It's not exactly our job to go to these lengths to track down relatives of a dead PoW. But like I said, this was one of those cases that had been gnawing at me since he escaped. So I sent that photograph to the military police because I wanted someone to search the archives out there for me. I wanted to find another picture of him.'

'Yes?' I'm not sure if he heard me, because my voice was a whisper whipped away by the wind.

'They make high-school yearbooks there, like they do in America, except they're more like magazines than proper books. So my man checked Mittenwald Library archives – it's a tiny little town, a village really, in the Bavarian Alps – and looked through a few different years and . . .' He was slipping another piece of paper from his envelope. 'This is him. Isn't it?' He leaned forward to point out an image on the page.

He looked so young! I nodded. Daddy leaned over to look as well.

It was another black-and-white image, and it was tiny, surrounded by dozens of photographs of strangers' faces. But yes, it was Hans as a teenager. I'd know his face anywhere.

Only—

(Hang on a minute.)

Only . . . the name under the boy with the shy smile wasn't Hans. It was Wilhelm. Wilhelm Gerhard.

40

...he sat next to the Snow Queen. She put her fur coat around him,
and it felt as if he lay down in a deep snowdrift.

From *The Snow Queen*

There was a quiet knock on my bedroom door.

'Oh,' Daddy said, when he poked his head into my room. 'I was going to ask if you need a hand with your tie, but I see you're already dressed.'

I was sitting on the bed trying to make my head feel the right way before Mother's funeral. I had that odd feeling of pressure in my skull again, that sensation of a kettle screaming inside my mind. 'I have to wear a tie every day for Densford Secondary,' I said.

'Ah.' I realised he'd never seen me in my school uniform. I still hadn't been back there since the snow. 'Well, Granny and Grandpa are downstairs if you want to come and say hello. Your other grandparents aren't here yet.'

'Yes, in a minute.'

He left and closed the door behind him. I fiddled with the pointed end of my black tie. I supposed the funeral would make Mother's death feel more real. So far, I hadn't felt very much. I'd always been so terrified of her leaving me. But it was like I'd always known she would leave in the end. It was like I'd been waiting for it. And, with Daddy home, things weren't so very bad.

He was doing all the cooking, like he'd done before the war. And he was trying his best with the shopping and cleaning, too. I hadn't realised how much I'd been doing for Mother, until Daddy started doing it for me.

Things were all right, really. Apart from the nightmares. Sometimes I woke up screaming, and Daddy would run into my room to tell me I was safe now, go back to sleep. But I couldn't tell him what monsters were making me suffer. I pretended I could never remember the dreams. He probably thought they were just memories of Mother leaving and how I was trapped in the house in the snow.

Daddy and I were both trying so hard to get better. But yes, he grew very quiet sometimes, and went to sit in the bomb shelter in the garden, and I remembered how I'd heard him crying in there once before. I left him alone when he went in there now. I thought he was maybe thinking about the war, which he never talked about, and Mother, who he didn't talk about much either.

I went to look out of my window. Tiny buds were starting to appear on the magnolia tree. Through the branches, I could see the pavement on the other side of the fence. Bunches of flowers and wreaths laid there for the village to see. Some of the neighbours, dressed in black, hovered nearby at a respectful distance. I saw Jean Bainbridge, who'd been friends with Mother, arrive and lay down a bunch of daffodils. She was wearing a black hat with a bit of black net falling across her face.

Mother was dead. And Hansel was dead, too. Did that mean they were together now?

'Your Hans was a naughty boy,' Detective Taylor had said. 'He wasn't who he said he was.'

Sitting at that table outside the Royal Oak I had felt a sudden rush of dizziness as if I was about to faint.

'What?'

The policeman was actually grinning at me. He was thrilled. He winked at Daddy, like he was playing a fun game.

'I love it when a hunch pays off,' he said. 'Now I knew his real name I could find out who he really was.'

'But . . . but . . . who was he?'

And he placed his beer down and turned again to his manila envelope and I suddenly didn't want to know. In a panic, I wondered how I could get Daddy to make him stop talking. I stood up, banging into the table hard, and my cup rattled in its saucer and a couple of the beers spilled over.

'Daniel!' Daddy cried, as the beer dripped through the holes in the iron table on to their laps.

I snatched up the photographs of Hans the woodchopper and Wilhelm the student and then grabbed at the envelope in the detective's hand. 'Sorry,' I said, 'I don't want to get beer on it all.'

He stood up too. 'I'm sorry, this was a shock. You said he was your, er, friend. I should have—'

'No, no, it's all right.' I stuffed the photographs back into the envelope. 'Sorry.' They were all gaping at me. 'I'll go inside and get a cloth.'

I stumbled off into the pub, which felt dark and stuffy after sitting beneath the cold sky, and I rolled up the envelope so that I was gripping it like a baton in my fist. I walked past the bar and threw myself down at an empty table in the corner, to try to force my breathing to slow down. The barman gave me a strange look, but a couple came in so he turned away to serve them. I knew Daddy and the policemen were waiting for me outside, but I needed a minute to myself. There was an empty pint glass on the table, a dirty ashtray, and a packet of matches. There were three still in there, when I slid open the box.

I decided to burn the envelope.

There was already a fire burning in the pub but I thought it'd be too obvious if I walked over and threw it into the grate. The matches would work though; I knew there was a little metal rubbish bin in the men's toilets – I could set it alight in there. I started to stand up. But the sudden memory of using another set of matches in another time, another place, to make a fire, made me hesitate. And then I felt sick. It would be like burning Hansel. And I leaned forward onto the table with my head between my hands.

It was a stupid idea anyway. How could I explain the missing envelope if I burned it? And the detective knew all the information inside it; destroying it wouldn't really make it disappear. My heart eventually stopped spluttering in my chest and settled down to a steady beat, so I sat back up. The envelope was on the seat beside me.

I didn't have long. They'd give me a few minutes, assuming I must be waiting for the barman's attention, but then Daddy would probably come looking for me. I wasn't sure if they realised that I'd taken the envelope with me. It didn't matter: I'd decided not to read whatever was inside. I'd just sit there for a minute, catching my breath, before getting a cloth and going outside to wipe up the mess.

But the envelope, the paper inside it, was like a siren's sly call to a lonely sailor at sea. There was a story inside those pages. And in the end, I wanted to be told the story.

I went into the toilets so I could shut myself in a cubicle, and I pulled out the detective's report. And I began to read.

Some of what Hansel had said was true. Wilhelm Gerhard's father, Kurt, was indeed a wealthy shoe manufacturer who had travelled around Europe with his family before the war. He was also a prominent figure in the local Nazi party, and his handsome son Wilhelm – the boy in the school photograph – had joined the Waffen-SS.

I didn't need to be told what that meant. Everyone knew the SS set up the German police state and used security forces like the Gestapo to crush any resistance. And now, a few years after the war, everyone also knew about the SS's other job too – running Germany's concentration camps.

I'd closed the lid and was sitting on the toilet but I reeled backwards so I could avoid looking at the words for a couple of seconds. Then, worried that my time might be running out, I quickly scanned the last couple of pages.

They were just dry facts, I understood that. Wilhelm's father may have forced him to join the SS. Wilhelm may have secretly been against everything they stood for. But why would he lie to everyone about his name? Why would he say he was called Hans?

Records had been hurriedly destroyed as the Germans lost the war and so – despite his best efforts – Detective Taylor was unable to find out exactly when and where Wilhelm had been at any given time. But, he wrote in his report, it was standard practice to rotate SS members in and out of the camps. They'd be moved around according to manpower needs or to give them a break from the front lines. There was a very compelling argument, he said, that every single member of the SS knew about the existence of concentration camps and, more than that, knew exactly what went on within them. That's why the whole organisation was deemed liable for crimes against humanity. That's why this report into Hans said he almost certainly knew about – and had, in fact, likely participated in – the extermination of the Jews (and the gypsies, and the homosexuals, and the religious, and the communists, and the handicapped, and all the others deemed unfit to live).

Hans was probably a Nazi after all.

Grandma and Grandad's car pulled up outside the house, and I saw them nod awkwardly at the mourners before walking up the path into the cottage. I heard Granny greeting them in the hall. I'd have to go downstairs in a minute. The hearse would arrive soon and then it would be time for Mother's funeral procession.

But I couldn't get thoughts of Hansel out of my head. I was back in the toilet cubicle, with the tall walls either side of me, as I tried to learn what I could about a man I'd once believed to be a woodchopper-prince.

Detective Taylor couldn't find Wilhelm's family. His report said some old neighbours claimed they'd been killed by a bomb, but he wasn't sure if that was true. They were well-known party members; they may have run away, changed their names. If they were still alive, then they still didn't know what became of Wilhelm.

Towards the end of the report, the policeman described Mother's necklace. It was found in the PoW's skeletal fist. The chain was broken, so they suspected he'd pulled it from her throat to rob her. He'd have to rewrite that page now, now that I'd told him it couldn't have happened that way. The report would say the chain had broken one day when Mother happened to be at the orchard, and the prisoner had stolen the necklace then. I thought about the broken chain. The tiny links had probably worn away with time and the weather. Or perhaps the delicate silver had snapped as Hans held it and waited for me to save him. I liked the thought of him looking at it. Why else would he do that if it wasn't love?

The last page of the document gave me another shock. Mr Higgins had walked into the police station in Densford, a week after Hans had been discovered at the bottom of the mine. He said he'd been walking in the woods when he'd tripped over and found a body. Bones, just about buried in what must have been a shallow grave. He'd been wracking his brains, he had, on the drive to the police station, and remembered an old tramp who used to be seen about the village sometimes, but who had disappeared around the same time the prisoner escaped. Mr Higgins could only assume – according to the desk sergeant, who told Detective Taylor, who wrote it in his report – that the PoW had killed the tramp at some point during his getaway. Perhaps the man had tried to stop him, and there'd been a struggle, a fight. Did the PoW have a weapon? A gun, a knife? No? Well, he was young and strong, wasn't he, from all that wood-chopping. Perhaps he'd grabbed a branch or log, from the ground, and used that? To batter the man. Mr Higgins wasn't a policeman, although he had been in charge of the Bambury Home Guard, so he'd leave it to the officers to investigate. But if he was a gambling man, he'd bet this new body he'd stumbled across in the woods was connected to the PoW. It must have been dislodged by the melting snow, which was why he'd found it that day. It was lucky, really, a funny coincidence.

But it was justice too. Now everybody would know the PoW killed the tramp, and that would be the end of the whole sorry mess.

Granny came up to fetch me. 'Ready, dear? Don't you look smart?' She squeezed my shoulder as she guided me downstairs. 'Things will get better after today,' she said. 'Let's just get through today.'

Then she took me into the sitting room and I let Grandma kiss me and Grandad shake my hand. And when the hearse came, men in black top hats put the flowers into the car, and we walked behind it, and the rest of the mourners walked behind us, for the short distance to the church.

The sun was out and I felt warm in my black school blazer, which Granny said would do for a funeral jacket with my white shirt and new black tie. I looked at Grandma and Grandad, because they were Mother's parents and I wondered how they would react. But they just looked sad, and neither of them cried. They looked like I felt. I remembered Mother's row outside the station with Grandma. I didn't know if Grandma was thinking about that, or other things.

The priest said: 'Forasmuch as it hath pleased Almighty God of his great mercy to take unto himself the soul of our dear sister here departed, we therefore commit her body to the ground; earth to earth, ashes to ashes, dust to dust...'

Then he started to speak about stories from the Bible, because even adults liked to listen to stories like that, and he talked about her eternal life. I wondered if Mother had met Hansel yet, in this new life she'd started. I wasn't quite sure what to think about Wilhelm, but I liked the thought of Mother and Hansel being together again. Daddy told me 'the PoW' had been given a pauper's burial – well, a cremation – since no one could find his family. So he'd been given a funeral at last, I thought, just like Mother.

Daddy led me over to a pile of soil not far from the grave. We each scooped up a handful of earth and threw it down into the hole; on to her coffin.

41

*They took each other by the hand and walked out of the
great palace . . . The winds were still; and as they walked,
the sun broke through the clouds.*
From *The Snow Queen*

There was something nice about packing everything away neatly
into boxes. The cottage was disappearing into wooden crates in
each room. The last of the clutter that Granny had missed, when
she came to clean the house after the snow, was being thrown
away. The rubbish piled high in cupboards and crammed into
drawers was a fluttering stream that trickled out of the house into
the bins outside, and Mother's clothes, and the ones too small
for me, were birds that flew away to the Red Cross to be given to
refugees.

The removal van was arriving tomorrow, and it would carry
Daddy and me and our things and our furniture all the way to
Norfolk. We were going to live in a house just two streets away
from Granny and Grandpa. Daddy said his war pension and the
money from the sale of the cottage were all we needed, but he was
talking about trying to get a job at a bank in Great Yarmouth.

I'd have to start a new school. I'd missed quite a lot of the
term, but Harry had written to me and promised it wouldn't be a
problem. The master was a good chap on the whole, he said, and
I hadn't missed much. And his friends were all looking forward
to meeting me. He'd told them all how I survived by eating snow

on my own for weeks without any parents there. They couldn't wait to meet a real-life hero, he said. And, his messy handwriting added, we'd be able to walk to school together every day because we'd practically be neighbours.

Starting a new school where I'd hardly know anyone made me feel nervous, but then maybe that was the best thing about it; I could be a completely different person there. In any case, I felt sick with relief that I'd never have to go back to Densford Secondary.

I looked around my room to see what else I still had to do. My small bedside table had to be taken downstairs into the front garden so I picked it up and carried it outside. Daddy had promised one of the neighbours she could have the bits and bobs we weren't taking with us, and there was a little collection under the magnolia tree for her to inspect. I put the table next to a pair of mismatched wooden chairs on the lawn, which was dotted with petals.

'What's all this?'

I turned around to see Mr Higgins just coming to a stop on the other side of our fence. He rested a thick hand on a wooden post, and I tried not to look at it.

'Ah, hello Higgins,' Daddy said, as he came out of the front door carrying a footstool.

'Patterson.'

'What are you doing here?'

'On my way to visit Evelyn Moore – my cousin's widow, by way of marriage. Like to pop by to check on her from time to time.'

'Ah, yes, that's nice. Please pass on my regards.'

'I might ask you the same question, anyway – what are you up to?'

And Daddy told him we were moving away. I looked up at Mr Higgins and saw something slowly change in his expression. His scrunched-up face seemed to get smoother. He's relieved, I thought. By 'finding' the Troll himself, he'd made sure no one would ask any questions and had managed to pin it all on Hansel. And now with Mother and Farmer Dawson dead, and me moving away, there were only a few people left who knew what he and the nice man did that day. And they had their own reasons for keeping quiet.

Mr Higgins congratulated Daddy on the move, then said to me: 'Well, you be a good boy for your father. Don't give him any trouble now, will you?'

Of course I could hear the threat creeping underneath his words, and I hated having to obey it. But I looked down at the table on the grass and pushed my thumbnail into the soft wood and said: 'No, sir. I'll be good.'

Sometimes I wondered if I *should* tell Daddy what had happened, just to tell someone so that I wasn't alone in the knowing of it. But how could I explain about the Troll without also explaining about Hansel and Mother and everything that'd happened that summer? I supposed I could keep some of it back from him, but even if I just told him about the Troll he'd be upset, and the thought of adding to his upset, of making him go to cry in the bomb shelter, sealed my lips. And, the truth was, I didn't *want* him to know what I'd done. I didn't want him to think badly of me. Things were so good now he was home again I didn't want to do anything to ruin it.

I slipped back into the cottage and went upstairs to my room to carry on packing. The cottage looked bigger, but barer, wiped clean of memories. Although if I looked for her, I could still see her listening to the wireless in the sitting room, or running to answer the telephone when Grandma rang to check up on her, or reading a magazine while she nibbled on some crackers in the kitchen.

And I could see her slumped on the floor outside the bathroom, or gulping gin like it was a cool glass of water, or squeezing out through a crack in the door to crawl into the snow.

The new house would not have these moments waiting for me

in the rooms, or around the corners. There was a sadness in that. But, if I was honest, there was a gladness in it, too. I supposed it meant I wouldn't be hit with a vision of Mother like an unexpected punch to my stomach from the boys at school. I would be more in control of the memories that came into my mind. Like that night we baked a cake together, and the fairy tales she read to me every night.

I picked up a book from my shelf. A woman wrapped in white furs and diamonds that glittered like icicles looked out at me from the cover, along with a little boy wrapped up next to her in her sleigh. I put it into the empty box at my feet marked 'BOOKS'. Was it silly to take these? I didn't want to read them any more. But she'd held them, and loved them, and they were a gift that she gave to me every day.

I'd take them all.

42

─❧─

'Gerda! Sweet little Gerda, where have you been so long?
And where have I been?' Kai looked about him. 'How cold it
is, how empty, and how huge!' And he held on to Gerda . . .
Now the Snow Queen could return, it did not matter, for
his right to freedom was written in brilliant pieces of ice.
From *The Snow Queen*

Daddy said he'd meant to come back to Bambury before now.
But this year had been so busy, what with the move, and getting
me settled into school, and his new job, that he couldn't believe
how the months had flown by. So now here we were, at the cemetery to pay our respects to Mother, and nearly at the year's end.

We crunched through snow as we made our way across the
churchyard. I felt it collapse and harden beneath my feet as my
soles crushed the water out of it. It wasn't at all like the strange
stuff that buried the world last winter; it was just a couple of
inches deep, but it seemed right somehow. A wintry sun made the
day bright and sharp.

'It's nearly the anniversary,' I said. 'Perhaps it was better to
come now?'

'Yes,' he said. 'Maybe you're right.'

'Perhaps we should always come at this time? You know – just
once a year, but . . . every year?'

'Yes.' He looked at me with a brief smile. 'Yes. Let's do that.'

We found her grave, and laid a bunch of yellow winter jasmine down in the snow. The headstone that loomed over the flowers didn't say much, but it described her as a daughter, a wife, a mother. None of those words seemed to explain who she was. They just described her in relation to other people. I didn't think of her that way. She was just herself.

When we started to feel the cold, we walked back towards the High Street. Daddy wanted to pop into the pub to catch up with his old friends before driving us home to Great Yarmouth.

I told him I'd join him later. Maybe he thought I had friends of my own I wanted to find in the village.

Instead, I walked down the lane, and slowed my step as I passed our old cottage. Different curtains hung at the windows but I couldn't see anybody inside. I was surprised to find that when I trailed my hand along the fence it only came up to my waist now; I'd grown.

I pushed on, and went into the forest.

At first, I thought I'd walk all the way to where Hans fell, because that was close to where they found Mother. But once I was inside the woods, I realised I didn't need to. Both of them were everywhere here. She wasn't in the headstone in the cemetery; she'd been here the whole time. I remembered that when I was little, I thought I could see and feel magic in amongst these trees. Well, this was a sort of magic too, wasn't it?

I took our old path towards the orchard. A stranger probably wouldn't be able to see the track because of the snow, which was lighter in the forest, but had still dusted the ground through the trees.

I usually managed not to think about these woods, and who'd died in them. But today I would face it.

I'm a killer, I thought. *I killed them all.*

In the night-time, the monsters didn't come to find me as often as they used to – things seemed to be different for me in Norfolk.

Weeks could go by without me remembering. But now, here, I thought about who didn't exist because of me.

I thought of Hans the woodchopper. Of course, this wasn't in Detective Taylor's report, but knowing about Hans's true past explained why he'd wanted to escape. I had no way of knowing for sure, but my best guess was that he managed to swap uniforms with an infantryman at some point, either before or after he was captured. He might have ordered the real Hans Müller to hand over his identity. I often wondered what happened to the real Hans Müller. Was he sent off to a special PoW camp for SS officers in Wilhelm's place? Probably not. The real Hans Müller would have talked, wouldn't he? So maybe Hans had died somehow, and Wilhelm just saw an opportunity to take his uniform and papers. That was what I hoped had happened. But when Wilhelm saw, that autumn in Bambury in 1944, that the Germans were going to lose, he was afraid he'd be caught. I remember telling him what I'd heard on the wireless, about how Germany was losing and the war would soon be over. He must have feared interrogation or maybe even the threat of a war trial. That must be why he had to run. And then there was the petition, the sudden threat that stricter controls might be imposed on the PoWs.

I still didn't know where he'd have gone. Was he really trying to get to Switzerland? How would he have crossed the Channel? Perhaps he'd have tried to get to Ireland to make his way from there to South America. That's where the rest of the Nazis ended up, people said.

I'd believed him to be a kind, brave woodchopper. And perhaps he was. Just because he ran doesn't necessarily mean he was guilty, does it? He might have run in fear of the discovery he'd stolen an identity, rather than fear of what he'd done as an officer. Because there *was* goodness in him. His kindness towards me, and that beautiful kiss he shared with my mother. Those things were real, I was sure of it. But now I also knew he may have had another

319

side altogether. Maybe it wasn't the Troll, but *Hans* who was the monster all along.

Perhaps no one sees what's right underneath their noses if only they'd really look. In the back of my mind, I dimly heard my mother's voice reading to me: 'Oh but Grandmother, what terrible big *teeth* you have!'

It was hard for me to think about Hans this way. To shine a new light on him and see he wasn't really how I'd remembered him, when I looked at him under the harsh glare. I realised he had, in a way, still remained something of a fairy-tale character to me, even now.

How strange that I was only just figuring out that he wasn't really a magical woodchopper-prince after all. I supposed human beings – all of us – are always more complicated than the cut-outs in the old stories. Real lives are so much messier, so much harder to understand.

Unlike fairy tales, that world of good and evil I used to love so much, life was as grey as the patch on Hans's back. Evil was perhaps just as often made up of things unsaid, and actions not taken, and looking the other way. Everyone was capable of terrible things – I knew that better than anyone.

A fallen tree blocked the way so I scrambled over it. I remembered how my mother and I had both hurried to find this path once, after we'd come across the Troll in the forest.

Did it have a dark side too? For a while, once I was a bit older, I managed to convince myself it really was a predator of children because I remembered it watching those boys playing in the stream. But I knew now, in my heart of hearts, it wasn't a monster; it was just waiting for them to leave so it could drink and wash.

He, not it! I was thirteen now; time to put aside childish things. I had to admit to myself that he was human after all. He must have had a name, though I'd never learned it. They'd cremated him too, I'd heard, with the same sort of pauper's funeral Hans was given.

My eyes suddenly watered, but I was coming closer to the orchard now, and I picked up my pace. The snow squashed by my shoes made a kind of ripping sound with each step. It had been years since I'd been here, but I recognised the individual trees now. I was very close.

I thought of that dark mirror sometimes; the one the Devil made, which shattered so that its evil shards were carried on the winds throughout the world. The tiny grains would pierce a human eye or a human heart and gradually turn to ice and make the person cold.

It seemed to me that it was like the Devil was simply planting seeds. Seeds that would grow – if left untreated – and push out the human warmth. Seeds of ice and snow.

It was just a story, of course, but – like most stories – it was also true. Probably, there were lots of people who had such seeds inside them. Seeds that made them cold or sick. I didn't know enough about Hans's life to know what planted his seed – what pushed him to join the SS and possibly commit horrors. War planted a seed in my father; I saw it damage him. And my birth planted a seed of darkness inside my mother that she never really recovered from. The mirrored shards in her heart and her eyes grew so big that she could no longer see joy in the world or her own place within it. If treated, perhaps these seeds could have been dug out before they took root. Daddy did not succumb to the ice, after all.

I had a seed inside me, too. But I was cold even before I killed Hans and the Troll. It must have been my mother who planted my seed in me. She was made of ice. And I was made of her. If she was the Snow Queen, then I was her boy made of snow.

The path seemed to peter out up ahead and there was now an unbroken wooden fence running around what used to be the orchard. Another PoW must have been brought in, because the job clearing away the dead trees had been finished. It was a field now. The wood cabin, the *shed*, was gone. There was just a smooth white blanket of snow laid out invitingly before me. I climbed over the fence and walked towards the place where the glade had been. My footprints would lead to the place where an oak stump once stood.

Mother was cold. But it occurred to me now that maybe she didn't want to be. She spent her life waiting for love to find her, after all. She was the Snow Queen – I always knew that – but now I was wondering whether she was Gerda, too. The little girl who went to war against her. Maybe that's what it was like for her. Maybe she was fighting a battle within herself, although she lost in the end.

I think she was looking for peace. And so she went to sleep in the snow. I hope she found what she was looking for.

But could there have been another way?

I wondered whether to launch my own battle, against my own cold heart. Kai was free of the Snow Queen in the end, and I wondered how it would feel for me to break away from the ice.

It all happened. Nothing would ever change that. But it was over now. Mother was dead and was never coming back. Hans was dead too, and the Troll, and even Farmer Dawson. But I wasn't dead. I was still here.

As I crunched towards the centre of the vanished orchard – towards a glade filled with apple trees and sunlight that only I could see – I thought how everybody's life is their very own story.

A lot of fairy tales are about paths and journeys. And as I walked through the snow and approached the glen it felt like I was coming to a crossroads. I must choose a path. And it felt very important that I choose the right one.

I did wrong here. I lied, and I watched a murder, and I let a man die alone in the bottom of a pit, and I'd stayed silent about all of it.

What would happen if I stopped being silent? What would

happen if I told one more story? What would happen if I told the truth?

I could tell Daddy first. And it would be hard, and it would hurt him. But I was doing so much *pretending* – the way Mother had pretended – that maybe it was time to stop. We could go to the police station in Densford together.

I wondered what they would do to me when they heard my confession. They might charge me with all sorts of things – I'd looked it up in the school library once; murder, or manslaughter, or perverting the course of justice, or even preventing the burial of two bodies. But I was just a little boy back then; I was just nine. So perhaps they'd do none of those things. Perhaps Detective Taylor would just listen to me, and then gather together some officers to find Mr Higgins and the nice man.

He might take me back to the woods so I could show him the places, though. He might let me through the fence they'd built around the mine. And I'd finally return to Hans's hole, which was empty now. I'd force myself to look down into the dark pit, and it would be like I had finally gone back for him.

And I could show the police where the Home Guard killed the Troll. Maybe the detectives would tell me his name, and at last I'd know him as the man he really was.

I wondered what else would happen to me if I did this. What would happen to my nightmares if the dead men were no longer a secret only I knew about? Neither of them were in the earth waiting for me any more – both had been brought up and turned into ashes. My mother was the only one in the ground now. I always thought they'd come up to take me, but maybe it would just be her who'd be waiting for me at the end.

My Snow Queen, my Gerda.

I sank down in the snow, and I could feel her there, and all around me. And I began to cry. And Hans and the Troll were there too, in the crumbling snow I scooped up in my hands, and in the distant trees, and in the wintry sky.

323

I took off my coat; I wanted to feel the cold. I wanted to feel close to her. Just for a little while, until it was time to go back to the village. And, I thought, if the police don't lock me up, then I'll come back here next winter. And the winter after that. And all the winters of my life.

And each time, I'll kneel down in the snow, and push my hands down to feel the hard-packed earth lying beneath, and I'll burrow with my fingers, so they go into the ground. Into the frozen earth that cradles my mother. It'll be like we're holding hands.

'I'm here,' I'll say, or something like that.

And – just for a moment – she'll come up and we'll sit there together. And one day, when I'm old, she'll come up to take me home.

The warmth penetrated to his heart and melted both the ice and the glass splinter in it . . . Kai burst into tears and wept so much the grains of glass in his eyes were washed away . . .

They took each other by the hand . . . Kai and Gerda looked into each other's eyes and now they understood . . . There they sat, the two of them, grown-ups; and yet in their hearts children, and it was summer: a warm glorious summer day.

From *The Snow Queen*

Acknowledgements

※

I never used to understand long acknowledgements sections at the backs of novels; only one person wrote it. But now I know how silly that is, and how many people there are behind the scenes helping in every way, personally and professionally.

Firstly, I would like to thank the person who made everything happen and turned my crazy dreams into a reality: my brilliant agent, Felicity Blunt. Thank you so much for taking me on, for having faith in me, and for all your help – not just on the business side of things, but also your invaluable editorial guidance and your patience with my endless questions! There's no one else I'd rather have on my side.

I'd also like to thank the rest of the team at Curtis Brown, particularly the unflappable Jessica Whitlum-Cooper, who is always ridiculously helpful, her predecessor Emma Herdman, for her early support, and Melissa Pimentel, for her work on translation rights.

Massive thanks and gratitude to publishing director Arzu Tahsin; an incredible editor who taught me the true value of a story that ends with a 'happily-ever-after' and (by giving me a book deal) gave me one of my own.

And many thanks to everyone else at Weidenfeld & Nicolson and Orion, especially Jennifer Kerslake, who went above and beyond anything I could have expected, as did Craig Lye, Paul Stark and Rebecca Gray, who have all been a delight to work with. I'd also like to thank copy-editor Sophie Hutton-Squire and artist Sinem Erkas for the truly beautiful cover design.

Thanks also to Penguin Random House for letting me quote

from Eric Christian Haugaard's evocative translation of *The Snow Queen* – and thanks to Hans Christian Andersen himself for inspiring me with such a beautiful, dark fairy tale. I used Victorian translations for the other tales quoted, and was struck by how little the wording has changed over the centuries because they're so perfect.

And now to thank the people who were there helping me from the beginning, or very close to it, starting with the obscenely talented author Jane Harris, who is also a wonderful teacher and has been a mentor and inspiration to me.

I've also been inspired by my writer friends – Carys Lawton-Bryce, Anjali Deshpande, David Harley and Clare Cowburn Baker – who suffered through my early attempts at this book and helped me try to make it better. As did Sophie Wilson and Karl French.

And thanks also to Akie Kotabe, who was there when I wrote the first word, and the last, of that very first draft and who never stopped encouraging me.

Lucy Cohen, who made sure the reporters' rota at work allowed me the time to write – and who never laughed at me for doing so – probably doesn't realise how much her help has meant to me; this book would never have been finished without her kind support.

Shout out to Bernadette Hood and also Ray Stephens, who bored everyone he knows banging on about this book in the pub (hopefully this mention gets you some free drinks).

My sisters Justine Mayer and Kristiana Meseg are wonderful, strong women I'm proud to be related to, and special thanks to my sister Nola Mayer, who moved me more than she'll ever know with her enthusiastic – and occasionally weepy – support.

And a huge thank you to my other fabulous sisters – who I also count as friends – Peony Mayer and Gillian Males, who both read an early draft and helped me immeasurably with it, as did Robin de Peyer, who cheered me on at every step, never doubted me, and who picked me up and swung me around in the middle of Oxford Street when I told him I'd be published.

Thanks also to my dog Bambi, who can't read these words but deserves them anyway, for faithfully sitting on my lap and keeping me company while I wrote, and in whose honour I named my village. My sister Peony demanded I name the town after her dog, Denzil; she says I have to thank him too.

Finally, I would like to thank my parents – Tom and Teresa Mayer – for their boundless support; not just with this novel, but throughout my life. I've been so lucky. The only similarity between my amazing, warm and loving mum with the mother in this book is that she shared her love of stories with me and ignited my lifelong passion for reading and writing. Thank you for your help with that early draft and for being someone to aspire to, and for always being – so fiercely! – in my corner. And thank you to my lovely dad, who has been supportive in every way a parent can be supportive – but who also insisted he wouldn't read a single page of this story until it was published and in the shops. I laughed long and loud at that, and told him the chances of that happening were mind-bogglingly slim to zero, but he stood firm. I'd like to thank him for believing in me. I hate it when he's right, but . . . Here you go then! You can read it now.

Chloë Mayer
London, June 2017